A TIME TO
DANCE

A TIME TO DANCE

THE SEQUEL TO *Timeless Waltz*

a novel

ANITA STANSFIELD

Covenant Communications, Inc.

Covenant.

Chapter 1

Salt Lake City, Utah

Dr. Alexander Keane felt a sharp rush of adrenaline as he snapped sterile gloves onto his hands the same moment he saw the ambulance come to an abrupt halt. The automatic doors of the emergency room willingly opened for the paramedics as they ushered the critically injured patient toward Alex and the medical personnel surrounding him. The call had come in a few minutes earlier while the ambulance had been en route. Eighteen-year-old male. Car accident. Unconscious and difficulty in breathing. Possible concussion and internal injuries.

"His name is Mark," one of the paramedics said to Alex as they exchanged responsibility for the patient. Alex knew the name could have been found in a wallet or on the vehicle registration; however, most of the paramedics were aware that, whenever possible, Alex was one of many doctors who preferred knowing the patient's name. For him, a name made his work more personal, and helped him focus his lifesaving efforts on a human being, rather than just a human body.

Within seconds Mark had been efficiently moved to a brightly lit trauma room where Alex worked earnestly to save his life, giving orders to the three nurses assisting him. As the situation became increasingly critical, Alex felt his brain gathering every possible bit of information stored there from his education and experience that might help him now. Habitually he coupled his knowledge with a silent, fervent prayer that his mind and hands would be guided to save this young man and give this life a second chance to be lived. But in his heart, as always, he knew he had to relinquish the matter to God. He knew from hard-won experience that no amount of medical technology or expertise could save a life that God meant to call home. But Alex knew it was his job to assume that every life was meant to be saved until the very last moment when nothing more could be done.

Alex felt his own adrenaline heighten as Mark suddenly flat-lined. "Don't you do this, Mark," Alex muttered as if words alone might convince him to live. He was grateful for state-of-the-art equipment at ready access and nurses who could practically read his mind as they worked together to get the heart started again. Seconds felt eternal as they tried again and again, then they all let out a unified sigh of relief when a steady beeping in the room let them know that Mark had come back to life. They continued working with practiced efficiency until the patient was stable, and then he was taken to surgery where the damage from the accident would be carefully repaired. By the time Alex's shift ended he'd been informed that the surgery had gone well, and Mark would be fine.

Driving home after midnight, Alex found comfort in knowing that whenever his odd shifts might end, and whatever his day might have entailed, Jane would be there waiting for him, making any day, no matter how difficult, worth living. Alex arrived home to find the house dark and everyone asleep. He found a plate of dinner in the fridge, covered with plastic wrap, waiting to be heated in the microwave. A little note was taped to the plastic. *Love you, Jane.* For a minute Alex just savored Jane's sentiment and stared at the food, trying to decide if he was more hungry than tired, or more tired than hungry. After four straight days of the usual twelve-hour shifts, he felt utterly and thoroughly exhausted. He was grateful to have the next three days off, but then he would be doing three days of an odd shift that would mess up his sleeping habits and bring on another bout of exhaustion. However, that was just part of the job and something he'd anticipated long before graduating from medical school. At this particular hospital, the ER physicians had staggered schedules so that a fresh doctor would always be present. It was a good system and a great hospital. He loved his work for the most part, and he just had to remind himself on occasion that the odd hours were worth it.

After staring at the food for a minute, Alex convinced himself that he needed to eat. He put the plate in the microwave, grateful that he would be home all day tomorrow, and he could sleep as late as he wanted. He thought of Mark and couldn't help smiling. It was nice to ponder the drama of a day's work that had a favorable outcome. More often than not, any given shift at the ER had some degree of tragedy laced into it.

After eating, Alex went quietly up the stairs and turned on the hall light. He peeked into each of the children's bedrooms just long enough to see evidence of them sleeping soundly in their beds. He moved silently into his own bedroom, not wanting to wake Jane. Then he realized the bed was empty, but light shone from beneath the bathroom door. She came out just as he sat on the edge of the bed to remove his shoes.

"Oh, I did hear you," she said and bent over to kiss him.

"I didn't want to wake you." He returned her kiss and pressed a hand to her well-rounded belly, where their third child was nearly ready to come into the world.

"You didn't wake me," she said, awkwardly getting back into bed. "For some strange reason I have to go to the bathroom fourteen times in the night."

He chuckled at her exaggeration. "You should see a doctor about that."

"I hate to break it to you," she said, settling her head onto the pillow, "but it's a doctor's fault I'm in this condition."

"So it is," he said and went into the bathroom.

A few minutes later he eased into the bed beside Jane and took a moment to touch her long, curly blonde hair, then he touched her face and kissed her. "I love you," he muttered quietly and nestled his head close to hers.

"I love you too," she replied and snuggled up close to him.

challenging, as was Jane's calling in the Primary. And just caring for two young children and preparing for the imminent arrival of a third one was often overwhelming. Still, they'd been greatly blessed, and the life they shared was good. So why did he feel this hovering uneasiness that something wasn't right?

Again Alex left Jane sleeping peacefully and got out of bed to check on the children. He walked through the house and found everything in order, then he opened the front-room drapes and watched the sun come up before he settled onto the couch with the scriptures. Through the years since he'd come to his senses and learned to fully appreciate what a great blessing it was to have the gospel in his life, Alex had grown to rely heavily on the scriptures. They had guided him through valleys of forgiveness and mountains of grief. They had helped him understand and cope with the seemingly senseless life-and-death situations he was confronted with daily. And they had helped him keep his focus on all that was truly important in this life. And now, while he struggled to understand why he couldn't shake the feeling that something wasn't right, he found peace in reading the words of Nephi.

"How come you're up so early?" Jane asked, drawing him away from his reading.

Alex looked up to see her standing in the doorway of the front room, her nightgown stretched tightly over her belly, her face drawn with exhaustion. "Couldn't sleep," he said, holding out a hand toward her. "What are *you* doing up? You should rest every minute you can."

Jane took his hand and snuggled up beside him on the couch. "Well, once I'd taken my seventy-fifth trip to the bathroom, I figured cuddling with you might be a better option. But you were gone."

"Sorry you had to come so far to find me," he said, pressing a kiss into her hair as she settled her head on his shoulder.

"It was worth the trip," she said and nuzzled closer. "What are you reading?"

"First Nephi."

"Read out loud," she said, relaxing with a loud sigh.

Alex cleared his throat and began to read from the middle of chapter seven. "'Yea, and how is it that ye have forgotten that the Lord is able to do all things according to his will, for the children of men, if it so be that they exercise faith in him? Wherefore, let us be faithful to him.'" Alex continued to read through to the end of the chapter, then he set the book aside and hugged Jane tightly. "I love you Mrs. Keane," he said.

"I love you too . . . *Dr.* Keane."

"I think I prefer just being Alex to you."

"Oh no," she said lightly. "You always make everything all better. You'll always be more of a doctor to me than to anybody else, even if what you do for me has nothing to do with being a doctor."

Alex just hugged her again and a minute later she asked, "Why couldn't you sleep? Is something wrong?"

Alex hesitated, wondering what to say, and how much to tell her about what he was feeling. He didn't want her to worry, but he'd learned long ago that he could never hide anything from her. They were committed to being completely honest with each other about their feelings—even when feelings were difficult to explain.

When he didn't answer right away, Jane lifted her head to look at him. "What?" she pressed, her eyes showing concern.

"I just had this . . . uneasy feeling." He saw her brow furrow and he hurried to try and explain. "I woke up in the night and just . . . felt like something was wrong. I checked you . . . the kids . . . the house. Everything was fine. I prayed that I'd either be guided to solve whatever was wrong, or feel peace. Then I went back to sleep. I woke up still feeling peace, but then . . . that uneasiness came back, and . . . I'm not certain what to make of it."

"You feel like something *is* wrong, or something *will* be wrong?"

"I don't know."

"Well," Jane said, settling her head again onto his shoulder, "there's no sense worrying or getting worked up over something you can't do anything about. You're already doing all you can do."

"What's that?" he asked, not liking the way her words contradicted his stark sense of helplessness.

"You're praying for guidance from the Spirit, and you already live in a way that will make you receptive to that guidance if you need it."

"Well . . . I try, but . . ."

"You're a good man, Alex. You don't have to be perfect to be worthy of the Spirit. If God wants us to know something, He'll let us know. We both pray every day that our family . . . our loved ones . . . will be protected and healthy. If something happens, then we have to know that it's God's will."

"You mean like the accident that put you in a coma for ten weeks?"

Jane looked into his eyes. "Yes," she said, "like that. It was hard, but we both know it was meant to be, and we had many miracles."

"Yes," he agreed, albeit grudgingly. "I can't deny that you're right, but quite frankly it was one of the most difficult things I've ever faced, and I don't particularly want to face any such thing ever again."

Jane smiled and touched his face. "And there's no reason to believe that you'll have to."

"Well, I hope not, but . . . I just can't shake this . . . unsettled feeling."

"Okay, but like I said, you're doing all you can do, so there's no sense in getting upset over it. You need to trust in the Lord to guide you. That would make it a matter of faith. Maybe it's Satan trying to get you all worked up."

"Maybe," he said, but he didn't think so.

"Or," she said, "maybe . . . it's just . . . well, I remember a time when I just felt like the Lord was trying to make me slow down and take notice of how blessed I really was. It's like the Spirit was simply telling me to stop and look around and count my blessings."

Alex made a noise of interest as he contemplated that. He liked that idea, and it certainly couldn't hurt for him to take an accounting of all that was good in his life, although he didn't really consider himself the kind of person to take his blessings for granted. Perhaps that stemmed from once almost losing Jane. Still, Jane's suggestions were not counteracting his deep, gut instinct that something wasn't right.

"Maybe," she went on, as if she could sense his ongoing unrest, "these feelings are preparing you for something."

"You mean for something to go wrong?"

"Maybe. Maybe not. I remember my dad saying that before he was called to be bishop, he had a feeling for quite some time that something was going to change, and it made him terribly uneasy."

"Oh, that would be just great," Alex said with sarcasm. "But I really don't think I'm bishop material."

"I would have to disagree with that," she said, "but the point I'm trying to make isn't literal. There could be a number of different callings in the Church that might bring on difficult changes. Or it may be something else. Whatever it is, the answer is still the same. We both need to trust in the Lord, do our best to stay close to the Spirit, and have some faith. If either of us feels prompted to do something, we'll do it. And whatever the future may bring, God will make us equal to it; He will get us through. He's proven that to us in the past. We must believe that He'll be there for us no matter what."

Alex smiled and had to admit he felt better. She was right. He kissed her quickly and asked, "How did you get to be so wise?"

"Just had good examples, I guess."

"I love you, Jane," he murmured and kissed her again.

"I love you too," she whispered, "and I . . . ooh!"

"What?"

She laughed softly. "I just got kicked." She pressed his hand to her belly and a moment later he felt the baby kick. They laughed together, since it was rare that he actually got to feel it. He kissed Jane again, truly grateful for all that he'd been blessed with.

The children were soon awake and filling the house with the typical sounds of morning. Barrett plopped himself in front of PBS cared for during the meetings so that Jane could relax and enjoy them. Except for times like this when she was so thoroughly uncomfortable with her pregnancy, he made the time to take her to the temple regularly. And he was rarely anything but kind and considerate to her and the children.

Jane watched him scanning through a magazine while he ate, and she smiled as she considered that in addition to everything else, he was certainly a pleasure to look at. While she felt bloated and less attractive than she'd ever felt in her life, Alex Keane could take her breath away just by sitting there. Being in his late thirties had only made him more appealing. He was tall and broad shouldered; his features were firm, and his dark hair was thick and touchable. And she loved him. Perhaps knowing that more than one of her sisters had married men who had turned out to have difficulties made her more mindful of the blessings she'd found in her own marriage. Whatever it was, she thanked God daily for giving her such a good man. She treasured moments like this when a day off gave him time to just be with her.

Alex pushed the magazine aside and glanced at her as he took a bite of his sandwich, then he muttered with his mouth full, "What are you looking at?"

"You," she said and reached over to put a hand in his hair, then she pressed it over his bristly face. It always felt bristly on days off when he chose not to shave unless they were actually going somewhere. And she liked it. "You're adorable," she added with a little laugh.

Alex chuckled and kissed her hand. "No, *you* are adorable."

"*You* need your eyes checked," she said, taking her empty plate to the counter. "In case you haven't noticed, I'm nearly nine months pregnant and I look like a balloon."

"Exactly," he said, coming behind her and pressing a kiss to her neck while he pressed his hands over her belly. "And you are more beautiful every day."

Jane turned to look at him. "If you keep saying things like that, Alex, you'll never get rid of me—even if such words are somewhat patronizing at the moment."

He smiled. "You're too wise to be patronized," he said and kissed her, wrapping his arms around her. She felt frustrated with the belly between them that forced distance into their embrace. But that didn't diminish the tenderness of his kiss, nor the love she felt from it.

"I love you, Alex," she muttered, again touching his hair. She could never explain the fascination she had with his hair, which usually had a way of looking like he'd tried to put it in place, but its gentle waves had chosen their own course. But the result was a combination of a look that was both rugged and boyish. And she loved it.

Jane was startled when he took her hand into his, put his other one on her back, and eased her into a careful waltz. "What are you doing?" she laughed.

"You, of all people, should not need me to explain a waltz."

"I don't think I'm in any condition to be dancing," she said with another laugh.

"As you can see, we're taking it slowly."

"But . . . the belly," she said.

"Clearly, I can reach around it," he said and continued to guide her through the steps. In spite of the lack of music, their feet moved together perfectly, as if they were thoroughly attuned to each other. Looking into his eyes, she felt certain they were. From the very first waltz they'd shared, practically strangers but already falling in love, she'd known he was meant to be her partner for life and forever. And she loved him more every day.

Alex contemplated Jane's expression while they waltzed lazily around the kitchen. He couldn't believe how much he loved her, and how blessed he was to have such a good woman in his life. He thought of what she'd said earlier, about stopping to take an account of his blessings. As he pondered briefly what their life together meant to him, his heart felt momentarily so full that he was almost moved to tears. He considered what he had felt earlier and wondered if he should be afraid of what the future might bring. But at this moment all he could feel was perfect peace, and his uneasiness vanished.

Jane soon declared exhaustion and insisted on sitting down. Alex gracefully escorted her to a chair before he put the food away and wiped off the counters, then he suggested she take a nap since he was there to watch Katharine. And she made no effort to protest.

That evening Alex got a call from one of the other ER doctors, asking if he would trade a shift with him. Alex would have to work the following day early, but then he'd only have two odd days and a few off after that. He gladly agreed, especially since this particular doctor had helped him out when he'd needed time off.

The following morning, a few hours into his shift, Alex realized he'd forgotten all about the uneasy feeling he'd had—only because it came back. At the first possible opportunity he called Jane to be assured that all was well.

"That feeling again?" she asked.

"Yeah."

"You're starting to scare me," she said, "especially since we're supposed to have a baby in a couple of weeks."

Alex didn't want to admit how he was scaring himself. Not wanting to alarm her, he said gently, "Hey, everything's going to be fine. We have every reason to believe the baby is perfect. You're healthy and you have a great doctor." The obstetrician who had seen her through the previous two pregnancies was one of the best. Even though Alex had actually delivered the babies, Dr. Terrence had been present through the process to make certain all went well.

"I have two great doctors, actually," she said. "But that doesn't mean something can't go wrong."

Alex repeated what she'd told him yesterday. "It's a matter of faith, Jane. We both need to trust in the Lord and do our best to stay close to the Spirit."

"Okay," she said quietly.

"Take care of yourself," he said.

"And you do the same," she replied.

Alex said a prayer and forced himself to get back to work. He was pleasantly surprised when his cousin Susan called to see if she could meet him at the cafeteria for lunch. It was something she did a couple of times a month, on the average, and he was grateful for the distraction today.

Susan Barrett Clark was old enough to be Alex's mother, since she was technically his mother's cousin. But Susan and his mother had barely known each other. Alex had met Susan following his mother's death, while Jane had been in a coma. He'd gone to a family wedding that had been held at Susan's home, mostly because he'd wanted to see the house. It was a spacious and beautiful ancestral home, built by one of their forefathers—Alexander Barrett, for whom Alex had been named. Susan had inherited the house, and she and her husband, Donald, had restored it to its present beautiful condition. The house held a tender spot in Alex's heart, not unlike his relationship with Susan. Her passion for the history of their family had quickly rubbed off on him, and they had spent many hours together discussing family history, searching out new branches of dead relatives, and doing temple work for them, usually with Jane and Donald being heavily involved.

Donald and Susan lived alone in the ancestral home, since their children were all grown and scattered across the country, raising their own families. Because they saw their children and grandchildren very little, Susan especially had latched onto Alex and Jane's young family, taking great delight in helping with the children and being involved in their lives. Alex and Jane loved her participation, especially since Jane's parents lived out of state, and Alex's mother was gone. Alex's father and stepmother lived half an hour away, but they were busier with other aspects of their lives, and Susan was the perfect surrogate grandmother. And she was almost as excited about this new baby as Alex and Jane were.

Since Susan only lived about fifteen minutes from the hospital, she enjoyed keeping track of Alex's shifts and coming by to have a meal with him occasionally. Over lunch Alex told Susan about his recent feelings, and she basically said the same thing that Jane had said the day before. She did, however, offer to go visit Jane before she went home, just to see that all was well. Alex was grateful for her efforts and for her positive perspective. Going back to work he uttered another prayer that all would be well, and then he tried to focus on all that he needed to do.

Chapter 2

Jane decided to put together an enchilada casserole early in the afternoon so that it could just be heated up for dinner. These days she simply had no energy left at all by evening, but she wanted Alex to have something decent to eat when he came home from a difficult twelve-hour shift. She knew he would never complain, but she still preferred to do everything she could to let him know how much she loved and appreciated him. After Barrett got off to preschool she started browning some ground beef and putting the other ingredients together. Katharine began to cry from upstairs, and she hurried to see what the problem was. It took her so long just to get up the stairs that she felt especially frustrated by the time she got there to realize that Katharine had not only broken a bottle of perfume on the bathroom floor, but she'd cut her foot on the glass. Between the blood, the glass, the potency of the perfume fragrance, and the screaming child, Jane almost felt nauseous while she did her best to take care of the wound, dry the tears, and clean up the mess. She gently scolded Katharine for getting into things that she knew were not for her, but realized how grateful she was that the cut on the child's foot had been minimal. And then the smoke alarm went off, scaring her so badly that she almost feared she might go into labor.

Recalling the meat she'd left cooking on the stove, Jane was struck with deep panic as the smell of smoke distinctly assaulted her senses. Heedless of being thirty-eight weeks pregnant, she scooped up Katharine and went down the stairs as quickly as she could manage. She screamed when she realized the kitchen was actually in flames.

Katharine immediately picked up on her mother's fear and began to wail. With no thought beyond just getting out of the house, Jane hurried toward the back door in the opposite direction from the fire, grateful to have Katharine in her arms and to know that Barrett was safely elsewhere. Once outside, she set Katharine down, unable to carry her another step. Keeping the child's hand in hers, heedless of her crying, she hurried up the driveway and considered it a huge blessing to find her neighbor, Sister McKenzie, pulling weeds in her front yard.

"Call 911!" Jane said the moment the woman looked up at her. "My kitchen's on fire."

"Oh my!" Sister McKenzie ran into her house and came out less than a minute later with the cordless phone in her hand to find Jane sitting on the lawn, trying to calm Katharine down. "It's done," she reported. "They're on their way. Are you all right, honey?"

"We're fine," Jane said, as contradictory tears rolled down her face. Her gratitude for their safety was sharply counteracted by the stark reality that her house was on fire. She couldn't believe it! Then she thought of Alex's uneasy feelings and wondered if this was the event he'd been unconsciously dreading. She prayed the damage wouldn't be too horrible, while she wondered how to tell Alex how stupid she'd been.

Sirens announced the coming of the cavalry to save her home, and within minutes the fire was out. Sister McKenzie stayed close to Jane through the drama, while other neighbors appeared, showing varying degrees of curiosity and concern. A friend from across the street quickly took Katharine to her home to distract her, and Jane was glad to have the child absent when she received the official report that her kitchen was gone but the rest of the house had been spared. The smoke and water damage, however, made the home unlivable until cleaning and repairs could be done. The fire officials offered a great deal of information concerning options, but Sister McKenzie took it all in better than Jane, who was more preoccupied with wondering how badly their belongings—specifically sentimental ones—had been damaged. She knew it could have been worse, but she still felt like the world had ended.

Watching the fire trucks drive away and the audience all returning to their homes, except for Sister McKenzie, who had a tight hold on her hand, Jane knew she couldn't wait any longer to call her husband. She almost prayed that he would be involved in some trauma and not be able to call her back for a couple of hours. But she knew that putting it off would make it harder.

"Come inside," Sister McKenzie said. "All of this can't be good for you in your condition."

"Thank you," Jane muttered and was relieved to be guided to a comfortable recliner, and then to have a tall glass of water put into her hand. "I'm so grateful you were here," Jane added.

"Me too, honey. And I'm grateful you and little Katharine are safe. I know it's hard, but everything's going to be okay."

Jane nodded but couldn't speak. Then she happened to see through the window a familiar car pulling into her drive. "Oh, good heavens," Jane said. "That's Alex's cousin. Will you . . . tell her I'm here before she panics? I don't think I can get there as quickly as you can."

"Of course, honey," the woman said and rushed outside.

She came back a couple of minutes later with Susan at her side. "Are you okay?" Susan asked, kneeling beside Jane and wrapping her in a motherly embrace.

Jane immediately started to cry. "Not really, but . . . well . . . obviously no one was hurt, and I'm grateful, but . . ." She couldn't go on.

"It's okay," Susan said. "Your family can live with us until everything's put in order. It will be okay."

Jane couldn't help feeling some relief. She hadn't even considered where they would go, but she had to admit staying with Susan was a comfortable option. The family had spent many hours in her home, and they were all familiar with Susan and Donald. There was no question about the space available, with the house being so huge.

"I need to call Alex," Jane said and became more emotional. "I don't know how to tell him. I feel so stupid. And I can't stop crying, and . . ."

"Do you want me to call him?" Susan offered. "I just had lunch with him."

"Would you?" Jane asked. He needed to know, but she didn't want to try to explain it through all of her blubbering.

"I'd be happy to," Susan said. She asked Jane some specific questions to make sure she had the story right, and then Sister McKenzie handed her the phone.

* * * * *

Alex was going over some paperwork when a nurse said, "You've got a call on line three."

"Thank you," he said and went to the phone.

"This is Dr. Keane," he said.

"Hello Alex," he heard Susan say.

"Is something wrong?" he asked, knowing she had been headed to his home.

"Everyone is fine," she said, but the way she said it made his heart pound.

"What's happened?"

Her voice was calm and even as she said, "There's been a fire, Alex."

"What?" he countered in a voice that made several staff members turn toward him, but he looked the other way and was glad when they all went back to their business. "What happened?" he asked again, more quietly. "Are you sure everyone is okay?"

"Yes. Katharine and Jane are fine. They got out without any trouble. Barrett is at school. Apparently Jane was cooking something and Katharine broke some glass upstairs and cut her foot. By the time Jane got everything taken care of, the kitchen was in flames." Alex put a hand over his mouth as he listened. "The fire is out. Only the kitchen area was affected. But there's smoke and water damage. That's why you're all going to come and stay with me for a while."

"I'm on my way home," Alex said, unable to keep his voice from trembling, wishing he couldn't be overheard.

"There's no need for that," Susan said. "There's nothing you can do right now. Just . . . finish your shift. I'm going to help Jane get some things together and I'll take them all home with me as soon as Barrett gets done at school."

Alex resisted the urge to ignore her admonition to stay at work, but he knew she was likely right. And he didn't want to leave the ER understaffed or have to call in another doctor if the need wasn't there.

"Okay," he said with hesitance. "Can I talk to Jane?"

"She's pretty upset, but . . . she's right here."

"Just let me talk to her," he said, needing to hear for himself that she was okay.

Jane looked up with alarm when Susan held out the phone, then nodded with encouragement as Jane took it from her, attempting to control her emotions.

"I'm so sorry, Alex," she said. "It was just plain stupid and I—"

"Jane," he interrupted gently, "it's okay. We didn't lose anything that's not replaceable. I love you and I'm just . . ." his voice cracked, ". . . so grateful that you and the kids are okay. That's all I care about."

"Okay," she said through a fresh bout of tears.

"I'll see you at Susan's as soon as I get off."

"Okay," she said again. "I love you too."

Alex hung up the phone and tried to calm his pounding heart. "Something wrong?" he heard a voice ask, and he turned to see Dr. Ray Baker, a friend and colleague of many years. A couple of nurses and a receptionist were also close by, looking concerned.

"Uh . . . there was a fire . . . at my home. But everyone's okay."

"Is there anything we can do?" one of the nurses asked.

"Uh . . . I don't think so, but thank you."

"Do you need to go?" Ray asked.

"My cousin's with Jane; she told me there was nothing I can do, that I should stay. I guess the drama is over."

"Relatively speaking," Ray said, putting a hand on Alex's shoulder. "Why don't you at least take a break? I'll let you know if anything comes in."

"Okay," Alex said and went to the lounge where he sank onto the couch, grateful to be alone when he couldn't hold back a sudden rush of tears. A mixture of fear and gratitude consumed him for a few minutes, then he just sat and stared, contemplating how much worse it could have been, but wondering how long it would take to undo the damages. It seemed they would be living with Susan until after the baby came. But maybe that wasn't such a bad thing.

* * * * *

Jane insisted she couldn't go back into the house, so Susan and Sister McKenzie went to gather some things the family would need. Jane told them where to find certain things and insisted they be careful, but Sister McKenzie reminded Jane that the house was sound and the fire was out. Jane had another good cry while they were gone, and was relieved when they returned to report that the upstairs bedrooms, where the doors had been closed, appeared to be fine and none of the clothes they'd gathered even had a vague aroma of smoke. Everything in the nursery—the farthest room from the kitchen—was just fine. The two women made a few trips into the house and came out with luggage packed for every member of the family with all of the essentials according to their logic and Jane's instructions. The luggage was all in the back of Susan's SUV when Susan and Jane went to pick up Barrett from preschool. Together they explained what had happened and why they would be going to stay with Susan. They picked up Katharine with the intent of Jane and the kids following Susan in her car, but Susan had barely pulled into Jane's driveway when Jane put a hand on Susan's arm.

"What?" she asked.

"I think I'm in labor," Jane reported in a calm voice that belied her desire to scream.

"Okay," Susan said with studied composure, "we'll put the children's seats in my car and I'll drive you to the hospital. I'll keep the kids with me. It'll be fine."

Jane sat in the passenger seat of Susan's car while she hurried to get the children buckled in safely. She could never put into words how grateful she was to have Susan with her. Of course she was always a phone call away, but it was nice not to have to even call.

On their way to the hospital the pains came on quickly. Susan dialed the ER with a speed-dial number on her cell phone. Jane was glad to hear that apparently she'd been put right through to Alex, and he wasn't in the middle of a trauma.

"What is it?" Alex asked, unable to help feeling panicked to hear Susan's voice—again. He glanced at the clock, noting there was less than an hour left of his shift.

"Jane's in labor," she said. "We're on our way."

"Okay," Alex said, his heart quickening for different reasons.

"I've got the kids in the car, so you need to meet us at the door. I'll turn her over to you and take the kids home with me."

"Okay," Alex said. "I'll be watching for you."

He hung up and hurried to call Dr. Terrence. He explained the situation to his coworkers who assured him that they'd take care of everything, and a few minutes later he saw Susan's SUV on the other side of the glass doors. He hurried out with a wheelchair and opened the passenger door to find Jane diligently breathing in short spurts as she endured a contraction. He squatted down beside her, waiting for the pain to relent. When she turned to him with tears in her eyes, he wrapped her in his arms, grateful beyond words to feel her there and safe.

"Hi, Daddy!" Katharine said from the backseat.

"Hi, princess," he said with a little chuckle.

"Mommy's going to have a baby," Barrett said.

"Yes, she is," Alex said and helped Jane into the wheelchair. Susan helped her get better situated while he opened the door to the backseat and hugged each of his children. "Now, you be good for Susan and I'll come and see you just as soon as the baby gets here."

He closed the door and hugged Susan, thanking her for everything, then he wheeled Jane into the hospital while he asked, "You okay?"

"Beyond pains less than a minute apart, I'm tolerable. How are you?"

"Knowing my family is safe and well, I'm fantastic."

Alex took her straight to labor and delivery, where the nurses barely had time to get her in a hospital gown before she was in transition and Dr. Terrence arrived.

"I'm just assisting," he said to Alex as he entered the delivery room.

Dr. Terrence made certain all was well while Alex coached Jane with her breathing and attempted to soothe her anxiety over there not being time for them to give her anything to ease the pain. Then a nurse held Jane's hand while Alex guided his new son into the world. He laughed when the baby let out a healthy cry, then he hurried to clamp the cord and cut it, leaving the rest of the work to Dr. Terrence while he moved to Jane's side and placed the baby in her arms.

"Oh," she said with tearful laughter, pressing a hand over the thick, dark hair on his head, "he looks like you."

Alex chuckled. "You have a vivid imagination," he said and kissed her.

"Is everything okay?" she asked, looking the baby over.

"He appears to be perfect," Alex said and wrapped his arms carefully around them both, silently thanking God for the miracles of this day.

Alex went with the baby while he was cleaned up and examined by the pediatrician. He was given a clean bill of health and Alex carried him into the room where Jane was recovering. She opened her eyes and smiled when she saw them.

"He's perfect," Alex said and set the baby close by her side. "And I think he looks like you."

Jane laughed softly and touched her baby's skin and hair, marveling at the miracle.

"How are you?" he asked, touching Jane's face.

"A little sore . . . tired, but not too bad, actually. It went so fast this time that I was scared there for a few minutes, but now that it's over I can admit that fast is better—only because I was close to the hospital and you were already here." Her chin began to quiver as she looked up at him. "I'm so sorry about the house, Alex."

"It's just a house, Jane," he said, kissing her brow. "People get distracted all the time. It's just one of those things. Everybody is safe and that's all that matters. No more apologies."

"You're so good to me," she said.

"No." He kissed her lips then looked at the baby. "It's the other way around. You make me happier every day."

Since Jane needed her sleep, and the baby was in good hands, Alex drove to Susan's house, and Katharine came running once he walked through the door. Barrett approached him more slowly, equally excited but less energetic. Alex laughed and picked them both up at the same time.

"You have a new brother," he announced, carrying them into the kitchen where Susan was making a salad.

"Everything's okay?" Susan asked eagerly as he set the children down.

"It's perfect," Alex said and laughed again. "And since I had the camera in my car, I have pictures."

The children made excited noises as they all followed him down the hall to the study where Susan's computer was kept. He'd spent many hours there working on genealogy with her, and he was comfortable using her equipment. He plugged in the memory stick from his digital camera, and within a couple of minutes the baby's plump little face filled the screen. They all laughed at the silly expression, then Susan said, "Oh, he's beautiful."

"He's a boy," Barrett protested. "He can't be beautiful. He's handsome."

"Oh, you're right," Susan said. "He certainly is handsome."

"I think his face looks kind of red and fat," Barrett said.

Alex chuckled. "He'll get over that."

He pulled up a few more pictures, including one of Jane holding the baby that he just couldn't keep from staring at until he scooped the children into his arms again, silently thanking God for how richly his life was blessed.

Alex was glad to have the next day off. He woke up finding serenity in his surroundings. He loved this house, but he'd never actually slept here. Lying in bed, he pondered the events of the previous day and felt immensely grateful. Then that uneasy feeling came over him again, and he almost felt angry. He'd been certain the fire should have justified all those feelings, and now that the baby was here he wanted to believe that all was well. He considered Jane's suggestion that he might be in for a new Church calling, or perhaps simply some kind of change. But that just didn't feel right. Examining his feelings closely, he truly felt that something wasn't right and he needed to be alert; he needed to figure it out. He prayed for guidance and tried to push it out of his mind and enjoy the reality of having a new member of the family.

He called Jane at the hospital to be assured that all was well. "This is a switch," he said. *"Me* calling *you* at the hospital."

"I think I prefer it the other way around," she said. "Although they are treating me very well."

"As they should."

She insisted that everything was fine and he should spend some time with the kids before he came in. He gave Katharine a bath, and then he turned her over to Susan to fix her hair. Donald had left early to go fishing with a friend.

While Alex was bathing Barrett he noticed a couple of nasty bruises on his legs. "What happened, buddy?" he asked.

"I don't know," Barrett said, seeming surprised by them.

"You didn't fall down, or . . . bump into something?"

"I don't remember," he said, genuinely puzzled, and Alex let it drop.

During breakfast Barrett seemed quiet and a little under the weather. Alex touched his face and found it mildly feverish. "Do you feel sick?" he asked.

"Kind of," Barrett said and left his breakfast untouched to go and lie on the couch.

"I guess he won't be going to preschool today," Susan said. "But don't you worry. I'm very good at taking care of sick children. He probably just has a touch of the flu."

"Probably," Alex said, not liking the idea of bringing home a new baby to a house with a virus in it. And he couldn't help feeling concerned for Barrett. It was never fun having a sick child, and he hoped that whatever it was passed quickly. He got Barrett a blanket and pillow and some children's Tylenol, making sure he was comfortable with one of his favorite TV shows. While Katharine was helping Susan load the dishwasher, Alex made some calls to arrange for a disaster cleanup company to begin putting his home back together. He then answered some messages that had been left on his cell phone from members of the ward who were concerned. He let everyone know that all was well, the baby had come, and they were staying with relatives. He made arrangements with a retired neighbor to help mediate with the people who would be repairing the damages. Then he called friends and relatives to tell them about the new arrival.

When his calls were finished, he found Barrett asleep and slightly feverish. Susan assured him that she was delighted to care for the children and he should stay at the hospital with Jane as long as he wanted. Carrying a dozen roses, he arrived to find Jane rested and looking radiant. And no matter what Barrett said, he had to admit the baby was beautiful. They sat together and just enjoyed their new son through the better part of the afternoon, settling firmly on the name Preston Alexander—Preston because they both had ancestors who had come from Preston, England, after joining the Church. And now a temple and an MTC were there.

Alex told Jane about the calls he'd made, and about the arrangements to have work started on the house. Jane shuddered visibly and said, "I don't know if I ever want to go back there. It just gives me the creeps."

Alex nearly suggested that they could certainly sell it and move elsewhere, but he figured that conversation would be better for another time. And perhaps by the time it was ready to move back into, she would change her mind.

Jane asked how the children were doing, and Alex mentioned Barrett's fever.

"He sure has gotten sick a lot this last spring," she said absently while she patted the baby against her shoulder in an effort to get a burp out of him. "I need to pump him up with vitamins or something to build up his immune system, I guess."

Alex fought to keep from letting on to how his heart had just begun to thud. Was this spiritual guidance or paranoia? he wondered. And the answer was immediate. All of his uneasy feelings culminated with one startling realization. *Something was wrong with Barrett!* And it wasn't the flu. But he didn't want Jane getting upset or panicking, so he decided that he wasn't going to say anything at all until he had something to tell her.

Feeling almost nauseous, he fought to keep his voice and expression steady as he said, "I think I'll go check on the kids and give Susan a break. I'll stop by this evening."

"Okay," she said, and he kissed her. They shared a smile and another kiss before he held the baby a minute and left the room. Once beyond the maternity ward he practically ran to his car. The drive to Susan's house left him impatient. He almost felt that if he didn't get to Barrett within minutes he might lose him, even though logic told him that was ridiculous. Praying silently, he felt a degree of calmness seep into him. He knew he'd been prompted, and that alone led him to hope that whatever the problem might be, he had caught it quickly enough to counteract any permanent problems. He thought of all the diseases he'd been well-versed on through medical school that could cripple children and leave them with brain damage. He forced his mind away from that, needing to believe that whatever it was couldn't be that serious.

Alex ran into the house and found Barrett sleeping on Susan's bed, wearing pajamas. She was sitting nearby crocheting something while she watched TV. "Donald took Katharine on an errand. Barrett was up for a while and seemed better, and then the fever went up again. I gave him more Tylenol, but he wanted to put on his jammies."

"Okay, thank you," Alex said and briefly pressed his fingers against Barrett's neck and under his arms, causing the child to stir slightly before Alex scooped him up.

"Where are you going?" Susan asked, following them out of the room.

"I'm taking him to the hospital," he said. "I just . . . want a blood test . . . to make sure it's not something serious."

"Okay," Susan said. "Call if you need anything."

"Thank you," he called and hurried outside.

Barrett came partly awake as Alex buckled him into his car seat. "You okay, buddy?" he asked.

"Yeah," the child said and yawned. "Where are we going?"

"I'm just going to have a doctor check you and see why you're sick," he said as he kissed the boy's forehead. Then he got into the front seat and drove back to the hospital. He'd never been so grateful for his job as when he walked through the ambulance entrance and said to the girls behind the desk, whom he knew very well, "This is my son. Get me the admitting papers, whatever it takes."

"Okay," they both said, and he was glad to observe that the place was quiet. He was even gladder to see Ray Baker standing nearby. Ray followed him into a vacant exam room where Alex gently laid Barrett down.

"What's up?" Ray asked.

"I need a CBC with differential, as quickly as possible."

"Okay," Ray said. "I'm on it."

Alex held Barrett close while the blood was drawn, and he was grateful for Becky, a nurse he knew well, who provided a red sucker that helped quiet Barrett's crying. While they were waiting, Ray came in and sat down. "Talk to me," he said to Alex, who had Barrett on his lap.

"He gets sick a lot," Alex said in a calm voice, not wanting to upset Barrett. "I hadn't really thought much about it until he got a fever today, but . . . it happens a lot—too much. He has enlarged lymph nodes. And what do you make of this?" He lifted the pant legs of Barrett's pajamas and showed him the bruises. "He can't even remember how he got them. Those are pretty deep bruises for a kid not to remember getting hurt."

"I'd agree with that," Ray said, but the look in his eyes was something Alex didn't want to ponder.

"I just want to know if there's anything going on, anything at all. Cover all the bases. Give it to me like any other parent in here with a sick kid."

"Okay," Ray said and pressed a hand over Alex's shoulder before he left the room.

Alex fought to hold back the temptation to cry. After the accident he'd been in with Jane years ago, he'd never wanted to be on the receiving end of this place again. But here he was. And what would Jane think if she knew that he was here? How would she feel about his train of thought? He never wanted to have to tell her. He told himself that maybe it wasn't anything serious, that perhaps his prompting had been to prevent it from turning into something serious. But something deeper, more profound, more *real* than any physical pain, told him they were on the brink of a nightmare.

Becky came in to ask questions in order to do the paperwork; she came back a short while later with papers for him to sign. Barrett fell asleep with the sucker in his mouth. Alex took it out and tossed it into a trash can where he had countless times thrown used gloves, bloodied gauze, and any other number of used medical items. But never a used sucker. He pondered the distant noises of the ER on the other side of that door, and the torturous feeling of waiting and wondering. Did God consider it necessary to occasionally give him empathy for being on the other side? Was this meant to help him understand how difficult it was for the patients he regularly dealt with to wait? Well, he considered that lesson learned and wanted to move on. He found himself listing diseases and symptoms in his head, wondering what words he might be confronted with. One word in particular kept circling in his mind but he couldn't bring himself to even consider it a possibility. But the symptoms were clear. And the very idea brought on a wave of nausea.

Alex held Barrett close and immersed himself in a silent prayer for strength, for guidance, for this child to be well. Surely it was coincidence, a mistake. The waiting became irrelevant when his prayers became all consuming, and he lost all sense of time. When Baker came through the door it startled Alex, then he realized that his arm was aching and his leg was asleep from holding Barrett in the same position for so long. His heart beat painfully hard, and his mouth went dry as Baker closed the door and took a seat. Alex wondered if his own countenance looked like that when he was about to deliver bad news. Alex stood and laid Barrett carefully on the exam table, grateful that he rolled over and remained asleep. Leaning against the edge of the table, he folded his arms and said, "Okay, let me have it."

"Okay," Baker said, but his hesitance was all too apparent. "I'm going to do as you asked, and give it to you like I would any other parent." He sighed loudly. "I'm arranging for you to meet with an oncologist immediately."

Alex felt his mind protest silently. *Oncologist? Immediately?* That much left him relatively certain even before Baker added, "It looks like leukemia, Alex."

That was it. That was the word he'd wanted to avoid. And it was ugly. He groaned and looked away as if he could hide from the truth.

"His white count is 140,000," Baker said, and Alex groaned again. He didn't even have to ask what that meant. It was serious. It was out of control.

"You need to take him next door," Baker said, and it took Alex a moment to realize what he meant. Primary Children's Medical Center was literally situated right next to the hospital where Alex worked. How could he not count that as a blessing in the face of this horror? He knew that people traveled long distances to have their children treated here. But for them it was as good as in their own backyard.

"I've already called," Baker went on. "It's all arranged. They're waiting for you. We've got to get that white count down and get him stabilized, and then find out exactly where it stands. If I were you, I would insist they move quickly. He needs a bone marrow aspirate, lumbar punctures, and CT scans. Then they'll know for sure, and know exactly what to do."

Alex squeezed his eyes closed. He knew what those first two tests entailed, and just the thought of his son enduring them made the sickness inside him smolder. But in his heart he knew that would only be the beginning. The road to surviving this disease would be hellish—plain and simple.

Certain he would lose control at any moment, Alex muttered quietly, "Thank you." His voice broke and trembled. "I need to be alone."

"I understand," Ray said and left the room, closing the door behind him.

Alex wrapped his arms around his middle and groaned as he sank to his knees and curled around the painful knots inside of him. "No," he muttered quietly, over and over. "No, no. No! Please God, no. Let it be something else, anything else." But he knew the diagnosis was correct. He just knew. The needed tests would confirm it beyond question, but in his heart he already knew. And if Barrett had been anyone else's child, maybe he would have spotted it much sooner, or figured it out from the symptoms more easily. Had it been some level of denial that had kept him from wanting to even consider that something was wrong? Logically he could assess that the symptoms had been vague, and anyone could have missed it. But that didn't keep him from feeling an onslaught of guilt. And beyond that, he had no idea how he was even going to make it through another hour, let alone all that lay ahead.

Reminding himself of where he was, Alex forced himself to his senses and scooped Barrett into his arms. Carrying him out to the car, he was assailed with the mental image of Abraham putting Isaac on the altar. But he wondered if Abraham had considered how he was going to tell Isaac's mother.

Chapter 3

In the car, Barrett came fully awake, and Alex had to resist the urge to give in to his grief during the few minutes it took him to park in a place closest to where they needed to go. Realizing what could be happening once they walked through those doors, he got into the backseat next to Barrett and struggled for the words to prepare him.

"Hey there, buddy. We're at a different hospital now. This is a hospital that is especially for children. I need you to be very grown up and listen carefully to what I have to say. There isn't time to talk much right now, but we can talk more about it later. Right now you need to know that the doctors think there might be something wrong with you that could be very serious, and we need to do some things to get it taken care of so you won't get more sick."

"Am I going to get another shot?" he asked, referring to the blood he'd had drawn.

"I'm afraid so," Alex said, not even wanting to think about how invasive all of this would be to Barrett's little body and tender emotions. "But I'm going to stay with you every minute. I promise."

Barrett nodded, and Alex carried him inside, but he wondered if the child was too sleepy to grasp what Alex had said, or too scared to talk about it.

Once inside Alex informed them of who he was and why he was there, and the concept of emergency medicine took on an entirely different perspective. He recognized the urgency of several people surrounding them all at once, working together efficiently to keep the child calm and do what had to be done whether he remained calm or not. He was grateful for an atmosphere and attitude that was clearly part of a facility specifically geared to treating children. They were kind and patient with Barrett, but no amount of soothing could counteract the effects of the pain being inflicted on him as an IV was inserted and more blood drawn. Alex found it difficult to stand back and not be actively involved when he knew exactly what to do, but at the same time he had no desire to actually be the one sticking needles into his own son.

When the chaos quieted down to torturous waiting, Alex held Barrett's little hand in his while the child became absorbed in a video that had been provided. *He couldn't believe it.* He'd experienced shock and horror in his life before, but somehow this felt worse. Barrett was a child, barely on the brink of beginning to discover his own independence, of embarking on his life.

Trying not to think too hard about what was happening, Alex realized the room they were in had a sense of familiarity. It only took him a moment to recall that he'd done r otations in this hospital. With one memory came another, and another. A series of disjointed events in his residency swirled together in his mind. Such memories were filed away in the part of his brain that exclusively held his professional life. He'd seen firsthand many medical horrors that were the result of accidents, crime, and disease. Many had been disturbing to a point of leaking over into his personal life, creating a certain level of depression. Before completing his residency he had learned to carefully assess a situation, remain emotionally detached beyond the need to be compassionate and offer an appropriate bedside manner, and then he would file the memories away into an imaginary box that kept him from ever having to look at them again. Of course, there were times when one medical trauma might trigger another. There was information in that box he often needed to draw on in order to deal with whatever he might be faced with. But never—*never*—had he believed that some of the most difficult memories would leak into his personal life. They were all filed neatly behind the label, PEDIATRIC ONCOLOGY. He'd seen every level of the process of children with cancer, from onset, through chemo and radiation, and the horror of bone marrow transplants. And he'd even been there for the final blow—delivering the news to horrified parents that nothing more could be done.

Alex turned to look at Barrett and felt the connection take place in his brain. The possible journey before them became excruciatingly clear. He felt suddenly ill and hurried into the bathroom, certain he was going to throw up. He managed to get it under control, but he had to take hold of the edge of the sink and hang his head lower than his heart to get past a sensation of losing consciousness while he gasped for breath. "Please God," he muttered hotly. "Why this? Why *this?*" He wondered why it couldn't be a localized cancer that could be removed surgically and treated locally. Chemotherapy and radiation for any cancer were a nightmare, but he couldn't even bring himself to wonder if Barrett would ever need a bone marrow transplant. The idea was just too horrific to swallow.

Alex had to pray away the images in order to even be able to find the strength to stand up straight. He took several deep breaths and went back to Barrett's side, but sitting there the battle going on in his head continued to rage. He became so immersed in the nightmare of the moment that it startled him to realize there would be people wondering where he was. He glanced at his watch, relieved to realize it wasn't as late as it felt.

"Barrett," Alex said, and the child turned toward him with no sign of fear or trauma in his eyes. How grateful he was for the resiliency of children! But if he knew the reality. . . .

"I need to go use the phone. I'll be back in a few minutes." There was a phone in the room, but he didn't want Barrett to overhear, and he couldn't use his cell phone in this part of the hospital. "You just watch your movie."

"You'll be back?"

"I promise."

Barrett nodded and turned his attention back to the TV.

Alex hurried to find a phone, but he knew there was nothing he could say to Jane that didn't need to be said face-to-face. Instead he called his father. While the phone was ringing, Alex briefly pondered the relationship he shared with this man. It was full of irony and poignancy, but they had come to a place where they were truly friends. At the age of thirteen, Alex had been devastated by his father's choice to leave the family for another woman. While Alex had spent twenty years being bitter over that choice and the challenges that followed, Neil Keane had eventually come to terms with his problems, done his best to make restitution, and had come back into the Church. The woman he'd been involved with had gone back to her family. Neil had regained a mutual respect with Alex's mother before she died, and he was now married to Roxanne, a wonderful woman who accepted Neil completely in spite of the challenges of his past. Eventually Alex had been able to forgive his father and let go of his own issues in order to do the same. He was grateful now to have his father in his life; there was comfort in just hearing him answer the phone, and knowing that a connection existed between them.

"Dad," Alex said, surprised by how emotional it sounded.

"Alex? What's wrong? Is the baby okay?"

"The baby is fine," Alex said, but the strain in his voice was evident.

"Jane?"

"Jane's fine. It's . . . Barrett. I just found out that . . . it looks like he probably . . . has leukemia, Dad." There. He'd said it. He'd actually let the word pass through his lips in relation to his own child.

"It can't be," Neil muttered.

"I'm at Primary Children's Medical Center. They're trying to stabilize him, and they're going to do some tests. I can tell you the details later, but . . . I need to talk to Jane. She doesn't know yet. But I can't leave him alone."

"I'm on my way," Neil said, and Alex told him where to find them. He felt some relief to know that a measure of support was on its way. Fearing Jane might be worried before he could get there, he called the nurses' station in the maternity ward and just asked that they tell her something had come up to delay him, but he'd be there in a while.

Alex then phoned Susan. She immediately said, "Something's wrong, isn't it. You've been gone for hours."

"Yeah," Alex said, "but . . . I can't talk about it right now. I'm at Primary Children's. Barrett will be staying and I'm staying with him. I do need to come home and get a few things later; we can talk then. Will Katharine be okay if—"

"Don't you even give her a second's thought. We'll take care of whatever you need us to do."

"Thank you," Alex said. "I'll try not to get there too late."

"It doesn't matter how late. We'll talk when you get here."

"Thank you," Alex said again and ended the call. He took a deep breath and returned to Barrett's room to find him still engrossed in the video. Something more connected in Alex's brain. He'd noticed that Barrett had been more drawn to quiet activities: watching TV, playing with puzzles, coloring, looking at story-books. Alex had simply credited it to a new stage. But now he had to wonder if it had been a lack of energy that had kept him from activities that were more physical. And how long had it been since the change had taken place? How long had this evil been growing in Barrett's body while they'd been completely oblivious?

Alex sat down and took Barrett's hand. The child glanced toward him but hardly seemed to notice. And that was fine. Alex was all for any distraction from the nightmare.

The video ended, and Alex turned off the TV. He knew that he needed to give a better explanation to Barrett in order for him to be more prepared for what lay ahead. But he couldn't bring himself to do it, not yet. He needed to think it through. Instead he spoke in an animated voice about the new baby, and learning to read, and they sang the ABC song together. Barrett asked if they could go to the zoo now that it wasn't winter anymore. Alex promised him that they would.

While a nurse was checking Barrett's IV and engaging him in conversation about preschool and his friends, Alex noticed his father at the door. "I'll be right back," he said to Barrett and hurried into the hall. He had expected to be relieved to see his father. What he hadn't expected was to have all the grief and fear and sorrow he'd felt in the last few hours come rushing out of him in heaving sobs as Neil wrapped him in a father's love. He was grateful that they were alone in the hall, although he doubted he was the only parent to ever fall apart in this place.

When Alex had managed to calm down, Neil said gently, "You need to tell me everything."

"Yes, I do," Alex said, wiping at his face. "But Jane doesn't even know yet. I told her I'd be back. I have to go. We'll talk later."

"Sounds good," Neil said.

Alex took a deep breath and went back into Barrett's room with Neil at his side. "Look who's here," Alex said in a bright voice.

"Hi, Grandpa," Barrett said eagerly. "I'm sick," he added as if it were something positive.

"I can see that," Neil said. "And I get to visit with you while your father goes to see Mommy and the new baby."

"Can I see the baby?" Barrett asked.

"Soon," Alex said. "Right now you just visit with Grandpa and be a good boy." He pressed a kiss to Barrett's forehead, momentarily lingering close to him as if he might never have the chance again.

"He'll be fine," Neil said. "Run along. We'll have a marvelous time."

"Thank you," Alex said and hurried out of the room.

Not even bothering to get in the car, he just hurried to the other hospital, running when he wouldn't disturb anyone by doing so. Exerting the energy helped suppress his hovering grief back to where he could handle it. Once in the maternity area, he found a men's room where he splashed cold water on his face and blotted it dry with paper towels, at the same time catching his breath. Just thinking of what he was about to do made him sick to his stomach. He thought of seeing the picture of Jane and the baby on the computer screen; what he had to tell her felt like throwing a rock at it, shattering the perfection of this joyous event in their lives and replacing it with one of horror.

Drawing courage, he looked at himself in the mirror, hoping he didn't look like he'd been crying. With a prayer in his heart he went to face his wife.

* * * * *

Jane got the baby to sleep and left him in the center of her bed before she took a careful trip to the bathroom. She made herself comfortable in a recliner near the bed and picked up a magazine that a friend had brought when she'd come to see the new baby. A minute later she looked up to see Alex leaning in the doorway, watching her. Just seeing him took her breath away, and she considered herself the luckiest woman alive to be the mother of his children. His hair had that neatly mussed look that made her want to touch it. He wore comfortable jeans with soft leather hiking boots—his shoe of preference for work or play—and a white T-shirt beneath a long jacket that was pushed behind the hands that were placed casually on his hips.

"Hi," she said, then something tightened inside of her as she paused to consider his countenance and the way he seemed stuck at the door.

"Hi," he replied, his voice solemn, no hint of a smile.

"What's wrong?" she asked, hoping he would hurry to tell her that everything was fine. Maybe he was just tired, or he'd been notified that something horrible had happened in the ER. But he said nothing.

"Alex?" she said. "Has somebody died, or what?"

No, came his silent response, *but our son has been given a probable death sentence.* He reminded himself that much could be done; Barrett's chances of survival could be high. Or they could not. But whether he survived or not, the journey ahead was one that no child should have to endure.

He forced himself into the room and moved a chair directly in front of her, where he sat and leaned his forearms on his thighs.

"Alex?" she said again.

"Uh . . . you know those uneasy feelings I've been having?"

"Yes," she said, her voice tightening.

"I was hoping it had to do with the fire, but I woke up with it again this morning. Only stronger. Now I'm thinking that maybe the fire was a blessing."

"A blessing?" she asked, wishing she could even begin to guess what was coming.

"I think it might be good for us to be living with Susan and Donald," he said.

"Okay," she drawled. "Get to the point."

Alex sighed and leaned back in his chair, but he couldn't look at her. "When I left here . . . earlier . . . I didn't want to say anything, but . . . I knew something was wrong." He glanced at Jane, but her overt fear made him turn away. He pressed on. "I took Barrett to the ER . . . asked for some blood work."

He heard her suck in her breath. Her voice was barely audible when she asked, "What are you saying?"

Alex felt his throat become constricted and his voice rasped as he said, "There's a reason he keeps getting sick, Jane . . . a reason he sits in one place while Katharine is all over the place . . . and the bruises." A sob jumped out of his throat and he pushed his hands brutally into his hair. "I should have seen it," he cried. "I'm a doctor, for the love of heaven. I should have known."

"Known what, Alex?" she growled, shaking his shoulders with her hands.

Jane became consumed with a dread unlike anything she'd ever experienced as Alex lifted his head to show tears tumbling from beneath his closed eyelids.

"It's probably leukemia," he said, and she felt herself tremble from the inside out.

"No," she muttered, and Alex pushed the chair back and went to his knees in front of her, burying his face in her lap, sobbing helplessly. The evidence of his grief shattered any hope she had to be spared from feeling what she'd just learned. As Jane also started to sob, Alex raised up enough to wrap her in his arms, urging her face to his chest. They held each other and cried only a few minutes before she took his shoulders into her hands again and looked into his eyes, saying hotly, "Tell me. Tell me everything." He looked hesitant and she asked, "Will he die, Alex?"

"I don't know," he said, his voice raspy. "He needs tests to determine exactly what we're dealing with, and how far it has progressed."

"Then it's not certain yet?"

"Every symptom is there, Jane. The tests are necessary to be certain, but . . . I just . . . know. All those uneasy feelings just . . . came together and . . . I knew." He hung his head. "I should have seen it sooner, Jane. I should have known."

"You can't blame yourself for this," she insisted.

Alex sat on the floor and leaned back against the wall. "I certainly didn't cause it, but I think I could have caught it earlier. When he kept getting sick . . . I should have suspected something."

"Lots of kids have strings of colds and flu, Alex."

"I know," he said. "But . . . I keep thinking about . . . how he'd say he was tired and he wanted me to carry him. He's done that a lot, you know. I thought he just . . . wanted attention because I carry Katharine more than him."

"I've noticed him seeming weak sometimes. I just thought that . . . I don't know. I thought kids can't be full of energy every minute of the day." She put a hand over her mouth and cried new tears. "I'm with him more than you are. I should have seen there was a problem, that he . . ." She became too emotional to speak, and Alex realized he could never blame her for not picking up on such subtle symptoms. And if he couldn't blame her, he certainly couldn't waste energy by blaming himself. The past couldn't be changed; they just had to move forward.

He took her hand into his. "It doesn't matter, Jane. What's past is past. I'd like to think that the prompting I had today means that it's being caught early enough to stop it. I know they can do a great deal to treat it, but it's one of those things where . . . the treatments that can save his life are often worse than the disease. And we have to face the fact that . . . well, I know they've made great progress. They save a lot more lives than they used to, but . . . still, a lot of people die from leukemia every year." He shook his head and groaned while Jane cried silent tears. "I'm a doctor, Jane. And there is absolutely nothing I can personally do to change this or fix it. Even if I were a cancer specialist, I could not take away what he's going to have to go through."

Neither of them said anything for several minutes while they were each lost in their own attempt to accept what they'd learned. Jane broke the silence by saying, "Where is he now?"

"Dad's with him; he's at Primary Children's."

"Already?" She sounded horrified.

"It's serious, Jane. They need to get him stabilized. His white blood count is completely out of control."

"What does that mean?" she asked as if he might have all the answers. He could answer the question, but he couldn't solve the problem. And he *hated* it.

"White blood cells fight infection," he said. "With leukemia, the body produces too many of one type of blood cells. Because the cells are abnormal, they don't function properly." He went on to try and give her a brief overview of the basics, feeling disoriented as he gave a discourse that didn't seem right within the context of his own family.

"So, now what?"

Alex reached up to take her hand. "They're doing some tests very early in the morning. I'm going to stay with him—tonight and . . . as long as it takes."

Jane watched her husband's visible anguish and wondered what he might not be telling her. Not that she felt he would withhold information from her, but just knowing he was a doctor made it evident he understood all of this at a level that she felt certain she could never grasp. She wondered if she should be frustrated by her lack of knowledge, or grateful. Either way, there were things she just had to know. "What kind of tests?" she asked, feeling as if she were viewing all of this from a distance. It couldn't be real. It just couldn't.

Jane saw something in his eyes that let her know he didn't want to tell her. He hesitated, and she was ready to prod him, but he said firmly, "They need a sample of his spinal fluid and his bone marrow."

She thought about that for a moment and felt a little sick. "Will he be put out while they do it?"

"I believe so. And . . . I believe they'll give him a drug that . . ." he hesitated, "well, it makes you forget."

"In other words, the procedure is traumatic."

Alex hung his head. "They're also going to install a central line."

"What is that?" she demanded, almost sounding angry.

"It's a tube that's surgically inserted into a vein just above the heart. It sounds awful but it's actually kept there through the course of the treatments and eliminates the need for all the needles and poking. The chemotherapy, blood draws, everything is done through that."

Jane was thoughtful and quiet, attempting to take it all in. "I need to be with him." She glanced at the baby.

"You need to be with the baby; you need to take care of yourself. I have tomorrow off, and I'll get more time off—whatever I have to. I can be with him. Donald and Susan said they'll do whatever we need. Katharine's in good hands."

Jane nodded. "Now I understand why you said that maybe the fire was a blessing." She looked at him hard. "You don't think that . . . it really *is* a blessing? That it . . . was meant to happen?"

"Who knows?" he said. "Probably not. But I can't deny being grateful to know that we're under the same roof with Donald and Susan. And I think that the baby coming early, and Barrett's symptoms . . . and the prompting . . . today . . . are all part of some very important timing. It's as if . . . we couldn't possibly wait any longer."

"Then . . . perhaps . . . we have hope that he'll make it through."

Alex sighed. "We can't give up hope, Jane." He recalled the spiritual impression he'd had the other day and repeated it to her, reminding himself that he'd been promised that trusting in God would see his family through any possible trial.

"We have evidence that God is with us." She squeezed his hand.

"Yes, I believe we do, and . . . we have family and friends who will help us get through this. But we also have to realize that . . . Jane, I work right next door to the best children's medical center in five states; it's one of the best pediatric cancer centers in the country. Do you have any idea what a blessing that is?" He went to his knees again, touching her face, and then he kissed her. "We're going to get through this, Jane. Do you hear me? It's going to be hard, but we're going to do it—together. You, me, and God. Do you understand?"

She nodded tearfully, and he held her close.

"Alex," she said, "we need to let people know. We need them to fast for him; we need the prayers of loved ones."

"Of course," he said. "Maybe Susan and Roxanne could help make calls."

"Have you told anyone yet?"

"Just my father. Donald and Susan know something's wrong but I told them we'd talk later."

"Mom and Dad are coming the day after tomorrow to see the baby. I talked to Susan. She said there was no problem with them staying there. Maybe the timing of that is good as well." Alex nodded, and she added, "Is he okay? Right now?"

"Oh, yeah, he's fine. He was acting like nothing was wrong. He's got an IV and he's dealt with a lot of needles. He wasn't very happy about it, but he's a brave kid."

Jane tried to smile but started to cry instead. She didn't want to admit that a part of her felt grateful she had the excuse of just giving birth to keep her from witnessing what Alex was having to face. She wanted to thank him for being there, for buffering her from the horror. But she couldn't find the words.

"Does he know?" she asked, wiping at her eyes.

Alex shook his head. "He obviously knows something is wrong. I told him the doctors needed to do tests to find the problem. But how do you tell a kid something like this?"

"I wish we could tell him together," she said, and then his pager beeped. "Who is it?" she asked as he looked at it.

"The ER," he said and stood up to use the phone in the room to call them. He was immediately put through to Dr. Baker. "What's up?" he asked.

"You okay?"

"All things considered, but . . ." He didn't finish.

"I just wanted you to know that your shift for the day after tomorrow is covered, and we'll work on giving you some more time, at least until Jane can recover. I know one of you needs to be with Barrett."

"Thank you," Alex said.

"It's not a problem. Let me know if there's anything you need. We'll be in touch."

"Okay, thanks. I owe you one."

"Nah. Just take good care of your family."

"I'll do my best." Alex hung up and said to Jane, "That was Baker. He's helping me get some time off." He glanced at his watch. "I don't want to go, but . . . I've got to get some stuff at the house, and talk to Donald and Susan, and Dad's with Barrett and—"

"It's okay," Jane said, coming to her feet.

Alex took her in his arms, holding her tightly. He looked down and gave a slight smile. "Hey, I can hug you again . . . now that the baby's over there."

"I love you, Alex. You're right. We'll get through this together."

He kissed her. "I don't want to leave you here alone with this to think about. I don't want to be alone with this to think about."

"It'll be okay," she said, but her chin quivered before she kissed him again. "Let me know. Call me whenever it's possible."

"I will."

Alex pressed a hand over the baby's wispy hair while he slept, then he kissed Jane once more and hurried out of the room. Driving home he phoned Barrett's room, and Neil answered the phone.

"How is he?"

"He's great. I think he must have gotten a lot of rest today because he's sure not interested in sleeping now. We're having a good time."

"Okay, I'm glad to hear it. I'm going home to get a few things, and I'll be back."

"Take your time," Neil said, but Alex felt like he needed to talk to Barrett tonight before he *did* go to sleep.

Back at the house, Alex found Donald and Susan waiting for him, and Katharine had gone to bed. Their anxious faces made it evident they'd been worried and speculating. "What did you find out?" Susan asked as he sat down across from them.

Alex couldn't even consider answering the question without feeling sick. He knew Susan had picked up on the depth of his anxiety when she said with concern, "Alex?"

"Just give me a minute," he said and pressed his hands through his hair.

As if to ease the tension, Donald said, "Congratulations on that new baby. Can't wait to meet him. I saw the pictures. He's a real cutie."

"Yes, he certainly is," Alex said.

"Just tell us what's wrong," Donald said gently, and Alex watched him and Susan exchange a concerned glance. He still couldn't get the words to form, and Donald added, "We're family, son. Tell us what we can do to help."

"Um . . . I . . . I . . . took Barrett for a blood test . . . on a hunch, perhaps." He watched their faces tighten with dread and Susan took hold of her husband's hand where it rested on the table. Alex looked away. "It's . . . very likely . . . leukemia." There. He'd said it again. And with the word came the tears. But Susan was crying too. They both looked horrified. "I . . . should have seen it. I'm a doctor, for crying out loud. How could I miss the symptoms?"

"What *are* the symptoms?" Donald asked.

Alex did his best to explain, at the same time trying not to hold onto regret for not seeing the signs sooner. They assured him as Jane had that anyone could miss the signs, but he was still having trouble with that.

"Have you told Jane?" Susan asked.

"Yeah. I didn't want to." His emotions got the better of him.

"She didn't want to tell you that she'd tried to burn the house down," Susan said with a smile. Alex only shook his head as if it might help him grasp all that had happened in two days.

"We'll do whatever we can to help," Donald said. "Consider us full-time child care and taxi service. Whatever you need."

"Thank you," Alex said. "I have to admit that maybe the fire turned out to be a blessing. Maybe we needed to be here."

"Maybe you did," Susan said gently. "Don't even worry about Katharine. For the next few days, you take care of Barrett, and we'll take care of Katharine and Jane, and she can take care of the baby."

"Thank you," he said. "I don't know what we'd do without you."

"I'm sure you would have figured something out," Donald said, "but we're glad to help."

They offered to help call family and friends, but Alex realized that he could actually email most of the people who mattered. Before he did that he called the bishop of their home ward and explained the situation. He told him what had been arranged regarding the house, assured him that they were in good hands where they were staying, and asked that ward members might pray, and perhaps fast, for Barrett. The bishop eagerly agreed to spread the word, and he made Alex promise to call if any needs arose.

Alex then sent out a group email that included every friend and family member who used the Internet. He attached a picture of the baby and began the letter with an official birth announcement, following it with the solemn news that Barrett likely had leukemia. He told of the tests that would be taking place the following day, asked for fasting and prayers on Barrett's behalf, and promised to send out future emails with information. He mentioned that he would likely not be available by phone, but he included Susan's phone number at her suggestion. After clicking the SEND icon, he hurried to call Jane's parents before they had a chance to check their email. He was glad they lived in California, as it was an hour earlier there. He told Jane's father the news and wasn't surprised by his shock. They were both glad to know that arrangements had already been made for Walter and Louisa to soon be here. Alex then checked the address book in his planner to figure out who else needed to be informed. Susan agreed to make those calls for him in the morning. He felt deeply relieved not to have to repeat the news over and over.

Having done all he could at the moment, Alex went to Katharine's room and watched her sleeping, praying that she wouldn't fall between the cracks and have emotional trauma over what was facing her family. He peeked into Barrett's empty room and wished he could think of his son without wanting to burst into tears. Through the drive back to the hospital he couldn't hold them back. He hadn't cried like this since Jane had recovered from that coma and he had come to terms with issues in his life that had caused him so much grief. Life had felt close to perfect since he and Jane had married. And now this. This was a nightmare. But he knew when he woke up tomorrow it was still going to be there.

Mingled with his tears was a fervent prayer. He asked specifically for guidance in knowing how much and what to tell Barrett about the situation. He was pleased when the words came to him, then disappointed when he arrived to find that Barrett was sleeping soundly while his father sat close by, reading a magazine. Alex sat on the edge of Barrett's bed and just watched him, touching his face and hair, praying that he would endure this well—and come through triumphant.

"Okay, talk to me," Neil said quietly.

Alex sighed and started at the beginning, telling his father of the uneasy feelings he'd been having that had led up to today's events. He wept as he expressed his guilt in not picking up on it sooner. Neil pointed out that obviously he had been prompted, and if God had wanted them to find the cancer sooner, He would have done something about it.

"You live close to the Spirit. You were listening. You did your part; you did the best you could. You've got too much on your shoulders to be carrying needless guilt around."

"I know," Alex admitted. "It's just . . . hard not to . . . wonder."

"Well, you can't," Neil said, and then he asked, "Do you need help with Jane and the baby? Katharine?"

"I think Donald and Susan have that covered. And Jane's parents will be here the day after tomorrow."

"What time are the tests in the morning?"

"I don't know. Early."

"Then I'll be back early."

"Dad, you really don't need to—"

"I'm going home to get a few hours sleep, and I'll be back. There's nowhere I would rather be than here with you."

"Okay," Alex said. "Thank you."

Neil hugged Alex tightly and admonished him to call at any hour if he was needed.

Alex was grateful that a parent was allowed to spend the night in the room with the patient, but he hardly slept at all. He prayed, he cried, he pondered all the potential outcomes of the situation, and he couldn't deny that he was simply not prepared for the possibility of giving up his son.

Chapter 4

Alex emerged from dozing to hear Barrett whimpering. He turned on a dim light and snuggled up close to him, reminding him gently of where they were so he might not feel so disoriented. Seeing what time it was, he realized it likely wouldn't be much longer before Barrett would be taken for the bone marrow aspirate. He decided to enjoy these quiet moments and considered them a blessing.

At first he spoke quietly of the baby and what a good big brother Barrett was going to be to Preston. And when he knew Barrett was fully awake, he said gently, "Do you know how you haven't been feeling well?" The boy nodded. "And remember before we came to this hospital we went to the other hospital so they could test your blood?"

"That's where you work," Barrett said.

"That's right. The thing is, they found something in your blood that's not very good, something that tells doctors you could be very, very sick."

"Like a germ?" he asked.

"That's right. Only this germ is called cancer, and it's very important that we find out exactly how much of it is in your body so that we can do things to get rid of it, so that you won't become more sick." Barrett looked inquisitive but said nothing. "That's why we have to be here. I know it's not fun for you to be here, but you've been a very brave boy. Now, I don't want you to be afraid, Barrett, but I need you to be very grown up and understand that cancer is very serious, and the things we have to do to make it go away can be very hard to go through; they can hurt and make you feel very sick. But if you don't do those hard things, cancer can . . ." He swallowed hard and forced it out. "People can die from cancer, Barrett. That's why we have to do whatever we have to in order to get rid of it, even if it hurts or makes you sick. In a little while they're going to have to do some more tests so that we can find out how sick your body is. Do you understand?"

Barrett nodded and asked, "Are they going to give me more shots?"

"I'm afraid so."

The child whimpered. "I hate shots, Daddy."

"I know," he said and held him close. "That's why they're going to put a special tube right here." He touched Barrett's upper chest. "It looks kind of funny, and it might feel strange for a while, but once they put that in, they don't have to give you so many shots, and you don't have to have this tube in your arm."

"I don't like this tube in my arm."

"I know," Alex said. "And I'm sorry it has to be there. I wish I could take it out."

"You're a doctor," he said. "You can take it out."

Alex looked into his son's eyes and chalked this up as one of the most difficult conversations of his life. "I know how to take it out, Barrett, but I don't want to do that because you need the medicine that's going into the tube."

Barrett looked thoughtful for a long moment, then he said, "Am I going to die?"

Alex swallowed carefully. "Everybody has to die eventually, Barrett. Some people do die of cancer, but lots of people get better too. We hope that you get better and grow up."

"So I can go on a mission?"

"That's right."

"And be a daddy like you."

"That would be great."

"And a doctor, so I can help people get better . . . like you."

Again Alex had to swallow. "I would love to have you grow up and be a doctor, Barrett. But even doctors can't make everything better. There are some things we just can't fix. And sometimes we try very hard to do everything we know, and it still doesn't make a person better. We just have to try and do the best we can. And that's why we need to have these tests done."

"Is it going to hurt?" Barrett asked, obviously preoccupied with the issue of pain—and for good reason. He'd already been confronted with a great deal of it.

"I'm afraid that some of it is going to hurt, yes."

"Like when they put the needle in my arm?"

"Yes, and it might even hurt more than that. But I'm going to be with you every second, and I know that you're a brave boy. You can cry if you want to, and you can even get mad if it will make you feel better. But you have to hold very still and let the doctors and nurses do what needs to be done. Do you think you can do that?"

His fear was evident, but he nodded stoutly, and Alex hugged him. "You're such a good boy, Barrett. I love you so much."

Barrett settled his head against Alex's chest and was quiet for several minutes. Then he said out of the silence, "Jesus died."

Alex almost choked. "Yes, He did, Barrett."

"He died to make things better for everybody else."

"That's right," Alex said. "But we don't want you to die, Barrett. We want you to stay with us until we're all very old."

A few minutes later Barrett said, "Dad, you forgot to give me a priesthood blessing."

And a little child shall lead them, Alex thought, feeling relatively stupid that he had overlooked something so important—and supposedly so obvious. "You're right, Barrett, I did forget. I guess I was just worried so much that I didn't think of it. I'm glad that you thought of it. You know what? Grandpa is going to come back to the hospital later, and he can help me give you a blessing."

"Okay," Barrett said. And a minute later he added, "You shouldn't worry, Dad. I'll be okay."

They snuggled for a long while until Alex realized Barrett was asleep. Holding his son close, he prayed with all the fervency of his soul that this sweet child would be spared too much suffering, and that he would survive and grow into adulthood.

A nurse came into the room to check Barrett, letting Alex know that he would need to be ready for the tests in about half an hour.

"Thank you," Alex said.

"Oh." She smiled. "And I think Grandpa's here. He got here about ten minutes ago, but didn't want to disturb you. He's down the hall reading."

"Thank you," Alex said again and eased carefully away from Barrett, hoping he would sleep a little longer.

Alex found his father, and they greeted each other with a common embrace. "Thanks for coming," Alex said. "It really is nice to have you here."

"Glad to do it. I always wake up ridiculously early anyway since I retired. I've brought a good book, and I have nowhere to go."

"Would you help me give him a blessing?" Alex asked.

"I would love to," he said, and they walked together to Barrett's room. They visited quietly and let him sleep a few more minutes, then Alex gently nudged him awake, knowing that time was short.

"Look who's here," Alex said. "Grandpa came to help with that blessing you asked for."

"Hi, Grandpa," Barrett said with a sleepy smile.

"Hey there, sport," Neil said.

"I have a new brother," Barrett said, and Neil chuckled.

"I heard about that. He's very lucky to have you for a big brother."

"I don't have a big brother *or* a little brother," Alex said. "I just have sisters."

"Like Katharine?" Barrett asked.

"Yes. Do you remember Aunt Charlotte and Aunt Becca? They're my sisters."

"Becca smells good, and Charlotte likes to do puzzles with me."

"That's right," Alex said with a chuckle.

As Alex put his hands on Barrett's head to give him a blessing, he wanted desperately to be able to say words that would indicate his son would live through this, but none came to his mind. Still, Barrett was told that his Heavenly Father was mindful of him and that through his great faith he would be a strength and inspiration to those around him as he endured these trials well. He was told that the pain and sickness were necessary, but their effects would be tempered. He was also told that those who loved him would be blessed with comfort and strength and much evidence of the Lord's blessings.

When it was done, Alex leaned over his son and said, "See, everything's going to be okay. And even Heavenly Father knows what a brave boy you are."

Barrett just smiled and said once again, "Don't worry, Dad. I'll be okay."

Alex looked up at his father, sharing a poignant smile.

"We have to go soon," Alex said. "You'd better use the bathroom first."

"Can I have something to eat?"

"I'm afraid not," Alex said. "But when the tests are done we'll get you something to eat; I promise. Anything you want."

"Ice cream?"

"Absolutely."

Neil found a place to wait and read while Alex went in with Barrett for the tests. Alex couldn't believe how squeamish he was about observing his son as the patient. He couldn't begin to count the medical procedures he'd observed and actually done through his years of medical school, residency, and as a practicing physician. But he'd never felt so startled by the reality of having bone marrow and a tiny piece of bone being removed from a patient's hip—Barrett's hip. That was just the beginning of a long, hard day with more procedures. And Alex knew they were barely embarking on a lengthy, harrowing journey. He didn't need test results to tell him the truth; in his heart he already knew it was leukemia. And observing Barrett's pain threatened to rip Alex's heart right out. If only he only could take it on himself. He felt as if he'd do anything—*anything*—to keep his son from suffering.

Late in the afternoon while Barrett slept, Alex left him in Neil's care and took Jane and the baby home from the hospital. She wanted to see Barrett, but he convinced her to go home and rest for a couple of days first. He assured her that Barrett was sleeping at the moment, and he was in good hands. He understood Jane's frustration in not being with her son, but he encouraged her to stay focused on the baby and her own recovery. He stopped her protests when he said, "If you get sick or have problems from over-doing it, you won't be any good to anybody."

Alex spent some time at home helping Jane get settled in. Donald and Susan fussed over the baby and were eager to help Jane with whatever she needed. Katharine was thrilled with her baby brother, and seeing them together was a delight. But Barrett's absence was difficult to swallow.

When Alex left for the hospital, Susan assured him that all would be well at home, and he needed to just take care of Barrett. He promised Jane that he'd have Barrett call her as soon as it was possible. In the car he shed a few tears, feeling torn between what should have been and the reality of what was really happening. He was relieved at least to find a message on his cell phone from Ray Baker telling him he didn't have to work for the next five days, and beyond that they could still be very flexible. Alex was grateful, and he just didn't think about what they might do about the lost wages.

At the hospital, Alex found Barrett awake but miserable from the procedures that had been done that day. He was cuddled in Neil's lap while Roxanne tried to distract him from the pain with a story. She reported quietly to Alex, "A nurse will be back soon with something to help him feel better."

"Thank you," Alex said and took Barrett from his father, settling into a chair with his son on his lap. "You should go," he said to Neil. "You've been here all day. And I'm grateful. But I'm here for the night now. You don't have to stay."

Much to Alex's relief Neil said, "If it's okay we'll just stick around a while longer."

The nurse came in with some pain medication, and Alex was relieved to see it given through the line, avoiding another shot. Alex waited for the right moment to call home, when the pain seemed to be lessening, but before Barrett got too sleepy. Roxanne dialed the number and held the phone base close so that Barrett could hold the receiver.

Jane heard the phone ring and reached for the cordless handset Susan had left within her reach. The caller ID let her know it was the children's hospital. One more taste of reality, she thought as she answered.

"Hi Mom," Barrett's little voice said, and she had to force back any sign of emotion. He sounded a bit groggy, but those two words were relatively cheerful.

"Hi, Barrett," she said brightly. "Are you taking good care of Daddy?"

She heard him giggle slightly then say away from the phone, "She wants to know if I'm taking care of you. Mommy is silly."

"Yes, she is," Jane heard Alex say.

Into the phone Barrett said, "I'm sick, Mommy. But there's lots of nice doctors and nurses and they're going to help me get better."

"I'm sorry you're sick," she said, "but I'm glad they're taking good care of you."

"They took out my bones," he said, "and it hurts really bad, but Daddy said I'm brave."

"I'm sure you are," Jane said and silently added, *Don't think too hard. Don't cry. You can cry later.*

"That's bone marrow," she heard Alex say. "Obviously your bones are still there or you would be like Jell-o."

Barrett giggled softly, sounding more groggy. "It was bone marrow, Mommy."

"I heard that."

The baby began to fuss where he lay in Jane's arms, and Barrett asked excitedly, "Is that my brother?"

"It is. He's getting hungry."

"The baby is hungry," Barrett said to Alex. "He's crying. I can hear him crying." More into the phone he asked, "When I come home can I hold him?"

"You sure can," Jane said. "He's going to need a big brother to teach him how to do all kinds of things when he gets bigger."

"Okay," Barrett said, sounding suddenly very sleepy. "I have to go to bed now, Mommy."

"Okay, buddy," she said. "I love you. I'll talk to you tomorrow, and I'll come and see you very soon."

"Okay. Bye, Mommy."

Jane then heard Alex say into the phone, "They gave him something for the pain and he's about out. How are you?"

"I've been better," she said, unable to hold the tears back now that it was Alex.

"I hear you," he said. "Is everything okay there?"

"Yes, it's fine. You just take good care of him and don't worry about us. Call me in the morning."

"I will," he said. "I love you, Jane."

"I love you too, Alex."

Jane hung up the phone and cried until the baby's demands to be fed distracted her into meeting his needs. She'd been thinking that the timing of all of this was horrendous, but as she watched Preston nursing, she considered that perhaps God had known she would need a distraction to help her cope.

The following day Donald drove to the airport to pick up Jane's parents, even though they'd only met twice before, at the baby blessings for Barrett and Katharine. Waiting for her parents to arrive, Jane told Susan how thoroughly grateful she felt for all she and Donald were doing for her family. She couldn't comprehend how they could possibly manage otherwise. Not only was Susan there to see that Katharine's every need was met, but she was close by to help Jane with any little thing that might be difficult. She helped care for the baby without being intrusive, and she always had something cooking that made meals a delight rather than a burden. But most of all Susan offered perfect compassion and a constant shoulder to cry on as Jane mourned over trying to accept that her son had a horrible disease that could possibly be fatal.

When her parents arrived Jane started into a whole new bout of weeping, and they too offered her compassion and understanding while shedding some tears of their own. The horror of Barrett's illness was starkly contrasted by the joy they all felt in Preston's arrival. He was a beautiful baby with a pleasant disposition, and Jane was finding great joy in him and in seeing the joy he brought to others.

Alex came home for supper and spent a couple of hours enjoying the baby and Katharine, and visiting with Jane's parents, then he returned to the hospital to once again spend the night. He assured them that Barrett was progressing and doing as well as could be expected, but he seemed to avoid wanting to share any details. And Jane wondered if that was best.

The following day Walter and Louisa took Jane to Primary Children's Medical Center to see Barrett. She left the baby with Susan, feeling it would be better. Alex had told Jane he would meet them in the main lobby—by the water, he'd told her, saying she couldn't miss it. After entering through the huge revolving door, Jane's attention was immediately drawn to a large rectangular, shallow pool, and in it was a complex structure created from a wide variety of steel parts and pieces. Water trickled through many moving parts, and little bronze sculptures were interspersed through the structure. She stood for a full minute, with her parents on either side of her, just taking in the scene with fascination. Looking down she noticed a plaque there that read, *Such is the kingdom of heaven.* She forced back tears and glanced around, wondering where Alex might be. Her watch told her they were early, and they sat down where there was an even better view of the sculpture and its moving parts. The sound of trickling water was mingled with the bustle of people going past. For nearly ten minutes she just sat there, taking in the atmosphere of this place. Doctors, nurses, and administrative staff, all clearly identifiable by their attire and ID badges, hurried back and forth. And there were the visitors bringing balloons and gifts. And parents taking children of all ages in and out. She watched children stop and put their hands in the water, watching the mechanisms with fascination. Many threw coins into the water, and she wondered what kind of procedures they were coming here for, or had just endured. She saw children in pajamas, some riding in wagons that clearly belonged to the hospital, some hooked to complex IV poles that followed after them. She felt an aura that was both magical and tragic as some children laughed, and others fussed. But Jane didn't have any trouble maintaining her composure until she saw a young boy go past in one of the little wagons. A tiny mask was over the lower half of his face, and his little head was bald. Jane put a hand over her mouth to keep from crying out, and she reached for her mother's hand, wondering what level of familiarity she was destined to gain with this place. How tragic and magical might *their* experiences be as they endured all that lay ahead?

"Hey there, gorgeous," she heard Alex say and looked up to see him standing beside her. She stood up and put her arms around him. "You okay?" he asked. She nodded and forced a smile, but she couldn't speak. He just hugged her again and seemed to understand.

Alex greeted Jane's parents, and then said, "Let's go. He's excited to see you." He kept his arm around Jane as they walked a long hall, got into the elevator, then walked down another hall. Jane noted the carpet was inlaid with brightly colored stars, and the walls were covered with children's artwork in beautiful frames. Jane had expected to find her son in a hospital bed, but Alex took them instead to a playroom, where Barrett was sitting at a Lego table, busily creating something with the brightly colored bricks. Jane was glad that he hadn't noticed them in the doorway. It gave her a moment to absorb the reality of what she was seeing. If not for the IV pole he was hooked to, and the hospital-issue pajamas, she wouldn't think anything was wrong.

Alex whispered to Jane, "They have these playrooms in every section of the hospital. The toys are all meticulously cleaned on a regular basis to avoid any spreading of infection." He laughed softly. "He's been having so much fun he might not want to go home." More loudly he added, "Hey, buddy, look who's here."

"Mommy!" Barrett said with excitement and she hurried to embrace him.

Barrett was also thrilled to see his grandparents who had come from California. He didn't see them often, but they talked on the phone regularly and he knew them well. He greeted Walter and Louisa with enthusiasm, and then he proudly showed them the central line sticking out of his chest. While he was talking with his grandparents, Jane discreetly asked Alex, "How long is he going to have that?"

Alex gave her that look she'd come to recognize lately. He didn't want to tell her. She countered his gaze, and he said, "At least three years." Jane tried not to show how horrified that made her feel. *Three years? But why?* As if to answer her silent question, Alex went on to say, "That's the standard time span for chemotherapy for a male in order to be certain it doesn't come back."

Jane turned her back to Barrett so he wouldn't catch her crying as new tears forced their way out. *Three years?* "He'll be nearly eight, Alex."

"I know," he said.

She wondered if his thoughts were the same as hers. Did he wonder if Barrett would actually *live* to be eight? She couldn't even consider the possibility of losing him. She *couldn't!*

"Mommy, look," Barrett said, drawing her attention to the toys that he was showing to her parents. She focused on her son and swallowed her grief, trying to pretend that for the moment all was well.

Walter and Louisa slipped out to give Jane and Alex some time alone with their son. When Barrett wanted to show Jane his room down the hall, she realized that he was limping. He only took a few steps before Alex picked him up. She knew the pain was from the bone marrow aspirate he'd had done. And while Jane didn't even want to think about it, Barrett was eager to show her the evidence of the procedure. He seemed excited about the room where he'd been staying, and showed her how he could watch movies from a large video library and play video games. His positive attitude was somewhat comforting, and he clearly enjoyed introducing her to friends he'd made. There were other cancer patients in different stages, but Barrett was most taken with his nurse friends. His favorite was a male nurse named Caleb. Barrett showed Jane the pictures of his brother that Alex had brought him, and it quickly became evident that he had shown the pictures to everyone.

Walter and Louisa returned and insisted on staying with Barrett while Alex and Jane went to the cafeteria and got something to eat together.

"And you thought I couldn't be original for a date," he said once they were seated with their meal.

"I never said that."

"I know, but it sounded good." He took her hand across the table. "Are you okay?"

"Not really, no. I'm in shock, Alex. I can't believe it's happening. I don't know what to expect, how to feel, what to say."

"It's okay. I don't either. We just have to take it one day— sometimes one hour—at a time."

"You're missing a lot of work."

"We'll manage somehow. There may be times when we just have to leave Barrett with the staff. They're wonderful. But he'll be coming home in a few days, and we'll go from there. All we can do is the best we can do."

"The Relief Society president from our ward called. They want to help. They're giving us a list of sisters to call who will come and sit with Barrett, or take the other children—whatever we need."

"That's nice," he said. "For the moment I think we're fine. After your parents go home we'll see what happens." He saw tears gather in her eyes and reached over to touch her face. "It's going to be okay," he said.

Jane nodded, but she felt certain he knew she didn't believe him.

The following day Alex sat next to Barrett while he slept, mostly due to the pain medication. He looked up to see his father enter the room. He stood and they embraced.

"How's he doing?" Neil asked.

"Not bad, all things considered."

"Any procedures on the docket that would require his father to be here in the next few hours?"

"Not that I know of. Why?"

"Because I think you need to let me sit with him while you go spend some time with that new baby of yours."

Alex felt choked up. He didn't even try to protest. "Thanks, Dad," he said and hugged him again before he hurried home. At the house he found no sign of anyone on the main floor. He took the stairs three at a time and entered the bedroom to find Jane curled up in bed, with the baby laying close to her, his eyes open as he looked around, serenely taking in the world he'd recently come into. Jane looked up when Alex came through the door. He could tell she'd been crying, but she showed him a courageous smile and held out a hand.

"Hi," he said, taking her hand as he bent to kiss her. "Where is everybody?"

"They all went shopping. How is he?" she asked.

"He's okay. He's sleeping right now. Dad's with him." Alex picked up the baby and sat close to Jane. "He told me I needed to spend time with my other son." Alex touched the baby's little cheek and smiled at the funny face he made. "I think he was right."

Alex couldn't help recalling when Barrett had been this size. If they'd known what was ahead, how heartbreaking it would have been! But they wouldn't have loved him any less or regretted any moment with him. Holding Preston now gave Alex balance somehow, and he was grateful for this tangible evidence that life was good, and that somehow it would go on—no matter what happened.

* * * * *

A week after Barrett had gone into the hospital, he came home to be greeted by a wide assortment of balloons, gifts, and stuffed animals that had arrived from his preschool classmates, and from friends and ward members from their neighborhood. Gifts had also been shipped from relatives out of state. Barrett had a marvelous time assessing his loot, and then with no prompting from anyone, he picked out several items to give to Katharine. Alex was so proud of him he could hardly stand it. How could a child so young understand that Katharine had also felt the strain of all this, and likely had trouble understanding why Barrett was getting so much attention?

The effects of the chemotherapy were already making Barrett ill. He had little appetite, and when he wanted something it was always a strange request. But his doctor had suggested giving him what he wanted as far as it was possible, so they did. He complained about food tasting like metal and was more often than not exhausted and nauseous. But Alex far preferred having him home as opposed to keeping a hospital vigil. Being with his family under one roof seemed a great blessing that he no longer took for granted. Even on the days when Alex had to work long shifts, he enjoyed being able to come home and stay there. Jane had her hands full with the baby and a three-year-old, on top of an ailing chemo patient. But Susan and Donald were marvelous to help out, especially during the hours when Alex was gone. Walter and Louisa helped a great deal as well until they had to return home, but they promised to come back when Preston was blessed, and they made it clear that one or both of them could come and help any time, should the need arise. Barrett loved his little brother, and they all found joy in seeing his interest in the baby. In spite of his ongoing illness and frequent outpatient trips to the hospital to continue his chemotherapy, the child kept up a positive attitude that was an inspiration to those around him.

Before the time arrived for Preston to be blessed, Barrett had already lost all of his hair. But Jane had found a variety of cute little hats for every purpose and season. Barrett took great pride in his hat collection, and he only seemed mildly self-conscious at church where it wasn't appropriate for a boy to wear a hat. He was usually too sick to go anyway, but he did insist that he was going for Preston's blessing.

Family came from all over the country to be present when Preston would be blessed in church and officially given his name. It was evident they had come to see Barrett as much as the baby, and everyone was careful not to let Katharine feel left out. Gifts were brought by many for all three of the children. Word had gotten out about the hat collection, and nearly every visiting relative gave Barrett a hat. Barrett found humor in the situation and purposely appeared with a different hat every ten minutes.

When they were able to attend at all, Alex and Jane had mostly been attending church with Donald and Susan rather than going to their home ward, working around Barrett's ongoing illness and Alex's work schedule. But their records were still in the ward where their home was located, and that's where the baby would be blessed. Jane's parents and siblings were all able to come, as well as Alex's two older sisters. For years his sister Charlotte had not been active. But she had returned to full activity, and while everyone was in town, most of the adults went to a temple session on Saturday morning. Alex felt a deep peace to be within temple walls and have Jane at his side, and also to have so many family members there with them. He was especially grateful for the eternal perspective he felt there. Losing Barrett would be indescribably difficult, if it came to that, but in his heart he knew it would not be permanent. They would be together forever.

Following the fast meeting where Preston was blessed, they all gathered at Donald and Susan's house for a lovely meal that consisted of some of Susan's best cooking, along with donations of salads and desserts from several sisters in both wards. Alex sat in the yard, beneath the huge trees, contemplating a thousand thoughts. Looking around at the love and support of family, he felt touched by the strength he found there. Most of them lived far away, but their phone calls, letters, and prayers had been greatly needed and much appreciated. Seeing Barrett spending moments here and there with his aunts, uncles, and cousins, he felt grateful that the child felt well enough today to interact and enjoy the day, at least to some degree. And for the moment his white blood count was at a good level. As always, Alex kept a constant prayer in his heart that the treatment would be effective and all would be well in the end.

For some reason Alex found himself looking at the house in a way he hadn't for a long time. From here in the huge, well-groomed yard, he was reminded of the first time he'd come here for a wedding reception and how taken he'd been with the house, even from the outside. He loved living here and had to admit that he dreaded the day when they would have to leave.

Alex observed his wife while she talked and laughed with loved ones. She was the most amazing woman in the world. He'd felt that way the first time he'd laid eyes on her, and the years had not diminished his fascination, or his love. Both only grew stronger with time as she grew more beautiful and incredible in his eyes. She was as spiritual as she was competent and wise. She was gentle and tender, but firm and strong in her opinions and beliefs. He'd seen her struggle a great deal with Barrett's illness, but she took on each new day with firm courage and determination. Oh, how he loved her!

Taking in the evidence of the blessings surrounding him, Alex was reminded of that day in the laundry room when he'd been struck with such a strong sense of gratitude. For the first time since all of this had happened, he recalled that moment and the impression that had come to his mind, that trusting in God would see his family through any possible trial. God had known this was on the horizon, and he'd been carefully preparing Alex to face it. He felt peace and comfort from the promise he'd been given. Surely God *would* see his family through this trial.

A few days after all of the relatives had returned to their homes, Alex took his family on an excursion to the zoo. Barrett loved the zoo and he'd been bringing it up for weeks. Preston and Katharine did well in the double stroller, and they rented a wagon for Barrett so he wouldn't have to walk. He had moments of seeming to enjoy it, but for the most part he just said he was tired and his stomach felt sick, and eventually he fell asleep in the wagon. The other two fell asleep soon afterward, so Alex and Jane sat on a bench while the children slept. He put his arm around her and said, "And you thought I couldn't be original for a date."

She looked surprised, and then she laughed. "Okay, you got me this time," she said. "This is pretty romantic stuff."

Alex took a long gaze at each of the children and said, "Yeah, actually it is." He placed a kiss on her brow and told her he loved her. And they both pressed forward, trying to pretend that life was normal.

Weeks dragged into months while Barrett continued regular chemotherapy. Alex felt a deepening frustration in being able to do so little to combat this disease. His life was committed to saving lives, but he could do nothing for his son. He did his best to trust in the experts and have faith that all would be well. But at times the waiting felt torturous and eternal. He found it difficult to accept that while the treatments were killing cancer cells and hopefully preventing them from ever coming back, they were also killing the good cells in Barrett's blood. Watching him become steadily weaker, it was hard to believe that this was actually doing the child good.

As Barrett's immune system became utterly battered, he was pretty much under house arrest beyond his regular trips to the hospital for treatments and tests. It was a blessing not to have the other children old enough to be in school, since they didn't want any germs brought into the house from exposure to other children. But this made it difficult to send Katharine and Preston to other homes to play. If there was even a hint of a virus in the air, Jane kept them rigorously away from others, which meant keeping them home from church more often than not. If Barrett were to contract a virus, the complications could be devastating.

Alex could feel the strain taking its toll on his wife. She had the blessing of being able to leave the children with Susan and Donald in order to run errands or go do whatever she needed. But he knew she found it hard to leave Barrett any more than absolutely necessary, and her greatest outings these days were rushed trips to the grocery store or the pharmacy, except for her regular excursions to Primary Children's where she spent endless hours with Barrett through each step of the process. Susan and Donald made themselves readily available if needed, and Alex knew Jane was grateful for that. But she didn't want to become a burden to them, and he sensed that something deeply maternal made her want to care for her own children as much as humanly possible. He loved and admired her for it, but he also felt concerned.

Alex could count a million reasons why he was grateful to be living with Donald and Susan, but there were simply aspects of life that they couldn't buffer. Susan insisted on manning the kitchen, and the main floor of the house remained clean and orderly, but the sections of the house upstairs that Alex's family had taken over were a disaster. The bedrooms, bathroom, and sitting room that had been converted into a little TV/ playroom for the family gradually became absolute chaos. Alex and Jane were both so busy just trying to keep up with the kids and Barrett's treatment and illness that keeping their belongings in order just wasn't a priority. They'd developed a system of laundry where the piles of clean clothes didn't get mixed into the piles of dirty ones, and anti-bacterial cleaners were always within close reach to keep the bathroom sanitized so that Barrett wouldn't be exposed to any germs. But the disorder was pathetic.

For Alex, having to go to work felt like a necessary burden. Income was mandatory to keep life's wheels turning, but he hated the hours away from his family. Coming home from a twelve-hour shift always left him facing a frazzled and weary wife. There were days when he would go to great lengths to get someone to cover a shift just to avoid that moment. If he could be at home, the burden was shared more equally. Jane could keep the younger children cared for while he dealt with Barrett crying and puking from the effects of chemotherapy. *At least we're not dealing with the effects of a bone marrow transplant,* he regularly told himself.

He was grateful daily that Susan usually kept meals available; she loved to cook and enjoyed having someone to feed. Alex knew that without her culinary hobbies they would be surviving solely on frozen and fast foods, or whatever might come out of a can. Jane had hotly declared that she had choices of where to spend her time, because she only had so much of it to give. And the kitchen would have been the first to go. She put her energy entirely into being a good mother to her children.

A new complication arose when Alex was unable to make a house payment. He'd been grateful to be able to get extra time off work, which had been the only option on many days to help get Barrett through, not to mention Jane. He'd known it would have adverse financial effects, but with the passing of time it had gradually gotten worse, and this reality hit harder than he'd expected. There had also been many other expenses: eating when and where they could, and a higher phone bill for all the communication with loved ones out of state. And while the house insurance had taken care of the majority of repairing the fire damage, there had been related expenses that weren't covered. But dealing with that was a piece of cake in comparison to the regular influx of medical bills. They had excellent health insurance and he was grateful beyond belief for that, but just keeping track of the bills and reconciling them with the insurance company and the separate doctors and facilities became a paperwork nightmare. And even with good coverage, the percentages left over on such an ordeal were proving to be a tremendous financial burden. *At least we're not paying for a bone marrow transplant,* he often reminded himself.

When the mortgage became more than thirty days late, Alex began to more seriously consider an idea that had been in the back of his mind for weeks. Maybe they should just sell the house, or perhaps rent it. But he couldn't bring himself to suggest it to Jane. He didn't want her to lose her home in the midst of everything else that was happening. She had friends in that neighborhood, and he knew she loved the house. Or at least she had in the past. But now, that home and the life they'd lived there seemed almost like another world.

Alex sat at a small desk in the bedroom he and Jane were using, the bills spread out in front of him, feeling helpless and not in control. Barrett was drifting in and out of sleep on his lap, and Alex turned his attention more to the child. He asked himself how much he would be willing to give up to save his son's life, and the house payment felt irrelevant. But wherever it might fall on his personal priority list, he was obligated to pay for it, and he knew he had to do everything in his power to be honest in those dealings and meet his financial commitments. The burden felt heavy and impossible to balance.

Alex eased his arms more tightly around Barrett, habitually praying that the chemo would be enough, that the child would survive, that his family could hold it together. He muttered aloud, "And avoiding foreclosure would be nice, too."

Katharine came running into the room jabbering that it was time for supper. While Barrett had learned to talk very clearly at a young age, Katharine had an adorable language all her own, full of mispronunciations.

"Okay, we're coming," he said, and she ran off.

Alex carried Barrett down the stairs and sat at the table where everyone else was already seated. After the blessing, Barrett perked up and showed some interest in being awake.

"You want something to eat, buddy?" Alex asked him.

Barrett just shook his head and buried his face against his father's chest. Alex exchanged a meaningful glance with Jane that spoke of the ongoing concern and heartache they shared.

About halfway through the meal that Alex could barely bring himself to eat, Susan asked, "What's wrong, Alex? Something different, I'm guessing, from that look on your face."

"Sorry," he said and focused more on his meal.

"Don't apologize. Just get over the pride and tell us what's wrong."

Alex sighed. "Getting nasty letters from the mortgage company, actually. And I'm not sure what to do about it." He thought about talking to his father, certain that Neil wouldn't be happy to find out that they were struggling and hadn't asked for help. Neil had financial surplus, but Alex truly didn't know how much. Seeking his help was certainly an option, but not something he felt good about at this point. It just didn't feel like the right course to take.

"I wish we had anything to loan you," Donald said. "Or even give you. But we've had to help a couple of our kids, and the retirement money is pretty tight at the moment."

"Oh, no," Alex said. "I wouldn't expect that, or even want it. You asked, so I told you. I'm certain something will work out."

"The house is nearly ready to move back into, isn't it?" Susan asked as if the idea were painful.

"It's getting close," Alex said. "But . . . truthfully, I think it's better if we stay here for the time being. We've prayed about it, and . . . we just feel it's better. Especially for Katharine. She's very attached to you."

"I agree," Susan said firmly, as if she'd prefer to have them never leave.

Jane clinched it when she said, "Why don't we just sell it?" Alex couldn't believe what he was hearing. He wondered if they'd both had the same thoughts but had been hesitant to voice them. "I really don't want to go back," she went on. "When Barrett is past all of this, we'll find another home. In the meantime, we can give Donald and Susan some rent if we're not paying a mortgage. And I suspect they'd take much less than the mortgage payment."

"I don't think any rent whatsoever is necessary," Susan insisted. "You already buy *all* of the groceries, most of the time. But I think your staying is a great idea. If the mortgage company knows you have it on the market, maybe they'll cut you a little slack."

Donald interjected, "We could get some family and ward members together and just pack up what's left over there. Get a storage unit for a while if we need to, although we have some room in the garage."

"A lot of the furniture on the main floor was ruined anyway," Jane said. "So, let's just empty it out and sell it. There, that's decided."

"Okay," Alex said and felt confident that prayers were being heard.

He put the house on the market the next day, and the following weekend, members of that ward, along with Donald and Susan, and Roxanne and his father helped pack up and empty the house. Jane supervised, deciding what should go to Susan's house, and what should go into storage. Most of what they used regularly was already at Susan's, but they made the decision to move in more fully, knowing that even the simplest battle with leukemia would take three years. They put only some furniture and appliances, holiday decorations, and some odds and ends in a storage unit. Everything else was in the house with them, or in the garage. The very next week they got an offer on the house and took it. They were able to pay off some debts, get all of their bills current, and the remainder of the equity was put into the bank to use when they were ready for a new home. It all came together so well that Alex couldn't deny, once again, that God's hand was in their lives, guiding and caring for them in spite of the horrors going on with little Barrett.

With the house sold, the family's membership records were transferred to Donald and Susan's ward. They were welcomed zealously with help and support, and the bishop kept regular track of Barrett's progress and the family's needs. Alex and Jane both felt it was important to be willing to serve in the ward, even though they weren't sure how they would ever manage time wise. But the bishop said that he felt it was appropriate for them to take this season in their lives to accept the service of others.

Preston cut teeth and crawled, and Barrett's chemo went on. Preston learned to walk and passed his first birthday. And still the chemo went on. He became Katharine's shadow, following her through their days of playing together, and she instinctively mothered her little brother with a tenderness that was touching. She also used her maternal instincts on Barrett, often tucking a blanket over him while he rested on the couch, or bringing him things that he asked for. Alex and Jane often discussed the affection and warmth between their children, and the rarity of contention. They felt certain that each of the children had been blessed with a level of understanding that helped buffer the challenges they faced. As parents they often just sat and observed their children growing and progressing, or just struggling to survive, and they felt deeply grateful for the simple pleasures and joys that they might have once taken for granted.

More than a year after the diagnosis of his leukemia, Barrett passed the requirements to graduate from kindergarten, even though he'd never actually attended. What he'd learned had been at home with Jane's help. It didn't hurt that Barrett's mother had a degree in elementary education and had taught kindergarten and first grade prior to having her first baby. She commented more than once how grateful she was for that training, and she couldn't help wondering if this was one of its greatest purposes, to help her son get his education in spite of not being able to go to school. Even when he felt well enough or had the energy, they were so worried about him contracting germs from other children that they couldn't even consider it.

Barrett became understandably focused on TV and video games, since he didn't have the strength to do much else the majority of the time, and he couldn't play with friends who might bring germs into the house. Alex and Jane just did their best to make sure that he was exposed to positive and educational aspects of his hobbies. They also focused strongly on other things he loved that didn't require energy. A new puzzle or a new coloring book and crayons always made his face light up. Some days were better than others, and in rare moments he almost seemed like a normal child. But the reality was too stark to ignore. Chemotherapy was stunting his growth and taking his little body through a process that seemed to be killing everything it could possibly kill and still keep him alive.

Donald and Susan remained dedicated beyond belief. Alex and Jane were both continually amazed at their eager willingness to do whatever needed to be done. Members from the ward, as well as members from the area Jane and Alex had moved from, pitched in to help with meals occasionally, and took Katharine and Preston on outings here and there when there was absolutely no danger of them contracting any illness. The help and support of others didn't go unappreciated, especially as time wore on and the ongoing treatments and related side effects became steadily more wearying.

Trips back and forth to the hospital were hard on Jane, but she often mentioned how grateful she was to be living so close and not to be needing to go hundreds of miles for treatments as some families they had become acquainted with were having to do. Facilities and assistance were available to help those who had to come from long distances, but it was still a huge challenge. Many times Alex and Jane had opened their home to such parents who needed a place to stay for a night here and there. Susan and Donald had also eagerly embraced the opportunity to do all that they could, and they considered their huge home a blessing in that regard.

Gratitude became a marvelous remedy for Alex and Jane. They often sat together in a quiet moment, or lay close together before they fell asleep, and verbally recounted all they had to be grateful for. It didn't take away the harsh reality of Barrett's illness or its related challenges, but it did offer some perspective. And perspective could be a marvelous thing.

Chapter 5

"I have a proposition for you," Susan said to Alex without preamble.

"Okay," Alex said. "I'm listening."

"You know that Donald and I want to go on a mission—at least one."

"Yes," he drawled.

"We've put it off because you know a couple of the kids have needed some financial help, and while that's winding down and they're doing better, truthfully . . . I think the Lord knew we needed to be here for you at this time. We've felt hesitant to submit papers without really knowing why. All along we've had two big concerns, but we've just tried to have faith that when the time came those problems would be solved. The first was being able to support ourselves. We do get some pension and Social Security, but we would need more. And our savings have been used up helping the kids. One of our children is now in a position to help us some, and that's good, but . . . the other problem is, well . . . the house." She looked around with nostalgia at the family room where they were seated, and sighed. Then she looked directly at Alex. "You know how I love this house."

"I do," he said.

"And you love it too."

"I won't deny that," he said and wondered if she was leading up to having them rent the house so it would be lived in while they were gone, and the income could help support the mission. He hoped so, because he liked that idea.

"My kids don't want it. They all have established homes and lives. If they inherit it they'll just sell it and split the money, and it would be turned into a bed and breakfast, or something." She focused more intently on him. "This house should stay in the family, Alex." She paused for emphasis. "Buy it from us, Alex. Raise your family here. Leave the house to Barrett when you die of old age."

Alex couldn't believe it. Her offer was too good to be true. And he really liked that last part. But he had to say, "You can't be serious. We can't afford this house."

"I don't intend to sell it to you for its value, Alex. We've been very blessed by this house. But in a way I've always considered it Alexander Barrett's home. It's always felt more like we were simply . . . taking care of it for him—renting it from him maybe, even though he's long gone. I inherited the house for reasons I don't quite understand. But it was in horrendous condition, so I think my relatives considered it more of a curse than a blessing. I'm absolutely certain that the amount of money we put into maintaining and restoring it were at least as much as we would have spent to purchase an adequate nice house. But we were blessed with the resources to do it, and those loans are all paid off now. And yes, the present value of the house is immense, I'm sure. But the only money we need is enough to serve a mission or two and see to our needs until we die. Our kids can find their own way. They don't need a big inheritance from us. I've already talked to Donald. We've prayed about it. We know it's right. We'll sell it to you for whatever you sold the other house for, but we're not going to sell it to you until Barrett's past this, and that will give you a chance to get ahead a bit."

"It's too good to be true, Susan," he said and couldn't hold back a little laugh. "I could never turn down such an offer. You know how I love this house, but . . . it's too one-sided. I really don't think I could feel good about it when the value of the house is so—"

"Oh, you haven't heard the catch yet," she said with a little smirk.

"Okay, what's the catch?"

"Except for when we're on our missions or visiting our children, we're going to live here with you until we're too old and decrepit to take care of ourselves. Then we'll either move in with kids or go to a care center or something. It really doesn't matter. We just want to be able to live here for as long as we're reasonably able to."

Alex chuckled and shook his head. "You call that a catch? I call that an added bonus."

Susan smiled as if the idea made her the happiest woman alive. "You talk to Jane and give it some time. Our offer stands. For now, we'll just keep doing what we're doing—working together to get Barrett well and get the family through this in one piece."

* * * * *

Alex found Jane in Barrett's bedroom, sitting in a chair near the bed, just watching him sleep in the glow of a little lamp on the dresser. Without a word he took her hand into his and urged her to her feet, easing her into a gentle waltz.

"What are you doing?" she asked softly, with a little laugh. It was good to hear her laugh, even if it was a little one.

"I'm dancing with you," he said. It merged into more of a simple slow dance than a waltz, but Jane put her head on his shoulder and sighed, and he loved just holding her close, swaying her back and forth to the silence of the room surrounding them.

"Guess what?" he said quietly.

"What?" She pulled back to look at him.

"I found a house. It's perfect. Not very far from hospital hill. Good neighborhood. The seller wants the same price we sold the other house for, and they're willing to wait to sell it until Barrett's doing better. And the house is beautiful, Jane. It's perfect."

"It sounds too good to be true."

"That's what I said." He laughed softly. "But there is a catch."

"What?" She stopped dancing and stepped back.

"Donald and Susan are going to live there with us except for when they're on their missions or visiting their kids." Jane's brow furrowed, and Alex added, "They want the house to stay in the family."

"*The* house?" She looked around. "*This* house?"

"That's right. What do you think?"

"I . . . can't believe it. They'd really give it to us for that price?"

"She said the offer stands."

"Oh, Alex," she said, throwing her arms around him, "it's a miracle. I love it here! I didn't want to admit it because I knew it was temporary, but it just . . . feels so right."

"Yes, it does," he agreed, and they continued to dance.

When Alex told Susan they wanted to accept her offer on the house, she behaved as if she'd just won a million-dollar lottery. He felt more like it was the other way around. She hugged him tightly then said, "There's something I want you to see. I came across it a while back; hadn't seen it for years before then. I was going to show it to you, but I found it right after Barrett's illness was discovered, and things have been pretty crazy."

Alex followed her to an attic that he hadn't realized existed. He laughed as they ascended the wooden steps and she pulled a chain to turn on a single light bulb. "This is the proverbial attic, you know," he said.

"Yes, I believe it is. And I know there are amazing treasures up here, but I've never had time to really go through everything. I've just scavenged a bit here and there. But what I want you to see is over there, against that wall. It's a painting."

He saw where she was pointing and moved between trunks and boxes to kneel beside the painting that was covered with an old sheet. "Let's have a look," she said, and he pulled the fabric away. What he saw left him so stunned he could hardly catch his breath. "Amazing, isn't it?" Susan said with a chuckle. "If you wore your hair differently, it would be almost like looking in a mirror." She paused as if expecting a reaction from him, but he couldn't give one. "It's Alexander Barrett," she said. "The original owner of the house."

Alex cleared his throat, but his voice was still raspy. "I know who it is." He took a deep breath, as if to inhale what he saw before him. He couldn't remember the last time he'd even thought about the illogical experience he'd had in this house several years ago. But what he saw now validated something that he'd kept in his heart since that time. Only Jane knew about it, and they'd not spoken of it for years. Alex had recorded it in his journal—there in the midst of the horror of Jane's coma had been one of the most marvelous experiences of his life. And now he was face-to-face with evidence that it had really happened. He quickly searched his heart and knew that it was right to share it with Susan. He turned to her and said, "I've seen this painting before."

She gave a dubious chuckle. "You couldn't have. It's been up here all along, and you've never been up here before."

He intensified his gaze on her and added, "I saw it in a dream, Susan."

Her eyes filled with deep interest. "What are you saying?"

Alex sat on the floor and glanced again at the portrait of his great-great-grandfather, Alexander Barrett. Then he looked back at Susan, who was sitting on an old wooden crate.

"Do you remember the night we met?"

"You came to the wedding. Of course I remember." She chuckled. "It was memorable the way you passed out on the floor and I couldn't get you to come around. You told me you'd just been in a car accident and had a head injury. You had stitches . . . and bruises . . . on your face."

"That's right. We were standing in the study, where the desk is built into the wall. And I dropped this." He took Alexander Barrett's ring out of his pocket, where he always kept it, and handed it to her. "I pulled it out to look at it because I was thinking about the man who had once sat at that desk."

"I didn't know you had this," she said. "It's like the one in the portrait."

"It *is* the one in the portrait. You inherited the house; my mother inherited that ring. It was always too small for me, and somewhat garish in my opinion. But I've always carried it with me, at first because I knew it had meaning for my mother. And then after I first came to this house, it took on great personal meaning for me."

He took the ring back and held it as he spoke. "When I got on the floor to pick it up, I bumped my head on the desk and it knocked me out cold. You said I was out for ten minutes at most, but for me it had felt like a few days. I had an experience, you see. It was like a dream. Well, it *was* a dream. But it felt so real. At the time, my life was a mess. I'd wasted years over issues that were tearing me apart. Jane was in a coma. I had prayed very hard to find my way back, but I felt lost." He sighed and glanced at the portrait. "It was as if I were seeing a little piece of his life through his eyes. I saw this portrait on the wall . . . in this house . . . except the house looked as it would have during his time."

"That's incredible," Susan said, mesmerized.

"Yes, it was. Especially when the events that occurred in my dream were things I later read in his journals. It was as if I had some . . . spiritual experience that allowed me to see a small portion of his life. A little like Alma the Younger, perhaps . . . as far as having some miraculous experience while he was unconscious. I can't explain it. I only know it was a miracle, and a great blessing to me. I woke up a changed man. I'd never had much interest in genealogy or my forebears prior to that time. But after what I'd seen and felt, I became obsessed to some degree—as you well know. And that has brought you and me closer."

He looked at the ring and stuffed it into his pocket. "Anyway, I thought you might like to know that story. I've never told anyone but Jane, and I'd prefer that it remain between us."

"Of course," she said gently. "Thank you for sharing it with me." She bent forward and pressed a hand to his face. "You are so precious to me, Alex. I love my children dearly, and they have all given me great joy. But I've never shared with any of them the friendship I share with you. I'm sorry that your mother didn't stay around longer; however, I'm grateful to be somewhat of a mother to you in her absence."

"The privilege is mine, Susan. I love you dearly. I could never tell you what a tremendous blessing you have been in my life. I think he brought us together." Alex nodded toward the painting. "We'll have to thank him for that one day."

"Indeed we will," she said.

"And by the way," he stood up and brushed off the back of his jeans before he held out a hand to help Susan to her feet, "you make a fine mother . . . and grandmother. My mother was an amazing woman and I miss her, but she was no more amazing than you are. The two of you would have gotten along beautifully."

"I wish we'd gotten to know each other beyond a vague acquaintance."

"Perhaps one day you'll have that chance," he said, and they left the attic together.

* * * * *

Alex came awake to the phone ringing and realized it was still dark. His heart pounded with panic, fearing that something had gone wrong with Barrett. It took him a moment to orient himself to the fact that Barrett was asleep in the other room, and not at the hospital. And he hadn't been for many months. He grabbed the phone but couldn't focus enough to read the caller ID before he answered.

"Alex?" he heard a woman's voice say, but it took his brain a second to grasp that it was Jane's mother.

"Yes," he said, aware of Jane sitting up next to him. "What's wrong?"

"We've got some bad news, Alex. I'm glad you answered. I need to tell Jane, but I need to tell you first."

The panic that had erupted at hearing the phone ring in the middle of the night heightened dramatically with such a preamble. Did Louisa know her daughter was emotionally fragile from the ongoing strain of Barrett's illness? Was she worried that whatever Jane needed to be told would be too much for her to handle alone?

"Okay," Alex said and met Jane's eyes, almost disappointed to see that she was wide awake, gazing at him expectantly.

Louisa's voice was surprisingly even as she said, "Walter passed away about an hour ago."

Alex was stunned into silence as a turmoil of grief and shock tightened his stomach. He finally managed to answer the silence

on the other end of the phone. "How?" was all he could manage to
squeak out.

"A stroke. There was no warning. That's all I can say right
now." Her voice trembled, and he felt sure she was struggling to
hold it together enough to inform her children.

"I understand," he said. "Is someone with you?"

"Yes," she said more firmly. "How is Barrett?"

"The same. He's doing okay, but it's tough."

"That's why I'm worried about Jane more than anyone," she
said. "I need to tell her. You'll hold her hand, won't you?"

"Of course," he said. "She's right here."

Jane absorbed Alex's side of the conversation with calm trepidation while she tried to guess who he was talking to and what had
gone wrong. His expressions and tone of voice let her know it
couldn't be good, whatever it was. But her dread tightened every
nerve in her body as he turned to look at her with a frightened
caution in his eyes, saying gently, "It's your mother. She wants to
talk to you."

Jane heard her breathing become audible as Alex carefully put
the phone into her right hand, then firmly took her left, holding it
tightly.

"Mom?" she said into the phone, her voice betraying her fear.

"Jane, honey," her mother said. "I've got some difficult news."
Jane said nothing; she could only wait for the guillotine to fall.
And it did when Louisa added, "Your father passed away about an
hour ago."

Alex heard Jane suck in her breath as if a harsh wind had
rushed into her face. She squeezed his hand painfully tight and he
tightened his hold in response, putting his other arm around her
shoulders. The remainder of the conversation was brief as Jane
managed to squeak out a few questions and exclamations of disbelief. Then she handed the phone back to Alex. Not certain if he
was supposed to hang it up or talk some more, he said hello.

"I need to make other calls," Louisa said. "I don't know exactly
when the funeral will be, but the sooner you can get here the

better. Is it possible for both of you to come? I know Barrett has needs that can't be brushed over."

"We'll figure something out," Alex said. "We'll let you know."

"Thank you, Alex," she said with the first sign of real emotion. "I'm so grateful you're part of the family." She sniffled and added, "You and I have been through crisis before. Maybe that's why I feel like I need you here. If there's any possible way for you to come as well . . ."

"I'll be there," he promised, knowing he could never send Jane alone anyway.

"Thank you," she said and ended the call.

Alex hung up the phone and turned his attention to Jane, who was practically hyperventilating. He felt his own shock starting to wear off while he took hold of Jane's shoulders and told her to breathe, much as he would if she were in labor. He watched her consciously try to take some deep breaths and blow them out, then she started to cry and literally crumpled in his arms. She sobbed helplessly until the sun came up, then she settled into a numb shock and stared at the wall long after the children woke up and needed attention. Alex left Jane to her grief and saw to the children's needs. As always he was grateful for Susan, who firmly declared that it would be best if they left the children at home with her.

"Barrett can't travel and the others are too young to know or care," she insisted.

"But Barrett has appointments," he said. "I don't want you dealing with this on your own. Dad and Roxanne could probably help."

"I'm sure they will," Susan said. "And there are sisters in the ward who would gladly watch the little ones if I need to take Barrett in myself. I know the drill, and we'll do everything we can to keep them all healthy and cared for. We'll work it out. You just get some plane tickets and get the time off work. I'll take care of the rest."

Alex first called his father, needing a shoulder to cry on as much as some help with the children. He eagerly offered to see that Barrett got to his appointments and was cared for. Neil and

Roxanne had spent a great deal of time with Barrett through the process of his chemotherapy, and Alex knew they could handle whatever might come up. They decided that Barrett would just stay with them while Alex and Jane were gone. And Barrett was actually pleased with the idea. He took the news of his grandfather's death with the faith of a child, taking for granted that he was now with Heavenly Father and Jesus, and everything would be okay. Katharine didn't seem to have any comprehension of death, and she just wanted to play. Alex was grateful not to have to deal with trying to console grief in his children when he had no idea how to console the grief in his wife. For himself, losing Walter was deep and painful. He'd grown to love Jane's father dearly. He'd gained a tender closeness with her parents through the course of Jane's coma when they had shared endless hours of bedside vigil, and that closeness had remained through the years. But the grief he felt came nowhere near to Jane's reaction to the news. He'd never seen her so utterly lost and inconsolable. Through the night and into the next day she did little but cry and sleep, and he could barely get her to eat anything at all. When Alex expressed his concerns to Susan, she suggested that perhaps Jane had unconsciously tangled her grief over Barrett's illness, and her fear over losing her son, into the loss of her father. "Maybe losing her father has just given an outlet for all of the emotions she's kept bottled inside."

"I'm sure you're right," Alex said, and the more he pondered the idea, the more it made sense. But he still didn't know what to do about it.

In making preparations to leave, Alex had to guide Jane through every step, as if she'd lost the ability to make the simplest decisions. Thirty-six hours after the news had come, they were in the air on their way to California. Alex kept Jane's hand in his through the flight. He tried to get her to talk about what she was feeling, but she had nothing to say, and for the most part her tears seemed to have been replaced by a deep shock. She seemed lost in a place where Alex was unable to find her.

After picking up a rented car at the airport, Alex drove to the home where Jane had been raised, well aware that she was feeling anxiety over facing the reality that her father wouldn't be there, even though she said very little. Arriving at the house, Louisa first hugged Jane tightly while they both wept, then she took hold of Alex as if he might save her. Through the course of completing funeral arrangements Louisa seemed to always want him and Jane nearby. He often found her holding his hand or turning to him when a decision needed to be made. There were moments when the situation felt a bit awkward, since she had all of her children around, but Jane's older sister pointed out when their mother was out of the room that the time Louisa and Alex had spent together during Jane's coma had likely spurred this connection. And they all seemed fine with it. Alex certainly didn't mind; he only wished he could do something to ease the heartache of such a loss. He couldn't help wondering what it would be like if Barrett didn't survive his bout with leukemia. If it were this painful to lose someone who had lived a full life and was now retired, how would it be to lose a child? He couldn't even think about it.

Through the viewing and the funeral, Alex remained between Jane and her mother every possible minute. At moments he wondered how he was supposed to be strong enough to carry them both through this, when something inside made him want to crumble to the ground and never get up. But he prayed continually for the strength he needed and was surprised to feel those prayers answered over and over. Somehow he always knew what to say and what to do in a way that felt surreal and distant, as if he were acting by a will beyond his own. He didn't question the reasons; he just thanked God for carrying him through.

They returned home to find all well there. Even Barrett had managed just fine without them. Alex found Jane wanting to be near the child more than usual, as if she feared that letting him out of her sight might cause her to lose him the way she'd lost her father. Alex repeatedly attempted to get her to talk through her feelings over the loss, but she insisted there was nothing to say.

A few days after their return, Alex found it impossible to sleep. For reasons he couldn't define, he felt drawn to the attic of the house. He turned on the light and ambled slowly between the boxes and trunks, pondering the history that might be buried in them. In another season of life, perhaps he'd have the time and motivation to start digging. At the moment, he preferred just being among memorabilia that represented his forebears. He thought of the family history he'd come to know so well, and how he'd always been particularly drawn to his mother's side—most specifically, his great-great-grandfather, his namesake.

Alex pulled away the fabric covering Alexander Barrett's portrait. As always, looking at it felt a little eerie. But he couldn't deny the closeness he felt with this man for a number of reasons. Since the illogical experience of seeing a portion of his life in some kind of dream, Alex had liked to imagine that this great man might be some kind of guardian angel in his own life. Alex had studied his history and journals over and over. He'd felt spiritually connected to him. But he wondered now if Alexander Barrett had any knowledge from his side of the veil of the challenges going on with this particular little branch of his offspring. Whether or not he did, Alex still found some comfort in the thought.

The following morning Alex was feeding the kids breakfast when a thought occurred to him. Once they had eaten and he'd helped Susan load the dishwasher, he went to the study and pulled out the Barrett genealogy, wondering if the memory teasing at his brain had any accuracy. He knew there was nothing about a particular event in the journals, or he would have remembered it. But looking at the pedigree chart, the dates told a story. The third child of Alexander and Katharine Barrett had died at the age of five.

"Good heavens," Alex muttered and felt chilled. He wondered why there was no reference to it in the parents' journals. Too painful, perhaps? He didn't know the cause of death. It didn't matter. There was no denying the deepening bond he felt with his great-great-grandfather. Perhaps he knew and understood after all.

* * * * *

Less than two weeks after their return from the funeral, Barrett came down with cold symptoms, seemingly out of nowhere. No one else in the household had a cold, and he hadn't been anywhere or exposed to anyone else since their return. There was no adequate way for Alex and Jane to express their concerns. Barrett's immune system was in horrendous condition, and they both knew it. In seemingly no time at all he was hospitalized with pneumonia. Alex saw his fears reflected in Jane's eyes, even though she still refused to talk about much of anything. The fear blew into full-fledged panic when Barrett was abruptly moved to the pediatric intensive care unit, and they were told that his chances of survival were dropping rapidly. Word went out through a well-used system of email and phone calls to alert family, friends, and ward members to fast and pray for Barrett. He was given a number of priesthood blessings as well, and within a couple of days he showed improvement, and they felt sure he would beat the pneumonia. But the deepening hollow look in Jane's eyes did not lessen with the positive prognosis. For all intents and purposes, she interacted with Alex normally, but there was an undercurrent in her behavior that frightened him.

Alex often found himself in the attic, if only for a few minutes here and there, between his comings and goings. He could never explain the subtle comfort he found there that helped him keep going. But he always felt a little better somehow after sitting there alone for a brief reprieve.

Barrett's recovery from the pneumonia was long and hard, but as the holidays approached he almost began behaving like a normal kid again—at least a normal kid with cancer. The holidays ended up being a bright spot in the ongoing struggles. Barrett did so much better than he had the previous Christmas that they couldn't help but find joy in simply watching him take in the holiday celebrations with his brother and sister.

Katharine was four and a half now and obsessed with baby dolls and play dishes. She was technically attending preschool, but every other parent had been alerted to let the teacher know if any child had even the slightest hint of a virus, in which case Katharine would be kept home. But the teacher always provided Jane with the materials that Katharine missed, and Jane helped her keep up. While Katharine enjoyed school, she didn't seem to mind being home with her brothers, helping care for them as if she had some maternal responsibility.

Preston was now old enough to attend the nursery class at church, but his attendance was often sparse there as well with the ongoing concern of bringing any viruses into the home. And Preston too seemed to want to help care for his older brother. He brought him toys and storybooks, and Barrett loved to read simple stories to his little brother. Their mutual favorite was *Hop on Pop,* by Dr. Seuss.

Preston had curly blond hair like his sister and a pleasant disposition, and he was greatly talented at making Barrett laugh. While the family often felt quarantined and left to their own resources for company and entertainment, Preston's comical antics of imitating cartoon characters or animals were always great fun.

The three children together thoroughly enjoyed the holiday celebrations, and Donald and Susan clearly appreciated being a part of it. If Alex had to find a silver lining in their present circumstances, it would definitely be the closeness they had come to find as a family while even the children seemed to have found friendship among themselves when the opportunities to play with other friends were rare these days.

With the spirit of Christmas in the air, Alex felt some hope blossoming that perhaps they might be moving into the downside of this. He felt his hope reflected in Jane when she seemed more like herself than she had since long before her father's death. She was still far from the woman who had once been so full of life and sparkle. But then he felt sure he'd lost something of himself through all of this as well.

After the first of the year, Barrett underwent the standard tests to gauge how the treatment was working. The hopes and prayers of everyone who knew and loved Barrett were all focused on the desire for positive results. Alex felt both afraid to believe, and at the same time certain that all would be well. Then the call came that the doctor wanted to meet with him and Jane. His hope for the best became immediately squelched by his fear of the worst. And when he told Jane about the appointment, he instinctively knew that she shared his every emotion. More and more it seemed they had nothing to say to each other. It was if they understood each other so well that words were not necessary, but at the same time, the lack of conversation only seemed to encourage an inability to express emotions that he knew were building steadily in both of them.

Alex held Jane's trembling hand in his while they listened to the test results. And then the axe fell. But even before it did, Alex realized that in his heart he had known what was coming. In that moment, he believed he'd known all along, at some level, that it would come to this. He'd fought it and wished it away and had done everything to convince himself that it wouldn't be necessary. But his deepest gut instinct told him that he'd been prepared for this moment, even if denial had attempted to keep the preparation at bay.

"He's going to need a bone marrow transplant," the doctor said, "if there's any hope for him to survive this."

Alex had to force himself to breathe. The memories of medical images didn't come hesitantly out of that secluded part of his brain. They burst into his conscious mind like a firecracker exploding with a startling pop.

Jane felt Alex's hand come down over her leg, gripping so tightly that it hurt. She turned to look at him and saw his focus still on the doctor. His expression showed some futile attempt to appear composed, but there was no missing the callow fear in his eyes. She had come here expecting to be told that Barrett would inevitably die. Being told that there was still a chance had given her a measure of hope she'd not expected. But this reaction in Alex left her feeling unsteady and frightened. Realizing the doctor was still talking, she did her best to give him her attention.

"I would suggest that you alert everyone who might be a possible match, who is willing and able to be tested for compatibility." He went on to explain that the testing was expensive, and insurance guidelines needed to be considered by those who might be a probable match. He added gently, "The odds of finding a match that's not a blood relative are much less likely, and we have to consider that time is an issue."

Alex let go of Jane's leg and put his arm around her shoulders, and for a moment she felt certain he was trembling. She felt drawn back and forth between the subtle evidence of her husband's anxiety and what the doctor was telling them. He talked of the tests that would be necessary to see if Barrett's organs were strong enough to handle the transplant, and he spoke of all the steps that would lead up to and follow the transplant. He said that he would refer them to people at the hospital who were there to specifically help prepare families for this, and to guide them through the process. When he asked if they had any questions, Jane's head was spinning far too much to even come up with a cohesive thought. She was grateful to hear Alex say, "We need to think about this."

"Of course," the doctor said with compassion. "We'll be in touch."

Chapter 6

Alex hurried Jane from the room so quickly that she almost tripped. With her arm in his hand he guided her out to the car without saying a word, but she could feel his anxiety. Once in the car he just sat, staring at nothing. Then he squeezed his eyes closed tightly, his expression anguished.

"Talk to me, Alex," she pleaded, and he turned toward her as if he'd forgotten she was there. "You know something I don't know; I can see it, feel it."

Alex took a deep breath and studied his wife's expression. The fear in her eyes was matched with an overt trust. She was trusting in him to know the answers. Well, he certainly knew something she didn't, but he had no inclination to share it with her. And he certainly didn't have the answers. He reminded himself that it was up to the two of them, together, to make this decision. And they couldn't do that effectively if he didn't tell her what he knew.

"Alex, please," she said to counter his silence.

"Yeah," he said, "I know something you don't know." He was surprised to hear the anger in his own voice. But anger at who, what? Anger to buffer the fear and heartache, no doubt. But given the choice, anger seemed much easier to cope with.

When he said nothing more, she said with stark courage in her voice, "Tell me."

Alex shook his head, and an anguished noise came out of his mouth. He heard himself curse aloud, and Jane gasped. She hadn't heard a word like that come out of his mouth since she'd recovered from that coma. He forced himself to go on. "I have *never* truly *hated* being a doctor until *this moment!*"

"Why?" she asked, courage and fear still battling in her voice. But what exactly she feared was hard to tell.

"Because I *know* what he's talking about, Jane. I spent some significant time in the children's bone marrow transplant unit during my residency. Ever since the day Barrett was diagnosed, I have prayed and pleaded that it wouldn't come to this." He cursed again. "You sit there and you listen to a doctor telling you we're going to do this, and we'll have to do that, and he'll respond like this. And it's the bare minimum, the tiniest tip of the iceberg. And by all I hold dear I wish to God that I didn't know what he was talking about, that I could go into this as blind as every other parent."

Alex paused to ponder Jane's horrified expression. He softened his tone. "And I wonder if it's right for me to take that blindness away from you."

She looked hard into his eyes. "I need to know, Alex. Maybe there's a reason that *you* know. Maybe that's a blessing, the same way your working so close to the hospital is a blessing."

"Or a curse," he countered, unable to avoid the cynicism.

"Tell me," she pleaded.

Alex attempted to push past his anger and fear, instead praying for some strength and guidance. He took a deep breath and muttered, "We have a choice to make, Jane. Just because they recommend this, doesn't mean we have to do it."

"And what's the other option? To just . . . let him die when we had a chance to save him? We can't do that, Alex, not when there's any chance at all to save his life."

He sighed and had to admit, "I know." He turned more toward her and added firmly, "But it still needs to be an educated decision, Jane. I can't change what I know, and if my knowing can make any difference at all, it would only be to . . . I don't know . . . help us be better prepared, maybe."

"I'm listening."

He sighed loudly. "I don't know if I can talk about this in reference to Barrett; it makes me *sick*."

He saw her swallow hard, and the courage in her eyes faded slightly. Still, she said with conviction, "Then talk about it like a doctor."

Alex attempted to put himself in the proper frame of mind, keeping the medical technicalities separate from the personal attachment. He cleared his throat and began, "Full-body radiation, combined with higher doses of chemotherapy, will in essence kill every living cell in his bone marrow. The process includes making a full-body mold to hold him completely motionless, and he will also be strapped down, with his eyes taped closed." He saw Jane put a hand over her mouth but he turned to look the other way. "Thankfully, he will be sedated. These repeated doses of radiation will quite literally take him to the brink of death with the hope of killing every single cancer cell that might be hiding in his body. Then the new bone marrow is given to him, and he will be kept in strict isolation for weeks. He will be put on drugs to fight the infections he can't fight, and drugs to keep his body from rejecting the transplant, and drugs to keep him from feeling the pain. His mouth and the lining of his esophagus—and possibly other places as well—will likely be filled with bleeding ulcers. The cells will slough off and he will vomit all this stuff out—over and over. He will need someone with him around the clock to be certain he doesn't choke on the mucus that will be coming up. His lips will swell and peel; his skin will turn splotchy and red, like a bad sunburn. He won't be able to swallow or talk . . . for weeks. *If,* after all of this, the graft takes hold and does its job, his healing will be slow and strained. And when he comes home he will bring half the hospital with him. The isolation we've been through to this point will seem easy in comparison. The road back to eating will be one of the hardest to traverse. The care and medication he will need is almost . . . incomprehensible." Still not looking at Jane he said, "Okay, as close as I can recall, that's the minimum, no-complications version."

He turned toward her, and the sickness smoldering inside of him exploded. She had an arm around her middle and a hand pressed tightly over her mouth, but he couldn't tell if it was meant to keep her from crying or throwing up. He put his arms around her and pulled her close as she clutched onto him and let out an anguished noise. He could feel her breathing sharply, but she didn't cry. After settling into normal breathing, she asked without letting go of him, "And that's our choice above letting him die?"

"That's it," he said coldly.

He felt her take a deep breath, but she didn't let go of him; she just kept her head against his chest. That determined courage returned to her voice as she said, "What would be the complications version?"

Alex held her tighter as if he could shield her from the harsh reality. He sighed. "There are many possibilities. Obviously, infection of many kinds is a risk. If his system tries to reject the transplant, then it's like a war inside his body, cells killing cells. Allergic reactions can happen. Sometimes the new blood cells move in and take over in a way the body can't handle, and the organs start to shut down. No matter how you look at it, Jane, there is a great deal of risk that something could go wrong, and that he may not even survive the process."

"But if he does?"

"If he does . . . if they can really kill every cancer cell . . . he'll have a chance to grow up and live a relatively normal life. But that's subjective, as well. He may survive the cancer but have permanent damage to any of his organs, including his brain."

Minutes of silence allowed the things he'd said to settle in. Jane finally tightened her arms around him and said, "We have to try, Alex. How could we ever live with letting him die without even trying?"

"We can't," he said. "I know that. I just . . ."

"What?" she asked, easing back to look at him.

Alex shook his head and met her eyes. "It's not fair, Jane. How can it be right for a parent to choose between letting a child die, and letting a child suffer unspeakably?"

"No, it's not fair, Alex. But that doesn't change it. I've heard you say a hundred times that in the ER you have to do everything you possibly can to save a life until you know beyond any doubt there's absolutely nothing more you could have done. Surely we must do the same for our son."

Alex looked at his wife for a seemingly endless moment while other memories crowded into his consciousness. What he'd seen the children suffer in the BMT unit had been horrendous in itself. But he recalled other casualties as well. The suffering of the parents had been equally unspeakable. He'd witnessed tears, exhaustion, anger, and bitterness that had become emblazoned in the recesses of his mind. But in that moment the clearest memory of all was something that had happened in the middle of a night shift. He'd just helped stabilize a kid who had come in on Life Flight, and he'd been asked to check on a kid who was in the first phase following a transplant. He turned the corner into a hallway that was empty except for the married couple who were engaged in a quiet argument. Alex had ducked back behind the corner, not wanting to intrude. But he'd been unable to avoid overhearing the woman say, "You and I made this child together, and if you can't stand by us through this, then you can just kiss us both good-bye—for good. Don't think you can walk out now and waltz back into our lives once the nightmare is over."

Alex didn't wait long enough to hear any more, or to see what her husband's response might have been. He'd gone elsewhere for twenty minutes and returned to find the hallway empty. He'd stuck to his duties and forced the conversation away, along with the images of bald-headed children and grieving parents. At the time, he and Jane had been engaged, but he'd had no comprehension of what it was like to have a child of his own, or any belief that he and Jane could ever be at cross purposes over anything. But he'd felt the distance between them growing since Barrett's illness had begun. There were moments when he knew they were in it together, gems of connection that kept him going. Still, the strain was apparent, and he wondered what might happen between them by raising the strain level several degrees.

Reminding himself to stick to matters of the moment, he took her hand and said gently, "I agree that we have to do everything we possibly can to save him, Jane. But before we sign those papers we need to absolutely know and completely agree that it's the right choice. It's the only way we can live with it. Do you understand?" She nodded. "We need to study this out, get every avenue of information we possibly can, ask questions until we get all the answers. We need to be as prepared as we possibly can. But even then, I don't know that we can ever be truly prepared for what we're in for. Even with what I know, Jane, I know it from a doctor's perspective, not a parent's. And it scares me. I'm not only afraid of what it will do to him, but to you . . . to us." She wrapped her arms around him tightly as if to say that she wouldn't let it come between them, but he couldn't bring himself to feel entirely confident on that count.

He added what he believed to be an important point. "There's something we need to consider."

"What?" she asked, easing back.

"We may not be able to find a match. If we start preparing ourselves for this and a match can't be found, then what?"

Jane drew a ragged breath. "Then we'll know we did everything we could."

He nodded and hugged her tightly, while he felt a battle ensuing in his mind. He felt the choices before him colliding with a gamut of emotions that clashed and contended for triumph.

Through the next several days the battle raged. Word went out quickly via emails and phone calls that they were considering a bone marrow transplant. Alex and Jane were both amazed at how many relatives who were considered a possible match were willing, even eager, to have the testing done to see if they might qualify. For some, insurance covered the expense; others found a way to pay for the testing. In the meantime they met with people who talked them more thoroughly through the process and answered their questions. They met with counselors and a social worker assigned by the hospital to their case to aid them through the process. Alex felt increasingly grateful for the brutal conversation he'd had with Jane, which did end up making it easier to ask specific questions about what to expect, and not be too blown away by the answers. They each devoured piles of reading material and diligently searched the web for any other facet of information they could find. But he felt sure that most of what they were reading only scratched the surface, giving minimal information from a medical perspective.

An added shock was the frank discussion they endured on the financial aspect of this endeavor. Even with health insurance, their out-of-pocket estimated cost was a six-figure amount with a large variable. They were given advice on ways to raise the needed funds as well as information to connect them to charitable foundations that could help. They were also frankly instructed on ways to possibly survive this without having to file for bankruptcy. While Primary Children's Medical Center was a charitable facility, Alex knew the money had to come from somewhere. And there were too many dying kids to expect the hospital to even begin to meet every need of every patient. Alex had to remind himself that Barrett's father was a doctor, and they lived close enough that they didn't have to rent an apartment or make expensive commutes for treatment. They were blessed in many ways, and surely they could find a way to survive this financially and leave the hospital's charity resources for people with more difficult circumstances.

Making a final choice was held up by the testing to see if Barrett could withstand the transplant, and by the need for a donor match. The battle in Alex's head became more intense as he felt the waiting drawing to a close. A part of him almost hoped Barrett's body would be declared unfit, or that a donor couldn't be found, that they would never have to face the horror. But with that came truckloads of guilt. How could he not want his son to live? How could he secretly have a death wish for Barrett? On the other hand, if he sided with the hope for a match that would give Barrett a second chance for life, a different kind of guilt reared its ugly head, making him feel like some kind of sick sadist. How could he knowingly toss his son into a pit of ravenous radiation that would eat him alive? He found himself leaning more toward the no-avail-able-donor wish. At least the waiting would be over. Death would be imminent, but at least they'd know where they stood. If a donor was found, death could still be a distinct possibility, but they would all be thrown into a sadistic game of roulette, torturously waiting for the spin of the wheel to determine if he would live or die, or if his suffering would have purpose or be in vain.

Testing revealed that Barrett was a prime candidate for a trans-plant. In spite of what his body had been through thus far, he was considered strong enough in every respect to withstand what would be done to him. With each revelation came new levels of hope and fear, running side by side like a couple of wild horses, dragging Alex and Jane headlong into unknown territory.

As they met once again with the people who were working to coordinate the death and resurrection of Barrett Keane, the final piece was laid out. "We have good news," they were told. "We've found a match for Barrett. There was only one possibility that came up, but it's enough."

In a split second the battle raging in Alex's head came to an abrupt truce. Gratitude squelched the fear. His son would be given a second chance to live. In the space of a heartbeat he saw in his mind Barrett's baptism, his receiving the priesthood, getting his Eagle Scout award, going on a mission, getting married in the temple, having children of his own. The briefness and enormity of this glimpse into the future felt visionary and momentarily real. And for that moment, the suffering and sorrow and grief and pain simply didn't matter. If only Barrett could live. In a breathless voice he spoke one word. "Who?" But the question echoed subplots in his mind. Who would be enduring the procedure and pain to give a portion of liquid gold? Who would be the means for life to come out of death for a child? Who would forever become a part of Barrett's DNA should the transplant succeed? Alex felt Jane take his hand in a painful, expectant grip, and he felt certain her thoughts were as his.

And then the answer came. "It's you, Alex."

Alex drew a rough breath, wondering why he had dismissed the idea that he could be the one. Perhaps he'd just been so focused on every other aspect of the process that the possibility seemed irrelevant. But knowing that he was the one filled him with a deepening sense of gratitude and a solid sense of privilege. He felt nothing but thoroughly honored to be given the opportunity to do this for Barrett. The bond between father and son deepened in that moment. He would gladly give his life in exchange for Barrett's. Giving up some bone marrow seemed insignificant. He only wished there was something he could give to spare Barrett the suffering that he knew was inevitable. But in his heart he knew this was the right course. And Jane knew it too.

It only took a minute for Alex and Jane to sign their names to the warrant—papers that gave permission for their son to be taken into the valley of the shadow of death. Then they took hold of each other's hands, silently and mutually investing every grain of hope that the end result would bring back to life every part of him that would be tortured and destroyed.

Once the decision was official, a shock wave of planning and preparation was set in motion. Family, friends, and ward members rallied up forces that they'd only seen glimpses of to this point. Fund-raising projects sprouted all over the place, even in other states where family members lived. A ward member with a media connection arranged for a story on Barrett to appear in the *Salt Lake Tribune*. Initially, Alex felt hesitant, not wanting to feel like the issue was being exploited. But with the encouragement of family and friends he realized this was a good opportunity to raise some much-needed funds to make it through this. He insisted that the article make it clear that all money donated would go directly to Barrett's medical bills, and if they collected more than they needed, it would go to help other victims of children's leukemia who needed support. And he wanted it made clear that Barrett was far from the only child going through this at Primary Children's; he was simply the only one at the moment facing a BMT who actually resided in Salt Lake City. A reporter and photographer arranged for an interview, and they decided to use the slant of Alex's medical career in contrast to Barrett's medical crisis. The picture that ended up in the paper was of Barrett sitting cross-legged on a table in one of the trauma rooms at the ER where Alex worked. Alex was wearing scrubs, leaning his hands on the table while Barrett listened to his father's heart with the stethoscope in his ears. Alex thought the picture was adorable, especially the crooked little smile on Barrett's face. But he wasn't terribly thrilled with the headline, "Doctor Gives Life to Dying Son." He quickly got over his negative feelings, however, when the bank account set up for Barrett's transplant began to fill up. He marveled at the generosity of strangers, not to mention friends and loved ones who continued doing all they could to help the situation.

Alex wasn't surprised to have his father approach him with a sincere desire to help. "We want to contribute to the medical expenses, Alex." He took a bite of his lunch on the other side of the table at the hospital cafeteria.

Alex sighed and looked down. "Listen, Dad . . . I don't know how much money you've got put away but—"

"Quite a lot, actually," Neil said, and Alex felt surprised. He knew his father had done well, that his partial ownership in a company had paid off significantly. But he still had no idea of the actual numbers, and he didn't want to.

"Okay, but . . . you don't need to spend it all on helping us get through this, or—"

"That's not possible, Alex," Neil said, and Alex leaned back, not feeling much appetite anyway. "Now be quiet and listen to me for a minute, son. People are rallying to raise money, and I think that's a great thing. It's good when others have the opportunity to give of themselves and pull together for a cause, and the life of a child is a great cause. I don't want to step in and save the day or make a big deal of it, and I don't want to deny these good people an opportunity to contribute. But you said that any excess would go to helping other families who don't have the resources you do. So I'm going to make a contribution that Roxanne and I can feel good about, and I'm going to do it anonymously. It's between you and me. In the end, if more needs arise, I want you to know there's more we can give, and I believe more and more that this hospital is a great place to be putting extra money."

"I can't argue with that," Alex said. He leaned forward again and picked up his fork. "Thank you, Dad."

"I'd give everything I have to save Barrett's life."

"Yeah, I know what you mean," Alex said, grateful beyond measure to have his father in his life. The money was wonderful, but it was secondary to the hours this man had spent at Alex's side through all of this, and the tender relationship he shared with Barrett. Neil and Roxanne were among a select few who had never seemed put off by the ugly side of cancer. Their regular visits and time with Barrett, and the support they gave the entire family, had been a treasure on many difficult days.

Beyond the financial concerns, plans were put carefully into place to handle the care Barrett would need. The hospital staff would take good care of him, but Jane was adamant that she wanted to be with her son every possible minute, even though it meant leaving her other two children mostly in the care of Donald and Susan, with Neil and Roxanne as an ongoing backup, regularly taking them for outings or overnight occasionally to keep from wearing out Donald and Susan too much. Alex would be with Barrett whenever work allowed, during which times Jane could be at home with the other children. Allowing for the possibility that there would be times when neither of Barrett's parents could be with him, Jane wanted a backup plan. As a mother she just felt better knowing that someone besides the nursing staff would be with her son as much as possible. Jane learned everything she could about what to expect and how to be prepared to handle it, and they arranged, according to the hospital's requirements, to provide other options for people who could sit with Barrett should the need arise. Knowing that his condition much of the time would be far more challenging than just a sleepy or whiny child, they were pleased when the Relief Society presented them with the names of a few women who had been sought out on a stake level conforming to specific requirements. These women were willing to come on short notice to sit with Barrett should one of his parents become ill, or should any other need arise. They either had some nursing experience, or had been exposed to severe health issues with their own loved ones in the past. The bottom line was that they could calmly handle caring for a child who would likely be puking up blood. Neil and Roxanne were also more than willing to be with Barrett if necessary and learn whatever they had to in order to help give the support that would be needed.

Now that family and friends had become actively involved in having testing done and raising funds, there was a huge increase in people wanting to be kept informed of Barrett's progress. Alex had been sending out mass emails when he could, but even that was beginning to feel overwhelming. He and Jane were both just too busy to talk with every concerned person, and they knew it was only going to get worse. He was grateful when Jane's brother-in-law, who lived in California, offered to put together a website where loved ones could go for regular updates, and they could also post pictures and positive aspects of Barrett's life and family. Being married to Jane's sister, he already had a lot of great photos and enough information from previous emails to set up the site. All he needed was for Jane or Alex to send him an email when there was any news to share, and he would post it for others to read. Alex and Jane agreed that it was a great idea, and the announcement of barrettkeane.com went out to family, friends, and coworkers.

With every test complete and all arrangements made, a day came in early March when Barrett officially began his radiation treatments. As they became more intense, he was checked into the hospital, and the vigil began. Intense chemotherapy was put into the mix, and the days became long and hard.

As much as they had studied and prepared, settling into the process did not confront them with any surprises—except that no amount of knowledge could have fully prepared them for the reality of Barrett's physical response to all he was being subjected to, or the inner parental paradox of their hopes and dreams battling endlessly against the grief and horror. Alex and Jane both worked hard to keep Barrett happy and distracted, resorting to ridiculous measures of entertainment and rewards for enduring his treatments with courage. In truth, Barrett's attitude was an inspiration to his parents, as well as all who came in contact with him. He rarely complained and never cried. But he did ask a great many questions that were, more often than not, difficult to answer. Still, Alex and Jane had uncompromisingly agreed that they would never lie to Barrett, or even try to sugar-coat the truth in order to temporarily appease him. At times his fear was readily evident and subsequently heart-wrenching to observe. Yet, Barrett's courage was equally distinct, touching Alex deeply and leaving him often feeling inadequate. He felt at times that Barrett was somehow far superior to his father in spirit, leaving Alex struggling to understand why *he* of all people would be entrusted to guide this valiant child of God through the depths of hell. His only hope in believing he could be equal to the task was in knowing that Jane was there beside him, every step of the way. She had strength that didn't surprise him, but it often left him in awe. Still, he felt her turning to him for answers and the means to keep her strength alive. And again he felt inadequate. But all he could do was keep putting one foot in front of the other, trusting that God knew what He was doing, even if cancer in children just felt senseless and horrid from a mortal perspective.

When the big day finally arrived, Alex sat at Barrett's bedside, watching him sleep, praying with all his heart and soul that when all was said and done, Barrett would live beyond this. Alex had spent the night with Barrett, but he hadn't slept well, and the hour preceding dawn felt well spent in observing his son. He knew it wouldn't be long before Jane arrived to sit with Barrett, and he would be going elsewhere to have holes drilled into his hips in order to remove the life-giving fluid. For the moment he felt suspended here with his son in a moment of perfect serenity, the calm before the storm.

"You're awake," Jane said, and he turned to see her enter the room.

"You're early," he said and stood to greet her. They shared a firm embrace.

"I couldn't sleep."

"Me neither."

"How is he?" she asked.

"He's slept well the last few hours."

"And how are you?" she asked.

"I'm fine."

"I wish I could be with you," she said. "I feel torn."

"It's okay," he insisted. "You need to be here. It's not a big deal. Besides, Dad will take good care of me. He'll be here soon."

"Alex," she said gently, "there's something I want to say."

"Okay."

She looked intently into his eyes. "The night we first met, you were a hero to me. I didn't know your name or anything about you, but I spent hours thinking about what you'd done for me at that restaurant. It may have seemed simple, but it meant a great deal to me. You've been there beside me ever since, caring for me and my children in every way imaginable. I can't begin to recount all the times you've been there for me, for things like crying babies in the night, a kid puking on the carpet, to a dance in the kitchen if only to make me smile. I just want you to know . . . you're my hero, Alex. You always have been. But never more than today. What you are giving today, Alex, has the ability to save my son's life. And I want you to know that I'm grateful."

"He's my son too, Jane. And it's not that big of a deal—at least not from my perspective. You would do the same if you had been a match." He looked at Barrett sleeping. "I only wish there was something—anything—I could give to take away the suffering."

Jane wrapped her arms around him, and he held her close. "Now, be nice to the nurses," she said lightly, still holding him tightly. "Remember you're not the doctor now; you're the patient. Try to behave."

"I'll try," he said.

More seriously she added, "And do what they tell you. Don't be up and around too soon. We'll be fine."

Alex wanted to believe her, but he knew the real trauma was about to begin. He could only pray that all went as well as it possibly could, and that in the end it would all be worth it.

The transplant went well from both ends, and Barrett's initial reaction to the new bone marrow caused only minor difficulties that were quickly remedied. But the child quickly became consumed with the expected side effects from all he'd endured. Jane told Alex more than once that she was grateful to have been prepared for what to expect, but that didn't make it any easier to get through. The hours dragged into days that felt eternal, even though they knew they had barely begun. But they simply did their best to keep pressing forward, praying fervently that the bone marrow would graft, and the road to healing could begin.

While Barrett struggled hourly, Jane became a genius at trying to keep spirits up. She found ways to decorate his hospital room according to the firm restrictions of being confined for months to a room where no germ could be allowed to enter. With Alex's help she covered the ceiling with Mylar balloons, and she covered the walls with laminated pictures of the people who loved Barrett, and many of his favorite things. His love for the zoo and jungle animals quickly dominated the room. There were pictures of animals everywhere, and plastic animals as well. No toy could enter the room unless it was new and had come straight out of the packaging, and then through a sterilizing process. And while Barrett rarely showed any interest in playing with toys, his parents and grandparents were all for trying anything that might hold his interest or light up his eyes even for a few minutes. His favorite toy quickly became a stuffed elephant that Grandpa had brought him after it had spent a great deal of time in a hospital dryer being sterilized.

Barrett had every possible access to TV, recorded movies, and video games, but he often just felt too sick to care. His love of coloring books and puzzles was difficult to appease when it wasn't possible to disinfect such things. Books could be brought into the room, but more for the purpose of the parents to read, keeping a safe distance between the books and the child.

Alex was pleased to see that the technology related to the complex air filtering system in this part of the hospital had changed in the years since he'd done his residency. While many precautions still needed to be taken, the atmosphere of the isolation rooms had become more conducive to the patient's social and emotional well being. Nevertheless, they still had to be extremely cautious. And while the hospital unit did well at keeping germs out, Alex and Jane both worked very hard to keep their home environment germ-free as well. They wouldn't be taking Katharine or Preston to see Barrett as long as his system was so completely vulnerable, since young children were tremendous germ carriers. But Jane was adamant that she and Alex needed to do everything possible to avoid getting sick themselves so that they could be with Barrett. Any hint of a virus and you simply wouldn't be allowed past the all-powerful double set of doors into the sterile world where life was fighting to be lived. And fight Barrett did! Alex only hoped that his son could keep up his apparent firm determination to conquer the battle going on inside of his body. He wasn't sure he could accept any other possibility.

Jane and Alex both quickly found themselves a part of a unique community within the hospital, and an even more closely knit group among the bone marrow transplant patients. The nursing staff and other workers affiliated with the program were gems among the human race. Occasionally Jane became frustrated with a nurse who seemed more intent on following orders than in the mood to show tenderness in a strained situation. But for the most part they were always there, calm and firm no matter the circumstances, behaving as if every child struggling to live was the center of the universe.

Among other parents who were sentenced to confinement with their ailing children, it was easy to find common ground and a firm consensus that until a parent had camped here, they could never comprehend the reality. There were moments of aggravation with other parents when the stress and anxiety couldn't help but make tension high and temperaments fragile. There were other moments when the connection was deep and profound, leaving them grateful to know they weren't alone in the torture chamber. And getting to know the parents was closely integrated with becoming attached to the children they were there to try to save.

They became especially close to a little girl named Andrea, who went by the name Andie. Her parents, Bruce and Karen, were LDS and the parents of five children, Andie being the youngest. Andie was about the same age as Barrett, but her leukemia had begun earlier, and she had progressed further in her treatments. Barrett and Andie had first played together during outpatient chemo treatments, and then Andie had ended up in the transplant war not many weeks before Barrett began that course. Bruce and Karen lived more than an hour from Salt Lake City, and the trips back and forth were difficult, but they had relatives in the city, and they had managed well enough. Still, Alex could look at these people and recognize the signs of strain in their faces that he found in Jane's and even his own. The nightmare felt as if it would never end.

* * * * *

Alex bent over the sink in the hospital restroom and splashed cold water on his face. He dried it with paper towels then took a good, long look at himself in the mirror for the first time in days. Or had it been longer? He was disappointed to realize that he looked as bad as he felt. The procedure he'd endured to give bone marrow had seemed fairly insignificant in the big scheme of things, but combining it with long hours at work and the ongoing vigil at Barrett's bedside, he couldn't deny the signs of strain.

Alex pushed his hair back off his face and realized he needed a haircut even more than he needed a shave. His hair hung to the bottom of his neck and was looking pretty shaggy on top. And the hair on his face looked more like a beard than an aversion to shaving. Realizing he didn't have time for a haircut and felt no desire to shave, he combed his hair back off his face as he'd been doing recently and called it good. He'd never worn it this way before, but combed into place it looked relatively well groomed. Returning to Barrett's room he found Jane in the usual place, apparently dozing in a chair near his bed, a familiar weary aura about her. But at least Barrett was sleeping for the moment. As miserable as he'd been, they counted every possible minute of sleep a blessing. Alex longed to see his son's eyes filled with the sparkle and laughter that used to be there. But now there was only pain and sickness in those sweet eyes, and he far preferred to see him sleeping.

Alex was debating whether or not to wake Jane to tell her good-bye when she turned her head and opened her eyes. "Time to go?" she whispered.

"I'm afraid so," he said, bending over to kiss her. "Let me know if anything changes."

"I will, of course," she said and touched his face.

"I love you, Jane," he said firmly. "He's going to be okay."

He saw tears well up in her eyes, and his heart burned with a desire to take away her pain, as well as Barrett's. She nodded, but he wasn't sure she believed him. And how could she? There was a part of him that felt reluctant to believe it himself.

Alex was grateful for a busy shift in the ER. If he kept moving he was more likely to keep awake. Once it was done he called Barrett's room. Jane told him the child was asleep for the first time in more than ten hours; he'd had a horrible day of repeated vomiting and inconsolable misery. Knowing that Alex was on his way, she told him she was leaving to go home for the night. Alex grabbed a sandwich in the cafeteria that he ate as he walked the well-beaten path to Barrett's room. Making himself comfortable, he settled in for the night. Compounded exhaustion had eliminated his difficulty in being able to sleep at odd times and in strange places. He got a few hours of sleep before Barrett was throwing up again. Thankfully he was back to sleep within an hour and Alex was able to get some more rest. He woke up to the now-familiar sounds of Barrett getting rid of all the garbage inside of him. When the episode was over and cleaned up, Barrett clung to Alex and drifted to sleep in his father's arms. Alex realized he'd dozed off as well when he woke to daylight to find Jane there, sitting close to Barrett, holding his hand.

"Hello, Dr. Keane," she said, turning to look at him as if she'd sensed his consciousness.

"How are you?" he asked.

"I'm okay," she said, turning back to look at Barrett. "How are you?"

"The same," he said. "How are Katharine and Preston?"

"They're fine. Susan's taking very good care of them, as always. I think they're beginning to believe Susan is their mother."

Alex struggled for something to say to help give her some perspective. He was glad to find a thought, and hoped it would help. "Jane . . . as hard as this seems now, one day . . . it will balance out. They will hardly remember this time. It seems insurmountable now, but we will be a normal family again . . . someday."

She glared at him, almost seeming angry, as if she would love to counter his words, but didn't know what to say. He hurried to add, "I don't know what the outcome will be, Jane, but I know that life goes on. Don't forget that I once spent nightmarish weeks in a hospital room with you, believing it would never end."

"And if I had died?" she snapped.

Alex swallowed hard. He didn't even want to go there—not in relation to her *or* Barrett. But he was able to say with confidence, "Losing you would have been devastating to me, Jane. But I reached a point when I knew that whatever happened, it was in God's hands, and somehow He would see me through it."

She turned abruptly away as if to say that she didn't want to hear it. Alex reminded himself that there had been a time when he had been stubborn and difficult to reach, lost behind a fog of anger and fear. She had the right to be the same. He just hoped that it would run its course and she could find some peace over this situation.

Alex went into the bathroom and attempted to clean up a bit, but he knew he needed to go home and take a shower. He was grateful to have the day off and sat with Jane for a short while, her hand in his, saying nothing while his mind vacillated between prayer and disjointed thoughts of the past and the present. A thought came to his mind so suddenly that it made him gasp. Or was it a feeling? Both.

"What?" Jane demanded, turning toward him.

Alex tried to examine the idea and at the same time come up with words to explain. It came down to one simple fact. "I need to see my father." He stood up as he said it.

"You think something's wrong?" she asked, sounding panicked. There was no need for words to express the fact that neither of them could face another family drama at this point.

"I don't know," Alex said, trying to remain levelheaded, for her sake if not his own. "I just . . . feel like I need to see him. Maybe it's nothing."

"Okay," she said, and he leaned over to kiss her. "I'll be here. Let me know."

"Of course," he said and hurried from the room, feeling distracted.

Chapter 7

Once in the car, Alex dialed his father's house on the cell phone. No answer. He glanced at the car clock and tried to figure out what day it was. Saturday. Logic said Neil would be at home, but they certainly could have made spontaneous plans to be elsewhere. He tried Neil's cell phone, but it went straight to voice mail. He simply said, "It's Alex. Call me back."

While he drove, Alex tried not to feel nervous. He tried to discount the impression he'd gotten, attempting to convince himself that he'd become paranoid, considering recent events. But he knew he'd been prompted to see his father. He didn't even want to consider what might be wrong. At this point, if something happened to anyone else that Alex loved, he felt certain he'd go over the edge. He was trying to be strong enough to hold both himself and Jane together, but it was all beginning to wear on him.

Again Alex tried to call both numbers, and again he got no one. He felt frustrated with the drive to his father's home, and even more so by sluggish traffic at a time of day when there shouldn't have been any. He finally pulled into the driveway of his dad's house and ran to the door. He knew it would be locked; it always was—even when they were home. But Neil had long ago given Alex a key so that he could check on the house and water plants when they were out of town. He quickly put his key into the deadbolt to open it and walked inside, locking the door behind him.

"Dad!" he called but got no answer. He did a quick perusal of the main floor and hollered up the stairs. He peeked into the garage and found both vehicles there. That was when his heart began to pound. No evidence that they were gone—but they were gone. He heard a noise that made him gasp and turned to see Roxanne coming into the kitchen through the sliding glass door, pulling off her gardening gloves.

"Oh, you scared me," he said, and she laughed softly. Obviously *she* was fine, but he hurried to ask, "Where's Dad?"

"He's in the garden, why? We've been out there all morning."

"I . . . tried to call, but . . ."

Her eyes widened. "Is Barrett okay? Has something—"

"He's fine," Alex said. "Well, as fine as he was yesterday."

Roxanne sighed visibly. "Then what's wrong?" she asked. "You seem . . . upset."

Alex peeked out the glass door to see for himself that his father was, indeed, kneeling in the garden, pulling weeds. He sat down hard at the kitchen table and let out a long, slow breath.

"Alex, are you okay?"

"Yeah," he said. "I just . . . I don't know. I just . . . felt like I needed to get here . . . be here . . . like something was wrong. When I couldn't get an answer, I kind of panicked." He looked up at her standing nearby, her expression concerned. He forced a smile and added, "Obviously everything is fine. I must be getting paranoid."

"Maybe," she said. "Maybe not." They stared at each other for a minute while he felt certain her thoughts were similar to his. They could analyze what he'd felt, and speculate over possible reasons that he'd needed to come. But words seemed pointless. He was relieved when she tossed her gloves into a basket by the door and went to the sink to wash up. "Have you eaten this morning?" she asked.

"Actually . . . no. But I'm fine. I can—"

"Oh, hush. We haven't eaten yet, either. We decided to get some work in before it got too hot. I bet you could use a home-cooked brunch."

"You talked me into it," he said. "Would you mind if I took a shower?"

"Not at all. You know you can make yourself at home. You could probably fit into some of your father's clothes if you need anything to—"

"I've got a bag in the car, actually. I keep extra stuff handy these days. I'll say hi to Dad first."

She smiled then opened the fridge. Alex stepped into the backyard and ambled toward where his father was working. "Hey there, old man," Alex said, and Neil looked up with a grin, pushing his cap back off his head as if to see him better.

"What brings you here?" Neil asked, coming to his feet and brushing the dirt off his gloved hands.

"Just . . . felt like I should come," he said and repeated the same explanation he'd given to Roxanne.

He was surprised when Neil said, "Maybe I didn't need you. Maybe you needed me."

Alex swallowed hard. "Maybe," he said, and then he smiled. "Or maybe I just needed some of Roxanne's cooking to keep me going. She's fixing brunch; I'm going to take a shower."

"Make yourself at home," Neil said, motioning toward the house. "I'll be in as soon as I finish this row."

Alex got his bag out of the car and went to the guest bathroom upstairs to shower. He considered shaving but only scraped away the hair on his neck that was feeling itchy and left his face as it was. This harsh schedule wasn't likely to let up anytime soon, and not having to shave every day had its advantages.

It felt good to be showered and wearing fresh clothes. He cleaned up after himself and left his bag near the front door before he found Roxanne and his father just sitting down to bacon, hash browns, and scrambled eggs. Over breakfast Roxanne complimented Alex on his new beard, then they asked questions about Barrett, and how Jane and the other children were doing. The answers concerning Barrett were all the same, but he enjoyed telling them how Preston was learning to talk and had a flair for coloring on things that shouldn't be colored on. And Katharine's obsession with constantly looking beautiful often found her digging in her mother's makeup or shoes, and trying them out.

"And how are you?" Neil asked firmly.

"I'm hanging in there," Alex said.

"Now tell me the truth," Neil prodded.

"What can I say? I think we're getting our own brand of chemotherapy. There are some things that must be endured in this world that just zap the life right out of you until it feels like you are barely alive." He chuckled without humor. "I guess we could call it refiner's radiation. Whatever it is, it stinks. But it could be worse."

"Yes, that's true. We just hope it doesn't get worse."

"We can hope," Alex said, not wanting to even think how easily life could get worse.

He helped clear the table and was wondering if he should just go back to the hospital, but he couldn't shake the feeling that he needed to be here. He called Susan to see how Katharine and Preston were doing. They were on their way out the door to go yard sale shopping, and the kids were doing fine. Alex talked to Katharine on the phone for a few minutes and felt completely convinced that both children were happy and at ease, and not feeling neglected by their parents in the slightest. Perhaps that was God's way of soothing the children's spirits and making this easier for him and Jane. He mentioned the theory to his father after he got off the phone, and Neil heartily agreed. While Roxanne left to do a number of errands and visit a friend, they sat in the family room to visit, and Neil mentioned that he and Roxanne would be going to the temple that evening, and they would put Barrett's name on the prayer roll—again.

"Thank you," Alex said, unable to remember the last time he'd been within temple walls. He missed it. But he knew he needed to be with his family; that was more important right now.

"And we'll put yours and Jane's names on, as well," Neil added.

Alex felt momentarily surprised then said, "Thank you," again. He felt sure they could all use some extra prayers. He was wondering again if he should just leave, and then the doorbell rang. Neil was stretched out with his feet on the coffee table and Alex offered, "I'll get it."

"Thanks," Neil said. "Whoever it is, don't scare them away."

"I'll see what I can do," Alex said and pulled the door open. He found himself facing a young man—middle twenties, he guessed. He was clean-cut and nice-looking with sandy brown hair, near Alex's height. He wore jeans and a dark blue polo shirt. His eyes looked troubled. He looked familiar, but not really. He also looked horribly nervous; visibly terrified would be more accurate.

While he was trying to figure out where he might have seen that face before, the kid said, "Is this the Keane residence?"

"It is," Alex said. "What can I do for you?"

"You're not Neil Keane; you're not old enough."

"Well, thank you . . . for saying I'm not old, anyway. I'm Neil's son, Alex." He held out a hand. The kid's eyes widened. He looked at the proffered hand, then at Alex's face, then the hand again. He took it almost reluctantly, but his handshake was firm—albeit trembling. Alex began to feel mildly uneasy about this—even before he recalled the feelings that had brought him here, and compelled him to stay. He saw this kid look into his eyes, as if he were searching for something. And he almost looked as if he might cry. "What can I do for you?" Alex asked as the handshake ended.

"I . . . need to talk to . . . Neil Keane."

"Okay," Alex said, motioning him inside and closing the door. "Dad!" Alex called. "There's someone here to see you." He added to the kid, "Can I tell him who?"

Again the kid gave him a soul-searching gaze and said, "I think I'd better do that."

"Okay," Alex said again, and Neil appeared in the entry hall, clearly confused. He'd obviously never seen this guy before. But the visitor's nervousness increased. For a moment Alex had thoughts dart through his mind that made him wonder if he'd let someone in the house who posed some kind of danger to his father. While he didn't think so, and his instincts said otherwise, he couldn't deny the uneasiness he was feeling.

"You're Neil Keane," the kid said with a definite tremor to his voice. Neil tossed a quick glance at Alex, as if to see if he too had noticed the weirdness of the moment.

Neil focused fully on their visitor and said, "Yes. What can I do for you, young man?"

The quaver in his voice heightened as he asked, "Do you remember Marilyn Morrison?"

Alex was wondering why that name sounded familiar, but his heart reacted with dread when he saw his father's face turn ashen in the space of a breath. "Yes, of course," Neil said in a calm voice that defied the change in his countenance.

The young man glanced at Alex and said, "Maybe we should talk alone."

"No," Neil said, again tossing a glance toward Alex, this time his eyes filled with some unspoken plea. But a plea for what? He only knew for certain that his father didn't want him to leave. If nothing else, he felt some validation for his need to be here. He didn't know what was coming, but he knew his father was upset. Neil turned and looked squarely at their visitor before he added, "There are no secrets in this household."

The kid looked pleased by the comment, or perhaps impressed. He quickly said, "Well, there aren't any secrets at my house either—not anymore." He held out his hand toward Neil. "I'm Wade Morrison. Marilyn is my mother."

Alex watched his father take the hand and hold it more than shake it. He watched their eyes connect, and the pieces of the conversation began to merge toward a memory that lured Alex to believe he had figured out who Marilyn Morrison was. It hit him just before Wade added with emotion clearly threaded into his voice, "And that would make you my father."

Alex sucked in his breath and watched the blood drain completely from his father's face. He trembled visibly while his hold on Wade's hand tightened. Alex watched the two of them exchange a gaze littered with a gamut of different emotions. Tears rose into Neil's eyes, and then he teetered and lost his footing.

"Whoa, Dad," Alex said, taking a quick stride to grab hold of him the same moment he let go of Wade's hand and put trembling fingers over his own eyes. "You okay?" he asked quietly.

"I need . . . to sit down," Neil said, his voice trembling. Alex guided him back to the sofa where he'd been sitting when the doorbell rang. Neil groaned and doubled over as if he were experiencing physical pain.

"You okay?" Alex asked again, putting a hand on his shoulder.

"I . . . just . . . need a minute," Neil said, brushing him away.

Alex turned to see that Wade had followed them and was standing in the doorway to the living area, looking frightened, defensive. The latter became more prominent as he said with an edge, "So now what?"

"You tell me," Alex said as he moved closer to Wade and put his hands on his hips. For a full minute they just stared at each other while Alex attempted to grasp what he'd just learned. *Unbelievable,* he thought more than once, but at the same time he felt strangely comfortable with Wade, as if their spirits were drawn together. He felt as if he'd just come face-to-face with a childhood friend that he'd not seen in many years. And while they might have both changed and grown, the underlying recognition was still there. Obviously they'd never seen each other before, at least not in this world. While he could never put into words what he felt, he absolutely had no problem with accepting this man as his brother. He felt sure the feeling was mutual when Wade spoke as if they actually knew each other well enough to interact completely uninhibited.

"Are you going to tell me where to go?" Wade demanded. "Tell me to leave and never come back?"

"No," Alex said quietly.

"Well, maybe you should."

"Is that what you expected when you came here?" Alex asked. Their eyes connected and Alex felt a fresh quickening of his heart as he pondered the reality that he had a brother. He'd never dreamed—and he felt certain Neil hadn't either—that something like this would ever come up as a result of those dark years that Neil so deeply regretted.

"Maybe," Wade said, anger appearing in his voice—and in his eyes.

Alex took it head on. "You're obviously very angry about this."

"Aren't you?" Wade demanded—as if they'd always known they were brothers.

"Stunned, yes. Upset, perhaps. Angry, no."

"Well, maybe you should be," Wade snapped quietly, as if he didn't want Neil to overhear.

"And maybe we should sit down and talk about this," Alex said. "Or did you just come here to vent some anger and then tell *us* where to go?"

Wade didn't answer. He glanced toward Neil, who still had his head down, pressed into his hands. Alex tried to get a feel for the best way to handle this. He moved to his father's side, put a hand on his shoulder and said quietly, "We're going to give you a few minutes alone, okay? We'll be back."

Neil just nodded without lifting his head. Alex guided Wade out the front door and to the driveway. "Get in," he said, pushing the remote to unlock the car doors. Wade looked momentarily hesitant, and Alex added, "What? You think I'm going to pull a gun on you or something?"

"Maybe."

"Well, I thought the same thing about you when you walked in the door. Get in."

Alex backed out of the driveway and turned the corner while Wade just looked out the window. "Look . . . Wade. It's Wade, right?"

"That's right."

"There is no point in our wasting time with chitchat. I'm sure there's a great deal you'd like to say, so why don't you just say it?"

A second later Alex's pager beeped and he resisted the urge to curse. He pulled it off his belt and looked at it. "Sorry. Just give me a minute." He pulled into an empty church parking lot, feeling far too distracted to drive and talk at the same time, then he dialed the ER. "This is Dr. Keane."

The voice at the other end said, "Dr. Baker wants to talk to you. I'll get him."

A few seconds later, Ray said into the phone, "Alex, I need a second opinion and there's no one else here with a brain."

"Okay, I'm listening."

Baker gave a two-minute explanation of a patient's bizarre symptoms and the conclusion he'd come to. Alex thought about it while he made a contemplative noise, trying to focus his mind on the moment. "Uh . . . yeah. I agree. I'd start the IV right away, then call Gosser. If he hasn't seen something like this, no one has. But I'd do an MRI anyway, just to make sure there isn't something else going on."

"Okay, thanks," Baker said. "I didn't get much sleep last night and I just needed to make sure I wasn't barking up the wrong tree."

"I'll get even," Alex said.

"How's Barrett?"

"He's the same. It's what we expected, but it's still ugly."

"Keep me posted. Let me know if I can do anything."

"Thank you," Alex said and ended the call. He turned to look at Wade, who was looking astonished. "What?" Alex asked.

"You're a doctor."

"That's right."

Wade made a dubious chuckle and looked the other way. While Alex was wondering what he had against doctors, Wade abruptly changed the subject, "Things like this don't happen to LDS people, you know. Things like this happen . . . on soap operas."

Alex was glad to hear that at least he'd taken the suggestion that they talk about this. He drew a deep breath and said, "Life happens, Wade. People are human and they make mistakes. That's what this earth life is about. LDS people aren't exempt from that. But they should know more about mercy and forgiveness and finding the road back."

Wade looked at him sharply. "How can you forgive something like this?"

Hearing the anger in Wade's voice that was amplified by his eyes, Alex said, "I don't think you're ready to hear the answer to that question."

"What makes you think so?"

"Because anger and forgiveness don't mix, Wade."

"Oh, and you're the expert, I suppose," he said like a snotty teenager.

"You bet I am," Alex said, feeling a little angry himself. When he realized *why* he felt angry, he quieted his tone and added, "Trust me when I tell you that you may have a right to feel angry, but if you hold onto it too long, it will destroy you."

Wade's voice was softer too as he said, "You knew . . . about the affair."

Alex felt years' worth of memories associated with that sentence pour into his mind. Certain that less information would be better at this point, he simply said, "Yes, I knew. As our father said, there are no secrets between us." He turned to Wade and added, "But you didn't know, did you." He gauged the trauma in Wade's eyes. "What you're feeling is raw . . . it's new. How did you find out?"

Wade said nothing. The silence became awkward. Alex searched for something to fill it. "Now I know why you looked familiar when I opened the door. You look like him, you know, like pictures . . . when he was younger."

"Well, that explains why I never looked like anyone else in my family," Wade said with a bitter edge to his voice.

"If it's any consolation, I don't look a thing like him; never did. Apparently I look very much like my mother's great-grandfather. But he wasn't around to make comparisons."

Wade's bitterness took on a sarcastic edge. "I didn't have any point of reference for comparisons either. But then . . . I never really thought about it." His voice became more even. "You never know how genetics can mix up. A child can be any combination of its parents' genes, and doesn't necessarily have to bear any physical resemblance to either of them."

"That's true," Alex said, then he repeated, "So, how did you find out? Or don't you want to talk about it?"

"Why do *you* want to talk about it?" he asked as if the question were deeply important.

Alex said carefully, "I just found out I have a brother. Isn't it natural that I should be concerned?"

Wade let out a harsh chuckle. "I don't know that there's anything natural about any of this. At best I'd hoped not to be thrown out before I had a chance to say what I wanted to say."

"And what did you want to say?"

"It really doesn't matter, *big brother*." His sarcasm was deep. "My *father* is obviously not very happy about my showing up, and is in no condition to talk about anything."

"I think *our* father is in shock. I wouldn't say he's not happy about your showing up. Don't judge him too harshly until he's had a chance to—"

"This man took my mother away from her family . . . her covenants . . . and *I* am the result!" His eyes blazed, and his voice rumbled. "Everything that I had always believed to be firm and true has now dissolved into . . . quicksand, sucking me into some . . . vacuum of . . . nothingness. I don't even know who I am . . . where I belong."

Alex spoke in a voice that he hoped would calm Wade's anger. "So . . . did you come to meet your father with the purpose of telling him off . . . or to find out who you are . . . and where you belong?"

Wade looked at him long and hard, then he looked the other way. "Both, I guess."

Alex realized that he still had no idea how this young man had come to discover the truth about his paternity. He wondered how to attempt once again to bring the conversation around to that, and then his cell phone rang. He looked at the caller ID and his heart quickened. He hoped everything was all right as he answered.

"Alex?" Jane said.

"Yeah. Is everything okay? Have you talked to the doctor today?"

"No, but . . . everything's the same. I just . . . hadn't heard from you. How's everything at your end? Is your dad okay?"

"He was when I got there, but I don't think he is now."

"What do you—"

"I can't really talk at the moment, but . . ."

"You'll catch me up later," she guessed, and he was grateful that she could almost read his mind.

"That's right," he said. "I called Susan. She and the kids are doing the yard sale quest. They sounded great."

"Okay. That's good."

"Will you be all right without me for a while?"

"Sure, I'm fine," she said, but he felt dubious on that count. "When do you have to work again? I can't remember."

"Tomorrow morning," he said. "I'll meet you later at the hospital." He paused and added, "I love you, Jane. Kiss Barrett for me."

"I love you too," she said and hung up.

"Your wife?" Wade asked, glancing at Alex's wedding ring.

"Yeah," Alex said, distracted with thoughts of the *other* drama in his life.

He was surprised to hear Wade ask in a voice of concern, "What's wrong?" Alex looked toward him, disoriented. "You asked her if she'd talked to the doctor. *You're* a doctor, but apparently you don't have all the answers."

Alex told himself not to feel defensive. He didn't want to admit how much that hurt. He forced a calm voice. "No, I don't have all the answers. I'm an ER physician. I turn special problems over to specialists."

"So, I take it from both of the phone conversations I've listened to that someone you care about has a special problem."

His concern was evident, but Alex looked the other way, not wanting to be on the receiving end of the questions. He cleared his throat and just said it. "My son has leukemia."

Wade's voice was surprisingly tender as he said, "I'm sorry."

"Yeah, well . . . so am I."

"How old is he?"

"He's six," Alex said.

"I'm truly sorry." He sighed loudly. "Maybe I should just go home and let you get back to your family."

Alex turned to look at him. "I am with my family." Wade looked at him sharply. "And would that be home to your mother, or home to your father?"

"That would be home to my apartment."

"So, that's it? You let us know of your existence and then you just . . . what? Turn and run?"

"Maybe that would be best. Maybe I shouldn't have come at all."

"Obviously you don't believe that. I suspect you weighed your decision to come very carefully. I suspect that maybe you need your father . . . and maybe you need a brother too."

"Half-brother," he clarified quickly. "I have three brothers . . . besides you. I guess that makes you my other brother."

"But they're half-brothers too," Alex said in the same tone, and anger flared in Wade's eyes. "And until you come to terms with that," Alex added, "you're never going to stop feeling angry."

"Listen, Alex. You did say your name is Alex, right?" He didn't wait for a response. "I don't need you telling me how to feel, and I don't need *our* father to make my life complete."

"What *do* you need, Wade?"

"I need to just forget that any of this ever came up."

"Well, that's not going to happen, now, is it? Unfortunately we can't ever go back and undo what's been done."

"You got that right, but I sure wish that it was possible."

"And what would you change? Do you wish that you'd not come to meet your father today? Or do you wish that—"

"I wish that my *parents* would have stayed where they belonged. They had absolutely no idea the lives they were messing up."

"No, they did not," Alex said firmly. "They were stupid and irresponsible, and their sins will have eternal consequences." Wade showed some surprise, as if the idea struck something in him. Alex added gently, "But that doesn't mean forgiveness isn't possible."

"Don't even go there."

"I don't intend to . . . not yet at least. I already told you that anger and forgiveness don't mix. But like it or not, I intend to be around when you *are* ready to talk about it."

Wade sighed loudly. "Listen, you've got a kid in the hospital. You don't need me adding to your problems. Maybe you should just take me back to my car and—"

"Don't use my son's illness as an excuse to hide from this now that it's become uncomfortable."

"Hey, it's been uncomfortable for weeks now." His voice softened. "I just . . . I mean . . . really . . . leukemia. I feel like an idiot for feeling sorry for myself."

"Other people's problems can help you keep perspective, Wade, but they don't diminish the reality of your own. What you're facing is no small thing. You have a right to grieve over what you've lost."

"Lost?" he echoed, as if he had no idea what he was talking about.

"You lost your belief that life was the way you always thought it was. Any loss requires grieving. But sooner or later, you have to just cut your losses and move on."

Alex wondered if Wade was just trying to change the subject, or if he was attempting to turn the theory back on Alex. "Is he going to die?"

Alex swallowed and unwillingly clenched a fist. "I don't know. It's a definite possibility."

"And you want me to believe that you don't feel angry over that?" Wade asked as if this had become some kind of competition.

"You bet I am," Alex said harshly. "But you know what? Sometimes life just stinks, *little brother*. Sometimes there aren't any answers that will ever make sense in this world. But it's life. And it happens. Sometimes innocent children suffer and die from horrible diseases. Sometimes people you love betray you and let you down. But it's not all black and white, kid. There's a lot of good in this world too—even in the midst of the horrors. At least my son has leukemia and didn't get shot in the middle of some gang brawl. I've dug bullets out of kids his age. And at least your parents actually *care* about you."

"And how could you possibly know that?" Wade snapped.

"Listen, I'm not going to argue with you, kid. Apparently you've got it all figured out, but I want you to know there was a time when I thought I had it all figured out too. I spent twenty years being angry over my father's bad choices—twenty years, Wade. That's half my life. But one day my life finally hit rock bottom enough that I was willing to really listen to what he had to say, and to see how far he'd come from the days when he had made those poor choices. You and I are both deeply affected—and deeply scarred by what they did. But we have our own choices to make. Are you going to let it keep you angry for twenty years? Or will you be smarter than I was and make something good out of what you've been given?"

Wade was silent, but Alex sensed his anger. His voice was tight when he finally said, "Listen, I think I just . . . need to go home. I think I have way too much to think about."

"That's likely true, but . . . I think before you go, you should at least see if your father has recovered from the shock. Just . . . give him a few minutes."

Wade looked reluctant but said, "Okay."

Alex started the car and pulled out of the parking lot. A moment later Wade said, "I can't believe you're a doctor."

"Why is that? You have something against doctors?"

"No. I'm in pre-med at the U of U."

"Really?" Alex chuckled. "I work at the U of U Medical Center. Maybe a passion for medicine is genetic." Wade shifted uncomfortably in his seat and Alex added, "Did I say something wrong?"

"Genetics. I've always been fascinated with them, obsessed perhaps. It was absolutely my favorite class; loved every minute of it."

"Maybe you should retake it . . . just for fun."

"Oh, I'm still in it."

"But you don't love it anymore?"

"Nope. I'm good at it, but I hate it."

Wade said nothing more, and Alex added, "Are you going to tell me why?"

"If you're interested."

"I am." He pulled the car into their father's driveway and put it in park, then turned more toward Wade.

"DNA matching. Genetic sequencing. The professor asked for some volunteers to take capillary tubes home and get blood samples from family members to study DNA patterns." Alex could feel it coming even before Wade turned to look directly at him and said, "Imagine my surprise when I discovered that something wasn't right. I took what I'd found to my professor, certain I'd screwed up, that I'd done something wrong. He double-checked everything; said it was right." He chuckled with no humor. "'You mean I was adopted?' I asked him. Fortunately he was discreet. Our conversation was private. He pointed out that I certainly had my mother's DNA, but not my father's—or the man I'd always believed to be my father." He made a dubious noise. "At least I understood why my parents had been so uncomfortable with my request for blood samples. I thought it was because they didn't trust that I actually knew how to use a needle."

"I can't even imagine how difficult that must have been," Alex said, and Wade's expression softened.

"Yeah, well . . . I still can't imagine it."

"What did you do?"

"I stewed about it for a few days, then I realized I had to know the truth, no matter how much it hurt. I hadn't been home since I'd taken the blood samples. We had a family gathering scheduled and I went early, asked if I could talk to them privately. What I saw in their faces already confirmed that they knew I was on to them. I just asked them why I had my mother's DNA, but not my father's. My mother immediately burst into tears and couldn't talk." Wade sighed loudly. "I had never before felt any different than any of my siblings, but in that moment I realized that she felt shame in my existence. My dad, he . . ." He hesitated and squeezed his eyes closed. His voice cracked as he said, "He's not my father; I don't even know what to call him anymore."

"Of course he's your father," Alex said. "If you *had* been adopted, you would have called the parents who raised you mother and father. In a way . . . he *did* adopt you. He raised you as his own, obviously."

"Yes, he did," Wade said. "He's a good man. He was completely composed as he told me the story; how she left him with three small children, had a lengthy affair, and then realized she'd made a mistake and came back, begging his forgiveness. And he took her back. I don't know that I would have been so noble."

"You can't say that without being faced with it, really. Obviously he loved her very much. Maybe there were reasons . . . other things going on that people on the outside wouldn't know about."

"Oh, there were. He told me about that. He said that he'd not been a good husband in those early years. He said he'd had a harsh upbringing, and without even thinking about it he was passing it on. He called himself a chauvinistic jerk. He said that she'd tried to get him to change the way he treated her; she'd told him she was unhappy. But he wouldn't listen. He said that in the end, they both had a great deal of repentance to do, that he felt some account-ability in her decision. I told him no matter how badly he'd treated her, cheating on him wasn't the way to solve it. He agreed, but . . ."

Wade became emotional and Alex put a hand on his shoulder. "What?" he pressed gently.

"He said . . . 'Who was I to cast a stone at her?'"

Alex felt emotional himself as he pondered the deeper meaning of such a statement. Through a stretch of silence he wondered for the first time in his life about the unwritten depth of the incident recorded in the New Testament. A woman taken in adultery, brought before Jesus as some kind of test to see how He would handle the situation. And how wise He had been! No one in the crowd had had a clear enough conscience to condemn her. But what had Jesus sensed about this woman that no one else could have seen? Had her choice to commit sin been distorted by other difficult circumstances in her life? If Jesus had been able to look upon the heart, had He known that God's judgment of her sin might have been far more complex than any mortal mind could have comprehended?

"So, he took her back," Wade said, bringing Alex to the moment. "She was excommunicated. And they started marriage counseling. But before they reconciled enough to sleep in the same bed, she realized she was pregnant. Apparently her decision to come back had been rather impulsive. It was his idea to keep the truth between the two of them, to make everyone else believe that I was his child. My three older siblings were still pretty young when it happened. Only the oldest remembers Mom being gone, but it's vague." He sighed again. "They all know the truth now. That was my fault. I exploded. I said awful things . . . especially to my mother. And she just took it. She told me she deserved my anger, that she had wronged me and she knew it. I insisted she tell me who my father was. She didn't want to. She said it was better left alone. She finally gave in, but she made me promise to be kind and not to expect him to be happy about the news. She offered to contact him first and warn him, but I asked her not to. I was hoping he would have lived in some other state—or country; that he might be difficult—or impossible—to find. Maybe she was hoping for that too. But it only took me five minutes on the Internet to realize that he lived right here—in the same valley where I'd grown up, where I live, work, go to school. I tried to talk myself out of it, but in my heart I knew I could never go on without at least meeting him."

"And now you have. But you haven't had a chance to say whatever it is you came here to say."

Wade looked toward the house with trepidation. "I didn't think it would be that upsetting."

"How upsetting was it for you?" Alex asked.

Wade sighed. "Okay . . . it was about like that . . . once I was alone. But . . . I don't know, maybe I thought he would have suspected, or . . . maybe he'd be indifferent."

"Indifferent would have been tough to swallow," Alex pointed out.

"Yes, I suppose it would be."

Silence fell again until Alex felt compelled to say, "God is mindful of your pain in this, Wade."

Wade looked angry again. "And how would you know that?"

Alex simply said, "He sent me to answer the door, little brother. I was so strongly prompted to come to my father's house this morning that I thought something had happened to him. When I got there nothing was wrong, but I couldn't bring myself to leave. I've rarely had such a strong impression. I needed to be here."

Alex sensed that Wade's anger was spilling over into his feelings toward God; perhaps Alex felt the signs because he'd been there— for a very long time. He doubted that Wade was in the frame of mind to acknowledge God's hand in any of this, but he did say, "I have to admit that I'm glad you were here. I didn't expect to find a father *and* a brother." He met Alex's eyes. "I appreciate your time, and I . . . I'm glad you didn't kick me out and tell me where to go."

Alex just nodded and said, "Let's go inside, shall we?"

"What's he like? Our father?"

"He's a good man," Alex said. "He readily admits to the mistakes of his past, and he's worked very hard to make restitution."

Wade made no comment as he visibly drew courage. "Okay. I didn't think I'd have to work up the nerve to go to that door twice."

"The worst is already over," Alex said and got out of the car.

Chapter 8

Wade followed him through the front door after Alex opened it with his key. It was barely closed behind them when Neil appeared in the entry hall, his countenance both troubled and relieved. He exchanged a long gaze with Alex, as if he could silently take in all that might have happened since they'd left. Then his eyes turned to Wade. The boy looked nervous and apprehensive; more scared than angry. Without speaking a word, Neil stepped toward him and took him in a firm embrace. Wade appeared stunned at first, then he returned the embrace, albeit somewhat reluctantly.

Neil drew back and put his hands on Wade's shoulders, looking into his eyes. "I had no idea. She never told me."

"I know," Wade said solemnly. "She never told me either."

"Then how . . . did it come to this?" Neil asked.

Wade glanced at Alex, as if seeking a rescue. Alex hurried to say, "I think that's kind of a long story."

Neil glanced at Alex with silent appreciation, then he motioned toward the other room. "I'd love to hear that story," he said, and they all moved to the couches where Alex had once sat with his father to talk about forgiveness and healing. He knew Wade wasn't ready for forgiveness yet, but perhaps this was a good step toward healing. Wade and Alex sat at opposite ends of the same couch, with their father sitting on the opposite side of the coffee table, facing them. Alex helped gently prod Wade to share with Neil all that they'd talked about in the car. At moments Wade's anger was readily evident, and at others he just seemed sad, lost, uncertain.

When he declared there was nothing more to talk about, Neil asked him, "Can you ever forgive me?"

Wade looked at his father with hard eyes. "For what? My existence?"

Neil looked taken aback but said nothing.

"I'm going to need some time with that," Wade said, but he said it as if he didn't believe it would ever be possible to let go of the bitterness he felt.

"Of course," Neil said, as if he completely understood. Alex considered his father's expression and felt tempted to cry. He'd waited two decades for Alex to forgive him, and now fresh consequences of his bad choices had come back to haunt him, clearly opening old wounds.

The silence was broken by Wade leaping to his feet. "I really need to go," he said. "Thanks for not kicking me out."

The other men came to their feet, but Wade hurried to the door so quickly that Alex wondered if he was struggling with some kind of emotion that he didn't want spilling over in front of them.

"Wait," Alex said, sensing that Neil shared his panic. "How can we contact you?"

Wade hesitated, then said, "I know where to find you." And then he was gone.

Neil looked at the door, then at Alex, then he hurried back to the couch as if he'd once again been overtaken by uncontrollable weakness. "I can't believe it," he muttered as Alex sat close to him. He lifted a trembling hand to his face and rubbed it absently.

"It is pretty shocking," Alex said.

Neil turned to look at him. "I can't even imagine what you must be thinking of all this," he said as if he expected Alex to start condemning him all over again.

"You said yourself that we have no secrets."

"You're not upset about this?" Neil asked.

"Surprised, yes. More concerned than anything—for you, for him. I guess I'm pretty amazed to realize I have a brother. I don't think that's really sunk in yet."

Neil groaned and pressed a hand over his eyes. "No, I don't think it has."

"Talk to me, Dad," Alex said. "You're obviously very upset."

"Yes, I'm upset."

"Do you think it would have been better to go on not knowing?"

"No!" Neil insisted. "I only wish I had known a long time ago . . . all along."

"And what? You couldn't have been a part of his life without creating more trauma. He was raised in a good home with parents who loved him. This is hard for him now, but eventually he'll come to terms with it—and so will you."

Neil looked at him and sighed. "How did you get to be so wise?"

"I owe it all to the women in my life."

Neil smiled sadly. "Your mother was a good woman, Alex."

"Yes, she was."

"I should never have left her."

"No, you shouldn't have," Alex said. "But it's in the past; it's forgiven."

"But never forgotten," Neil said, rubbing his forehead.

"Forgiveness and repentance will never erase the natural consequences of our choices, Dad. But that doesn't mean the forgiveness isn't real."

"I know that," he said firmly. "But there's a hurt and angry young man out there who believes I am responsible for the misery in his life. I guess I *am* responsible. What if he can't forgive me?"

"That's his burden to carry, Dad. Your choices are between you and God, and it was all reconciled a long time ago."

"Okay. I know that too, but . . . he's my son, Alex. How can I help him?"

"Maybe you can't."

"But maybe *you* can," Neil said. "You know his pain, don't you, Alex."

"Not really, no. I grew up knowing who I was and where I came from."

"Still . . . you understand it . . . better than most people would. What I did hurt you deeply."

"Well, I already tried to open that door with Wade. Whether or not he chooses to ever contact me again will determine whether I have any opportunity to connect with him. I'm concerned too, but all we can do is . . ."

They heard the garage door opening and a car pulling in, and Neil groaned. "How can I tell her?"

"You just tell her," Alex said. "You have no secrets from her, either. Right?"

"Right." He looked at Alex. "I'm grateful you're here."

"So am I."

"You *were* prompted to come, Alex. I needed you. *He* needed you. I would have hated to have to call you right now and tell you what I just found out."

"I'm glad I was here, Dad. You know how to reach me if you ever need me."

Neil nodded, and Roxanne came into the kitchen at the far end of the living area, her arms full of packages. Before either of them could stand up to help her, she deposited them all on the counter. "Hi," she said, then her eyes narrowed as she perceived the mood in the room. "What's wrong?"

"Maybe you should sit down," Neil said, and her expression became panicked.

"It's not Barrett, is it?" she demanded, moving toward them.

"No," Alex hurried to say. "Everyone is safe; nothing's changed with Barrett."

"Then what is it?" Roxanne asked, sitting on the other side of Neil and taking his hand.

Neil looked at Alex, as if to draw courage, then he turned to Roxanne. "My past sins have come back to visit me, my dear." He paused and took a sharp breath. "Marilyn had a son—my son. She never told me. He was just here."

Roxanne looked at Alex as if he might verify this. He just returned her gaze until she said, "I can't believe it."

"That would be the consensus," Neil said. He went on to tell her all that had happened, with Alex filling in details. He wasn't surprised by Roxanne's compassion and support of her husband. She'd always been that way. Like Neil's first wife, she was an amazing woman, and Alex was glad to know his father had someone like her in his life.

Certain that they could manage on their own, Alex pleaded the need to be with his family at the hospital. They each embraced him and thanked him for coming, and he promised to keep them informed of any changes in Barrett's health.

Through the drive across the city, Alex pondered the events of this day and felt stunned all over again. A brother? He couldn't believe it! He wondered what Wade was doing now and wished he'd been more insistent about getting some contact information. He felt sure there would be ways of finding him, especially since he was taking classes at the U. But perhaps it was better—at least for now—if they just allowed him some time and space. He only hoped that with time Wade might feel that he could be a part of their family, as well as the one he'd been raised in. He didn't know if such a thing was possible, but he wanted to think so.

Realizing he was hungry, he drove through and got a burger that he ate on the way, knowing Jane would have gotten herself something to eat by now. He arrived to find that nothing had changed. He kissed his wife and touched Barrett's face as he slept.

Once their greetings were complete, Jane asked, "So what happened at your dad's house? You said he wasn't necessarily all right. Is he okay now?"

"He will be, eventually." Alex moved toward the window, looking out at the view that had become dreadfully familiar. "When I got there everything was fine; they were working in the garden. I was wondering if I'd imagined what I'd felt, but I still felt like I shouldn't leave. I took a shower, had something to eat. Roxanne left, and I visited with Dad. Then the doorbell rang."

At his dramatic pause she asked, "Bad news?"

"More good than bad, I think—at least from my perspective. Shocking news, to say the least."

"What?" she asked.

He turned and leaned on the windowsill. "You know, of course, that my father left when I was thirteen, lived with a woman for a couple of years."

"Of course," she said, her brow furrowed.

"It was my brother at the door, Jane." She gasped, and he added, "He's about fifteen years younger than I am. Dad never knew."

"Good heavens!" she said breathily. "A *brother?* I can't believe it."

Alex let out a harsh chuckle. "Yeah, well . . . neither can I. And Dad's having a really rough time swallowing it."

"Is he okay?"

"Not really, no. How do you deal with knowing that every possible avenue of repentance has taken place in regard to some bad choices, and then have new consequences open it all up again?" He let out a long breath. "And we're talking about the existence of another human being."

"What's he like?" Jane asked in a tender voice that made him realize for the first time in weeks she was concerned about something besides her father's death or Barrett's health and the effect it was having on her other children.

"He seems like a great kid, actually . . . but he's got a lot of anger, which is understandable. This is all raw for him. He's only known for a few weeks. Can you imagine . . . making a discovery like that? To find out that what you'd always believed to be true wasn't true after all."

"No, I can't," Jane said, her voice verifying that the idea was difficult to swallow. "How did he find out?" she asked.

Alex went on to repeat all that had happened, all that had been said. When he recounted the part about casting stones, she got tears in her eyes.

They talked a while longer before Jane went home to take care of some things while Alex stayed with Barrett. A couple of hours after she left, the phone in the hospital room rang. Since cell phones were not allowed in this area of the hospital, people knew this was how Alex and Jane could be reached. He answered it to hear his father, sounding upset.

"What is it, Dad?" Alex asked. "Take a deep breath and talk to me."

Neil began rambling in a way that Alex had never heard before. His father had long ago told him of the years of struggling and heartache that had followed leaving his family for another woman. And when the other woman had impulsively gone back to her family, he'd been left with only the harsh consequences of his bad choices. Alex knew that his father had undergone a great deal of counseling, and had even been suicidal. But until now he'd never truly comprehended the state of the man who had been through all of that. Alex had come back into his father's life long after it had all been settled. Neil's membership in the Church had long been in good standing by then, and he'd come to terms with all that had happened. But this new discovery had brought it all back. Neil was crumbling with raw emotion, as if the sin were as fresh now as it had been twenty-five years ago. While Alex listened to him babble about the lives he'd destroyed and the unfixable results of his choices, something starkly uneasy consumed his instincts.

"Dad," he said firmly, "listen to me. I'm on my way over. I'll be there in half an hour. Just . . . try to stay calm and . . . put Roxanne on the phone." Alex knew he'd probably get further with her.

"Alex?" she said into the phone almost immediately, and he knew she'd been sitting close by through the entire conversation. She too was obviously upset.

"I'm coming over. Do you have . . . a home teacher? A friend close by? Someone you can trust with this? Someone with the priesthood?"

"Uh . . . yeah . . . we do."

"Good. Call him—whoever it is. When I get there we need to give Dad a blessing, and we'll go from there. Okay?"

"Okay," she repeated.

"Are you going to be all right until I get there?"

"Yes, of course," she said, but she didn't sound convincing.

The second Alex hung up, he grabbed the list of names and phone numbers of sisters in the ward who had indicated they would be willing and able to help if needed. Neil and Roxanne had often been there for backup, but obviously that wouldn't work in this case. He knew that he could leave Barrett with the nursing staff, and he'd be fine, but he also knew that if Jane found out Barrett was alone she would turn around and come back. And she needed a break.

The first woman he called didn't answer. The second, a woman named Linda, was eager to come and sit with Barrett when he told her something had come up with his father and he needed to go. He was only vaguely acquainted with her, but she obviously knew the situation well.

"Is Jane all right?" Linda asked.

"She's at home with the other kids. She's exhausted, but otherwise fine."

"Okay, I'm on my way. You go ahead and leave. I'll not be ten minutes. I promise."

"Thank you," Alex said and hung up. He kissed Barrett's forehead while he slept, then he let the nurses know what was going on, and hurried to where he'd parked the car.

While he drove, Alex called Jane to tell her what he was doing. He assured her that she needed to stay at home and everything would be fine. After he hung up, he prayed through the remainder of the drive that he would be guided, that he would have the strength to combat whatever evil had taken hold of his father. Out of nowhere a childhood memory came to mind. Elementary school recess. He couldn't recall how old he'd been, or what events had led up to it. He only remembered that he'd done or said something stupid and he'd been feeling very foolish over it when a group of playground bullies had decided to really punish him for it—to the point of giving him a bloody nose on top of the repeated verbal insults they'd hurled at him. For a moment Alex wondered why such a disjointed memory would come to him now, then he gasped as he felt the answer come into his mind.

Alex arrived at his father's home to find him pacing and ranting about how he would never be free of what he'd done, that no miracle could ever be big enough to make this right. Alex noted Roxanne sitting on the couch crying, her hand being held by an elderly gentleman who looked relaxed but concerned. Neil was apparently oblivious to Alex entering the room until Roxanne stood up and greeted him with a hard embrace that spoke volumes of the fear she was feeling on her husband's behalf. "I've never seen him like this," she whispered.

"Neither have I," Alex whispered back. "But it's going to be okay."

Roxanne forced a smile, as if she wanted to believe him but didn't dare. She turned toward the visitor as he stood and held out a hand toward Alex. "This is Brother Harris," she said. "He's been our home teacher for many years."

"A pleasure to meet you, Brother Harris," Alex said.

"The pleasure is mine," he replied. "I've heard such good things about you. Your father is always bragging about his son, the doctor."

Alex just chuckled humbly, thinking that perhaps with time Neil could brag about *both* of his sons, both doctors. His eyes connected with his father's just before they shared a firm embrace. Never had Alex imagined himself being a strength to this man, especially at a time when his own life was such a mess. But he felt deeply comforted to realize that he knew what to do, and he had the power to do it. He briefly thought of the many years of his life when he'd not lived worthy to hold the priesthood, and he felt immeasurably grateful to be worthy now of that power. Now he could be the instrument in God's hands, through His power, to help solve these problems. He felt calm and secure in spite of the dark feeling in the room and the stark fear in his father's eyes.

Alex put his hands on his father's shoulders and said quietly, but firmly, "Brother Harris and I are going to give you a blessing, and then we'll talk. Okay?"

Neil nodded like an obedient child. Alex turned to Roxanne and said, "Before we do that, could you offer a prayer?"

She looked surprised but said, "Of course."

They were all seated and Neil held tightly to Alex's hand while Roxanne offered a tearful, heartfelt prayer on behalf of her husband. She asked that the power of the priesthood would guide these good men to help get them through this crisis, and that healing could take place within their family. When the prayer was finished Alex guided his father to a chair where he and Brother Harris could comfortably put their hands on his head. Alex was spokesman for the majority of the blessing, striving to open his mind and speak the words that he felt guided to speak. He heard himself stating plainly that followers of Satan had quickly moved in to take advantage of the opening of old wounds, but their bullying would not be tolerated in a home where faith and hope in Christ were lived daily. In the name of Christ he commanded the evil influence to depart, and then he said nothing for several seconds while a nearly palpable serenity seemed to drive the darkness away. Alex went on to bless his father with strength and guidance to work through this new chain of events, and he reiterated firmly that these sins had long ago been forgiven and wiped clean through the power of the Atonement, and it was through that same power that Neil's son would be made whole. Neil was told that as he embraced the healing power that had been with him for many years, he would become a stalwart to the people who had been adversely affected by his choices of the past, that he would lead them more fully to Christ and the deepest powers of His atoning sacrifice. Neil was admonished to cling fervently to study and prayer, and all else that would keep him close to the Spirit, that Satan would not easily give up his efforts to weigh Neil down with his past mistakes, and that he needed to hold fast to all things that would keep his armor fully in place to combat the influences of the adversary. He was told that the path ahead, with many challenges in his family, would not be easy, but by trusting in God the journey would bring them to joy and healing.

When the blessing was finished, Alex squatted down beside his father and found tears streaking his face. "It's okay, Dad," Alex said.

"Yes, I think it will be," Neil said, taking his hand and squeezing it tightly. "Thank you, son."

Brother Harris spoke some kind words to Neil and excused himself, saying that they would probably like some time to talk privately. They all thanked Brother Harris for coming, and he promised discretion over what they'd shared with him, and that he was always available if needed.

Once Brother Harris had gone, Alex sat close beside his father on the couch, while Roxanne sat on the other side of him. When the silence dragged on too long, Alex shared with them the childhood memory that had come to him during the drive over, and how he felt he'd been shown an understanding of what was taking place. This opened conversation about all that had been said in the blessing and how important it was for Neil to record these things in his journal and remember them through the journey ahead.

When the conversation ran down, Roxanne said to Neil, "Perhaps we should go ahead and go to the temple . . . like we'd planned. There's still time if we—"

"I can't," Neil said as if the very idea were absurd.

"Why not?" Roxanne demanded gently.

Neil shot to his feet and started pacing again. Alex rose and stopped him, putting both hands firmly on his shoulders. "Listen to me, Dad. Did you hear what that blessing said? You have to hold onto those words and claim them in your life; they didn't come from me, you know. You have to remember that what you've learned today does not make you unworthy to go to the temple all of a sudden. You've got to talk back to the voices in your head that are lying to you. Do you hear me?" Neil looked stunned, and Alex added, "Listen. You may not have known all these years that you had a son, but God knew. And you and I both know that He forgave you a long time ago—even knowing what we didn't know. This does not change your present worthiness in the slightest, and you've got to let go of believing that it does. You cannot have the strength to help others come to terms with this if you don't remember that you are worthy of every possible blessing, because you have lived your life accordingly for many years. Are you hearing me?"

Neil gave a barely perceptible nod, and Alex added, "I think you should go. I think it's the best thing you could possibly do right now."

Again Neil seemed almost childlike as he asked, "Will you go with us?"

Alex felt taken off guard. "I . . . don't have the right clothes with me or—"

"You can borrow something; you've worn my clothes before."

"I know, but . . ."

"Do you need to be with your family?" Roxanne asked gently.

Alex thought about it and had to admit, "No, they're fine." He looked at his father. "I'd love to go to the temple with you."

He called Jane, who eagerly agreed that he should go, and less than an hour later, Alex walked through the doors of the Jordan River Temple with his father and Roxanne. He was ashamed to realize he couldn't remember the last time he'd been within temple walls. It had been difficult for Jane to go during the final months of her pregnancy, and before she'd recovered, life had turned upside down. But now that he was here, Alex realized that one of the best things he could do for his family was to make some time occasionally to draw the strength that could be found here in order to buoy them up.

He stopped with his father to put some names down for the prayer roll. Alex watched him write down Barrett's full name, *Barrett Neil Keane.* Then he did the same for Alex and Jane, while Alex recalled their conversation about this earlier today. Alex wrote down his father's name, and Roxanne's. And Wade Morrison. Then he noticed Neil writing down the names of Wade's mother and the father who had raised him.

During the session Alex was aware of his father shedding some silent tears, and he occasionally reached for Alex's hand and squeezed it tightly. He was glad to be there, for many reasons. In the celestial room they sat together and spoke quietly of the peace and strength they had all found here to help them press forward through a variety of struggles. Alex commented that it would have been tragic for the negative voices in their heads to keep them from coming to this place that had more power in counteracting them than anything else on this earth ever could. Neil agreed.

After leaving the temple, they all went out for a late dinner then back to the house where they talked some more, this time focusing on their concern for Wade and a need to remember him in their prayers.

Back in his own clothes, Alex left his father and Roxanne with tight hugs at the door. They thanked him for all he'd done for them that day, and Alex walked to the car feeling as if they'd lived a week since he'd first come here this morning.

In the car Alex checked the messages on his phone to be told that shifts had been set up for someone to stay with Barrett until the following afternoon so that he could go home and get some sleep before he had to work, and Jane could go to church before going back to the hospital. A meal had been taken to the house to give Susan a break in the kitchen, and two sisters had taken Katharine and Preston to their homes for the evening so that Jane could relax. The message clearly stated that they would get a call if anything changed and to know that Barrett was in good hands. Alex couldn't hold back a sudden rush of tears as he deleted the message and tossed the phone in the passenger seat. He'd hardly cried at all since they'd become caught up in the bone marrow carnival. But this day had pressed him to both extremes of emotion. He felt as if he'd descended to the depths of hell with his father, but together they had risen again to a level where the power of the priesthood and the evidence of God's love and mercy had been visibly evident. And now he'd been blessed again with that love being given through the hands of these sweet sisters who were not only willing but also eager to ease his family's burdens.

Alex entered the house to find it dark and quiet. He peeked in Katharine's room to find her sleeping peacefully. He sat on the edge of her bed for several minutes, just watching her sleep and counting his blessings. In the nursery he spent a quiet minute with Preston as well, amazed at how fast he was growing. In spite of certain challenges, they had much to be grateful for.

* * * * *

From where she lay in bed, Jane heard Alex come up the stairs. She predicted the few minutes he spent in each of the children's rooms, and then he came into the room they shared, guided by the glow of the hall light. She watched him sit in a chair where the light clearly illuminated his face. He took off his shoes then just sat there, as if he couldn't find the motivation to move any farther. Taking the time to just look at him, she couldn't help noticing how quickly his beard had filled in. He'd never worn one before in all the years she'd known him, but she had to admit that she liked it. Until she'd seen her husband with a beard, she'd never given much thought to how differently the hair on a man's face could grow. Alex had no hair growing on his cheeks at all, but it framed his jaw line and blended smoothly into his mustache, giving the appearance that it was neatly groomed without his even trying. She also liked the way he'd taken to wearing his hair a little longer. It wasn't long enough to look rebellious or unkempt, but it was thicker and hung down the back of his neck. He combed it back off his face where it usually stayed put, except for a stray wave that occasionally came loose and hung over his forehead. Simply put, no matter how he wore his hair, or whether or not he shaved, he was the most handsome man she'd ever known. And she loved him.

Seeing the weariness in Alex's expression, she pondered how difficult this day must have been for him, and all that on top of the way he worked hard to provide for his family and see that their every need was met. Through the ongoing crisis of Barrett's illness, Jane had certainly seen Alex become emotional and struggle with accepting the reality that this was happening to their family. But he was always strong, and firm, and positive. He was the shoulder she cried on, the ear she complained to, and the arms that held her when she had no strength to hold herself up another minute. And she loved him.

"Hello, Doctor," she said, alerting him to the fact that she wasn't asleep.

"Hello." He turned toward her. "I didn't want to wake you," he said, moving toward the bed.

"You didn't. I'm afraid I took a late nap while Jeanie and Paula were tending my kids."

"Paula left me a message," he said and sat beside her, pressing a kiss to her brow. "We're very blessed."

"Yes, we are," she said, and Alex realized she sounded more at peace than he'd heard in weeks. Perhaps his visit to the temple, combined with the help and support of these sweet sisters, had given her something good to hold onto. "How's your dad?" she asked gently.

"He's better, I think. But it could be rough for a while."

"How was the temple?"

"It was good, but I missed you."

"Better that one of us go, than neither of us."

"Yes, I'm sure you're right. But I look forward to when we can both go there together again."

"Yes, that would be nice."

She pressed a hand into his hair and urged his face close to hers. "I love you, Alex Keane," she said and kissed him.

"I love you too," he said and kissed her again. Passion crept into their kiss and he eased into the bed beside her without taking his lips from hers. "Ooh," he muttered close to her ear, "how long has it been since we've slept in the same bed at the same time?"

"It seems like forever," she said, "even though it hasn't been all that long."

"It's going to get longer," he said, and she kissed him again, making him realize that this most precious aspect of marriage was something else that had become lost in the struggles of their lives. Holding her close he felt rejuvenated and replenished by her love in a way that nothing else could.

"Oh, Jane," he murmured, "you're the best thing that ever happened to me."

"No," she said and kissed him, "it's the other way around."

He looked into her eyes and touched her face. "I don't know; I'm pretty stubborn. You had to wait a long time for me to come around."

"It was worth the wait." Her voice cracked as she added, "You're as stubborn about living the gospel as you were about resisting it. You are a strength to me, Alex."

"It's the other way around," he said and kissed her long and hard.

Afterward, she pressed her face to his shoulder and wept beyond control. He cried with her, certain it was good for them to let go of some degree of this grief they'd been carrying around. No words were necessary for them to share the emptiness of knowing that Barrett was not beneath their roof, as he should be, and that the nightmare was far from over.

* * * * *

It was difficult for Alex to get up early and leave his family in order to go to work. But he left feeling more strengthened emotionally and spiritually than he had in weeks, albeit he still felt physically drained. On his lunch break he went to check on Barrett and found that Linda had come back to sit with him after someone else had taken a shift. Barrett was asleep, and apparently he'd had a fairly good day so far. Alex sat close to him for a short while before he returned to work. He went back as soon as his shift ended that evening and found Jane there. She stood as he walked into the room. Their eyes met, and he saw a sparkle of something there that reminded him of the intimacy they'd shared the previous night. Like a moment of magic in the midst of a world of madness, the memory of what they'd shared strengthened the bond between them as they continued to endure whatever life threw at them.

"How are you?" he asked and kissed her quickly.

"I'm fine," she said. "And you?"

"I'm fine."

"Have you talked to your dad?"

"Yeah. He's good for the moment. And how's our little hero?" he asked, sitting on the edge of Barrett's bed, pressing a hand over his little bald head.

"The same," she said sadly. "I'm afraid it's been a rough afternoon."

Barrett's eyes came open and he showed a wan smile. But he couldn't speak.

"Hey there, buddy. Have you been a good boy for Mommy and the nurses?"

He nodded, and Jane said, "He's been a *very* good boy. He always is." She added more quietly, "If I were going through what he is, I don't think I'd be nearly so agreeable."

"Me neither," Alex said.

A week later Barrett had shown no progress, and there was no evidence that the new bone marrow was doing any good at all. Alex felt on the verge of losing it. He wasn't sure what he was about to lose, but he knew that whatever *it* was, losing it wouldn't be pretty. If he wasn't preoccupied with worry over his son, or his wife, he was worried about his brother. Every day Neil called at least once to see if Alex had heard from Wade. They had discussed contacting his mother, or seeing if they could find him somewhere on campus, but neither of them felt that would be appropriate—at least not at this point. Both with Barrett and with Wade, all they could do was wait.

Chapter 9

About five hours into a shift in the ER, one of the nurses found Alex, saying, "Your wife's on the phone. She sounds upset."

Alex became consumed with a dread and fear he'd never experienced as he worked his way to the phone. "What's wrong?" he asked without preamble, but Jane was crying too hard to speak. He felt tempted to just hang up and get there immediately, but that was too many minutes to have to wonder. "Calm down and tell me," he ordered gently. "Is Barrett—"

"Nothing's changed with Barrett," she managed to say, and he sucked in a breath of relief that was halted by a new dread over what else might have gone wrong to complicate their lives. "It's Andie." His thoughts went to Barrett's little friend, and her parents, and the many times their paths had crossed during the hospital vigil. "They're losing her, Alex."

That's all he had to hear to fully understand Jane's sorrow. They had all grown to love Andie and her family, but there was the deeper meaning that couldn't be ignored. Was Barrett doomed to follow her? Everything that had been done for Andie was being done for Barrett. But would it be enough?

"We're in PICU," she hurried to add. "Karen asked me to come with her."

"I'll be there in a few minutes," he said and hung up the phone. He was grateful to have the ER quiet as he announced that he was taking an early lunch break. When a nurse asked if he wanted her to call someone to fill in, he eagerly accepted the offer and hurried to the other hospital. He found Jane standing in the hallway outside of Andie's room. He caught a glimpse through the open doorway of Karen sitting in the chair, holding Andie in her arms, weeping. Bruce was kneeling beside her, crying as well. Alex turned his attention to Jane, who had a hand pressed over her mouth, her eyes squeezed closed with tears pouring from beneath her eyelids. He barely touched her to make her aware of his presence before she clutched onto him and wept without restraint, albeit quietly, fighting to keep others from hearing.

"She's gone," Jane muttered and cried harder.

Alex felt something tighten painfully in the deepest part of himself as he looked over Jane's head toward the grieving parents, desperately clinging to their lifeless child. "Heaven help us," he muttered and felt hot, harsh tears overtake him as well.

"It happened so fast," Jane said, and then she couldn't speak.

Once they'd both managed to calm down somewhat, Alex felt compelled to enter the room where he put a hand on Bruce's shoulder and spoke quietly. "Is there anything we can do?" Bruce came to his feet, and they shared a long, firm embrace. "Just keep fighting," he said to Alex as their eyes met. Alex nodded, unable to speak, then their eyes both moved to Andie, lying motionless in her mother's arms. Alex was surprised to see how serene the child looked. He'd seen her suffer so much, but now she looked as if she were sleeping peacefully.

He turned back to Bruce. "Can we . . . call anyone for you, or . . ."

"It's all taken care of," Bruce said. "Thank you."

"You know how to reach us. Please . . . if we can do anything—anything at all."

Bruce nodded and his chin quivered. "Please keep us informed," he said, and instantly Alex saw two scenarios in his mind. Would he one day call this man to tell him that Barrett had gone on to join his little friend on the other side of the veil? Or would he call to say that Barrett had conquered the disease and would be given the opportunity to grow up and live a normal life, when Andie had not? He wondered which it would be, and what kind of poignancy and sorrow there would be between them either way.

"Of course," Alex said.

"We'll keep praying for Barrett," Bruce said, and Alex nodded, unable to hold back a new rush of tears.

Family members arrived to be with Bruce and Karen. Alex slipped out of the room and guided Jane to Barrett's bedside where they knelt together and prayed for Andie's family and loved ones to be comforted and strengthened, and they prayed that Barrett would be spared from having this horrible disease take his life. Then they held each other and cried while Barrett slept, and Alex dreaded having to tell him that Andie was gone.

When the moment came, Alex sat on the edge of the bed and held Barrett's hand while Jane stood beside him, her hand on his shoulder. He looked into his son's young eyes and just said, "Andie died, Barrett. She's not sick anymore. Her spirit has gone to live with Heavenly Father."

Barrett looked thoughtful but surprisingly serene. Alex knew Jane shared his own frustration in seeing Barrett's eyes attempting to communicate something that he wasn't capable of saying with the radiation damage in his mouth and throat.

"What, honey?" Jane asked. "Are you sad that Andie is gone?"

Barrett just turned slightly and pointed toward a laminated picture of Jesus that had been put on the wall. "Andie is with Jesus now," Jane said, and Barrett's eyes agreed. Apparently that's what he'd wanted to say. Then his eyes filled with sadness. Or was it yearning?

"What, honey?" Jane asked again. "Are you thinking about Andie?" He showed no response. "About Jesus?" His eyes responded eagerly.

"Do you want to see Jesus, too?" Alex asked. He felt Jane squeeze his shoulder tightly as Barrett nodded and his eyes filled with innocent peace.

"You will one day," Alex said, amazed that he wasn't sobbing— although it was taking every ounce of self-control to keep from doing so. "But we don't know when. That's up to Heavenly Father. He's the only one who knows when it's time for you to go."

Barrett absorbed this, looking even more thoughtful until he drifted easily to sleep, aided by the morphine in his system. Alex hurried into the bathroom where he let the water run to buffer the sound of his weeping. He could never put words to the depth of guilt he felt in standing back to watch this child suffer, when Barrett himself seemed to prefer going where his little friend had gone, as opposed to facing any more of this torture.

The following evening Alex and Jane sat with Barrett, reading together from *Hop On Pop*. It was Barrett's favorite book, and Roxanne had dissembled a copy of it, laminating each page, and then had it spiral bound so that it could be thoroughly cleaned. Barrett was easily capable of reading the simple Dr. Seuss book, and it was one of his favorites, but being unable to do so, Alex read to him in an animated voice.

"Oh, this is my favorite part," Jane said.

And Alex read, "'Dad is sad. Very, very sad. He had a bad day. What a day Dad had!'" Alex chuckled. "Sounds like I had to give too many shots to little boys and girls at the hospital."

Barrett showed a subdued smile and Alex read on. "Oh, I like this page," he said, pointing to the big yellow furry father with two little yellow furry children jumping on his belly; one of them had a pink bow on its head. "There's you and Katharine jumping on your daddy." Alex then read, "'We like to hop. We like to hop on top of Pop. Stop. You must not hop on Pop.'" Alex read on until a page near the end. "'Father. Mother. Sister. Brother. That one is my other brother.'" He stopped as his mind went unexpectedly to Wade.

"Is something wrong?" Jane asked.

"I was just . . . wondering if Wade's okay." He let out an ironic chuckle. "He called me his other brother."

"Maybe he grew up reading *Hop on Pop*."

"Maybe he did."

Their story came to an abrupt halt when Barrett needed to throw up. They were just getting the situation under control when Bruce and Karen came into the room. Bruce held a cluster of brightly colored Mylar balloons. Karen was holding a large giraffe with a big purple bow around its long neck. He was sure it had taken some planning to get that thing in here following the standard sanitation process. He pondered the fact that they'd probably spent the day making funeral arrangements, but they'd taken the time to come here.

Before Alex could think of anything to say, Karen smiled at him and Jane, and then she eased to Barrett's side and tucked the giraffe into his arms. With a firm voice and peace in her countenance, she said to Barrett, "I think Andie wants you to have this. She knew how much you love giraffes." Barrett was clearly pleased. "And I want you to remember something very important," Karen added. "Andie is an angel now. Like your Grandma Angel, and your Grandpa Angel. She will always be your friend, and she will help watch out for you. Can you remember that?"

Barrett nodded, then his attention turned to Bruce and the balloons he carried. While Bruce teased Barrett as if nothing in the world was wrong, Karen turned to Alex and Jane and they all stepped into the hall, knowing that having that many people in the room at a time was discouraged.

"Thank you," Jane said tearfully. "But . . . you shouldn't be here. I'm certain you have your own—"

"No," Karen said. "This is where we need to be right now. We miss being here, in a way." She glanced through the window into the room where her husband was making Barrett show some semblance of a smile. Tears rose in Karen's eyes. But as she turned to look again at Alex and Jane, Alex was struck by something in her countenance that took his breath away. A serene smile crept through her tears as she said, "We knew we needed to tell you . . . face-to-face that . . ." Her emotion increased, but it was not sorrow that caused her tears. There was an indefinable tranquility that flowed into her words. "There is no describing," she said, "the perfect peace that fills every cell of your being, driving away every minuscule bit of the horror." She closed her eyes and actually smiled. "It was her time to go," she said. "We know it beyond any doubt." She opened her eyes, and her gaze was penetrating. "She is free now, and her freedom has set free all who love her. You are the ones still held captive with the waiting and wondering." She sniffled and wiped her face with a tissue that she pulled out of her pocket. "There are things worse than death, you see. We have felt her close, and her happiness is beyond description." She pressed a fist to her heart. "I have felt it as if it were my own. I know we will miss her; I know it will be hard. But I will always have the memory of such feelings to carry me through." She focused on Alex and Jane again. "We just want you to know that whatever God's will is for Barrett, whether he is meant to stay or go, you will find peace."

Alex realized that Jane was barely suppressing a torrent of audible sobbing by holding a hand tightly over her mouth. Karen wrapped Jane in her arms and together they wept while Alex looked on, feeling strangely comforted and deeply terrified while the events taking place around him felt distant and hazy. The emotion eventually subsided, and Bruce and Karen stayed just a few more minutes, talking and laughing as if the death of a child had never occurred in their lives—let alone the previous day. Barrett fell asleep before they left, but for more than an hour following their departure, neither Jane nor Alex had a word to say. He finally broke the silence by speaking the words that wouldn't stop scrolling through his mind. "Maybe we're praying for the wrong thing, Jane."

"What do you mean?" she asked as if he'd suggested something criminal.

Remaining calm, he said, "I mean that . . . I think she was right. There are things worse than death, and—"

"I can't believe you'd say that to me . . . now." Her anger was evident even though she kept her voice low to avoid waking Barrett. "I'm not giving up on him that easily."

"I'm not saying that we should give up," Alex insisted. "I will fight with everything inside of me to keep him with us, Jane."

"But?" she snapped. "Come on. What's the but?"

Alex leaned back in his chair and sighed. She had him figured. He had to say it. "But . . . if it's God's will for him to go, no amount of fasting, or fighting, or prayer is going to keep him here." Her anger heightened visibly but he pressed on. "The bottom line is accepting God's will, Jane."

She turned to glare at him, and he felt a wall slam down between them as she growled quietly, "I'm not giving up that easily."

Alex wanted to say that she misunderstood his meaning; he wanted to tell her that's not what he meant at all. But she hurried from the room, leaving in her wake the distinct message that he had just betrayed her somehow. He sighed and pressed a hand through his hair, wondering when this nightmare would end.

The next day Alex found Andie's obituary on the Internet. He printed it out and cried when he read it, then he took it to Jane who held it and stared helplessly at Andie's picture and the printed words. She commented only on the request that in lieu of flowers, donations be made to Primary Children's Medical Center.

"We should go to the funeral," he said.

"I can't," she countered, but offered no explanation.

"Maybe it would help . . . give us some perspective."

"I can't," she repeated more firmly, and he didn't bring it up again.

Alex felt strongly compelled to go, but he felt as strongly that he shouldn't press Jane to go if she wasn't comfortable with it. He simply told her that he'd traded a shift, and he was going to the funeral. She told him to give her love to Bruce and Karen.

Alex prayed through the long drive that he would remain composed and strong—at least while he was around other people. At the viewing he was surprised by the mood in the room. The receiving line of family members near the casket felt more like a wedding than a funeral. There was talk in the room of the tragedy and heartache, and tears were being shed. But the peace of Andie's family was almost palpable. Andie looked like a perfect little angel, sleeping soundly, dressed in white, the serenity in her countenance even more pronounced than it had been at the hospital. Alex embraced Karen and Bruce, feeling their peace and hope soak into him. He passed Jane's message on to them and they expressed compassion and understanding for her not wanting to be there. They promised to keep in touch, and Alex went into the chapel to find a seat near the back. He wanted an easy escape should his grief get out of hand. While he waited for the funeral to begin, he thought of Karen saying that they knew it had been Andie's time to go. He recalled his mother's funeral, when his sisters had firmly declared the same thing. But at the time he'd been too angry and lost in his own pain to feel that kind of peace. Eventually he'd come to terms with that, but he pondered on the power of fear and anger and bitterness to block peace from coming into a person's heart. He wondered what kind of fear Jane might be holding in her heart. He understood it, and he felt compassion for it. He just didn't know what to do about it. He was silently praying for her when he heard a familiar voice say, "Is this seat taken?"

Alex looked up to see his father standing at the end of the bench. "It is now," he said, sliding over. Neil sat down, and he added, "What are you doing here? It's more than an hour's drive from your house."

"A hunch," Neil said. "I thought you might be open to some company through a difficult event." Their eyes met, and he added, "I owe you one."

Alex took his father's hand. "You don't owe me anything. But I won't deny being glad to see you."

"You okay?"

"Not particularly. But if I don't ever have to face this with my own child, I'll be a lot better."

"We can't give up hope," Neil said and put an arm around Alex's shoulders.

"Where's Roxanne?" Alex asked.

"She went to the hospital to sit with Jane," he said, and Alex wanted to cry. With any luck Jane would vent to Roxanne and release some of the thoughts and feelings that she'd been hesitant to share with him—especially since he'd suggested that they needed to accept God's will.

Alex did pretty well with the funeral until a young woman did a musical number that crept into his heart. Following the song, while Alex barely managed to keep his tears back, Bruce stood at the pulpit and spoke of the joy Andie had brought to all who knew her, and that her life had not been in vain. She had been a child of perfect faith, and a peacemaker from her birth. He asked that those who'd had the privilege of knowing her would move forward by using her example to spread joy and peace and the testimony of knowing that her life had not ended, but she had moved on to a greater purpose.

Alex managed to gain his composure through the bishop's talk on the plan of salvation, and his firm and touching testimony of the power of the Atonement to heal the pain in losing this child. Then the Primary children of the ward gathered at the front of the chapel to sing "A Child's Prayer." The first phrases did him in. *Heavenly Father, are you really there? And do you hear and answer every child's prayer?* With that Alex had to hurry to the men's room, grateful to be alone while he sobbed without constraint. While he was still crying he found his father beside him and he eagerly accepted his warm embrace and the shoulder that muffled his sobs.

"It's going to be okay, Alex," Neil said. "Barrett will be fine."

"We can't know that," Alex cried. "We can't possibly know that."

Neil took Alex's face into his hands and looked at him hard. "Whether he lives or dies, he will be fine—and so will you."

Alex sobbed. "And what about my wife? How do I get her through this if we lose him?"

"She's stronger than she thinks she is," he said. "And so are you. The best thing you can do for her is love her without question."

Alex nodded firmly and said, "I have to go to the hospital."

"Okay. I'll follow you."

Alex prayed through the long drive and arrived to find his father pulling into the next parking space. As they walked into the hospital, Neil said, "Do you suppose Wade is okay?"

"I don't know," Alex said. "I worry about that too."

"Do you think we should try and find him?"

"I don't know. Maybe we just need to give it some time."

Silence fell again until Neil said, "I keep thinking about Marilyn . . . and Brad, her husband. I would really like to talk to them, but . . . I don't want to make it worse."

"If you pray about it and feel like you should do it then . . . you should at least try."

"If I feel like it's right, would you go with me?"

"Sure . . . if you want me to."

"Yes, I do, but . . . I don't know yet if it's right or not."

"Let me know."

"We should tell your sisters . . . about Wade."

"Yes, that would be a must," Alex said. "Do you want me to tell them?"

"Probably, but . . . not yet."

"Why not?"

"I don't know. Just . . . not yet."

"Okay," Alex said, and they hurried on to Barrett's room.

Alex barely spoke a greeting to Roxanne before he swept Jane into his arms and held her as if it was her he feared losing. "I love you, Jane," he said and looked into her eyes. "We mustn't give up hope." She nodded, and he felt that wall disappear from between them before she pressed her face to his shoulder and held to him tightly.

* * * * *

The day after the funeral, Alex was finishing up some paperwork, getting ready to take a lunch break, when one of the nurses from the front desk approached him, saying, "There's somebody here to see you; says he's a friend."

"Did he tell you his name?"

"Wade . . . something," she said. "Should I tell him to—"

"I'll be right there," Alex said. "I'm due for lunch anyway."

Alex couldn't keep his heart from pounding as he hurried to sign the reports on a couple of patients and get out to the waiting area. Wade was looking out the window and turned when he heard the door open. He had a beard not much different from the one Alex had taken to wearing.

"Hey kid," Alex said, then hesitated only a moment before he hugged Wade tightly, feeling some relief to have him return the embrace.

"You seem glad to see me," Wade said when Alex stepped back.

"Yeah, I am. I've been worried about you."

"No need for that," Wade said, glancing away. Alex didn't feel convinced on that count.

"Hey, what's this?" Alex asked, lightly rubbing the hair on Wade's face.

"I thought I'd follow your rebellious example."

"I'm not a rebel," Alex said proudly. "I just don't have time to shave."

"Well, I think I prefer being a rebel at the moment, if it's all the same to you."

"What are you saying? That you stopped going to church?"

"Yes, actually," Wade said without apology. "And I've pretty much stopped doing just about everything else I was raised to do."

"Do you really think that will help?" Alex asked, pondering the years he'd avoided church attendance as well as prayer and scripture study.

"Right now I don't think anything will help. If you don't want to hang out with a rebellious guy like me, just say so."

"I had my day," Alex said. "I'd be happy to hang out with you under any circumstances."

Wade seemed anxious to change the subject as he hurried to add, "I came yesterday; they said you were off, that you'd be here today."

"I'm sorry I missed you," Alex said. "I was at a funeral."

Wade looked panicked. "Not your son?"

"No," Alex said. "A friend of his. She was near the same age, died of the same thing."

"Whoa. That's got to be tough."

"Yeah," Alex said.

"How is your son?"

"It's hard to say. Right now the cure is worse than the disease, but it's the only way to combat it." Not wanting to talk about that he asked, "You hungry? Your timing's good; I've got a lunch break, even though it's a weird time for lunch. The cafeteria here is tolerable. It's on me."

"Okay, I could stand to eat," Wade said, and they walked together down the hall.

"So, how are you?" Alex asked.

"I don't know how to answer that," Wade said. "And I don't know how to explain the way I feel like I could talk to you about anything, when, for all intents and purposes, we're complete strangers."

Alex stopped walking and put a hand on Wade's arm, forcing him to stop as well. Their eyes met, and Alex said, "We're brothers, Wade. We may not have known that until recently, but that doesn't make the bond any less real."

"Well, I can't think of any other reason that I couldn't keep myself from coming to find you. I can't bring myself to face my parents *or* my father. My siblings . . . my *other* siblings are all whacked out over this too. They all just seem like they'd rather not talk about it at all, that maybe it would be better to pretend we didn't know. My genetics professor asks me how I'm doing here and there. Other than that, I can honestly say I've never felt so alone in my entire life. Truthfully, you're the only reason I could think of not to just end it all a couple of days ago."

Again Alex stopped walking and forced Wade to face him. "Please tell me you're saying that for shock value or something."

"If you think that then you don't know me at all."

"Actually, I *don't* know you at all," Alex said. "Which is why you're going to have to give me a chance to know you." He paused and said firmly, "Are you telling me that you were really suicidal over this?"

"If I answer that question honestly, are you going to think less of me?"

"I would never want you to be anything but completely honest with me, and there's nothing you could say or do that would make me care any less."

"Well then," Wade leaned his back against the wall of a long, mostly deserted hallway, "that's the truth of it. I don't know that I really could have gone through with it. But I was certainly tempted." He blew out a long breath and looked down. "At first I could only think of how it would hurt my parents—all three of them. And I *wanted* to hurt them, the way they'd hurt me by hiding the truth from me, by being so . . . stupid . . . in the first place. Then I realized that for all they'd done or not done, they didn't deserve that kind of hurt."

"You got that right," Alex said. He kept to himself that Wade had just admitted to knowing that his parents loved him, and he obviously loved them as well.

Wade gave him a hard stare then continued walking. "I'm hungry," he said. "How far is this cafeteria?"

They were seated with their food before any further conversation took place. "So, how's school?" Alex asked.

"Pretty intense, actually. But I'm managing to keep up. It's the only thing I can think about and not be upset. I lost my job, though. I need to look for another one, but I can't find the motivation."

"What happened?" Alex asked.

"I was just . . . so upset that I honestly forgot to go . . . one time too many. I hated that job anyway, but . . . I've got to pay the rent."

"Do you have what you need for the moment?" Alex asked.

Wade looked immediately angry. "I didn't tell you that to get you to feel sorry for me, or to have you start handing out cash."

Alex calmly said, "I have no intention of rescuing you from your need to get another job, Wade. But I know how difficult it can be to get through medical school and keep the bills paid. I certainly can't afford to solve all your problems, but I have a twenty in my wallet I won't miss."

"Keep it. I'm fine."

"Are your parents helping you with school?" Alex asked.

"They can't afford to, as much as they'd like to. Or I'm assuming they were telling me the truth when they said that they'd like to."

"You can't just assume that your parents are suddenly dishonest in every respect, just because they were trying to protect you."

Wade's anger was evident once more. "I have no comment on that, big brother."

"Have you talked to them at all? Do you think they're worried about you?"

"I don't know, and I don't care. They've called and left messages. I haven't felt like calling them back."

"Well, maybe you should . . . just to let them know you're okay. Maybe they're fearing the worst; maybe they think you could become suicidal." Wade gave him a sharp glare, and Alex added, "Dad's been worried sick about you. He calls me at least twice a day to ask if I've heard from you."

Wade looked mildly upset before he took a bite then said, "So call him. Tell him I'm fine."

"Are you?"

"Obviously. We're sitting here having lunch together. Call him."

Being away from the patient area, Alex pulled his cell phone out of his pocket and turned it on. "Okay, fine," he said lightly, "if it will help ease your guilt."

Alex dialed his father's house and was glad to hear him answer. "Hey, Dad. I just have a second, but I wanted to let you know that I'm having lunch with Wade. He appears to be fine at the moment."

Neil's relief was blatantly evident. "Thank you," he said. "Call me later."

"I will," Alex said and hung up the phone.

Wade immediately stated a phone number and pointed at the phone before he took another bite. "Dial it," Wade said when Alex hesitated.

"Who is it?" Alex asked while he punched in the number, glad to know that it would be kept in the phone's memory.

"My mother. If she's not there, leave a message."

Alex looked at the phone and groaned as a low battery warning came on. He certainly didn't want it to die in the middle of a crucial call. Noting a courtesy phone a few steps away he turned off the cell phone and stood up to dial the number he'd just been told. "Do you want me to tell her who I am?" Alex asked as the phone began to ring.

"To be truthful, I don't care." His words rang with definite bitterness.

Alex was hoping for a machine, but a woman answered. "Uh . . . is this Sister Morrison?"

"Yes," she said, sounding panicked, and he wondered why.

"Wade asked me to call and let you know that he's fine."

Following an audible sigh of relief she asked, "What's happened to him?"

"Nothing," Alex said firmly. "He just—"

"The caller ID is from a hospital number," she said, and he understood her panic.

"Sorry," he chuckled, "I work here. He's fine, really."

"Okay," she said, sounding upset. "Why won't he call me himself?"

"I can't answer that," he said, looking right at Wade who was focused on his food as if he'd not eaten for days. Alex suspected it was more accurate that he preferred to be distracted by it. "He just asked me to call you."

"You're a friend of his?"

"In a way," Alex said, wondering how much he should tell her.

"May I know your name?" she asked.

He wasn't about to lie to her. He could certainly say that he preferred not to tell her, but he felt that maybe it was better she knew. "My name is Alex Keane," he said, and Wade's attention perked up.

A long silence on the other end of the phone preceded her saying, "You're Neil's son."

"That's right."

Another long pause. "How is your father?"

"He's pretty shaken up, but all in all he's doing okay. I think he's worried about you."

"I've been worried about him as well." Her voice became teary. "Tell him I'm sorry. Maybe I should have tried harder to find him and tell him a long time ago."

"And maybe you did the right thing," Alex said. "But I'll tell him. Believe it or not, I think he understands."

"Tell Wade I love him. He may not believe it, but . . . tell him anyway."

"I will," Alex said, sensing a humility and graciousness in this woman that touched him.

He expected her to say good-bye, but instead she asked with some hesitance, "Are you . . . active . . . in the Church?"

"Uh . . . yes. Does it show in my voice, or something?"

"You called me *Sister* Morrison."

"So I did. Is that a problem, or—"

"No, of course not. I'm just . . . glad he's . . . with you, rather than being with . . . other people who would more likely lure him away from . . . the answers he needs . . . to get through this."

"I'll certainly do what I can," Alex said, noting that Wade had stopped eating now.

"Let me know if there's anything I can do."

"I'll do that," Alex said.

"Thank you."

"Not a problem."

Alex ended the call and sat down to his lunch. Wade asked, "You'll do what you can about what?"

"About keeping you from being too big of an idiot," Alex said and took a bite of his lunch.

Chapter 10

Wanting some conversation that might not be so strained, Alex asked, "So tell me about yourself, Wade. What do you do besides pre-med and losing your job?"

"Not much at the moment."

"Okay, but . . . before your life took a nosedive, you must have had a hobby."

"I ski in the winter. I like camping and hiking."

"Good hobbies for living here; easy access in several directions."

"Yeah," Wade said, clearly bored.

"You got a girlfriend?"

"No. I had a girl before my mission; said she'd wait, but she didn't. Typical story. I've dated a little here and there. Haven't felt much like doing that for a while, either."

"And where did you go on your mission?"

"Africa," he said. "How about you?"

Alex hated this question, but he'd gotten used to it coming up as a part of Mormon culture. "I didn't go on a mission," he said, and Wade looked surprised.

"Why not?" he asked, and Alex thought how good they'd both become at asking tough questions of each other.

"Because I quit going to church when I was fifteen, and I didn't start again until after I'd finished my residency and had been a practicing physician for a year or so. If you add that up, that's a lot of years. I got married in the temple, if that redeems me at all." He gave in to the temptation to add, "But that was after my Ferrari was totaled in an accident that left my fiancée in a coma for more than ten weeks. I'm very stubborn. It takes great drama to shake me out of apathy—or stupidity." Alex studied Wade's expression. "You look surprised."

"I just . . . assumed you'd always been . . . you know."

"Well, I wasn't. In high school I was smoking . . . getting drunk. Thankfully I had the sense to avoid sex and drugs. And I gave up the others—for the most part anyway—once I decided I wanted to be a doctor and I wouldn't make it happen by abusing my own body."

"Why?" Wade asked, apparently not interested at all in his food anymore.

"Why what? Why did I want to become a doctor? Why did I give it up? Why did I—"

"Why did you do stuff like that . . . not go to church?" Alex just stared at Wade a long moment until the kid added, "If you don't want to tell me, fine."

"Oh, I don't have a problem with telling you. I'm just wondering if you're ready to hear it."

"What's it got to do with me?"

Alex just said it. "I was blindly angry with my father, Wade, because he left a wife and three children for another woman—a woman who had lived in the same ward." Wade's eyes revealed that it wasn't what he'd expected, that he *didn't* want to hear it, but Alex pressed on. "Her family moved. We didn't. We got the brunt of the judgment; people looking at my mother as if it had been her fault. Some people came right out and asked her what she'd done to drive him away. Unlike in the case of your parents, my mother did nothing but treat him like a king. He admitted it to me later. He'd felt unworthy of how well she treated him, so he left her—left us. While he was traveling with his girlfriend, my mother was working night and day to take care of us kids and keep us fed. I was angry over his betrayal and hypocrisy. I was angry with members of the Church who had no idea the damage they'd done with their self-righteous judgment." Alex leaned closer to his brother. "I spent twenty years being angry and bitter, Wade. Twenty years of denying myself the blessings and privileges that life was willing to give me because *I* had become self-righteous and judgmental too."

"How did you stop it . . . the anger . . . the bitterness?"

Alex leaned closer still. "I forgave him."

"I don't know if I can do that. They have no comprehension what this has done to my life."

"Oh, I think they have an idea," Alex said. "But whether or not they do is irrelevant. If they were nothing but selfish and belligerent about the whole thing, forgiveness would still be the only answer to ever being free of what you feel right now."

"You make it sound so easy."

"It's not easy, Wade. You can't just snap your fingers and say, 'Okay I forgive them,' and it's done. But you need to understand something. Forgiveness does not mean you condone what they did, or that their accountability is wiped away. Forgiveness just gives it to God, who is the only one capable of judging their sins according to the intents of their hearts and the repentance process they both went through a long time ago. We're blessed in that regard, you know. At least in our case they've worked hard to make restitution. There are millions of people out there who have been hurt and betrayed by people who don't care and never will."

Wade looked thoughtful for a minute, then said, "You really think it's possible for me to let go of this?"

"I know it is."

Wade turned to look across the room. "I don't know; I need time."

"That's understandable."

Wade stood up. "Thanks for lunch. I need to go."

Alex resisted the urge to ask for his phone number, knowing he likely wouldn't answer messages from him any more than he would his mother. Instead he tucked a card with his own phone numbers into Wade's pocket and said, "I'm off at seven. Do you think you could meet me again in the waiting room? There's something I'd like to show you."

Wade contemplated it a moment then said, "I guess I can."

"Okay, I'll see you then."

Wade took a few steps then turned back and said, "You had a Ferrari?"

Alex chuckled. "Yeah, but I'm a family man now. Those baby seats don't fit too well in a car like that."

Wade nodded and smiled before he walked away. Alex called Jane once he was finished eating to catch her up. She was glad to hear he'd spent some time with Wade, and he was glad to hear that Barrett seemed to be having a good day.

A few hours later an eleven-year-old girl came in unconscious following a drowning. It didn't take much to determine that she was brain dead, but Alex had to be the one to tell her parents. He sat with them through the initial shock, grateful he wasn't needed elsewhere, praying that he would never be on the receiving end of this conversation. Once they'd calmed down, Alex used well-rehearsed diplomacy to ask if they would be open to letting their daughter's death give them an opportunity to save the lives of other children. He waited for the answer, wondering if these were the kind of people who would consider such an option, or if they would yell and swear at him. He was pleased when they were not only open to the idea, but also even eager to share what their daughter no longer needed. Before Alex's shift ended he had helped make arrangements to save three other children elsewhere in the country. He thought about the parents of these children who had been hoping and praying that matching organs could be found before their children died. He knew that feeling to some degree. Then he thought of the parents who had lost a child today and his heart felt heavy. He'd contemplated that feeling a great deal, and prayed he would never have to actually go there.

Wade wasn't in the waiting room when Alex came out, and he wondered if he would get stood up. But five minutes later he arrived, apologizing for being late.

"So, what did you want to show me?" Wade asked.

"Let's walk," Alex said, and they moved deeper into the hospital, around a couple of corners to an elevator.

"Where we going?" Wade asked as they stepped into the elevator, and Alex pushed the button to go from the main floor they were on, down one level to the first basement floor.

"The skywalk," Alex said, and Wade's brow furrowed.

"I hate to point out the obvious, but we're going down."

Alex smiled at him. "How observant of you. A metaphor I've considered many times as I've made this trek."

They stepped out of the elevator, went around a corner, and immediately into the long skywalk that connected the two hospitals. As the hill sloped down from the U of U Medical Center, the skywalk entered into the fourth floor of Primary Children's.

"Oh I get it," Wade said, noting the slope of the hill through the windows along one side. He then looked ahead and asked again, "Where are we going?"

"We are going to *that* hospital." He pointed ahead. "As opposed to *that* hospital." He pointed behind.

"Primary Children's?"

"That's right. You don't have any hint of a virus do you? No sore throat? Sniffles? Anything?"

"No, why?"

"Sick people can't go where I live most of the time these days."

Wade stopped walking. "You're taking me to meet your son?"

"And my wife. Is there a problem with that?"

Wade looked as if there was, but he started walking again and said, "I guess not."

"What?" Alex asked. "You don't want to get too attached to a family that you're not certain you want to be a part of?"

Wade looked surprised but said, "Maybe."

"Well, it's too late," Alex said.

As they approached the door that entered into the other hospital, Wade asked, "Why a metaphor?" Alex felt confused and he clarified, "You said something about a metaphor . . . when we were going down."

Alex stopped near the door a moment and pointed back to where they could see the slope of the hill and the perspective of the basement they'd just come out of. "When you walk through the doors to this hospital, there is absolutely no question that you are entering a world that exists on a higher plane. Especially doing it over and over. There's just a feeling . . ." He pushed the door open, and Wade followed him. He paused a moment to discreetly check Wade's expression. He didn't say anything, but Alex knew he could feel the difference. He couldn't resist sharing what a number of staff members had mentioned more than once. "They say angels walk the halls here. But only the children can see them."

Wade glanced around and said, "That's not so difficult to imagine."

They began walking the long, wide corridor from one end of the hospital to the other, and Alex shared his own observation, one that he and Jane had discussed many times. "This place is as magic as it is tragic."

Wade said nothing, and they walked in silence, while Alex's mind wandered back to the significant events of his workday.

"What's wrong?" Wade asked, and Alex was surprised by his sensitivity.

"Uh . . . a kid died today; one of my patients."

"What happened?"

"Drowning. The paramedics got her breathing, but she never regained consciousness."

"That's got to be tough. Do you lose patients often?"

"Regularly," Alex said as if it didn't bother him. "We save more than we lose, but we are a trauma center. It's just part of the job."

"I think I'll . . . deliver babies or something."

"Very wise," Alex said.

"What made you choose emergency medicine?"

"I just always knew that was my gift, so to speak. I work well with adrenaline pumping, I suppose. But it has its downside. I saw stuff during my residency that still haunts me."

"Like what?"

"I don't think you need to be haunted by it too," Alex said.

"Like what?" he repeated.

Alex settled for a blanket description. "Violent crimes, gang wars, high-speed car accidents, fires. When you work in teaching hospitals in inner cities you see it all. And then through residency you do rotations all over the place; every disease and illness imaginable."

"What's the worst thing you ever saw on the job?" Wade asked as if he were genuinely interested. Perhaps his desire to be a doctor gave him a sick fascination with trauma.

Alex had no trouble answering the question, but he wasn't sure Wade would get out of it what he might be hoping for. "It was a woman in her mid-fifties, DOA from a heart attack." Wade looked confused, and Alex added, "No blood. No gore. But it was the worst moment of my career. She was my mother."

"Whoa," Wade said. "I'm sorry."

"Yeah, well . . . that's life. My third-worst moment in an emergency room was when I came awake there and found out my fiancée was in a coma. But as you can see, that all turned out okay, eventually." He sighed loudly. "And the girl who died today, her parents consented to organ donation. There are at least three very happy families elsewhere. They're still working on matching up some other possibilities while she's on life support." He paused for emphasis then added, "Sometimes good things come out of the worst of circumstances."

"Is that supposed to mean something to me?"

"If it doesn't you need your head examined."

"Maybe I do."

"Wouldn't hurt."

"What was the second?" Wade asked.

"Second what?"

"You told me about the first- and third-worst experiences in the ER. What was the second?"

Alex inhaled and just said it, realizing he still hadn't recovered from this one. "When I was told that my son had leukemia." Wade made no comment.

They went through the first set of large double doors, and Alex told Wade, "He's in isolation. You'll need to wash up before we can go in."

Wade looked hesitant but followed Alex's example, asking while he scrubbed his hands, "Why isolation?"

"The brief version is that his immune system is completely shot. He was given a bone marrow transplant. We're waiting to see if it will help, but so far we haven't seen any improvement."

Alex picked up the security phone and waited for a nurse to answer. He simply said, "Hi, it's Alex. I have my brother with me." And the second set of double doors came open.

Alex said to Wade as they stepped into the hallway, "The unit has an amazing air filtering system, but we still have to be very careful with what goes into Barrett's room."

Wade said nothing, but he seemed somber and perhaps apprehensive as they moved down the hall and stepped into Barrett's room. Alex was surprised to find Linda there. Since the first time he'd called her, she'd become a common backup and had sat with Barrett a couple of times when neither he nor Jane could be there. She had once worked as an LPN, and she was a tremendous blessing in their lives right now.

"Where's Jane?" Alex asked, and she looked up from the plastic dinosaurs she held in each hand to entertain Barrett, who looked mildly interested.

Barrett's attention turned to his father, and his eyes showed recognition but little enthusiasm.

"Look, your daddy is here," Linda said. Then to Alex, "Susan called me earlier; said she thought Jane could use a break but she wouldn't take one if someone wasn't here with Barrett every minute."

"Yeah, she's like that," Alex said. "As always, we're grateful."

"It's not a problem," Linda said. "Barrett and I have become good friends." She set the dinosaurs close to Barrett and said to Alex, "Jane is actually here with Katharine. She got here just a while ago. I guess Katharine's been begging to come to the hospital."

"Yes, she certainly has," Alex said.

"She had a peek at Barrett through the window; now they've gone to the playroom."

Alex smiled at Linda and moved closer to Barrett as she moved aside. "And how's our little superman?" he asked.

"Not bad at the moment. Your timing is good. He's been pretty relaxed. A little longer and he might have been asleep. I'll give you a few minutes, then you can go see your wife. I can stay as long as you need."

"Okay, thanks," Alex said, and Linda left the room.

"Hey there, buddy," Alex said, and Barrett gave a weak smile. Alex scooped him up and sat on the bed to hold him. He got comfortable, then Barrett's eyes were drawn to the man hovering near the door. Alex answered the silent question. "That's your Uncle Wade." He motioned for Wade to come closer. "Wade, this is my son, Barrett."

"Hi," Wade said somewhat timidly, but he sat down and picked up the dinosaurs that Linda had left behind. He made growling noises that got Barrett's attention as the T-rex attempted to devour the stegosaurus. But Barrett only showed interest for half a minute before he laid his head against his father's chest. Alex held him near, only vaguely aware of Wade watching Barrett closely. The child was quickly asleep, but they remained in silence a few minutes before Wade said, "He looks like you."

Alex caught some sadness in the way he'd said it, and he couldn't help wondering if that somehow represented a sense of belonging to Wade. He looked nothing like the father who had raised him, and everything like a man he barely knew.

"So I'm told," Alex said. He sensed Wade's curiosity over Barrett's condition, but perhaps a hesitance to ask. And while Alex had certainly wanted Wade to meet his family, he couldn't deny that a portion of his purpose was to perhaps help give Wade some perspective. Barrett's suffering did not discount the challenges in Wade's life, but it never hurt to see things from a different point of view.

Wade finally said, "He had a bone marrow transplant?"

"That's right."

"What does that entail exactly?"

Alex looked down to make sure Barrett was asleep before he started talking about this in anything but tender terms. In a quiet voice he said, "They use full-body radiation and high doses of chemotherapy to kill every cell of his bone marrow—hopefully."

"Why hopefully?"

"Because if one cancer cell survives, then it's all for nothing. It will multiply into the new bone marrow and take him anyway. Right now he can't talk, or even laugh, because of the ulcers in his mouth and throat from the treatments. He's been extremely ill from the side effects, and will continue to be that way for a long time. Right now we're just waiting and hoping that the new bone marrow works."

"What's the tube in his nose for?"

"That's lunch," Alex said.

"Spoken like a true medical professional."

Alex only said, "I'm not much of a professional here, Wade. I'm just one of the mass of parents struggling to understand." He sighed and added, "It's called an NJ tube. He can't eat because the radiation and chemo have basically burned his mouth and throat. The tube puts nutrition straight to his intestines, but so far nothing that's gone into the tube has stayed down, so he's being fed through his veins. But we can't do that forever because it can damage other organs."

"What's that?" Wade asked, pointing at the tube taped in the center of Barrett's chest, which could be seen where the buttons of his pajamas were open.

Alex pushed the pajamas aside and explained the purpose of the central line. Wade asked for a clarification of the specifics of leukemia, and Alex began to tell him the explanation he'd given to countless friends and relatives. Wade interrupted him and said, "I'm a pre-med student, Alex. I realize I haven't gotten into the big stuff yet, but just tell me the real thing. If I don't understand something, I'll let you know."

"Okay," Alex said and began a medical oratory on a topic he'd come to know inside out. Wade only stopped him a couple of times to ask what something meant. While they talked Alex carefully shifted Barrett into his bed and covered him up, pressing a kiss to his face. They continued their conversation in the hall. Linda had been waiting there and went back in once Alex appeared.

When he'd finished a basic summary of the disease and the treatment, he was surprised to hear Wade say, "Okay, now tell me about Barrett."

"What do you mean?"

"How old was he when it was diagnosed?"

"He was four, almost five. That fifth birthday was a real kicker. He couldn't keep anything down because the chemo was making him sick, so cake and ice cream were not an option. His sixth birthday wasn't much better. We'll be coming up on his seventh in a few months."

"What does he like to do?" Wade asked, and Alex wondered why he felt so surprised by the questions. But as he began telling Wade about Barrett's love for animals, and his favorite movies, and his passion for ice cream, he realized it felt good to be talking about him this way.

Alex concluded by saying, "His very favorite thing, however, is going to the zoo. He kept asking to go after he got sick, but when we finally thought we could manage, it was a wash. He felt sick and went to sleep in the wagon." Alex sighed. "I would really like to take him to the zoo and have him enjoy it. Even if he doesn't end up surviving, a trip to the zoo would be nice."

"Sounds great," Wade said. "Would I be intruding to come along? I'm rather fond of the zoo myself."

Alex smiled at him. "We'll make a party of it."

Wade smiled back, then asked seriously, "Do you think he's going to make it, Alex?"

"I don't know."

"So, you go to work and watch children die and give the bad news to their parents, then you come here and have to sit on the other side."

"That about covers it," Alex said.

Wade looked hard at Alex and spoke with a level of compassion and maturity that completely contradicted the anger and belligerence Alex had seen most prominently in him. "It must be tough for you to dedicate your life to saving lives, and not be able to do anything to help your own son."

Alex felt momentarily speechless as Wade's words validated his deepest heartache. Even though he'd tried to explain that feeling many times to his loved ones, he'd never felt like they could ever fully understand such a perspective. But Wade understood. He'd never actually been in that position, but it was evident that his desire to practice medicine was rooted in a core understanding of its deepest emotional aspects.

"Yeah," Alex said, his voice cracking.

Wade looked away and added in a voice of reverent speculation, "I wonder if that wasn't how our Father in Heaven felt when His Son was on the cross. God of heaven and earth, capable of performing any wonder, but unable to save His own Son from dying a painful death."

Alex felt as if he'd turned to stone. The analogy struck his heart so deeply that he felt real pain there. Was that what he was meant to learn from all of this? Empathy for God the Father? Well, it was working. And meshed into the startling spiritual metaphor he'd just heard was the reality that it had been shown to him by this young man who claimed to be a rebel, who was, by every evidence, floundering with his faith. It was evident that for all of Wade's present challenges, he had a deep understanding of the gospel and a keenly sensitive spirit.

Wade glanced toward Barrett's room. "He's a great kid."

"Yes, he is," Alex said, feeling torn between the conversation and the thoughts swarming in his head. Focusing more on the moment, he added, "Come on. You've got to see the playroom."

"Awesome," Wade said after they'd gone back through the two sets of doors and to the playroom. "Now this is what I call a hospital."

"Indeed," Alex laughed softly. He was glad that only Jane and Katharine were there. It was nice to have the room to themselves.

She turned at the sound of his voice and smiled. "Hi," she said and stood to greet him with a kiss.

"Hello, gorgeous," he said and kissed her again.

"Have you seen Barrett?"

"Yeah, I was just with him. He's asleep."

"When Linda offered to stay with him, I thought it would be a good time to bring Katharine, but I wanted to see you before I left."

"I'm glad you waited," he said and turned toward Wade, which drew Jane's attention to him. "This is my wife, Jane," he said.

"Hello." Jane smiled at him.

"Jane, this is my brother, Wade."

"Oh, of course," Jane said and gave him a quick hug and a kiss on the cheek, which left him looking startled. "Welcome to the family," she added.

"Thanks," Wade said, then Katharine noticed her father and ran to hug him.

"And this is Katharine," Alex said.

"You have two kids?" Wade asked as Katharine returned to playing with a set of large Legos.

"Three actually. Preston is with my cousin at the moment. Well, Susan is actually my mother's cousin, but it works out the same."

"Have a seat, Wade," Jane said, sitting back down. Alex watched Wade sit on the floor close to Katharine and immediately start to play with her. Alex exchanged a warm glance with Jane and sat down beside her.

After watching them play for several minutes, Alex said to Wade, "Maybe you should consider pediatrics."

"Maybe I should," Wade said.

While Wade and Katharine played happily together, Jane occasionally asked Wade questions about himself, and Alex just listened.

"Are you hungry?" Jane asked Alex. "You haven't had supper, have you?"

"No, but I'm fine. I'll wait a while. How about you, Wade? You hungry?"

"No, thanks. I ate before I came."

A few minutes later Alex said to Wade, "I should warn you. Dad could be here in a few minutes. You're welcome to leave if you don't want to be here when he comes." Not wanting Wade to think he'd purposely set this up, he quickly added, "He called just a few minutes before I got off work. Said he had a surprise for me and wanted to know when I would be here with Barrett." Wade said nothing, but Alex could tell he was weighing the situation. Alex went on to say, "As I said, you're welcome to leave, but . . . I know he'd love to see you. It's up to you."

"Okay," Wade said and went back to playing with Katharine, although they'd exchanged Legos for plastic ponies. Alex was glad to have the large playroom to themselves for the moment. He could almost believe they were sitting in the family room at home if he used his imagination. He wondered if Wade had just lost track of the time, or if he really didn't have a problem with seeing their father again.

When Neil and Roxanne arrived, Wade was still there, playing ponies with Katharine on the floor. There wasn't even time for a hello before Neil said to Alex with an animated voice that contradicted something cautious in his eyes as he glanced at Wade and then intently back to Alex. "You'd never believe who called me from the airport, asking for a ride over here to see Barrett."

Alex didn't have time to guess before both of his sisters walked into the room. Before he had a chance to hug them, he caught a discreet sharp glance from his father, and a little shake of his head. Alex understood that his sisters didn't yet know about Wade, and Neil didn't want them to be told in Wade's presence. *Isn't this awkward,* Alex thought as he grinned and hugged his sisters, knowing he needed to say something to set the tone before anyone else blurted anything out.

"Wow, this is a surprise," Alex said.

"Oh, you look good," Charlotte said, "even with this." She touched his beard.

"I don't have time to shave."

"I like it," Becca said.

Jane exchanged hugs with Charlotte and Becca while Alex noticed that Roxanne was cautiously observing Wade and Katharine. When the women turned to Katharine to make a fuss over her, Wade stood up and eased toward Alex. Before anyone else could speak, Alex said, "Charlotte, Becca, I want you to meet a dear friend of mine. This is Wade. Wade," he said, discreetly, "these are my sisters, Charlotte and Becca, and you've met my dad."

"Of course," Wade said, nodding toward the women. "It's nice to meet you." Then to Neil, "And it's good to see you again." He seemed to mean it.

"How are you?" Neil asked.

"I'm fine, thanks."

"And this," Alex said to Wade, "is my father's wife, Roxanne."

"Hello," Wade said as Roxanne took his hand and squeezed it.

"It's so good to meet you," Roxanne said intently. "You must come to dinner sometime soon."

"That would be nice, thanks," Wade said, but Alex wasn't sure he meant it. "I should probably get going. I've got a lot of studying to do." Then he added, including everyone in the room, "It was nice meeting all of you." And to Katharine, "I'll come back and play again sometime." Katharine smiled and waved.

"I'll walk you out," Alex said and left the room at Wade's side. "Sorry about that," he said once they were several steps down the hall. "I had no idea they were coming. They don't know yet; we just haven't had a chance to tell them, and that wasn't the right time."

"Okay," Wade said, not sounding upset, but perhaps disconcerted.

"What's wrong?"

"They're my sisters too."

"Yes, they are."

"It's just so . . . weird. Do I have any other siblings I should be looking out for?"

"That's it," Alex said then added, "You were great with the kids. They like you."

"They're great kids," Wade said. "I hope Barrett comes through okay."

"Yeah, we all do."

"Hey," they heard Neil say and turned to see him trying to catch up. "Sorry about that," he said to Wade.

"It's okay. Alex already explained it."

"We'll tell them while they're here, but I didn't think this was the right setting."

"Of course. I understand," Wade said.

"Are you doing okay, son?" Neil asked, putting a hand on Wade's shoulder.

Wade looked a little startled. "As good as could be expected, I suppose," he said, but there was something sad and borderline angry in his eyes.

"May I ask you something?" Neil said.

"Sure," Wade said, and Alex took a step to move away, but Neil grabbed his arm to stop him without moving his other hand from Wade's shoulder.

"You're going to school?" Neil asked.

"That's right."

"I would like to help with that," Neil said, and Wade looked astonished before fresh anger clouded his countenance.

"I didn't come to meet you looking for a handout."

"I didn't think you had," Neil said. "But getting through school can be tough. I may not have been there for you up to this point. But I'm here now, and I want to help."

Wade turned to Alex. "Did you put him up to this?"

"I haven't said a word," Alex said, lifting his hands in the air.

"I'm your father, Wade," Neil said, "and I want to help. It's my moral obligation to help."

Wade countered, "Do you think that money is going to ease your conscience over screwing up my life?"

"No," Neil said without even a hint of defensiveness. "I would never expect it to." He stepped back and added, "You think about it, and we'll talk soon. It's good to see you again. I hope you'll keep in touch."

Neil walked away, and Wade watched him go before he made a frustrated noise and stuffed his hands in the back pockets of his jeans. Alex just said, "He paid off my student loans . . . anonymously. I was furious when I found out it was him. I thought he was trying to prove something. But he genuinely wanted to help me. That's not such a bad thing. He *is* your father."

Wade looked at him for a long moment then said, "It was nice meeting your wife and kids."

"Keep in touch," Alex said as he walked away, but Wade didn't respond.

Alex went back the way he'd come and found his father in the hallway some distance from the playroom. "You okay?" Alex asked.

"I don't know. It was good to see him; I'm glad he's made contact with you. I just hope I didn't blow it."

"You did just fine. He'll be back." Alex chuckled and added, "He likes the kids."

Back in the playroom they found Charlotte and Becca now playing with Katharine. They asked Alex questions about Barrett, and while the others waited in the playroom, he offered to take his sisters to see him, one at a time, once he was assured they had no sign of illness. Charlotte went first. After they'd washed up she followed Alex into the room, but they'd barely gotten through the door before Barrett started throwing up. Alex and Linda both rushed to help him, and thankfully the disaster missed the pajamas and bedding. Charlotte hung back while Alex soothed Barrett, but he was aware of his sister struggling quietly with emotion. He'd seen it before as friends and loved ones had come for a visit. And very few ever came back; they seemed to prefer keeping in touch from a distance. And that was fine. The reality was hard to face, and Alex knew it. He was grateful for Linda's calm efficiency, as well as her practical experience in such matters. Once the mess was cleaned up she slipped out of the room, saying she'd be close by. Alex sat close to Barrett and motioned Charlotte closer, saying, "Sorry about that."

"Does it happen often?" she asked, apparently horrified but composed.

"All the time," Alex said as if it were nothing. He then said to Barrett, "Look who came to see you. You remember your aunts. Remember how you told me that Becca smells good, and Charlotte likes to do puzzles?" His eyes showed recognition but looked weary. "This is Charlotte, and Becca's going to come and see you in a few minutes."

"He really said that?" Charlotte asked with a little laugh.

"He really did."

Charlotte spoke tenderly to Barrett. He focused on her but his eyes looked tired, and within a couple of minutes he fell asleep. Once Charlotte wasn't concerned about upsetting Barrett, she wept openly, and Alex couldn't hold back a couple of tears himself. He answered her questions about Barrett's present condition and couldn't deny being glad that his sisters had shown up. They'd shared an impulsive decision to make arrangements for their families and come in order to help give him and Jane a break. But Alex wondered if they had any idea that their father could use some family support, as well.

With Barrett settled into his bed, Alex escorted Charlotte back to the playroom and took Becca in to see her little nephew. Even though she only saw him sleeping and didn't observe the drama Charlotte had seen, she still wept and asked Alex all the same questions before Alex turned Barrett back over to Linda and they returned to the playroom. They visited for a few minutes with the others until Jane said, "Alex hasn't had any dinner."

"Then we should all go and get a little something," Neil announced. "It's on me."

Alex realized then that Jane had been in on the surprise, and that's why Susan had asked Linda to come and sit with Barrett, so they could all spend some time together. He was grateful she had. He didn't know what it was doing for her, but for him it was good to just be with his wife and Katharine to enjoy this visit with family.

They left the hospital together and visited over a simple supper out, then Jane insisted that she wanted to go back to the hospital and spend the night in Barrett's room, and Alex could take his sisters to the house and help them get settled. Since Jane and Susan had known they were coming, it had already been arranged for them to stay in Susan's home, and she was thrilled to have them. It was a much better option for them to stay there rather than at their father's house, since it was so much closer to the hospital.

Alex walked with Jane back to Barrett's room. The others had taken Katharine home with them. Once he made certain all was well, he left her with a kiss. "One of these days," he said, "we'll get to sleep in the same bed again."

"One of these days," she said.

Through the drive home Alex pondered the day's events and didn't have to wonder why he felt so exhausted. He arrived at the house to find that Neil and Roxanne had escorted his sisters inside. They were on familiar terms with Donald and Susan, with all the joint efforts they'd put into helping the family survive Barrett's illness. Susan had already guided the girls to a couple of guest rooms where they had deposited their luggage, and she was now getting Katharine to bed. Alex wondered if Neil and Roxanne would stick around to visit, but it quickly became evident they were leaving. He walked his father to the door, needing the answer to a question. He didn't even have to ask before Neil said quietly, "You tell them. I don't want to hear it."

"Oh, thanks a lot," Alex said with light sarcasm.

"You're a good kid," Neil said and gave him a hug.

Roxanne hugged him as well. "Let us know if we can do anything," she said, and they left.

Alex locked the door behind them and found his sisters sitting in the family room, their shoes kicked off, making themselves completely at home.

"Where's Preston?" Becca asked.

"Asleep. Susan takes good care of the kids. She's been a huge blessing."

"Do you think it would be okay if we help with them for a few days?" Charlotte asked. "We could take turns. Maybe Susan could use a break."

"Whatever you want to do is fine. I'll let you work it out with Susan. I just want the kids to be as comfortable as possible, but they're pretty adaptable—thank heaven."

"We could help with the cooking too," Becca said, "or do vigils at the hospital. We want to see Barrett some more when he's up to it."

"Whatever you can do will be great, but the hospital vigils can get ugly. Just be sure you can handle it because they don't appreciate whacked-out visitors."

"What do you mean?" Becca asked, and Charlotte told her about Barrett's episode when she'd been in the room. Alex felt the need to point out that what she'd seen had been mild in contrast to what was typical.

"We'll do whatever we can to help," Charlotte said firmly.

"Ask Jane what she needs. I just do my best to get my shifts in at work and make sure everybody stays as happy as possible."

"So . . . other than Barrett," Charlotte said, "is everything okay? You seem kind of tense."

"You've seemed uptight all evening," Becca added.

"Okay, well . . . so you've proven I can't put anything over on you."

"What's wrong?" Charlotte asked.

"Well, it's not really that anything is *wrong*," Alex said, glad to have the subject opened. He needed some sleep and didn't want to drag this out any longer than necessary. "It's just that . . . something has come up that's thrown us all for a loop—Dad especially."

"Okay," Becca drawled.

Charlotte added, "Don't keep us in suspense, little brother."

Hearing her say it that way, Alex realized that he'd said it to Wade the way he'd always heard his sisters say it to him.

"You know all about Dad's affair," Alex said, and they both looked surprised; obviously this wasn't what they'd expected.

"Of course," Becca said as Charlotte said, "Yes."

"Something's come out about that. Dad wanted me to call you, but I think he wanted to let it settle in a little more first. Perhaps it's better face-to-face. I consider it one more good reason for you to be here." Their expressions became more expectant, so he just hurried to say it. "Wade, the kid you met at the hospital. He's our brother."

They both made noises of disbelief, then assaulted him with questions. Alex put up his hands. "Hold on. I'll tell you the whole story . . . the brief version, anyway. And then I need to get some sleep. I have to work tomorrow. I'll bring you more up to speed later."

He went on to tell them how he'd felt prompted to go to their father's home, and the events that had ensued. He told them how Wade had found out, and a brief summary of Wade's state of mind, and their father's initial—and ongoing—struggle.

"I can't believe it," Charlotte said when Alex said that was basically it.

"Neither can I," Becca added.

Alex stood up and stretched. "Well, it is pretty tough to accept something like this. But the fact is that it's real and we're going to have to adjust. Wade is having trouble knowing who he is and where he belongs. He feels like his parents have lied to him, and his siblings don't know how to act around him anymore. I'm hoping that this side of his family can help him adjust and come to terms with it. That's all I have to say. I'm beat. It's good to have you here. I know I don't have to tell you to make yourselves at home."

"No, you don't," Charlotte said, and they both hugged him before he went to his own room and barely hit the pillow before he was asleep.

The following morning Alex called his father on a break to let him know he'd told his sisters. Neil was relieved, especially to hear that they took it well and hadn't seemed upset.

"While the girls are in town," Neil said, "I'd like to have everyone get together for a family dinner. Are you working Sunday?"

"I get off at three, I believe. That sounds great."

Neil was silent a moment, then asked, "Do you think Wade would come?"

"It certainly wouldn't hurt to ask. I'll see what I can do."

The next day Alex hadn't seen or heard from Wade, and he wondered if he should just try to find him. Pondering the matter, he felt good about calling Wade's mother to see if she knew anything about his class schedule. She didn't, but said Wade had a brother who occasionally met him for lunch on campus. She would ask and call him back. She called later that day to tell Alex the time and place that Wade should be coming out of a particular class. He promised to keep her informed if there was anything worth repeating, and she thanked him for his efforts on Wade's behalf.

Chapter 11

Alex was glad to have the next day off so that he could be at the right place at the right time. He leaned casually against the wall in the hallway where he couldn't possibly miss anyone walking out of the room where Wade was supposed to be. He was relieved to see Wade come out, and his stunned expression made Alex chuckle.

"How did you find me?" Wade asked.

"You didn't want to be found?"

"Not really."

"Well, I talked to your mother who talked to your brother— one of your *other* brothers." Alex reached into his jacket pocket. "Oh, that reminds me. I found something about me in a book, so I copied the page for you. I thought you might appreciate it."

"A medical journal, no doubt," Wade said, sounding facetiously bored.

"Not exactly," Alex said and unfolded the page before he held it in front of Wade's face. Alex thoroughly enjoyed the surprise in Wade's expression as he took in the typical Dr. Seuss artwork of a little family. Flying onto the page was a smiling little boy. At the bottom of the page it read, *That one is my other brother.* He waited for a reaction, wondering if Wade would be disgusted or indifferent. But he actually chuckled.

"It's from Barrett's favorite book," Alex said.

"Dr. Seuss must have been inspired. But I think that's *me* flying into the picture."

"Maybe. It works either way. Hang it on your wall or something."

"I might do that," Wade said, tucking the page into his backpack. "So, what do you need?"

"Dad wants to have a family dinner while our sisters are in town."

"They know?" Wade asked.

"They do now."

"And?"

"And . . . they were surprised, as we all were. But they're good with it. What do you say? Will you come to Sunday dinner? Everybody's going to be there except Barrett; well, and . . . obviously our sisters' families aren't here. They have husbands and kids. But we'll take it one step at a time."

Wade sighed loudly. He stared at the ground, then at the wall. Then at Alex. "Why?"

"Why what?"

"Why . . . are you all being so nice to me? Why . . . does it not seem like such a big deal to you people?"

"It *is* a big deal. That's why we want to help you through it. And . . . well . . . we're family. Please say you'll come; give it a shot. It would mean a lot to all of us, especially Dad."

"You talk about the family as if . . . they're really *my* family."

"They are. We are."

"It doesn't feel that way."

"Does the family you grew up with feel that way?"

"Not anymore."

"Well, I think that will get better with time as well. Say you'll come. Sunday at six, at Dad's house. It's casual. Just show up. Everyone promises to be nice, and Dad said he won't bring up anything to do with money."

Wade gave a dubious chuckle and conceded. "Okay, I'll be there."

"Great," Alex said with a laugh. "We'll look forward to it. Everything okay in the meantime? No . . . suicidal tendencies or anything?"

"Not this week," Wade said a little too seriously. "I did get a job."

"Great," Alex said again.

"It's not much, but it'll keep me from being thrown out in the streets."

"That's not a bad thing," Alex said. "I'm sure you have another class to get to. I'll see you Sunday. You know where to reach me in the meantime if you need anything."

When Sunday came it was difficult to leave Barrett at the hospital. Alex had to talk hard to get Jane to leave. They knew Barrett was in good hands, but he'd been extremely ill and struggling. The result had been a deepening of their weariness as parents, but especially for Jane, who spent far more time with Barrett than Alex did. Beyond that, they both hated the idea of having a family gathering without Barrett. Jane finally agreed to leave, but she was especially somber during the drive to Neil's home, even though Katharine and Preston were chattering happily in the back seat. Alex held her hand and kissed it more than once, but he couldn't think of anything to say that hadn't been said a thousand times.

They arrived a few minutes early to find everyone there but Wade. They all worked together to put the meal on while visiting with each other. Alex truly did enjoy having his sisters around, and he knew the time they'd spent with Jane and the kids the last few days had meant a great deal to all of them.

At twelve minutes after six Wade still hadn't arrived, and Alex began to feel nervous. Had he decided not to come? Or worse, was something wrong? Conversations of suicidal thoughts began spinning in his mind. At 6:18, Roxanne announced that they were ready to eat.

"Let's give it a couple more minutes," Alex said. But at six twenty-three, they decided to go ahead and be seated. Alex didn't want to share with the others what Wade had confided in him, about how deeply difficult this had been for him. But his uneasiness was worrisome. And it was even worse knowing that he had no idea how to contact him, or where to find him. They were about to offer the blessing on the food when the doorbell rang.

Alex jumped to his feet, offering to get it. His relief at seeing Wade was indescribable.

"You had me worried," he admitted, giving him a quick embrace.

"Sorry," Wade said. "I was studying and fell asleep."

"It'll do that to you," Alex said, silently offering a prayer of gratitude to know that his brother was safe—and apparently coping. "Come on in." He closed the door. "We were just about to say the blessing."

"You made it," Neil said with jubilance as they entered the dining room.

"Come sit down," Roxanne said, coming to her feet. She pressed a kiss to Wade's cheek and guided him to a chair at her side.

"Thank you," Wade said, visibly nervous as he took in the faces around the table.

Alex wasn't impressed with the way his sisters were trying too hard to accept Wade as their brother, but Wade's attention was quickly drawn to Katharine and Preston. He teased them both a little bit before Neil said, "Shall we bless it, then?"

Neil offered the prayer himself, expressing gratitude to be together as a family, and specifically to have Wade among them. He thanked God for bringing them together and prayed on Wade's behalf that he would find peace and healing. He then prayed for Barrett, that he would yet conquer this illness, and that they could work together as a family to get through this trial. After the amen was spoken, Alex saw Wade look directly at their father, and Neil returned his gaze. But there was no sign of anger or discomfort in Wade's eyes. Instead they expressed some level of appreciation, and perhaps even a hint of serenity. Alex concluded that they were making progress.

While they ate Wade was asked polite questions about himself. When he said that he was taking pre-med, everyone was clearly impressed, and a few jokes were made about the advantage of having doctors in the family.

"So, will you keep studying at the U?" Roxanne asked.

"I'm not sure. I need to decide a specialty before I finish up my undergraduate. That'll make a difference in where I go to medical school. I guess we'll see."

Charlotte said lightly, "If nothing else, you've found someone who can help you with your homework." She smiled toward Alex. "I remember drilling him with exam questions when he was doing pre-med at the U. The knee bone connected to the ankle bone and all that stuff."

Alex and Wade both let out a snigger at the same moment, but apparently everyone else had missed it. "What?" she demanded.

"You weren't paying attention when you drilled me on that stuff," Alex said. "There is no way you will ever find an ankle connected to a knee without something significant in between."

"Is that what I said?" she asked and laughed. "Oh, well. That's why I'm an interior decorator."

"Stick with curtains, sis," Alex said.

They continued bantering back and forth, mixing memories with reports of what was happening in the present. They all finished eating but stayed at the table visiting, except for Katharine and Preston, who went to the toy room to play. Charlotte and Becca both talked about their husbands and children, then the conversation was directed again at Wade.

"So," Becca asked him, "is there a girl in your life?"

"Not at the moment," Wade said. "I don't find much time for dating."

"Don't harass the kid," Alex said. "I hardly dated at all through college, and I turned out okay."

"Eventually," Charlotte said. "Thanks to Jane. You were positively horrible until she pulled you out of the gutter."

"I won't argue with that," Alex said, winking at his wife.

"You know," Becca said, motioning across the table where Alex and Wade were seated side by side, "the two of you really look like brothers."

"We do not!" Alex said, sounding comically insulted. "Wade's much better looking than I am. He looks like Dad. Besides, I look like my mother's great-grandfather. And there's a painting of him at my house to prove it."

"I'd like to see that," Becca said.

"So would I," Jane interjected, sounding surprised.

"It's in the attic," Alex said to his wife. Then to his sisters, "You're dreaming. We don't look like brothers."

"No, I can see it too," Charlotte said. "Maybe it's because you both have beards at the moment, or . . ."

"They wear their hair a lot the same," Becca added.

Wade and Alex exchanged a comical glance as the sisters went back and forth.

"Look how their beard line is the same on their faces."

"Yes, it is. And there's something about . . . their mannerisms. The way they talk."

"Well," Charlotte concluded, "you may have different features, but you still look like brothers. You *act* like brothers."

"You know," Roxanne said, "I saw this program on TV once where twins who had been separated at birth were brought back together, and it was amazing how they did so many things the same." She immediately added, "I agree with your sisters. The two of you look a great deal like brothers."

"Well," Wade said, "if he would shave and get a haircut, and stop trying to imitate me, we could keep that a secret." His sarcasm became evident when he added facetiously, "I can understand though why you *would* want to imitate me, with me being such a cool guy and all."

"I stopped shaving first, little brother," Alex said with the same humor. "Who is imitating whom? And don't forget that I'm *already* a doctor. Besides, you should know by now there's no keeping a secret around here."

Wade's voice became more serious. "So, if I had been born into this family, do you think I would have known all along I was the misbegotten brat?"

Following a moment of tense silence Alex said, "Are we all supposed to feel shocked or uncomfortable to hear you say something like that over the dinner table?"

Wade glanced around. "Obviously you are."

Alex felt Jane take his hand beneath the table, as if to offer silent support in an awkward moment. He returned her tight squeeze and attempted to discern what might really be going on. He hurried to say the first thought that occurred to him. "Or maybe you're just uncomfortable with all of this and you want to put us on the same level."

Wade shot him a gaze that betrayed the accuracy of the statement. Alex returned his stare boldly, watching Wade's anger diffuse into something more humble as he admitted, "Maybe I am."

"Would you prefer that we not talk about all of this so openly?" Alex asked, his tone clearly expressing genuine concern.

Wade sighed and shifted in his chair. "If you want to know the truth, I appreciate the way you talk about it. And it's nice to sit here and not feel like you're ashamed of me. I guess I'm just . . . trying to get used to all of this, and . . . I guess I'm not so uncomfortable with having it in the open, as I can't help wondering why you all seem okay with it. Why are you treating me like a brother, when the siblings I grew up with are . . . angry with me or something, like it was my fault?"

Neil leaned his elbows on the table and said gently, "My children have known all along about the indiscretions of my past. It's not such a shock to discover something's wet when you already knew there was a flood. For you—and obviously for your siblings—this is a shock. And it just takes a human being a certain amount of time to adjust to shock."

Wade sighed loudly. "So it's the fact that it was kept a secret that's the problem."

"Perhaps," Neil said, "but at what point do you tell a child something like this about himself? It's a bit different from being taught that you're adopted. At what age does a child understand something like this? Would it have been easier when you were a child? A teenager? Not likely. I'm not saying that keeping you ignorant was necessarily the right approach—or the wrong one—but it is a sensitive situation."

Wade looked thoughtful but said nothing. Charlotte asked her father, "Why do you suppose Wade's mother never told you?"

"That's what I'd like to know," Wade said, as if he found validation in having someone else bring it up.

"I've wondered about that myself," Neil said.

Wade seemed suddenly uncomfortable and said, "You people really don't need to sit here and listen to me whine about my life. It's not a requirement of suddenly finding out I'm your brother."

"I was thinking of it more as moral support," Becca said, and Charlotte made a noise of agreement.

Roxanne said, "But if you would prefer more privacy . . ."

"It's not that," Wade said. "I'm getting used to this 'everybody knows everything.' But I'm not prone to enjoyable conversation these days."

"It's okay," Alex said. "Just say what you need to say."

Again Wade sighed. "I think I can understand why my mother didn't tell me. I mean . . . you're right. When do you tell a kid something like that? But at the same time, my not knowing . . . and then knowing . . . has been tough. And I have to wonder why she didn't tell you." He looked at Neil.

"Maybe you should ask her," Alex suggested.

"I'm not sure I can even have a civil conversation with her at this point," Wade admitted.

"You mustn't blame her for this," Neil said.

Wade was only slightly curt as he countered, "And if I don't blame her, would that mean I blame you?" Before Neil could answer Wade added, "As I see it, she and you are equally to blame, because the fact stands. You are my parents."

"Yes, we are," Neil said. "And I wish I could even begin to understand, let alone express, all the thoughts I've had churning over that since I discovered your existence. When your mother left me, Wade, she left impulsively. It was like she woke up one day and realized how big a mistake she had made. Brad had never filed for a divorce because he kept trying to convince her to come back. I guess he finally got through to her. Obviously I never heard from her again. I did hear through the grapevine that she had found her way back into the Church, and she was doing well. For me, the

road from that point was ugly. Through the course of my relationship with your mother, the idea of consequences never entered my
mind. Then one day they knocked me flat on my backside. At first
I tried to attribute my regret to religious teachings that had incited
me to feel guilty. But I soon realized the emotional results of my
ugly choices were simply a matter of cause and effect. Finding my
way back to a place where I could even look at myself in the mirror
and not shudder was more difficult than I could ever tell you. But
even then, I believed that it was only me I had hurt. I somehow
deluded myself into thinking that my family had been better off in
my absence, that I had done them a favor. And I convinced myself
that Marilyn had made her own choices, and they had nothing to
do with me. Little by little, through the years, I've uncovered the
damage. It's like sifting through the wreckage of a tornado that
flattened your home and left your loved ones bruised and broken.
It hasn't been so many years since I thought I'd finally put the last
piece back together." He looked at Alex. "Being forgiven by my
son was one of the happiest days of my life. And I came to believe
that it had been put to rest at last."

"And then I showed up," Wade said.

"Yes, that certainly threw a cog in the wheel for both of us,
didn't it? And all of the pain and regret has washed back over me,
again and again. In spite of the excruciating struggles I'd endured
to come to terms with all of this, it wasn't until recently that I
finally grasped the reasons why *this* sin is often compared to
murder in its grievousness."

Alex noticed Wade straighten his back and take a deep breath
while he watched Neil intently.

"When murder is committed, a life is taken, and it can never
be given back. In this case, a life was created, and it can never be
undone. The power to create life should be taken very seriously,
and should only be used within the bonds of marriage. When it's
treated so lightly these days, especially in the media, it makes me
sick. The world has no idea what it's messing with, and the damage
that can be done with such attitudes. Few people know better than

you or I, Wade, how devastating the results can be." Neil's gaze intensified, and he leaned father forward. "But the paradox in all of this is that I cannot bring myself to regret that you exist. How can I look at you and not feel some . . . measure of gratitude to know that you are my son?"

Alex sensed Wade feeling unsettled as he looked down and folded his arms over his chest. Alex put a hand on his shoulder, but nothing was said for several moments until Wade spoke without looking up. "You know one thing that's really tough for me? I *hate* having my existence put in the same sentences with words like sin, and ugly, and regret. How am I supposed to believe that being born into this world was a good thing when nobody can talk about it without . . . guilt coming up all the time? Convince me that my existence is condoned by God, while the means by which I was conceived is not."

Alex felt the helpless anguish in the question at the same moment Jane squeezed his hand tightly and Neil met his eyes with a silent plea. But what was he supposed to say? He wanted to know when he'd gotten the job of supposedly having all the answers. And could there be an adequate answer to such a question? Whatever words Alex might be able to come up with would never appease the hole in Wade's aching spirit. Through an ongoing silence, the only possible answer came to his mind. He doubted it would sink in at the moment, but he simply had to say, "We are all children of God, Wade. In the grand scheme of things, it's all that really matters."

Wade turned to look at Alex, his eyes betraying the same doubt that had hovered there since they'd met. His voice held no bitterness when he spoke; it was sadder, more resigned. "When I get to the other side of the veil, Alex, I'm certain the grand scheme of things will have meaning for me. But right now I'm trying to cope in *this* world, and I'm having a hard time knowing how to fit myself into two families."

Charlotte suggested, "Just try to think of it like a divorce."

"But there wasn't a divorce because there was never a marriage," Wade said. "I realize that's the only possible way for me to find some point of reference to work from, but even that doesn't cover the bases." He looked around. "If this is making anyone uncomfortable, feel free to say so . . . or get up and leave. You won't offend me."

Roxanne said gently, "We didn't invite you here to just chat and laugh and pretend that everything's okay when it isn't. This is far from the first challenge that's ever come up in this family. We've had many dinner-table conversations about Barrett's leukemia, just to name one. It may not be pleasant to talk about. None of us likes to dwell on it, but his illness is real and it's not going to go away by pretending. We believe in sharing our burdens as a family."

Wade made no response. Charlotte said, "May I ask you something, Wade?"

"Of course."

"Did your parents ever treat you any differently from the other children? Did you ever feel, even subtly, a different attitude?"

"Never," Wade said firmly.

"Well, I think that's amazing," Charlotte said. "Obviously the man who raised you has a great love for you *and* your mother."

Wade looked puzzled, frustrated. His voice expressed it when he said, "You know what? I can't talk about this anymore. Maybe I should just go and—"

Alex put a hand on his arm to stop him from standing. "And maybe you should stay, and we'll change the subject. I think we've had enough brutally honest and thought-provoking conversation for one night."

"Agreed," Neil said. "Let's get these dishes washed, and we'll have some fun."

Everyone stood up and started carrying dishes to the kitchen. Wade picked up what he could carry and whispered to Alex, "What would define fun in this family?"

"I guess you'll have to stick around and find out."

"Yippee," Wade said with sarcasm. Alex just chuckled and followed him into the kitchen.

Wade asked Roxanne what he could do to help, but she insisted that he didn't need to. "Alex, why don't you take him downstairs, and we'll catch up with you."

"Yes, Mother," he said facetiously, and she winked at him. "Come along, little brother," he said to Wade, who followed him down a carpeted stairway to the basement. A small TV room was at the bottom of the stairs, and directly off of it was the toy room where Katharine and Preston were playing. Alex checked to make sure they were behaving themselves, then he led Wade into the game room and flipped on the light.

"Whoa," Wade said as he entered. The room was huge and painted in bright colors. At one end was a semi-circle of seating formed by couches and a couple of recliners, along with some beanbag chairs. A genuine jukebox filled one corner and looked dwarfed by the presence of a pool table, an air-hockey table, and a ping-pong table.

"All kinds of possible fun," Alex said. "So, what's your game of preference, little brother?"

"Are you challenging me to a duel?"

"Maybe."

"I'll try my hand at air hockey."

Alex chuckled. "You'll lose." He flipped the switch to turn the game on and tossed the plastic puck into the middle of the table.

They played for a few minutes with Alex definitely taking the advantage. He'd spent many hours playing this game with his father, intermixed with long conversations. While they slid the puck back and forth over a layer of air, Wade asked, "How long has it been since you reconciled with your father?"

"Our father, you mean."

"Our father," he corrected.

"It was just before I married Jane, and that would be about ten months before Barrett was born."

"Ten months, eh?"

"I was in my thirties when we got married. We were running out of time."

Wade nodded, and then returned to his purpose. "Not so many years, then."

"Nope."

"It's hard to imagine the two of you being angry with each other."

Alex chuckled. "Not for me it's not. Being angry with him was a deeply ingrained habit that wasn't easy to break."

"But you did it."

"Yes, I did it."

"How?" Wade asked.

Alex sunk another point and put his hands on his hips. "Why do you want to know?" he asked, but Wade said nothing. "Are you angry with him?"

"Not as angry as I feel toward my parents. At least he didn't lie to me."

"Do you really think they lied to you?"

"Okay, so they omitted the truth. It comes down to the same thing. How did you do it?"

"Are you sure you're ready to hear the answer?"

"Try me."

"I've told you before, and obviously you didn't get it. But I'll say it again. I forgave him, Wade." Alex saw anger flare in Wade's eyes, and he added, "When you're ready to talk about it without wanting to bite somebody's head off, you let me know."

"I'll do that," Wade said and tossed the puck back onto the table. The subject was dropped.

A few minutes later the family all came downstairs and gathered for a game of Pictionary. With a white board attached to one wall, they divided into two teams, the men against the women, with Roxanne being the referee and watching out for the children. Wade's mood lightened as the game picked up in momentum. He teased Alex about being a terrible artist, but gave both him and their father a jubilant high five when they won the game. Alex enjoyed seeing this side of Wade, and he could tell that his father did too.

They all went back to the kitchen for dessert, where Roxanne had left a fondue pot of chocolate melting. She produced fresh strawberries that had been washed and were ready to dip. Alex liked the way Jane laughed when he fed her a chocolate-dipped strawberry. It was good to hear her laugh. She fed one to him but pretended to lose her balance as it got close to his mouth, and she smeared chocolate around his lips. He laughed as he grabbed her wrist and guided the strawberry into his mouth, then he pulled her close and tried to kiss her. She squirmed away and ran, laughing as he chased her around the living area with everyone laughing and cheering him on. He finally pinned her on the couch and pressed a kiss on her lips, getting more chocolate on her face than he had on his own. She laughed and tried to protest; then their kiss became momentarily tender, and she reached her arms around his shoulders.

"Okay, none of that," Neil called in mock anger.

Alex laughed as he stood and took Jane's hand to help her up. Everyone's attention went elsewhere, so Alex kissed her again before he attempted to wipe away the chocolate from around her lips with his fingers. He was surprised to see tears form in her eyes when a moment ago she'd been laughing.

"What is it?" he asked softly. A tear fell, and he caught it with a finger that didn't have chocolate on it.

"I love you, Alex," she said, then wrapped her arms around him. "I miss you. I miss having a normal life."

"I know," he said, holding her close. "Me too. We just have to take these moments of normalcy when we can get them."

She looked up at him. "I guess we won't be sleeping in the same bed tonight."

"Do we ever?" he asked, wishing he could give her the answer she wanted to hear. "But it could probably be arranged."

"It's a nice thought," she said, "but I need to be with Barrett, and you have to work early."

"Yeah," Alex groaned, knowing it was *very* early. He hugged her again and glanced toward the kitchen end of the large living area to see that everyone else was distracted there, except for Wade, who was discreetly watching them. When their eyes met, Alex couldn't miss his concern.

Later when good-byes had been said and Alex walked Wade out to his car, Wade said in a quiet voice, "Is Jane okay?"

"Not really, no."

"It's more than just Barrett," he said, and Alex wondered if he was always so perceptive.

"Her father died very suddenly, not so long ago. Since the day Preston was born she's spent her life going back and forth to the hospital, either to be with Barrett or to take him in for chemo. She's exhausted and scared."

"And so are you."

"Yes, well . . . maybe I'm not quite as fragile as my wife right now."

"Or maybe you can't afford to be." Wade opened the door to his car. "Who will hold everyone together if you fall apart, big brother?"

Alex couldn't even respond to that without doing exactly as he'd suggested—fall apart.

"Thank you," Wade added. "It was nice."

"Glad you could make it," Alex said, and Wade got into the car. "Call me," he added just before Wade closed the door and drove away.

The following afternoon Alex was on duty when three teenaged boys were brought in from a car accident. Thankfully it wasn't serious. One had a broken leg and needed surgery to have it set. Another needed several stitches on his forehead, and the third had a nasty gash on his lower arm. They were all bruised and scraped up a little, but nothing they wouldn't recover from. Alex was always grateful to see a favorable outcome, especially when he'd seen so many cases of death, or altered lives, as the result of carelessness on the road. In this case, the hardest part was usually calming the shaken parents who had been called to come and give permission for the medical procedures to take place. When Alex was told that the kid with the bleeding forehead had a mother who had signed the papers, he went to that particular exam room to take care of the stitches. The kid was lying back on the table, holding a piece of gauze over the wound. He looked like he'd just gotten past that major high-school growth spurt that made him look more like a man than a boy.

"How you doing, kid?" Alex asked, sitting on a stool and rolling it toward him.

"I've got a headache," the kid said.

"Well, at least you'll recover," Alex said, snapping gloves onto his hands. "Which is more than we can say for that shirt. It is now evidence of the fact that head wounds bleed profusely."

"Yeah, my mom will appreciate that," the kid said, and Alex chuckled.

"What's your name?"

"Brian," he said.

"Okay, Brian. Let me have a look." Alex lifted the gauze and said, "I need to inject some anesthetic here. That's the only part that'll hurt worse than the headache."

"Great," Brian said with sarcasm.

Alex gave him the shot, then pressed a clean piece of gauze over the wound while they waited. It continued to bleed, though not too badly. He was just about to begin the stitches when Brian's mother was brought into the room.

"Are you okay?" she asked, rushing to the other side of the table where Brian was laying.

"I'm fine," he said.

"Is he really?" the woman asked while Alex focused on his work.

"Absolutely," Alex said. "I got a wound much like this myself once. As you can see I recovered nicely. He just needs about twelve or fifteen stitches here, but the possibility of scarring should be pretty minimal."

"What happened?" the mother asked, taking her son's hand.

Brian gave a brief explanation of the accident scenario: his friend had been driving, and someone else had been ticketed for not yielding the right of way. The mother expressed her gratitude that no one had been seriously hurt, while Alex took careful stitches, and Brian kept his eyes closed, showing no evidence of pain.

"How did you get a wound like this?" Brian asked Alex, as if he couldn't stand the silence.

"Some idiot in a truck ran a four-way stop. Totaled my Ferrari," he added with mock sorrow, and then he chuckled to make it clear he didn't really care about that. "I got a mild concussion and some pretty stitches much like these. My fiancée was in a coma for ten weeks, however."

"Is she okay?" the mother asked.

"Oh, yeah," Alex said. "We have three kids now."

"Oh, that's nice," she said.

"You totaled your Ferrari?" Brian asked as if that were far more tragic than a coma.

"I'm afraid so. But that's okay. Eventually I learned there was more to life than a hot car."

"I don't know about that," Brian said facetiously.

Chapter 12

When Alex finished the stitches, he cleaned around the wound once more then said, "There now. He's much better off than that shirt. Hope you're like my mom—good at getting stains out."

"Not necessarily," she said. "But we'll give it a try. Thank you, Doctor. Is there anything else we should be concerned about?"

"No," Alex said, "he's fine. He should probably take it easy for the rest of the day and not be doing anything too strenuous for a few days. He's going to be pretty sore—besides the stitches. But I think he can wash dishes and take out the garbage in a day or two." He stripped the gloves off his hands and tossed them into the trash, and then he scribbled on a prescription pad. "I'm giving him just a few pain pills to get through the first couple of days, then Tylenol or ibuprofen should be fine."

"Thank you," she said again, taking the prescription from him.

Alex helped Brian sit up and asked, "You okay?"

"Yeah, I'm fine," Brian said and moved toward the door, seeming steady on his feet.

"Can you make it to the waiting room, honey?" his mother asked him.

"Sure."

"I just want to ask the doctor a couple of questions, and then I'll be out."

Brian waved as if he understood, and then he headed out. Alex was well accustomed to having people use an emergency room visit as an excuse to have other concerns addressed. And he was fine with that, as long as it remained reasonable. He'd gotten very good at knowing when to stand up and move toward the door.

"Forgive me, Doctor," she said, "but . . . I just have to ask . . . do you think he's telling the truth about the accident?"

"As far as I know," Alex said, "but you'd have to see the police report to verify that."

She nodded then said, "The prescription . . . it isn't anything he could become addicted to, is it?"

"No," he said firmly. "At least not with that amount. I never write out more than I think a patient reasonably needs, for that very reason." Alex sensed that her concern was much deeper than she was letting on. He felt compelled to ask, "Are you concerned about drug addiction?"

He saw her tear up and steeled himself for another common side effect of emergency medicine. Some people, when faced with any degree of trauma, often confused the doctor for some kind of counselor and began to pour out their troubles. Again Alex had learned the balance of listening, being compassionate, and not allowing it to get out of hand. "I don't think so," she said. "Right now I'm just . . . concerned. He's become very distant lately. We've had a bit of drama at our house, and . . . well, I'm just concerned."

"There are many places to get information on such things," he said. "I would suggest learning all you can about the signs and ways that a parent can help, and then just do the best you can." He stood up and moved toward the door, stopping when she looked at his ID badge, then at his face, while her eyes widened as if she'd encountered the devil himself.

"You're Dr. Keane?"

"That's right," he said, wondering if she had encountered him here before and perhaps not liked the outcome of something that had happened to someone she cared about.

"You're Neil Keane's son?" she asked, incredulous.

"That's right," he said again.

"You told me you worked at the hospital, but . . . you're a doctor? The same Dr. Keane who called to tell me that my son was fine?"

As the connection settled in, Alex felt a little unsteady and put a hand on the nearby counter. "This is a little too weird to chalk up to coincidence," he said.

Her tears increased. "How you must hate me!"

"And why would you think that?" he asked, leaning against the counter and folding his arms over his chest.

"How could you not? I tore your family apart."

"Sister Morrison," he said, noting that she looked old and tired. The years had been hard on her. It was no wonder he didn't recognize her. He'd not seen her since he was thirteen and she'd attended the same ward.

"Please, just call me Marilyn," she said.

"Okay, Marilyn. My father made that choice, and I forgave him a long time ago. The present circumstances have nothing to do with me beyond my hope that I can help Wade get through this."

"Have you seen him . . . since we talked? I've prayed so hard for him, to know if he was truly okay."

"I saw him yesterday."

"Where?" she asked eagerly, her concern evident.

"He had dinner with us at my father's home."

She appeared shaken by that and moved to a chair. "I see," she said. "And was he well?"

"He seemed fine; he seemed the way he has since I met him."

"And how's that?"

"Like he's struggling with feelings of anger and grief, and he doesn't know who he is or where he belongs."

Marilyn squeezed her eyes closed with a self-punishing grimace, and tears slid down her face. "Do you suppose he'll trade his old family for a new one, then? That would certainly be better than no family at all, but . . ."

"We're not trying to replace your family in his life, Marilyn. We're simply trying to give him a place among us. I would think that with time he can find a comfortable place in both families."

"Do you think that's possible?" she asked as if he had all the answers. And he truly wished that he did.

"Anything is possible," he said.

She gave a wan smile. "I'm glad that he has you in his life, Doctor."

"Please . . . call me Alex. And I think my being in his life was an answer to prayers on Wade's behalf. Most likely yours. We didn't know at the time there was anything wrong."

"And perhaps our being able to talk now is an answer to prayers as well," she said and came to her feet. "Thank you for your time, Alex. And for caring about my son."

"He's my brother, too," Alex said. She nodded, silently expressing mixed feelings on that count.

"You'll watch out for him?"

"I'll do the best I can." He handed her his card. "Call me if you have any concerns, and I'll let you know if anything changes."

"Thank you," she said and left the room.

"Wait," he said, following after her. "Do you know where he lives?"

"Yes, but . . . he told me to stay out of his life. I haven't wanted to go there. I felt it was better to honor that and give him some time."

"It probably is, but . . . he hasn't told *me* to stay out of his life. Maybe I could drop in and let him know that I met his brother today."

She smiled slightly then told him where the apartment building was located, and which number Wade lived in. Since the ER was fairly slow, he walked her out to the waiting room where Brian was sitting with his eyes closed. When he opened them, Alex saw no resemblance to Wade, but he did see the same anger in his eyes. Apparently he too had felt betrayed by his mother.

"Put some ice on that when you get home," Alex said to him.

"Thanks, Doc," Brian said and followed his mother outside.

While traffic remained minimal in the ER, Alex called Jane to tell her what had happened. She was amazed and felt certain that prayers were being heard. She said that perhaps it was good for Alex and Marilyn simply to meet face-to-face in order to best help Wade.

"So are you going to see him?" she asked.

"I'm going to try. I don't know his schedule, but I think I'll go as soon as I get off and give it a try. A prayer that he'll be there wouldn't hurt."

"I'll do that," she said.

Alex had no trouble finding Wade's apartment. It was close to the U, and therefore only a few minutes from the hospital. He felt that maybe his prayers—and Jane's—were being heard when he spotted Wade's car in the parking lot. He climbed the stairs to the second floor, found the right door, and knocked on it. Wade pulled it open then scowled. "How do you do this?"

"Would you believe I'm psychic?"

"No."

"May I come in?" Alex asked.

"I suppose," Wade said with sarcasm, but with a light edge that led Alex to believe he wasn't entirely disappointed to see him here. "So, what's up? Another dinner invitation?"

"You have an open invitation at either my house, or our father's, I believe—provided someone's home. That's how it works with family."

"Is it?" Wade asked as Alex sat down on an old, fairly tacky couch. The place was small but relatively tidy. Wade obviously lived alone. More and more he reminded Alex of himself at that age. "So, did you just come to chat, or what?"

"I came to tell you that your brother was in a car accident today."

"What happened?" he demanded, panicked.

"He's fine."

"Which brother?"

"Brian," he said.

"How do you know? Did my mom call you or—"

"I stitched up his head," Alex said. "And I didn't know it was him until he'd gone out to the waiting room and your mother saw my ID badge. I think she nearly fainted. I told her I'd let you know about Brian. She's worried about him. Apparently anger is running rampant in the family. Maybe he'd be less angry if his brother came home once in a while. Maybe your example could help your siblings come to terms with this."

Wade made a scoffing noise. "My example is not going to have anything to do with coming to terms, Alex. At this point, the only thing they're going to get from me is more anger. It would be better if I stayed away."

"Okay, have it your way," Alex said. "I'm just the messenger."

He glanced around and noticed that the decor was most prominently African, a result of his serving a mission there, no doubt. Alex's eye was drawn to a framed photo of a younger Wade surrounded by a beautiful African family, and they were all wearing white.

"Baptism day?" Alex asked, pointing at it.

"Yeah," Wade said with a little smile.

Alex then noticed, taped to the wall, the copy he'd given Wade from the Dr. Seuss book. "Fancy artwork there," he said.

"It has sentimental value," Wade said.

"Really?" Alex asked, sounding ridiculously impressed.

"Did you want to . . . to just chat, or what?"

"Sure, why not?"

"I think we pretty much covered the bases yesterday."

"I think there was a lot said yesterday that could be hard to swallow. Why don't you tell me how you're feeling?"

Wade sighed, sounding annoyed at having it brought up. "The same. How do you expect me to feel? I had a good time last night, but I left with the same old feeling. I just . . . don't know who I am anymore. I don't know where I belong."

"Okay, I can give you that."

"I have no point of reference in this, Alex. Is there a support group for illegitimate Mormon boys who were brought up under false pretenses?"

"Not likely," Alex said. "But I'm certain there are a lot of Mormons out there who are struggling with similar feelings. The world is full of divorces and adoptions and poor choices, Wade. And Mormons are not exempt from that. You're far from the only person walking the earth who wasn't born under conventional circumstances. If people only came to this world under planned situations, there would be a heck of a lot less people."

"Well, sometimes I think it would be better if there was one less particular person walking the earth. And don't ask me to expound on that; don't ask me if I really mean it. I'm fine. I just . . . need some time. Change the subject or leave."

"Okay," Alex said, wishing he didn't feel horribly uneasy. "How's school?"

"The term ended. Look, I really need to be alone. I appreciate your coming by. I'll be in touch."

Alex gave Wade a hard look for a long moment, then stood up. "Okay," he said and moved toward the door. "Call me if you need anything."

"I'll do that," Wade said.

Alex drove away feeling deeply concerned for his brother but completely helpless to do anything about it.

* * * * *

Over the next few days, Barrett's condition showed no improvement, and the shadows in Jane's eyes darkened. While Alex contended with a growing dread on behalf of his wife and son, he couldn't rid himself of an equivalent dread in regard to Wade. He asked himself a hundred times if he should go and try to talk to him again, but something held him back.

It was nice having his sisters in town, and difficult to see them leave. He wished that they'd had more time to spend together, but it had still been good to see them. Apparently they had a marvelous time getting to know Susan better than they ever had before, since they were staying in her home. Susan was their cousin too, but it was Alex who had introduced them to each other. When Charlotte and Becca were telling him good-bye, he was surprised to hear that Susan had taken them to the attic to show them the painting of Alexander Barrett. They teased him about how much they looked alike.

"At least without that beard," Charlotte said.

"Still," Becca insisted, "you and Wade look like brothers. It's unmistakable. Maybe not in pictures side by side, but seeing the two of you talk and interact, you're definitely brothers."

Alex was completely fine with that. He only wished that Wade could be.

* * * * *

On the second day of a three-day stretch with shifts beginning at three A.M. Alex found himself on the helicopter pad at dawn as Life Flight arrived with a five-year-old boy who had been in a car accident with his mother. The mother had received only minor injuries, but the point of impact had left the child critical. Alex did his best to remain detached and not think of his own son as he fought with everything he had to save this little boy. But how could he *not* think of Barrett? At least with this kid he knew what to do to help him. Still, in the end, the child died. And Alex felt furious. Helpless, and lost, and crumbling with fear and grief. And just downright furious. He declared the time of death and hurried to the staff lounge, grateful to find himself there alone. He sank into a chair and pushed his hands into his hair, wondering if he should scream or sob.

The door opened, and he looked up to see Ray Baker. He wondered if they commonly got put on the same shifts because the ER director knew they worked well together, or if everyone here knew that Baker was close enough to Alex to keep him from going over the edge.

"You okay?" Baker asked.

"No, to be truthful."

"That was a tough one."

"Yeah," Alex said with a cynical edge to his voice, "but at least he died quickly. Once that car hit him he didn't feel a thing. Better than *torturing* a child within an inch of his life—quite literally."

"It's not going well, I take it," Baker said, sitting across from Alex.

Alex sighed and again pushed his hands into his hair, tugging at it fiercely. "There's still no evidence that the graft is taking. They keep pumping him full of everything they can to keep him alive, but . . . if it doesn't take hold soon . . ." He couldn't finish.

"Is there anything I can do?"

"Yeah, you can tell the parents that their kid just died. I can't do it. I'll lose it."

"Okay," Baker said. "Anything else?"

"No, thank you," Alex said. "I just need a few minutes."

Baker pressed a hand briefly over Alex's shoulder and left the room. Alex slumped back in the chair and groaned, wanting to just curl up and die himself. Life was just too blasted hard! But ten minutes later he had to talk himself into slithering back into the ER to make himself available for whatever might come through the doors.

Hours later he was glad to know that his shift was drawing to an end, even though it meant sitting helplessly at Barrett's bedside in order to help him each time he threw up. He kept glancing at the clock, feeling anxious and unsettled without understanding why. He was getting ready to take a few stitches in the forehead of a guy who had run into a cupboard door, when Baker came into the room. In a voice that was quiet and forcibly calm he said, "I'll take this. You need to go." Alex met his eyes, feeling panic grip his heart. Baker added firmly, "Barrett's on his way to PICU. Something's gone wrong; I don't know what. Hurry."

Alex ran every step while his mind filed through the possibilities of what could have happened. How could he not think of how Andie had died unexpectedly when rushing her to the pediatric intensive care unit hadn't been quick enough? The dread and terror that consumed him were indescribable. A nurse let him immediately into the secured area, apparently having been warned that he was on his way. He turned a corner to see Jane sitting on the floor, her back against the wall, hugging her knees, her head down.

"What happened?" he demanded, and her head shot up.

"I don't know," she cried, and she'd obviously been crying a great deal. "He just . . . he just . . . couldn't breathe, and . . . I can't go in there . . . I can't watch."

Alex helped her to her feet and held her close for a long moment, then took her shoulders firmly. "You wait here. I need to find out what's going on." She nodded, and he went into the room, then he almost wished that he hadn't. Barrett was surrounded by so many people he could hardly see the child. Alex knew this kind of scene well. This was trauma. Hands were working furiously; communication was going back and forth. And Alex was usually in the middle of it, often giving the orders and making the decisions. He understood the terms they were using, knew what they were doing. And he knew why. At least he knew the technical reasons for such procedures. But the reasons for Barrett's little body to suddenly crash remained somewhat of a mystery. He stood with a hand over his mouth, forcing himself to hold back, pacing an imaginary three-foot line, waiting for some evidence that Barrett was stable. He wondered if this was how it would end. Would he have no chance to even tell Barrett good-bye? He thought of the child he'd tried desperately to save earlier today and wondered if Barrett was doomed to join him. Then suddenly all was calm. For a split second he feared they'd given up, that it was too late, then he focused on the equipment that showed clear evidence of Barrett's heartbeat, breathing, and blood pressure.

A doctor Alex had never met before, who was mostly respon-sible for just saving Barrett's life, turned to see Alex standing there. He introduced himself and concluded from the scrubs Alex wore and his ID badge that he was a doctor. Alex was grateful, as he often was, to be told in straightforward medical terms what was taking place. He thanked the doctor, and then went out in the hall to find Jane there. She met his eyes and said, "He's dead, isn't he."

"No," Alex said quickly, "they've stabilized him." He put his arms around her and let her cry. When she'd calmed down he explained to her the different things that had seemed to go wrong all at once. Barrett had been put into an induced coma, and a ventilator was helping him breathe. He was receiving new drugs, and transfusions of blood and platelets.

Jane listened and wiped stray tears, finally saying, "This is the complications version, then."

"Yeah, this is it," Alex said.

She drew a deep breath. "Okay, well . . . you know what they say. Faith in every footstep." He watched her pull her shoulders back, lift her chin in a courageous gesture, and walk into the room where Barrett had almost died minutes earlier. Only one nurse was there now, meticulously checking the tubes and equipment overwhelming Barrett's little body. Jane stopped in her tracks at what she saw, and Alex was right behind her, holding her arms with his hands, attempting to lend some silent support. She turned her back to Barrett and pressed her face to Alex's chest, crying again until she found new courage and moved tentatively to his bedside.

Alex hated the memories that assaulted him of Jane spending ten weeks in a coma. He hated the sounds of the equipment and the helplessness that washed over him in new abundance. He concluded, however, that there was one silver lining to this. "At least he's not suffering at the moment. A coma isn't such a bad place to be when you're as sick as he's been."

Jane didn't comment. She just held Alex's hand as if he could save her. He wished that he could, but he felt increasingly doubtful that he had the strength to spare his family from becoming a casualty of this war that was raging.

"What if he doesn't come out of this, Alex?" she asked. "What if he never breathes on his own again?"

Alex could only wrap her in his arms and mutter quietly, "I can't answer that question, Jane. We can only pray that he does."

Neil and Roxanne arrived soon after Alex called them. Alex was grateful for Neil's offer to help give Barrett a blessing. As upset as he felt, Alex was only too glad to have his father be the mouthpiece. He felt a deep relief to hear a promise that Barrett would be shielded from any further suffering related to this illness. The way it was worded did not imply that he would be released from suffering, as in death, but rather protected from it. He was also told that the strength of his spirit would bless many lives while he remained upon the earth. Of course, no one knew how long that would be exactly, but it was still a nice promise.

Neil and Roxanne didn't stay long, but it was nice to feel their love and support. After they left, Alex and Jane sat together in Barrett's room until he insisted she go home. The sound of the ventilator breathing for Barrett, combined with the grueling silence of his parents having nothing to say to each other, threatened to send him over the edge. Alex told Jane he would stay with Barrett until he needed to go to work, and she should just come in the morning when she felt up to it. Having Barrett in a coma put an entirely different dynamic on their need to be with him, and he wanted Jane to get some rest and a little distance from the horror of waiting and wondering.

Nothing changed with Barrett through the hours that Alex stayed near him, drifting in and out of sleep in the recliner, while memories of Jane being in a coma littered his dreams and memories. He hated having to leave in the middle of the night to fill his shift, but knew that Barrett was in good hands with the nurse who was assigned only to care for Barrett.

Through all of this Alex had gained a deep respect for the nursing staff at this hospital. For the most part they were compassionate and kind, and they worked hard to soothe the pain—both emotional and physical—for both patients and parents. As a doctor, Alex had learned years ago the value of those gifted in the nursing profession, men and women alike who seemed to always have the right thing to say. Even if a doctor might have the answers, a nurse was often required to interpret and assuage the fears and concerns. He didn't even want to think where he would be without them, both personally and professionally.

The hours of his shift dragged. Jane called from Barrett's room to let him know she was there and nothing had changed. After getting off work in the middle of the afternoon, Alex went to see Barrett and was told that Jane had just left for home a few minutes earlier. He sat there for a short while, watching his son cling to life, praying with a weary intensity that this child's life would be spared. He also prayed for Wade, unable to rid himself of an ongoing uneasiness on his brother's behalf. He just didn't know what to do about it.

Alex felt suddenly restless and unable to just sit there. He felt like he needed to leave and hoped that his instincts were not somehow drawing him away from Barrett as some kind of preparation for Barrett no longer needing him. He couldn't even entertain the idea as he got into the car and headed toward home.

He'd not gone far when his cell phone rang. He already had the hands-free set in place, as he always did when he drove. He glanced at the caller ID but didn't recognize the number, so he answered with the standard, "This is Dr. Keane."

"Alex?" a woman's voice said, sounding panicked.

"Yes."

"This is Marilyn Morrison. I hope you won't think me strange, but . . . I'll get straight to the point. I have the most uneasy feeling about Wade."

"Okay," Alex said in a tone that encouraged her to go on, while his own recent feelings all came back to him.

"I've been trying to figure out if I'm just being neurotic or something, but . . . I just can't shake this feeling. I've wondered if I should go to his place, even though he's told me to stay away."

Alex didn't wait any longer before he pulled an abrupt U-turn and headed toward Wade's apartment.

"I felt better about calling you," she said. "I can't say any more than that. I'm just . . . asking if there's any possible way for you to check on him."

"I'm on my way," Alex said, and he could tell she was crying.

"You'll let me know?"

"Of course," he said and ended the call.

Traffic flowed so smoothly, along with hitting every light green, that Alex began to wonder what circumstance might await that required him to get there quickly. He felt sick with dread as memo-

ries of prior conversations blended into his own ongoing concerns
for Wade. He'd prayed every day that he would be prompted and
guided to help his brother, and he felt sure that Marilyn had been
doing the same. He wanted to think that her prompting was
nothing, but instinctively he believed something was truly wrong.

Alex prayed as he drove and unclipped the phone wire and
tossed it into the passenger seat, stuffing the phone in his pocket
just before he pulled into the parking lot of the apartment
building. He took the outside stairs three at a time. Seeing Wade's
car let him know that he was likely home. While he prayed for
guidance he knocked at the door and got no response. He
pounded and listened. Then pounded again.

"Open the door, Wade!" he shouted. Still nothing. He tried the
knob and found it locked. Alex didn't even have to think about it
before he took hold of the doorframe with both hands, and the
lock broke beneath his shoe. Obviously the deadbolt hadn't been
locked. He heard African music playing from the other room and
wondered if that was why Wade might not have heard him. He
wondered if his breaking down the door was going to make him
look like a fool. He glanced in the kitchen and bedroom and
found nothing but a CD player with the volume fairly high. Seeing
the bathroom door slightly ajar, Alex pushed it open just as the
sound of heaving sobs overpowered the music. Then he saw the
blood.

Alex held his breath, grateful for the sound of Wade's crying
that let him know he was alive and breathing. Between the music
and the tears Wade obviously hadn't heard him come in. But what
Alex saw shoved his heart into his throat. Wade was sitting on the
floor, his back against the side of the tub, his head hanging in
consummate despair. His elbows were set on his knees. His right
hand was gripping his left forearm. And from his left wrist, blood
was dripping onto the floor. His bare feet were flat on the floor
with blood pooling around them. And in the midst of the hideous
puddle lay a box cutter.

"What are you doing?" Alex shouted, resisting the urge to curse.

Wade shot his head up, so completely startled that he let out a gaspy scream before he started sobbing harder, barely able to say, "What are you doing here?"

"Saving your life, apparently," Alex growled and grabbed a washcloth, going to his knees beside Wade. He grabbed his arm and pressed the cloth over the wound, wrapping his hand tightly around the wrist and holding it firmly while he elevated the hand. He reached for a towel with his other hand and tossed it over the puddle to cover the gruesome sight, if not to soak it up.

"What are you doing?" Alex repeated, unable to keep anger out of his voice.

"I . . . don't know. I just . . . I just . . ." Wade was crying so hard he couldn't put a sentence together. He kept his head down, refusing to look at Alex.

"You couldn't call me?" Alex shouted.

"I . . .was . . . I was . . . going to, but . . ."

"But what?" he snapped. "Look at me and tell me why you would do something like this!" Wade just shook his head and cried. Alex leaned toward him and took hold of his hair, lifting his head, forcing Wade to face him. "How *dare* you do something like this to me!"

Wade's confusion was evident, but his crying had calmed down enough that he could speak intelligibly. "To *you?*"

"You'd better believe it. Do you have any idea how much effort I put into *saving* lives? I would have *never* gotten over this. *Never!*"

"You barely know me."

Alex yanked gently on his hair, resisting the urge to knock him across the side of the head. "You're my *brother!*" Again he resisted cursing. Alex let go of his hair and wrapped an arm around his neck, pressing their foreheads together. "You're my brother," he repeated, his voice husky.

Wade sobbed and took hold of Alex with the hand that wasn't being held with applied pressure.

"Do you have any idea how precious life is, Wade?"

"My life is *nothing!*" Wade cried. "Nothing but a *lie!*"

"Your life is *real.* Do you hear me? It's doesn't matter what choices your parents made. *God* gave you this life, and no one has the right to take it away but God. And obviously God wants you to live."

Wade drew back, looking startled. "What . . . do you mean?"

"I'm here, aren't I?"

Wade looked perplexed, and stunned, and completely overwrought. Then he pressed his head to Alex's shoulder and cried like a baby. Alex shifted from his knees to sit on the floor while he kept his hand clamped tightly over Wade's wrist, glad to note that very little blood was soaking through the washcloth. He kept his arm tightly around Wade, who poured out unfathomable anguish, holding to Alex with his free hand as if he might drown otherwise.

"I don't want to die," he muttered in the midst of his tears. "I just . . . I just . . . don't want to feel like this anymore. I didn't know any other way to stop feeling like this."

"Only Satan would tell you that you have no options beyond self-destruction, Wade. There are *always* options."

He waited for Wade to calm down before he peeked at the wound on his wrist to find that the bleeding had slowed down but hadn't stopped. He pressed Wade's free hand over it to replace his own before he stood up and looked in the cabinet and the medicine chest.

"You got any gauze or anything around here?"

"Probably not."

Alex went into the kitchen and found a drawer with towels in it. He found a large, lightweight dishtowel, then he noticed that a simple floral pattern was embroidered in one corner. Obviously it had some value. But he reasoned that the blood could be soaked out, and it was the only one the right size and weight to do the job. Returning to the bathroom he knelt on the floor and replaced the blood-soaked washcloth with the towel folded and wrapped tightly around his wrist, with the ends tied together firmly right over the wound.

"Did you steal this from your mother?" Alex asked lightly, pointing out the embroidered flowers.

"Actually, she gave it to me."

"Well, she'll be glad to know it was put to good use. Obviously you haven't washed a dish in about three weeks. No wonder you're depressed. Do you do anything besides sit around and feel sorry for yourself when you're not at work?"

"Actually, I lost my job."

"Again?" Alex asked but didn't wait for an answer. "Come on," he said, helping Wade to his feet with a firm grip on his arm. "Let's get you cleaned up and get out of here."

"Where are we going?" he asked, panicked.

"I need to stitch that up. Obviously I can't do it here. Be glad I didn't have to call 911 and have the whole neighborhood knowing what you tried to do to yourself."

As Wade looked down at the towel on the floor, saturated with blood, and the red spattering on his clothes, his expression took on a measure of horror and repulsion. With no warning he dropped to his knees by the toilet and threw up.

"Yeah, I know what you mean," Alex said and sat on the edge of the tub and waited until Wade's stomach was empty and the heaving had subsided. Wade sat down hard on the floor and Alex handed him a clean washcloth that he'd moistened with cool water. Wade pressed it to his face and attempted to catch his breath. Alex handed him a little paper cup with mouthwash in it then walked out of the room, saying, "Where might I find some clean clothes? Or is the laundry in the same condition as the dishes?"

"The stuff in the basket on the bedroom floor is all clean," Wade called back after Alex turned off the CD player.

Wade followed him into the bedroom, and Alex tossed him a wrinkled pair of jeans, noting that he looked pale and a little unsteady. While he was changing his clothes, Alex used his cell phone to call Jane.

"Something's come up," was all he said, knowing Wade could hear him. "I'll be a while yet. I didn't want you to worry."

"Okay," she said. "Did you see Barrett?"

"I did. They told me you'd left just before I got there."

"Yeah," she said, her voice strained, "I couldn't sit there any longer."

"It's okay," he said gently. "I felt the same way. He knows you love him. You don't have to be there every minute; you can't. *We* can't."

"I'm going back to spend the night," she said. "But I needed some time with Katharine and Preston."

Alex knew that meant she needed some time with happy, healthy children. "I understand," he said. "I'll get home as soon as I can."

"Is something wrong?"

"Yes."

"What?" she demanded. "Where are you?" She would have known he wasn't with Barrett or he wouldn't have used the cell phone.

"I'm at Wade's place."

"What happened?"

"I'll talk to you later," he said casually.

"He's close by, and you can't say," she guessed.

"That's right."

"Is he okay?"

"In a manner of speaking. You relax and take it easy. I'll see you when I get there."

"Okay. I love you, Alex."

"I love you too, babe."

He hung up and found Wade dressed in jeans, a dark T-shirt, and a long-sleeved shirt unbuttoned over it like a jacket. The unfastened cuffs of the sleeves covered his bandaged wrist to some degree. On his feet he wore flip-flops.

"You ready?"

"I suppose," he said, and they walked to the front door.

When Wade noticed the evidence of his apartment being broken into, Alex just shrugged and said, "I'll pay to fix it. I think the deadbolt will still work."

Wade took nothing with him but his keys, easily locking the deadbolt of the door as they left. Alex noted that Wade seemed a little unsteady on his feet, which he suspected was more from some level of shock than the actual loss of blood. In truth, he really hadn't lost much more than if he'd gone to the Red Cross to make a donation. But Alex wasn't about to tell him that at the rate he'd been bleeding it would have taken a while for him to die. Alex wanted him to believe that he'd been at death's door, and he hoped it scared him out of his mind. Still, if something hadn't been done, he *would* have died, and the thought made Alex feel downright sick. If the blood in the wrist had started to clot, which it likely would have, would he have cut deeper, tried something else? It was more his state of mind that concerned Alex.

He took hold of Wade's arm to help him walk, noting that he looked a little queasy. "You okay? You're not going to puke again, are you?"

"No, I'm fine."

Once Alex had helped Wade into the passenger seat, he said, "I need to make another quick call. I'll just be a minute."

With Wade inside the car, Alex stepped a few feet away and turned his back to call Marilyn.

"Hello?" she answered after half a ring. "Is that you, Alex?" She'd obviously been watching the caller ID.

"It is," he said. "And Wade is fine. But he wouldn't have been."

"What?" she insisted. "Tell me."

"Are you sitting down?"

"No, just tell me."

"Sit down."

"Okay, I'm sitting down."

"He cut one of his wrists."

Marilyn whimpered. "No. I can't believe it."

"I'm afraid it's true. He's going to be fine, physically at least."

"You're a doctor," she said tearfully. "You knew what to do."

"Well," he drawled, "I don't think it takes a rocket scientist to apply pressure to a bleeding wound. But I don't freak out at the sight of blood like some people do."

"Thank you, Alex."

"I'm glad you called me. I'm *very* glad you called me. He's pretty much stopped bleeding, but I'm taking him to the hospital to stitch it up."

"And then what? What if he tries it again?"

"I'm still working on that. I'll keep you informed. I promise."

"Thank you," she said again.

Alex put the phone in his pocket and got into the car.

"Who was that?" Wade asked.

"Your mother."

Wade became immediately angry. "You did *not* have to call her and tell her about this!"

"Yes, actually, I did," Alex said with underlying fury. "I'm not the one who was prompted to come and save your life, kid. Your mother called me and asked if I'd check on you. Maybe you should call her and thank her for caring enough to pray for you every hour of the day. Maybe you should thank her for being the kind of woman who lives close to the Spirit and respects its promptings."

Wade made a scoffing noise that provoked Alex's fury to the surface, even before he added, "She committed adultery, Alex."

Alex quickly checked the blind spot to his right then swerved the car to the curb, screeching it to a halt. He slammed it into park and turned hard eyes on his brother. "What are you saying? That her sin automatically makes her a bad person eternally?"

"The consequences are obviously eternal."

"But the sin is not. When are you going to figure out the difference?"

"When are *you* going to figure out that you have absolutely no idea how I feel?"

"You're right. I don't. I always knew who my father was. I always *knew* that he'd cheated on my mother and left us high and dry. And I wasted half my life over it. When are *you* going to grow up enough to realize that their choices are irrelevant to your life now? When are you going to be man enough to act like a man and face the truth? It's up to *you* to take what you've been given and do something about it. The path before you is yours. What are you going to do with it, Wade? Live your life as an angry derelict, unemployed and living in squalor? Or will you make the most of what you've got and realize that when it comes right down to it you have much to be grateful for?"

"Like what?" Wade snapped and Alex resisted the urge to just belt him in the jaw.

"Like people who love you and care about you enough to save you from your own stupidity. The prompting your mother got this afternoon was no small thing. She's a good woman, Wade. And I think you'd better be careful about the judgment you're throwing around. Go ahead and cast a stone, kid. As I see it, you're now guilty of attempted murder. Put that in your self-righteous edicts."

Wade squeezed his eyes closed and turned away as if he'd been slapped. Then he pressed his right hand over his eyes and started to cry. Alex sighed and put his arms around Wade, which made him cry harder.

"Maybe you would have been better off with somebody a little more tender and compassionate right now," Alex said.

"And maybe you're the only one who isn't afraid to tell me the truth."

Alex tightened his hold. "Sometimes the truth can be tough to hear. I've been there, you know, having someone who loved me telling me truth that hurt. Maybe this isn't a good time for that."

"And maybe you're right. Maybe it's time I grew up and started acting like a man."

Alex glanced down and noticed blood soaking through the towel tied around Wade's wrist. "I need to get this stitched up," he said and tousled Wade's hair as if he were a kid. He put the car into drive and eased back onto the road while Wade found a couple of napkins in the glove box and got his crying under control.

"I've never cried so much in my life."

"That's not such a bad thing."

Wade made a dubious noise and added, "And I can't believe you sat there with me while I was puking."

"And bleeding," Alex pointed out. "I'm a doctor, Wade. It's not a big deal—the puking anyway. I do have an aversion to watching people bleed, especially people I care about."

"You see people puking often?"

"You have no idea. I can't even count the times that patients have puked in front of me, around me, *on* me. It's just part of the job."

"Maybe I should consider a change in my education."

"Maybe you should work on staying alive long enough to finish your education."

While the drive was completed in silence, Alex's mind wandered through what had just happened. Then he thought of Barrett, and he felt angry all over again. He fought to keep it from showing, and then he wondered if it was just as well that Wade knew how he felt. Maybe it *was* necessary for him to hear the truth—however difficult it might be.

Chapter 13

At the hospital Alex walked through the automatic glass doors with Wade at his side. Wade kept his left hand tucked inside the open front of his outer shirt. A nurse looked up and said to Alex, "You're back." She glanced at the blood on his scrubs that wouldn't have been there when he left.

"My brother here had a little accident. I need a suture kit along with the usual. And of course, the paperwork."

"You got it," she said, and Alex led Wade into an empty exam room.

Alex pulled sterile gloves onto his hands, and the nurse brought what he'd asked for, setting it down before she left and closed the door behind her.

"Sit on the chair, and put your arm up on the table," Alex said tersely.

"You sound ticked off again."

"Yeah, I am." He untied the towel and peeled it off the wound to see that it was still bleeding, but only a little. "I'm tempted to do it without anesthetic, just so you'll remember the pain."

"You wouldn't, would you?"

"No," Alex said and immediately stuck a needle in to deaden the area.

Wade winced and scowled at Alex. "Are you always so gentle?" he asked with sarcasm.

"No, for you I'll be especially gentle." He dropped the needle into the sharps container and added, "I'll be back in a minute. Try to behave yourself."

Alex closed the door behind him and went to the desk, saying quietly to one of the girls there that he knew well, "Hey, could you get me some information on the recommendations we give with a suicide attempt?" Her eyes widened, and he added, "Confidentially, please."

"Of course," she said.

"Thank you," he muttered and returned to find Wade just as he'd left him. They waited in silence for the anesthetic to take effect, while Alex kept gauze pressed over the wound.

"I don't understand why you're so ticked off," Wade said.

"Well then, let me explain it to you. Do you have any idea of the effort and the anguish that is going into saving my son's life?" Wade looked stunned but said nothing. "And you have the *gall* to even *think* that you have the right to bring death into this family."

"I don't know how you can say we're family when we've only known each other for what? A few minutes?"

"Or forever. I don't know how you can say that we're *not* family when we share the same blood—blood that you're so eager to spill all over the floor. Do you have any idea how many people would have suffered over this? Do you know how many people love you, are praying for you day and night? Do you have any idea how losing you would affect those people? Your kid brother, for instance."

Wade looked away, his expression sour. "Yeah, you think about that long and hard, little brother. And while you're thinking about it, you tell me how I'm supposed to let you out of my sight without being terrified that you'll try it again."

"I won't try it again."

"Convince me," Alex said, but Wade remained silent. "Do I have to take you home with me? Hire a nanny?"

"Now you're just being stupid."

"You started this stupid thing, kid. What's it gonna be next? Pills? A bullet?"

"No."

"Convince me."

Still Wade had no apparent response. Alex remained silent while he stitched up the wound, and Wade watched closely, as if he might be pondering some kind of symbolism in seeing his mutilation being repaired. Alex wrapped the wrist and tugged the sleeve of Wade's shirt down to cover it.

"I hope it leaves a scar," Alex said and snapped the gloves off, tossing them into the trash.

"Thanks," Wade said with sarcasm.

"You need some counseling," Alex added without preface. "I can't talk you out of these feelings, Wade. Right now you're scared and you say you don't want to die . . . that you won't try it again. But what happens when those feelings come back? More powerful next time."

"I don't know," Wade admitted. "I don't know what to say, Alex. You're probably right. I do need counseling; I need something. I can't go on this way. Something's got to give one way or another."

Alex sighed. "Okay, well . . . tomorrow we'll see what we can figure out. Tonight you're coming home with me."

"That's really not necessary."

"Convince me."

"I can't."

"Then you're coming home with me."

On their way out, Alex was handed a large manila envelope with a wink and a smile.

"Thank you," he said and winked back.

In the car Alex broke the silence by saying, "You know why I feel so angry?"

"Why?"

"You scared me. I'm angry with you the same way I would be angry with Barrett if he ran into the street."

Wade sighed then asked, "How is Barrett?"

Alex felt a different kind of sickness envelop him as his thoughts went to his son. It took him a minute to reply. "Not doing well, I'm afraid."

"Why, what's wrong?" Wade asked, panicked.

Even as Alex tried to think of answering, a surge of grief grabbed his anger and shoved it down his throat. He attempted to quell the grief that was demanding to be heard, well aware that Wade was waiting for an answer and was clearly concerned over the silence. Alex knew he only made the tension worse when he put a hand over his mouth to stop the trembling of his lower lip.

"Alex?" Wade demanded.

"Um," Alex croaked, "he's . . . in PICU . . . for reasons I'm not going to get into right now. We almost lost him. He's in an induced coma and breathing with a ventilator. Besides that . . . the bone marrow graft isn't taking. He's getting worse, not better. If something doesn't change soon, then . . ." He couldn't even consider finishing that sentence.

Wade said nothing for a couple of minutes, then a quiet, "I'm sorry, Alex. I'm sorry for what I just did. I'm sorry for being another burden in your life. Most of all, I'm sorry about Barrett. It's just not fair."

"No, it's not."

Nothing more was said until Alex turned onto the street where he lived. "You're not a burden in my life," he muttered and pulled into the driveway.

Wade gave him a long stare, and then looked up at the house. "This is where you *live?*"

"It is," he said. "But don't go getting all impressed. We're living with my cousin and her husband. We had a fire in our house just before we found out Barrett was sick."

Wade looked surprised. "A fire? Boy, you've had more than your fair share of trials, haven't you? A fire. Barrett. And me."

"Don't even go for trying to be a martyr about this," Alex said. "I'm *grateful* you came into my life. *Losing* you would be a trial, Wade." Wade just opened the car door, and Alex snarled, "And that would bring us right back to where we started." As they walked through the front door, Alex added, "Oh, and . . . be warned. We don't keep secrets around here."

Wade scowled, and Alex closed the door. Little footsteps came running, and Preston jumped into Alex's arms with a fit of giggles that couldn't help but make him laugh.

"There's my little buddy," he said and kissed his cheek loudly, tossing aside the large envelope he was holding. "What have you been doing today?"

"We go to woomut."

Alex chuckled, then said to Wade, "That's Wal-Mart."

"Oh, of course," Wade said.

"Mommy make peanutter sammies."

"That's wonderful," he said and added to Wade, "That's peanut butter sandwiches."

"I caught that one," Wade said.

Preston looked at Wade, and Alex said, "That's Uncle Wade."

"Wade," Preston said with a crooked smile, then he held up two fingers. "I two."

"Wow!" Wade said with exaggerated excitement.

"We just had a birthday, didn't we," Alex said.

Preston scrambled down and ran away as fast as he'd appeared, calling over his shoulder, "I see Too Stoowy."

"Toy Story," Wade said to Alex.

"Very good." He pointed at him. "Pediatrics."

With subtle sarcasm he replied, "Right now I think I'll stick with suicide prevention."

Alex put a hand on his shoulder. "Good plan."

Wade followed Alex down the hall, saying, "This is a really great house."

"Yes, it is. I'll give you a tour later." They entered the room where *Toy Story* was playing on the television, and Jane was relaxing in a recliner, with her feet up. Preston and Katharine were playing close by with a variety of toys scattered around them. For a long moment Alex paused and pondered the weariness of Jane's countenance and the hollow look in her eyes that had become so familiar. He felt the crack in his heart growing wider and quickly forced reality away, fearing he might crumble irreparably right here and now.

"Hi," he said, alerting Jane to his presence.

"Hi," she said with a careworn smile, reaching her hand toward him. He took her hand and bent to kiss her, lingering over the connection as if it might give them a brief oasis of oneness in the midst of all the nightmares.

Katharine noticed her father and came to greet him with a hug and a kiss. She said hi to Wade, then returned to her playing.

"Is everything okay?" Jane asked.

Alex motioned toward Wade. "As you can see, my brother is still alive."

"Good," she said skeptically, tossing a smile at Wade as if she thought the statement was meant to infer some kind of humor. "Is this supposed to be . . . a revelation, or something?"

"Maybe," Alex said and grabbed Wade's arm, ignoring his attempt to resist as he lifted it to Jane's view and pushed the sleeve back. Jane gasped, and Alex said, "Can you imagine? He thought that dying was a better option than being my brother." He tossed Wade's arm out of his grasp. He moved toward the hall, adding, "Come on. Let's see if there's anything to eat."

Jane followed them into the kitchen, saying, "Susan left some soup on the stove. There are rolls to go with it. They went to the temple."

"Okay, thank you," Alex said and opened a cupboard to get some bowls out. To Jane he asked, "Have you eaten?"

"Yes," she said with something timid in her voice that made him look at her. She looked downright terrified of him. Was his anger so evident?

"What's wrong?" she asked.

"What's wrong?" he echoed, making her wince visibly. But something irrepressible rushed out of him, and he couldn't hold it back. "My son is *dying!*" he shouted and slammed the cupboard door closed. Jane winced again, and the terror in her eyes deepened. "And there is *nothing* I can do about it." He kicked the chair closest to him. It fell on its side and slid across the floor. "I can save *him!*" Alex motioned to Wade, who was leaning against the wall, staring at the floor. "But he doesn't *want* to live! His *mother* wants her son to live, just like *you* do. So, who gets what they want when all is said and done? And in the meantime, how is a human being supposed to *choose* between death and torture? Whether it's physical or emotional, it's still torture, and it's *not fair!* What should we do? Flip a coin? Tails you die; heads you suffer! Even then, it would be nice to make a choice and have it stick! Funny how I can wish that my son had just been smashed in a car. At least it would have been quick and easy. But no, he's one of the lucky ones. If you're really lucky, you get to suffer and *then* you die!"

Alex stopped shouting long enough to realize that tears were running down Jane's face. Wade was staring at him fiercely, wearing an anger that matched his own. Alex hurried from the room, not certain where he was going until he ended up in the attic, just sitting on an old trunk, staring at the portrait of Alexander Barrett, as if it might somehow give him the answers or the strength to keep up this juggling act of life and death, anger and grief—and fear.

* * * * *

Jane watched her husband leave the room and turned to meet Wade's eyes. For a long moment it was evident that neither of them knew what to say, but it was also evident they both shared the same concerns.

"Maybe I should just go," Wade said while she wiped at her tears.

Jane wasn't certain what made her suddenly able to reach beyond her own habitual pain to see a bigger picture, but she felt instinctively concerned for Wade, as if letting him go right now wasn't right. She also felt concerned for Alex and believed that Wade might be able to reach past whatever had just happened better than she could. Either way, she felt more prone to facing Alex in numbers.

"No, I think that would only make things worse," she said. "You can't leave without at least talking to him."

"I don't know that he'd appreciate what I want to say right now."

Jane took Wade's arm into her hand, guiding him out of the kitchen. "Maybe he needs to hear it. Either way, you're not leaving hungry, and you're not eating without Alex."

Jane didn't even have to wonder where he'd gone. She'd long ago picked up on his habit of going to the attic for a few minutes here and there, even though she'd never actually been up there herself.

Alex heard footsteps coming up the wooden steps but couldn't find the motivation to move. He glanced their way just long enough to be assured that it was both his wife and his brother. While he was expecting some kind of outburst or reprimand, Jane said, "That's incredible."

"What?" he asked and turned to see her staring at the portrait.

"You look just like him."

"Who is it?" Wade asked, as if the previous exchange hadn't taken place.

"It's my great-great-grandfather," Alex said. "The man who built this house."

"Your namesake," Jane said tenderly.

Alex stood up and covered the portrait as he always did when he left the room. He wanted to leave, but Wade and Jane were between him and the door, making it clear by their expressions that the conversation they'd started downstairs wasn't over.

"There's something I need to say," Wade said.

"Okay."

"You're obviously pretty upset."

"Yeah, I am," Alex said, not willing to try to hide the fact.

"If you're so ticked off at me," Wade insisted, "why don't you just hit me or something and get it over with? But don't yell at your wife. And don't blame me for crap in your life that has nothing to do with me. You just told me that I'm not a burden in your life, and I'd really like to believe that, because . . ." His voice broke and his chin quivered. His anger melted into humility. "Quite frankly . . . you're the only person in my life that I really feel like I can trust. But I know things are tough for you right now. You've been good to me, Alex, and the last thing I want is to bring more grief into your life. I didn't do this to get attention or create havoc. I know I need help; I'm willing to admit that. But maybe I need to go elsewhere to get it, and give you some time with your son."

Alex blew out a long, harsh breath. Needing a minute to quiet his churning emotions, he moved past them and down the stairs, saying over his shoulder, "Let's eat. I'm starving."

They followed him to the kitchen where the tension hovered like London fog. Alex picked up the chair he'd kicked and set his hands firmly on its back. "Forgive me for my anger," he said quietly. "I was angry before your mother called me, Wade, so yes . . . much of it has nothing to do with you."

"But some of it does, I know," Wade said. "And maybe I needed to know that." Their eyes met, and Wade added intently, "You really do care what happens to me, don't you? It's not just . . . some . . . obligation or . . . duty . . . because you know I'm your brother."

"Yeah," Alex said, "I really do care."

"Okay, but . . . maybe . . . my being here isn't the answer. You need to be with Barrett."

Alex sighed loudly and turned to Jane, who was still visibly upset. He held out a hand for her, and she came into his arms, where he held her tightly. "There's nothing we can do for Barrett right now but wait and pray," Alex said. "I'm certainly not going to baby-sit you, but I can help you figure out some options. I have tomorrow off. We'll see what we can do."

Jane eased back and looked up at Alex, her eyes letting him know that she understood his anger even before he said, "Forgive me."

"It's okay," she said, touching his face. "It was a lot easier to pick up the chair than it was to clean up the glass I threw at the wall yesterday." Alex felt his eyes widen, and she added, "I know exactly how you feel, Alex."

He hugged her again. "I know you do. Seeing you suffer is almost as hard as seeing Barrett suffer."

"And vice versa," she said, then she drew away and turned to Wade. "Come and eat. You guys must be hungry."

She moved to the stove to ladle soup into two bowls while Alex crossed the room and took Wade into a brotherly embrace. "It's going to be okay, little brother," he muttered. "We're going to get through this." Wade just nodded, too emotional to speak.

Alex was grateful for the way Jane gracefully guided them to the table and began talking of trivial things, ushering the mood into some semblance of normalcy. She left the room to check on the kids and came back with the manila envelope that Alex had left in the entry hall.

"Is this yours?" she asked, tossing it onto the table.

"Yes, thank you." He opened it and pulled out a small stack of papers. Glancing through them he saw standard information sheets provided by the hospital with suicide crisis numbers, local organizations available for help, and basic information to help loved ones handle the problem. There were also some pages printed off the Internet with more details of some local counseling options. He made a mental note to express his appreciation to the young woman who had gone the extra mile. Perhaps some chocolate wouldn't hurt, either. He knew she loved chocolate.

"What's that?" Wade asked. "You got it at the hospital." Alex slid all of the papers across the table except for the one he was reading. "Oh, I see," he said.

"Did you get enough to eat?" Alex asked.

"Yes, thank you. Tell your cousin she's a marvelous cook."

"You can tell her yourself. She'll be home in a while." He stood up and added, "Come here. I want to show you something."

Wade followed him down the hall, bringing the papers with him. Alex led him into the study where a huge hardwood desk had been built right into the room. He didn't bother explaining to Wade the significance of this room for him personally. Perhaps another time. He just motioned toward the computer and said, "Maybe you could get on the Internet and see if you can find some information that might help. What you've got in your hand might be a place to start." He motioned to the other side of the room where there were bookshelves and an old leather sofa. "Make yourself at home. There's a bathroom across the hall. I'm going to spend some time with my wife before she goes back to the hospital, and once I've got the kids to bed, we'll talk. Okay?"

"Okay," Wade said. "Thank you."

"It's not a problem. Are you all right for the moment?"

"Yeah, I'm fine. Thanks."

Alex left Wade there and found Jane upstairs bathing Preston, while Katharine was supposed to be picking up toys in her room. He told the child if she did a good job they'd have time for a story before bed. She grinned and increased her speed. He went into the bathroom and closed the toilet lid to sit there while Jane bent over the bathtub, rinsing shampoo out of Preston's hair while he kicked in the water and giggled.

"You okay?" she asked without looking at Alex.

"I'm coping for the moment. How about you?"

"The same." She lifted Preston into a big towel and handed him to Alex while she drained the tub and tidied the bathroom a bit. Then he followed her into Preston's room where she found his pajamas while he dried Preston and put a diaper on him. Jane handed the pajamas to him and said, "Do you want to tell me what happened?"

Alex sighed. "I stopped to see Barrett, but felt restless, like I was needed somewhere else. I was driving when Marilyn called me, said she had a horrible feeling about Wade. But she'd felt more like it was right to call me, rather than checking on him herself. I turned around and went to his apartment. He didn't answer so I kicked the lock in and found him in the bathroom. He'd cut his wrist and was sitting there crying like a baby, bleeding all over the floor."

"That's horrible," Jane said breathlessly.

"Yes, it is." He finished snapping Preston's pajamas and set him free. He ran toward his favorite toys and began to play.

"But you knew what to do."

"It didn't take much effort to get the bleeding under control. Fortunately he's not well educated on how to *really* slit a wrist. I took him to the hospital and stitched it up." He shook his head. "I just can't fathom what kind of pain would make a person feel that desperate. I've been through some tough things, but I never felt remotely tempted to end my own life. It scared me, Jane. But I'm afraid he saw a lot more anger than fear."

"Like he said in the kitchen, he knows you care."

"I guess. I just hope I wasn't too hard on him."

"I'm grateful you found him," she said.

"I'm grateful Marilyn called me."

"You let her know?"

"Yeah, just briefly. But she knows he's okay."

"So, now what?"

"We need to get him some help. He's not in school and he lost his job again, so I'm thinking we need to get some inpatient care. Something full-time, for a few days at least, to help him get to the core of the problem and learn some coping skills. I know Dad will pay for it."

"Have you told him?"

"Not yet. I need to call him."

Jane kissed him quickly. "Why don't you do that while I bathe Katharine."

"Why don't you let me bathe Katharine while you go to the hospital."

"Thanks, but . . . I need a few minutes with her. I'll go back when they're in bed. You deal with your brother right now."

"Okay," he said. "Thank you." She walked toward the door, and he added, "Jane." She turned back. "You're a good mother. These kids couldn't ask for better, and I'm grateful."

He saw something tender in her eyes before they filled with tears, then she hurried into Katharine's room. Alex took Preston and his toys with him to the bedroom he shared with Jane, where he found a cordless phone. He dialed his father's number, praying he would be home. Roxanne answered, then asked if everything was all right.

"Barrett's the same," he said. "But Wade's having some challenges. I'll let Dad tell you."

"Okay, I'll get him."

"Thank you."

"Alex," Neil said into the phone. "What's up?"

"I'll get straight to the point," Alex said, "as long as you're sitting down."

"I am," Neil said with concern.

"Wade tried to kill himself today." Only silence followed, and Alex finally said, "Dad, are you with me?"

"Yeah," he said, barely audible. "What happened?"

Alex repeated the story, bringing it to the conclusion, "I'm going to see that he gets some help. We're looking into the options. I have tomorrow off, and I'll do whatever it takes. But you have to pay for it."

"I'm glad to do it," Neil said. "I only wish any amount of money would take away his pain."

"And what about *your* pain?" Alex asked. Neil said nothing, and he added, "You feel responsible, don't you."

"Yes, I do."

"Well, you can't. Your part in this is in the past, Dad. He's got to—"

"The effects of my choices are very much in the present, Alex. And no one has more accountability in this situation than I do."

"I'm not sure Marilyn would agree with you."

"I'm not sure Marilyn would have made the choices she did if it had been any other man in my position. I was so utterly messed up, Alex. I made it easy for her to leave her family; I gave her every possible opportunity without giving a second's thought to how it might affect *her* life. I was selfish and egotistical. When she left me to go back to her family, I was furious. Not because I was concerned about her, but because misery loves company. And I didn't want to be alone in my misery. Marilyn is a good woman with a strong conscience and more courage than I could ever hope to possess. And Brad took her back—no questions asked. Raised my illegitimate child as his own, treated him no differently than the other children in the family. Now, my sins may have been forgiven a long time ago, but there is no disputing my accountability in Wade's present situation. I just don't know what to do about it."

"Maybe you should be telling all of this to Wade."

"Maybe I should. But at this point, I'm not sure if that would hurt or help."

"One day at a time, Dad. He's a great kid. I really think he's going to be okay."

"I hope so, because if he's not, I'm not sure I could ever live with that."

"You've got to find peace with it, Dad. Your love for him is important; he's going to need it. But you can't alter—or take accountability for—his free agency."

Neil was quiet a long moment, then said, "I'll cover the costs, whatever they may be."

"Good," Alex said lightly. "For starters, the hospital will be sending you a bill for the stitches."

"You let me know. Don't go too long without talking to me."

"I promise," he said.

"And . . . tell him I love him."

"I don't know if he'll believe me, but I'll tell him."

Alex tucked Katharine into bed and read her two stories, while Jane cuddled with Preston and put him into his crib for the night. Back in their bedroom together he repeated what his father had said, and she simply commented, "It's tragic to see the heartache that goes around in this world, even among good people who just have . . . problems."

"Yeah," he said. "Sometimes life just stinks."

She couldn't help agreeing with him.

Once they knew the children were asleep, Alex walked Jane out to her car and kissed her goodnight. "I'll call you in the morning," he said. "You call me any time if anything changes, or if you just need to talk."

"Okay," she said and kissed him again.

"Call when you get there so I know you're okay," he added just before he closed the car door between them and she drove away.

Going back into the house, he found Wade lying back on the couch, his flip-flops on the floor. He was reading from a book held above his head.

"Anything good?" Alex asked, and Wade looked at him over the top of it.

"Yes, actually," he said, and Alex realized it was the history of the Barrett family. "You gave your son your mother's maiden name."

"Yes, I did. It's also my middle name. I was named after my great-great-grandfather, Alexander Barrett." Alex glanced around as he sat down and crossed an ankle on his knee. "This is his house."

"Really?"

"Really."

"That's awesome."

"Yes, it is." Alex paused and then added, "Dad said to tell you he loves you."

Wade set the book aside but remained as he was on the couch. "You told him."

"I did. There are no—"

"Secrets in this family. I know. And what did dear old Dad have to say?"

"He feels responsible."

"Maybe he is," Wade said.

"He's accountable for his choices, and you are accountable for yours."

"*I* am the result of his choices."

"So you are. And were you not, would you still be the same man? Physically, your genetics would have been different. But if we believe that our spirits were born and lived long before we came here to receive physical bodies, then the technicality of your paternity really does not change who you are in an eternal perspective, does it?"

Wade said nothing, but Alex sensed it had given him something to think about. A minute later Wade asked, "And speaking of eternity. . ." His voice had that cynical edge Alex had heard him use a great deal. "Where do I belong exactly in the next life? Provided I can be forgiven for attempted murder and casting stones, that is."

Alex felt a little pang of heartache at the answer; they weren't and never could be sealed into the same family. But he reminded himself as he said it, "It's not so important who you are sealed to as the fact that you are sealed. You were born under the covenant."

Wade made a scoffing noise. "What covenant is that exactly? The covenant my father—if I can call him that—claims to have made void through treating his wife badly and driving her away? The covenant my mother willfully broke when she committed adultery? Is that the covenant you mean?"

"The covenant that was mended when everyone involved went through a full repentance process. Your mother was excommunicated and worked very hard to regain her membership in the Church, Wade. They did everything they possibly could to make restitution."

"Forgive my pessimism, Alex. But I find it difficult to swallow that their lying to me about who my father is wouldn't throw a cog in the wheel of that restitution."

Alex sighed. "That's between God and your parents."

"And what about the religious leaders who were representing God in my mother's disciplinary council? Were they not to be told every aspect of the situation? Did *they* know a child had resulted from the affair?"

"Obviously I don't know the answer to that. Maybe you should be discussing this with your bishop."

"And maybe I've done enough futile reasoning for one day," Wade said, his voice heavy. "I think I'm just . . ."

He stopped when a door opened in the distance, and Susan's voice called, "We're home."

"I'm in the study," Alex called back.

Wade sat up and put his flip-flops on just before Donald and Susan appeared in the doorway. Their attention went immediately to Wade.

"Hi," Susan said.

"Hi," Alex replied. "This is my brother, Wade."

Donald crossed the room and held out a hand, saying with a smile, "It's a pleasure to meet you, son. We've heard a lot of good things about you."

Wade stood and accepted Donald's handshake, passing a subtly skeptical glance toward Alex. "It's good to meet you as well," Wade said.

"This is my cousin, Susan," Alex said.

"Hello," she said to Wade.

"Actually, she is my mother's cousin. But we're still cousins. And her husband Donald. They've been good enough to take us in and provide daily babysitting services, and Susan is a marvelous cook."

"Did you get some soup?" she asked.

"Yes, thank you," Alex said. "It was wonderful."

"It was very good, thank you," Wade added.

Alex's cell phone rang and he answered it to hear Jane tell him that she'd arrived at the hospital, and nothing had changed. They exchanged "I love yous," and he got off the phone before he said to Donald and Susan, "Wade is spending the night. We have some things to take care of in the morning."

"Okay," Susan said with a smile. Then to Wade, "Could I interest you in a home-cooked breakfast before you do whatever it is you need to do?"

"You don't want to pass that up," Alex said.

"That would be nice, thank you," Wade said.

"What time do you need to eat?" she asked Alex.

"There's no hurry. Whenever you're in the mood to cook is fine."

"I'm always in the mood to cook," she said.

"For which I am eternally indebted," Alex chuckled. He gave Wade a cautious stare before he added, "Donald, I wonder if you could help me with something. Only if Wade is agreeable, of course."

"Sure, anything."

"Wade," Alex said, "would it be all right if we give you a priest-hood blessing?"

Wade looked hesitant, and Alex held his breath. It wasn't diffi-cult to imagine him boldly turning down such an offer, considering his present feelings. He finally said, "Okay. That would probably be good."

Susan gracefully said, "I'm going to take care of some things in the kitchen. When you're finished, I've got some of that cake I made yesterday stowed away, if you're interested."

"Thank you," Alex said, and she left the room.

Donald closed the door and Alex motioned Wade to the chair in front of the desk.

"What's your full name?" Alex asked.

"Wade Moses Morrison."

"Moses? Really?"

"Really," Wade said, sounding mildly annoyed that Alex would question him.

"Well, I mean . . . of course, but . . . does it have significance?"

"I have no idea," Wade said, and they proceeded with the blessing. While Alex heard himself promising that with faith and trust in God, Wade's spirit would be healed, he felt an impression that there was something significant about the name Moses, and it made him want to ask Marilyn. Focusing on the moment, he opened his mind to feel the Spirit and felt guided to tell Wade that as he worked to gain understanding he would be blessed with peace. He was also told that the only path to true healing led to the Savior, and only through Him and by Him could he ever completely be free of the pain he was feeling. He was reminded of his Father in Heaven's love for him, and that he should not be afraid to rely on the love of those whom God had sent into his life to assist him in this difficult time.

When the blessing was finished, Wade hugged Alex tightly, then shook Donald's hand, saying, "Thank you. Both of you."

"A pleasure, son," Donald said. He left the room saying, "I think I'll have some of that cake."

Alex knew it was his way of making a gracious exit to leave him alone with Wade. Alex met Wade's eyes and saw something different there. He was glad when Wade attempted to explain. "That was incredible."

"Was it?"

"For the first time since all of this happened, I actually felt a glimmer of peace, like I really *could* get through this."

Alex smiled and hugged him again. "You hang on to that feeling, kid. It'll get you through."

Wade nodded and said, "I think a piece of cake couldn't hurt, either."

Chapter 14

"No, I'm sure it couldn't hurt," Alex said, and they went to the kitchen to find Donald and Susan sitting at the table, sharing cake and milk.

"Have a seat," Donald said. Alex noted that plates, forks, and glasses had already been set out for them.

"Thank you," Wade said.

They all chatted casually while they ate, then Alex noticed Wade unconsciously pulling up his sleeves, exposing the bandage. He hadn't necessarily planned on telling Donald and Susan about the problem, but Susan was quick to say, "Oh, what happened to your arm?"

Wade looked so startled, so completely guilty, that Alex knew any attempt to justify it away with some trite explanation would only appear foolish. Apparently Wade realized this when he said to Alex, "Go ahead and tell them. I'm coming to accept that there are no secrets in this family."

Alex shrugged. "They're my family, not yours. My *mother's* family. It's up to you. But I can assure you that Donald and Susan are very compassionate and understanding people."

Wade simply said, "It doesn't matter. Just tell them."

"Wade cut his wrist," Alex said.

"On what?" Susan asked with a perfect naïveté that he would have found humorous if not for the weight of the subject.

"It was a box cutter, I believe," Alex said.

"Oh," Susan said with compassion. "How did that happen?"

"I think," Donald said to her, "what he's trying to say is that it wasn't an accident."

Susan didn't look astonished or upset, but the compassion in her eyes deepened as she looked at Wade and said, "Oh, you poor dear. Are you going to be okay?"

"He'll be fine," Alex said. "Tomorrow we are going to figure out what the options are for getting him some help. He's just been a little depressed."

"Might I recommend a great counselor?" Donald asked.

"Absolutely," Alex said, thinking this might be an answer to prayers.

"A member of our stake presidency is a counselor at a facility that specializes in suicide prevention. He's a wonderful man. I know him well. Perhaps I could call him in the morning; it might be a place to start."

"That would be great, Donald. Thank you." He tousled Wade's hair. "Maybe we're being blessed already, eh?"

"Maybe," Wade said.

They both thanked Susan for the cake, and again for the soup, then Alex discussed with her the plans for the children the following day. Alex then led Wade up the stairs and to a room that he could use. "And the bathroom is there," he pointed to a door across the hall. "Just make yourself at home. Maybe we'll get that tour in tomorrow, if you're interested."

"I am, yes. Very much."

"You okay?" Alex asked.

"Yes, really. I am. Thanks for everything."

"I'll see you in the morning then." Alex left the room and closed the door, saying a silent prayer that they could all get a good night's sleep.

Back in his own room he remembered something and returned to knock on Wade's door. He opened it after Wade called for him to come in and tossed something on the bed that landed next to where Wade was sitting.

"What's this?"

"It's called a toothbrush. We keep a few new ones on hand. Is there anything else you need?"

"No . . . thank you."

"Should I set my alarm every hour to check and make sure you're alive?"

"There's no need for that."

"Probably not. No need to set the alarm, anyway. I'll probably be wide awake all night wondering if you're alive."

"Now who's being a martyr?"

"Touché," Alex said. "You got me there. I'll see you in the morning. Susan's breakfast is worth living for, if nothing else." Wade actually smiled before Alex closed the door.

Alex was surprised at how well he slept and figured that exhaustion must have overruled his concerns and the emotions he'd struggled with. Or perhaps his bedtime prayer for peace had been heard. He woke to daylight hearing Preston on the monitor near his bed. With Preston in his arms he went to Wade's room, knocking lightly, hoping he wouldn't wake him but not willing to avoid checking on him.

"Yeah?" Wade called, and Alex pushed open the door to find him standing near the window.

"Did you get any sleep?" Alex asked.

"Off and on. How about you?"

"Yeah, I did. Listen, you're welcome to borrow clothes, anything you need."

"Thanks. I'm okay for the moment."

"I've got to get the kids dressed. I'll meet you downstairs in a few minutes. Make yourself at home."

A short while later Alex was sitting at the kitchen table feeding Preston scrambled eggs with a spoon, knowing that some help would prevent a big mess to clean up afterward. Katharine sat beside him, playing with her eggs more than eating them. Donald was in the other room on the phone. Susan had gone outside to put water on her newly planted garden. Katharine got down and ran out of the room just a moment before Wade appeared.

"You're alive," Alex said.

"You're surprised?"

"Just pleased. Have a seat. Susan will be right back, and she will take great pleasure in waiting on you hand and foot."

Wade sat down, and Katharine shouted from the other room, "Daddy! I need help at the potty!"

Alex chuckled and handed the spoon to Wade, motioning for him to feed Preston. "Pediatrics," he said with a wink and hurried into the bathroom. He returned with Katharine to find Wade managing rather well. "I think you have a gift," Alex said. Wade didn't answer, but he did seem rather preoccupied with watching Preston eat.

He did ask while looking into the bowl, "What is this stuff?"

"Scrambled eggs with ketchup. His favorite. Yum. Yum."

"As long as Preston likes it," Wade said and kept feeding him.

Alex got Katharine situated again in front of her breakfast, then asked, "You want me to take over?"

"We're okay."

Susan came in before Preston was finished eating. True to Alex's word, she fussed over Wade and fed them a breakfast that Wade declared would keep him full for a couple of days. He repeatedly thanked Susan for her hospitality and her fine cooking. She just teased him a little and made him laugh. Donald came in during the meal and handed Alex a piece of paper with a name and phone number written on it.

"I've already talked to him. You can call his assistant at this number, and she'll answer your questions and help you make arrangements."

"Thank you," Alex said.

Alex felt good about this option, but he decided he wanted to make other calls as well, just to hear about different options and weigh what might be best. He left the children and Wade in Susan's care and shut himself in the study to use the phone privately. After a number of conversations with different people, he felt good about going with the person Donald had recommended, and the facility this man was associated with. But he needed to know what Wade wanted to do.

Alex found his brother sitting in front of a PBS children's show, coloring with Katharine, while Preston played with little trucks on the floor.

"Yes, I know," Wade said, "this is great practice for pediatrics."

Alex smiled at him. "Let's talk."

Katharine was so engrossed in the TV program that she didn't notice Wade leaving the room with her father. Preston said, "Bye, Wade," and waved. Wade waved back and chuckled.

Back in the study Alex closed the door and motioned Wade to the couch. Once they were seated he said, "There are a number of different options here. I'll tell you what I believe would be the best, and then you tell me if you can live with it. If you can't, we'll try something else."

"Okay."

He explained his process of assessing information and how he'd come back to Donald's recommendation. "I really think if you actually stay somewhere for a few days, they can help you get through the worst of this more effectively, as opposed to dragging it out. You can check yourself in and out. Nobody's going to make you do it or take control of your life. This isn't like drug rehab or something. But you can get some help in big doses straight up front, and then work down to some outpatient counseling if you need it. What do you think?"

"Truthfully?" he asked, and Alex wondered if it would be a fight to get him to do this. "I'm relieved."

"Why?"

"I'm scared to go home and be alone, Alex. You were right when you asked me what I'll do when the feelings come back. I don't know what I'll do. Even in the night I had thoughts of . . . well, maybe some level of regret . . . that I hadn't succeeded. I know you'd let me stay here, but we both know you can't help me with this—even if you didn't have a life." He sighed with resignation. "I only see one big problem. I can't pay for it, Alex, and I'm not going to let you even—"

"Dad's paying for it. And don't get all prideful about that. You just told me yesterday that he has some responsibility in this. And maybe he does, depending on how you look at it. Either way, he's more than willing to do this. He's your father, and you need his help. Just say this is what you want, and I'll arrange it."

Wade blew out a slow breath. "Okay. But . . ."

"What?"

"Before I go . . . move into this place . . . will you come back to my apartment with me? Obviously I need to get some clothes and stuff, but . . . I dread going back there, knowing there's still blood in the bathroom, and . . ."

"I'd be happy to," he said. "We'll clean the place up and pack your things. It's not a problem."

"Are you sure you shouldn't be at the hospital?"

"I've talked to Jane this morning. Nothing has changed. She's coming home to be with the kids. Some friends are sitting with Barrett today. I'll see him this evening. He won't miss me."

"Why's that?"

Alex hesitated, then said, "He's in a coma."

"Oh, yeah," Wade said grimly.

Alex quickly excused himself to go make some calls. He got everything arranged for Wade, then called his father. Neil agreed to take care of the financial arrangements immediately, then Alex left the children in Susan's care until Jane got home, and he went to Wade's apartment with him. Once inside the door, Alex said, "You work on the dishes. I'll take care of the bathroom."

"Thanks," was all Wade said beyond letting him know where the cleaning supplies were. Within a couple of hours, the apartment looked relatively decent, the dishes were washed and put away, and laundry had been gathered for a trip to the Laundromat. Alex added to it the stuff he'd been soaking in cold water in the tub to get the blood out. He helped Wade pack a bag, then they went to a Laundromat and talked quietly of anything but suicide and counseling until the clothes were washed and dried. Wade added some clean clothes to his luggage, and then they drove to the facility.

In spite of Wade's visible nervousness, he admitted more than once to Alex that he couldn't deny some relief in getting the help he knew he needed. Alex promised to keep in touch and invited Wade to call him anytime. "Leave a message on my cell phone if I don't answer. I check it as often as possible between work and being with Barrett."

Wade nodded and hugged him tightly before Alex left him in the care of people who clearly cared and had the tools and training to get them through this. Driving away, Alex felt so depressed that he wondered if he needed some counseling himself. People at the hospital had talked with him and Jane regularly about the emotions associated with what they were going through with their son, but he still felt like a volcano waiting to explode. Or perhaps it was more implosion that he feared, as if he might just curl up and never be able to function again.

Being with Barrett only heightened Alex's fear of completely crumbling. The signs were becoming more clear. Tests indicated that the problems that had put him in PICU were showing improvement, but there was no sign whatsoever that the new bone marrow was making any difference at all, and at this point it was becoming less likely every hour that it would. The more time that passed, the more it seemed they were going to have to accept that Barrett was going to die. And while Alex had no idea how he would ever even respond to such a verdict, the thought of Jane's probable response provoked actual pain in his chest and stomach.

Two days after taking Wade to the facility, Barrett was doing better physically but still comatose, and beyond that there was no change. And Alex had heard nothing concerning his brother. He'd just finished a shift and was doing some errands when he answered his cell phone to hear Jane say, "You need to get here, as fast as you can."

Alex felt his heart plummet. Was this the moment? Was Barrett dying? "Why?" was all he could say while he headed the car toward the hospital.

Jane was crying too hard to answer. By the time she finally did he felt as if life as they'd known it had ceased. She managed to sputter, "I'm sorry. I didn't think I was going to cry like that." She exhaled and something akin to laughter crept into her voice. "They took the ventilator out. He's breathing on his own."

Alex found himself crying and had to pull over to avoid being a hazard on the road. Dread and grief turned instantly to elation and delight. Jane went on to say, "The word miracle is flying all over the place here, Alex. They're saying they've never seen such an abrupt turnaround from such critical problems."

Alex finally managed to say, "Okay, I'm on my way." He arrived to find Jane hovering just inside the doorway, while three people were doing something with Barrett, blocking the view. Alex took hold of Jane and felt her weeping silently in his arms.

Their attention turned toward Barrett as they heard a voice say, "Look, your mommy and daddy are here to see you."

Alex and Jane moved closer to the bed, where the absence of numerous tubes and equipment couldn't be missed. But something else was missing as well. Barrett looked up at his parents, but there was no apparent acknowledgment. They'd become accustomed to his not being able to speak, but there had been distinct messages in his eyes. But now, there was nothing. Barrett's eyes looked hollow and lifeless. It was as if his body had come back from the dead, but his spirit had remained wherever he'd come back from. Still, they sat close to him and spoke in animated voices, while Alex could only hope that with time Barrett's spirit would catch up with him.

The doctor's report was full of positive news related to the way Barrett's organs had come back to life and were functioning well, especially considering all he'd been through. But he finished by saying, "Now, if we could just get that bone marrow to kick in."

Following twenty-four hours of observation in PICU, Barrett was taken back to his old room in the BMT unit, and the routine fell back into place. His illness induced by side effects had lessened considerably, but it had been replaced with a heartless stagnancy that brought its own level of torture. Forty-eight hours after

Barrett had decided to start breathing on his own again, he had done nothing but sleep or stare with empty eyes.

Through the drama with Barrett, Alex had kept a prayer in his heart for Wade, and his thoughts often strayed to his brother, wondering how he was doing. He was relieved to finally get a call from Wade's counselor, who was also a member of the stake presidency. There was some consolation in hearing that Wade wasn't nearly as bad off as many people this man had dealt with. Dr. Hadley had apparently worked with others whose lives were so out of whack that it was extremely difficult to guide them to any kind of peace. He pointed out that in spite of Wade's present sense of dislocation from his family and his values, his upbringing had been strong and deeply rooted in emotionally healthy thinking. And there were no issues of mental illness or chemical imbalance to complicate the matter. He simply felt that Wade needed to reconnect with his true self, then he would be able to find peace with what had happened.

"And it's always easier," Dr. Hadley went on, "to work with someone who has the gospel in their life. Professionally I have to be careful with mixing my religious beliefs with my work, but when that's already in place I can help patients understand that the only way to truly make the healing complete is through the Atonement. Wade understands that; he's just not sure he believes it anymore. But deep down, I think he does, and I think eventually he'll come to that."

"So, what now?" Alex asked.

"Well, this might be somewhat . . . uncomfortable. But I truly believe it's the right way to go for Wade. I think it would be good for both sets of parents to meet together with Wade. From what you've told me, they've all come a long way spiritually with the issues of the past. If they were not living appropriately or still had challenges this might not be the right course. But under the circumstances, I think if Wade can see peace between people who have hurt and betrayed each other in the past, and hear for himself that each of these people loves and cares for him, and accepts him for who and what he is, it could go a long way toward his coming to terms. What do you think, Alex?"

"I think I agree . . . especially with that *uncomfortable* part."

"Do you think they would be open to the idea?"

"I think Wade's parents would do just about anything to help him. What does Wade think?"

"I haven't proposed it to him yet. I wanted to hear your opinion first. I don't want to propose the idea and then tell him that someone involved isn't willing to come. So I think it needs to be arranged before he even knows it's being considered."

"And if he doesn't want to do it?"

"We'll respect that. But he's pretty reasonable and trusting. I think he'll agree to it. And whatever we do, I think it would be well for you to be there. It's very clear you're the only person Wade completely trusts right now. Would you be willing to talk with his parents and see if it can be arranged?"

"I can do that," Alex said, and Dr. Hadley gave him a couple of time slots that were available.

After the call ended, Alex got on his knees and offered a fervent prayer to be guided in discussing this sensitive issue, and to know for himself if this was the right course. He didn't want something to happen that might make it worse rather than better for Wade. He came away feeling simply that it was the right course, and even if the meeting had some challenges, it would still work toward a positive outcome.

Alex first called his father. "Do you remember when you said you'd like to be able to talk with Marilyn and Brad about all of this?"

"Yes," Neil drawled cautiously, as if he feared what might be coming.

"Well, now's your chance, Dad. Dr. Hadley thinks it would be good for Wade if both sets of parents meet with him—together."

"I see," Neil said.

"And what do you think of that?"

"I'll do whatever I can to help Wade."

"That's what I told Dr. Hadley you'd say. It could be awkward."

"Yes, it certainly could."

"Aren't you glad you haven't been trying to keep any of this a secret?" Alex asked, attempting to offer a positive perspective. "Think how this might be if Roxanne hadn't known about your past. Or if your children hadn't known."

"Yes, that would be colorful, wouldn't it," he said with sarcasm.

"So, you're okay with it?"

"Yes."

"Is there anything you need to work around in the next few days?"

"No, we're flexible. We can be there anytime. Just let us know."

Alex ended the call, said another quick prayer, and dialed Marilyn's number. He was glad to know that her only job was doing book work for her husband's company, and she was almost always reachable at home. He hadn't talked to her since he'd let her know that Wade had checked himself into a crisis facility. As always, it was evident when she answered that she was expecting him according to the caller ID.

"How is he?" she asked.

"Coming along. His counselor, who is also a stake president, by the way, has asked that both sets of parents meet with Wade together. He thinks this would help him put some pieces together positively."

"Oh," was all she said.

"If you're not comfortable with it, Marilyn, just say so. We don't want to make the situation worse, but we really think it might help him to see evidence of the healing that's taken place in people who went through a lot to get where they are now."

"I'd do anything to help Wade," she said, and Alex told her what he'd told his father.

"What about your husband?"

"He won't have a problem with it, I'm certain. He's been wonderful about all of this. He loves Wade dearly."

"Well then, I'll arrange it." He told her the times that were an option, and they settled on meeting the following afternoon.

Alex called Dr. Hadley to tell him it was arranged, then he asked if he could come and visit Wade. He wanted to be the one to tell him their plans.

With his lunch hour spent making phone calls in between gulping down a sandwich, Alex returned to work and phoned Jane on his break to catch her up to speed. He told her he was going to see Wade as soon as he got off work, and then he would meet her in Barrett's room.

At the facility, Alex was taken to a small room with only a few chairs and a low table. A few minutes later Wade was brought in, and the door closed behind them.

"Hi," Wade said, and Alex rose to greet him with a hug. "When they said I had a visitor, I hoped it was you. I couldn't think of anybody else I wanted to see right now."

"Well, I'm flattered," Alex said as they were both seated, "but I've come to tell you that you're going to have more company tomorrow. In fact, it's going to be somewhat of a party."

"Who?" Wade asked skeptically.

"Your parents—all of them."

"At the same time?" he asked incredulously.

"Yeah."

"You've got to be kidding!" Wade stood up and began to pace. "That's like throwing me into the lion's den."

Alex chuckled, attempting to keep the mood somewhat light. "What do you think they're going to do? Get in a catfight to see who gets to keep you? You should know them all better than that."

"But . . . together? What's the point?"

"I don't know exactly," Alex said, feigning ignorance. "But Dr. Hadley believes it would be good, and I think he knows what he's talking about. I think we can trust him. What do you think?"

Wade stopped to look out the window and stuck his hands in the back pockets of his jeans. "I think it's insane. What if it's a disaster?"

"Then . . . we'll chalk it up to experience. Either way we'll move forward and keep working things out. If it starts to get disastrous, you can leave. The good doctor just thinks it would be well for a little discussion to take place with everyone directly involved."

"And who would that be exactly?"

"Your parents and—"

"Which would include my mother, but do you mean my blood father, or the one who raised me?"

"Both. And Roxanne."

Wade sighed loudly. "Will you be there?"

"Do you want me to be there?"

"Yes."

"Then I'll be there." Following a minute of silence, Alex added, "So how are you doing?"

"Better, I think," he said. "I'm glad I came. Maybe it was good that I did something stupid and desperate. Maybe I needed drastic measures."

"Maybe you did. Come here. Let me see your wrist."

Wade sat down and held out his arm, which was no longer bandaged. Alex looked at the stitches and pressed his fingers around them. "Does it hurt?"

"Not really."

"You're taking the antibiotics?"

"Yeah."

"It looks fine. I'll take the stitches out in a few days."

"How's Barrett?" Wade asked, and Alex felt sick. The child was always hovering in his mind, but each time the situation was brought to the foreground of Alex's thoughts, a palpable, smoldering sensation rushed into his stomach to accompany the reminder.

"He's out of PICU, but he's not doing well. We're still holding out for a miracle."

"I've been praying for him—and for you."

"You've started praying again?" Alex pretended to sound surprised.

"I have."

"Well, I'm glad to hear it. I've been praying for you, too."

They talked a short while longer, then Alex left for the hospital. His heart cracked open a little further to see that nothing had changed with Barrett, but there was a deepening of that sunken look in Jane's eyes. He'd never felt so utterly helpless in his life. But he did what he'd developed a habit of doing. Knowing he simply couldn't handle the reality on his own, he silently asked God to take the burden, and then he fought to focus his thoughts on trusting that God actually knew what to do with that burden. Seeing Barrett's condition, he couldn't help recalling, over and over, Karen's words to them following her daughter's passing. *There are things worse than death,* she'd said. Alex felt sure she was right, but he still couldn't even contemplate the thought of losing Barrett. He feared most of all what it would do to Jane. While she managed to function and interact with people around her on a seemingly normal level, he knew her well enough to know that emotionally she'd descended to a place that he didn't know how to reach.

Wanting desperately to just connect with her on any level of commonality, he took her hand without saying a word of greeting and urged her to her feet. He brought her close with his arm around her waist and eased her into a gentle dance. She went with it for only a few steps before she moved abruptly away and turned her back. "I can't; not now."

"Why not?" he asked, his voice strained.

"This is not the time for dancing, Alex."

He tried not to sound insulted. "I thought that you and I could always find time for a dance."

"Well, maybe you were wrong," she snapped. Then as if she were willing herself not to be angry or impatient, she took a deep breath and said in a forced voice, "This is a time to mourn, Alex." Tears came, and she added, "A time to weep."

Alex couldn't argue with that. He only prayed that one day they might have cause again to laugh—and to dance.

Chapter 15

Alex insisted that Jane go home, and he would stay the night with Barrett. She left so easily that he wondered if she had begun to separate herself emotionally from their son. While it broke his heart, he wondered if that might not be better. Alex slept in Barrett's room and stayed with him until it was time to go to the meeting with Wade. He pressed a hand over his sleeping son's face and murmured an unheard "I love you" before he slipped away, praying still that a miracle would save him, that something would change.

Alex arrived early to find Wade pacing and wringing his hands, wearing a long-sleeved shirt. "Hey, it's okay," Alex said, urging him to sit down.

"I haven't seen Brad and my mother at all since all this broke loose," he said, and Alex wondered when he'd come to calling the father who had raised him by his given name. He doubted that Brad would be happy to hear himself referred to that way. "I don't know what to say to her . . . to them."

"You don't have to say anything," Alex said. "Just . . . let Dr. Hadley guide the discussion and go with the flow." Wade was still visibly tense, and Alex suggested, "Would you like to say a prayer together before they get here?"

"Yeah," Wade said eagerly. "Would you do it?"

"Sure," Alex said and took his brother's hand before he bowed his head and prayed verbally, on Wade's behalf, that this meeting would go well, that communication would be effective, that hearts would be softened, and good things could result for everyone involved. He specifically prayed that Wade would be comforted and guided to understand the things that would bring him peace. Wade firmly echoed Alex's amen, then they went together to the room where the meeting would take place.

Dr. Hadley was there and greeted them kindly. He told Wade to just relax, but to feel that he could use this opportunity to ask any questions he needed to have answered. Wade just nodded and took a seat. Alex sat right next to him, and Wade said quietly, "Thanks for coming. I know this can't be fun for you, but I'm grateful."

"It's okay," he said. "Truthfully, I almost consider it a blessing to have something to worry about besides Barrett, when worrying has become so pointless."

"No better?"

"Nope."

"How's Jane?"

"Not good at all," Alex said. "I think I worry more for her than anyone."

Wade sighed. "Forgive me if this question sounds harsh, but . . . we seem to have that kind of relationship."

Alex couldn't help but smile. "So we do. Let me have it."

"Do you think he's going to die, Alex?"

"I don't know," Alex said, actually finding it a relief to talk about it without any volatile emotions flying around. "I've prayed over and over for God's will to be done, and I've done my best to accept that we might have to let him go, at the same time praying that he'll be spared. I've asked that I can be prepared to let him go if that's inevitable, but truthfully . . . I just don't feel anything at all. I feel numb, in shock maybe. Or just . . . past feeling. Maybe it's hurt so much for so long that I've just learned how to avoid feeling it. And a part of me is terrified of what might happen when I am confronted with those feelings."

"That sounds a lot like conversations we've been having around here lately."

"Well, I've spent some time with counselors at the hospital, but probably not enough. Maybe next week you can visit *me* in here."

"Whatever it takes," Wade said and their eyes met. Alex almost felt moved to tears by the implication, but he fought for control, certain that even a trickle of tears would break the dam holding back the entire torrent of all he was terrified to feel in regard to Barrett.

He was surprised to hear Wade say, "Someday . . . on the condition that I can get past all of this . . . I want to love someone . . . the way you love Jane. I want someone to love me, the way she loves you. I can see it in your eyes when you look at each other. What you're going through right now would tear some people apart, but it's like the two of you just . . . have something that holds you together so strongly that nothing could ever break it."

Alex couldn't think of a response. He felt touched by Wade's sentiment, and he certainly agreed that the love he shared with Jane was deeply profound. But at the moment he wasn't sure their relationship truly could survive anything—at least not the death of a child. He could never stand to let her go, and he believed that she would hold to the commitments between them regardless of anything else. But he'd felt varying degrees of walls between them through the course of Barrett's illness, and it broke his heart to think that losing their son could build walls between them that might never be brought down.

Alex was glad for a distraction when Neil and Roxanne were shown into the room and Wade became visibly apprehensive. Alex stood and greeted his father with a hug, hoping to melt a little ice in the room. "Thanks for coming," he said, and then he hugged Roxanne.

"Hello, Wade," Neil said to him, holding out a hand. "How are you?"

Alex could tell his father was more nervous than Wade as the two men shook hands. Wade answered almost facetiously, "The doctor here tells me he'll take the stitches out in a few days."

"And besides that?" Neil asked, raising his brows.

"I'm hanging in there. How are you?"

"I'm glad to see you," Neil said, then the tension was broken somewhat by Roxanne stepping between them to give Wade a hug. The two of them had never shared any serious conversation, beyond what had come up at the dinner table in her home, but she had a way of offering him acceptance and warmth without hardly saying anything at all.

Wade gave a timid smile as she eased back, saying gently, "It's good to see you, Wade."

"You too," he said and put his hands into his back pockets. Following an awkward moment of silence, he added, nodding to Neil, "I wanted to thank you . . . for making it possible for me to stay here. I think it's helping, and I'm grateful. I just wanted you to know that."

Neil smiled at him. "I'm happy to do anything I can," he said.

Dr. Hadley approached Neil and Roxanne, sparing them from another labored exchange. While Alex introduced them, Wade sat back down. Alex sat beside him while the others chatted a short distance away. Brad and Marilyn appeared in the doorway, and Alex could almost feel how Wade wanted to shrink and fade away.

"Oh help," he muttered quietly, and Alex realized his brother was shaking.

"It's okay," he whispered, putting his arm on the back of Wade's chair, resting a hand on his shoulder.

"Not really," Wade whispered back, then a stark silence descended over the room as the two couples stood silently facing each other and everyone seemed momentarily frozen. "It's like a shootout in an old western," Wade whispered, and Alex couldn't hold back a little snigger at the analogy. But Wade immediately glared at him, apparently not finding the humor. There was a familiar anger in his eyes that Alex hadn't seen in their last couple of visits. Apparently the presence of people he felt angry toward had brought it bubbling back to the surface.

Alex waited for something to happen, for someone to speak. He expected Dr. Hadley to break the ice, and then he realized that he was standing back, waiting to see what might happen.

"Hello, Wade," Marilyn said tenderly, and Alex could tell she was refraining from an attempt to actually approach him. "It's good to see you."

"We've missed you, son," Brad added cautiously.

"Hi," was all Wade said, and then the tension descended again.

Just when it seemed nothing would ever happen, Brad Morrison stepped toward Neil and held out a hand, saying somewhat nervously, "Neil, it's been a long time."

Alex felt stunned and in awe as he watched these two men share a firm handshake. They had once lived in the same ward, and then Neil had taken Brad's wife away, and they had likely not seen each other since. But there wasn't even the slightest trace of malice or bitterness in Brad's countenance.

"Yes, it has," Neil said. "I wish there was something I could say to apologize sufficiently for the heartache I've brought into your life."

Brad shrugged. "There's no need for that."

"You see that?" Alex whispered to Wade. "Now that's a miracle."

"Well, they're better men than I am."

"Maybe," Alex said, not willing to argue with him. "Or maybe they just have more practical experience in the futility of anger and bitterness." Wade scowled at Alex, and he added, "And maybe one day you'll stop looking at me like that when I tell you something you don't want to hear."

Their attention shifted back to the awkwardness among the people standing in the room. Again it seemed as if something was supposed to happen, but it didn't. Alex saw Marilyn and his father exchange a long gaze. Wade apparently noticed when he murmured, "Oh help. I think I'm going to scream."

"Well, don't," Alex said, putting a hand firmly on Wade's thigh, as if it might keep him more calm.

Marilyn seemed to break past some invisible barrier to cross the room and give Neil a hug. Their embrace was brief and strained, and Alex couldn't help considering how much they must have

ANITA STANSFIELD

cared for each other at one time. It was tragic to see how their relationship had been so thoroughly tainted by the sin that had been
at the center of it. Marilyn started to cry as she looked up at Neil,
saying with conviction, "I am so sorry. I should have told you."
She pressed a tissue beneath her nose for a long moment. "We
believed it was better not to tell Wade, but . . . we should have told
you. You had a right to know, and . . . I'm sorry."

"I understand," Neil said, his voice trembling. "Truly I do. It's
okay."

"I think I'm going to be sick," Wade whispered to Alex, as if he
couldn't handle the very idea of these two people once having been
close enough to be his parents.

"Well, if you're going to puke," Alex whispered back, "give me
fair warning. I'm not wearing scrubs."

"I'll do that," Wade said with sarcasm.

Another lapse of growing tension was broken when Dr. Hadley
stepped in and introduced everyone by name, as if this were a
social gathering. He finished by motioning in their direction. "And
you all know Wade. And that's Alex, his brother."

Alex noticed Marilyn bristling slightly over that, but she still
smiled at him before they all took Dr. Hadley's invitation to be
seated. They sat in some semblance of a circle, with Wade and Alex
facing Dr. Hadley, and the two sets of parents facing each other.

"Nothing like being caught in the middle," Wade whispered.

Dr. Hadley chuckled and said, "The two of you are over there
whispering like a couple of kids in school. Anything you want to
share?"

"Not really," Wade said, but Dr. Hadley winked at him to
relieve any implication that his words might have been scolding. It
was clearly more an effort to alleviate the tension.

"Now that we're all here," Hadley said, "I think we should start
off with each of you stating how you feel about the present situation. There's no need to repeat the circumstances; we all know
what we're dealing with. It's your feelings that are important here.
Would anyone like to begin?"

It was only silent a moment before Neil said, "I'd like to, if I may." Hadley motioned for him to go on. Looking directly at Wade, Neil spoke firmly. "When you first showed up and told me about our relationship, you know that I was pretty upset. Ever since that day, I have longed to go back and change that moment, because I didn't want you to believe that I was unhappy to learn of your existence. In truth, it was quite the opposite. There are parts of my life that I would like to go back and erase, things that I am mortified now to even think about. There are a great many things I've done that I regret, Wade. But I do *not* regret your existence. Much of my behavior was stupid, unquestionably wrong. However pathetic and unacceptable my choices may have been, God knew I would make those choices. And God is merciful, Wade. As I see it, He sent you here to be raised in an environment where you would be given a strong foundation to be able to rise above my bad choices. I want you to know that I love you, Wade. I only had to look once into your face to feel it. But I'm not here to take your father's place, or infringe upon relationships that are far more important than you could ever share with me. I just want you to be happy and at peace. I want to do whatever I can to help you meet your goals and live a good life, to somehow try to meagerly compensate for what I've inadvertently put you through." He sighed and added, "That's all I have to say for the moment."

"Thank you, Neil," Hadley said. "And how do you feel right now?'

"Just . . . glad for the opportunity to say words that have been running over and over in my head. I hope he knows they're from the heart."

"You still feel like puking?" Alex whispered to Wade.

"Yes."

Hadley smirked toward them in response to their whispering. Alex was surprised to hear Wade blurt, "He asked if I still feel like puking, and I told him yes. But there's no need for anyone to be offended by that. I've felt that way on a regular basis for a long time now. I'm almost getting used to it. Please continue." He motioned with his hand. "Don't let me hold you back." There was a subtle bite of sarcasm in his tone that Alex felt certain wasn't easy for the others in the room to hear. But their purpose for being here was to vent feelings and deal with them. And maybe these people needed to know the level of hurt this had created for Wade.

Brad spoke next, humbly expressing his love for Wade and his regret over bringing any grief into his life. He repeated what Wade had once told him he'd said, that he felt some accountability for driving Marilyn into an affair, due to his neglect and unkindness to her. He said that he'd felt it was right to keep the truth from Wade, even though he'd always felt that eventually he would find out. He sincerely, even tearfully, declared how his love for Wade was no less or no different than for his other children. To Brad, the joy Wade had brought into their home had been tangible evidence of the beauty of forgiveness and healing, and a constant reminder of his gratitude for having his family put back together. He finished by saying that in spite of certain choices in the past, Wade's mother was a good woman and she deserved Wade's respect no less now than she had before. Alex wanted to cross the room and hug the man. If more men were like Brad Morrison, the world would surely be a far better place. Throughout the oration, Wade leaned his forearms on his thighs, staring at the floor, his expression unreadable.

Roxanne spoke next, saying only that while she was the least involved of those present, she had nevertheless spent years with Neil, seeing his regret over his past mistakes, and watching him earnestly living the gospel in the years since he'd come back into the Church. She expressed her personal concern and tenderness toward Wade, and told how she had witnessed Neil's anguish and worry over Wade. She repeated Neil's adage that they didn't want to take the place of his rightful parents, but they cared for him and wanted to help in any way that could make his life better and more fulfilled.

The pattern of the meeting would have indicated that Marilyn would go next, but she said nothing. Hadley finally asked her, "Do you have something you want to say?"

"There's nothing I can say to Wade that I haven't already said. I've made it clear that I love him beyond measure, and I find no shame in his existence, even though there is shame in his conception. I've told him that I am more than willing to take full accountability for my choices and his pain that is a result of those choices. But that won't take away the pain, and it won't solve the problem. I have nothing more to say."

"Wade," Hadley said, "is there anything you want to say at this point?"

"Nothing that wouldn't be better left unsaid," he muttered. "Like my mother always taught me, if I can't say anything nice, then it's better to keep my mouth shut."

"I have something to say," Alex interjected before Hadley could push Wade into expressing his anger.

"Please feel free," Hadley said.

"I spent twenty years being angry with my father for his betrayal and his hypocrisy." He motioned toward Neil. "We can talk about all of that now without any anger or bitterness, but it took me a long time and a lot of heartache to come to that. I think I have a pretty good idea how Wade must feel, but in truth, none of us can truly know how he feels. We've all had heartache and regret in our lives, but not one of us has ever been in the position he is in. I keep thinking about the stitches I put in his wrist."

He took hold of Wade's arm and turned it over, pulling up his sleeve so everyone in the room could see the evidence. Wade glared at Alex and pulled his arm away, putting the sleeve back in place. Alex said to Wade, "It's not like it's a big secret."

"Just say what you have to say and get it over with," Wade said, but it was more impatient than angry.

"I only want to say that the more I think about it, the more I realize that I have no comprehension of the kind of pain and desperation that would press a person to do something like this. But I want to understand, and I want to help. Wade is a fine young man. In spite of how difficult this has been for him, I've seen a great deal of evidence that he has a strong sense of integrity, and he truly does care about the people he loves, even if he has trouble feeling it in the middle of his present confusion. I just want him to know how grateful I am to know that he's my brother, and to have him in my life. And I'm glad that it's come out in the open."

Alex took in the expressions in the room, seeing that Marilyn looked especially agitated. Apparently Hadley picked up on that as well when he said, "Marilyn, how are you feeling about all of this coming out in the open?"

"To be quite honest, Doctor, I wish that the secret could have remained forever. Maybe someday I'll feel differently, but right now I am weary of suffering the consequences of my choices in ways I'd never fathomed. Wade is not only my son; he's always been a friend. He, of all my children, has a personality that's always understood me. We could talk and laugh together as equals. He's withdrawn that from me with a great deal of contempt. My other children all know the truth now, and they've all come up with different ways of looking down on me."

"That would be my fault," Wade said. "I have to apologize for blurting it out like that; they didn't need to know."

"If you know, they certainly need to know," Marilyn said. "And I don't blame you. I don't blame anyone for any of this but myself. I only wish that any amount of punishing myself for this would put my family back together." Grief overtook her anew. "As it is, I can only wish that we could go back to the way it used to be. A futile wish, I know. But that's the way I feel."

"Since going back is a futile wish," Hadley said, "now that it's come to this, what do you want to have happen?"

Marilyn looked at Wade, who countered her gaze. "I want my son back. I want the love and respect of my children that I used to have. When God let me know that He had forgiven my sins, He didn't include the stipulation that I would lose my children. That price feels too high."

"I have a hypothetical question," Hadley said. "What if your sin had given you AIDS, and you had passed it on to your son? What if he were now dying from the disease you had given him?"

Marilyn looked horrified by the question, and he added, "I had a family in here a few weeks ago dealing with *that* issue."

"If that were the case," Marilyn said, "I don't know how I could go on living. I would wish that I had just died when . . ." She stopped so abruptly that everyone in the room immediately focused on her. Alex saw guilt in her eyes that reminded him of something more recent and familiar.

"When what?" Wade demanded.

Marilyn turned to look at Brad, as if seeking his wisdom. He gave a nod of encouragement, and she turned back to face Wade. "There's something you need to know," she said. "But first let me make it perfectly clear that once I got beyond a certain moment in my life, I never once regretted bringing you into this world. Even with where we are now, I would not trade away a moment of being your mother. I think you need to know, however, that I *do* know that kind of pain and desperation. I *do* understand, Wade. Truly."

She was unusually calm and free of emotion as she stood and moved directly in front of Wade. Pulling up her left sleeve, she put her wrist directly in front of his face, giving Alex a perfect view as well. The scar was faint but undeniable. Wade looked up at her, astonished and questioning.

"When I found out I was pregnant," she said and yanked the sleeve back down, "in my head I could hear the anger of my grown child, cursing me for my sins. At that point I decided I would prefer to die than ever face such taunts. When I was baptized again, I found peace with all of that, and I knew I had been wrong. Even with where we've come, I'm glad to be alive, Wade. And I'm grateful for the life we've shared, even if what's past is all we will ever share."

She returned to her seat, and Alex noticed his father furtively wiping tears while Roxanne held his hand. Silence reigned for several minutes, and Hadley seemed content to let it stand, as if he knew the people in the room needed time to gather thoughts and assess feelings. Wade finally whispered to Alex, "I can't stand this."

"Then say something. This is your chance to say what you need to say, get your questions answered."

Their whispering captured the attention of everyone in the room, but even Hadley didn't comment. Wade finally said, "I need a minute alone with my brother."

"Okay," Hadley motioned toward the door. "We'll be here when you're ready."

"And while we're gone you can talk about us," Wade said, leaving the room with Alex right behind him. The hallway was empty as they came into it, and Wade closed the door. "How am I supposed to feel about that?" he growled quietly.

"What?"

"My mother trying to kill herself when she found out she was pregnant with me?"

"That's a tough one," Alex said, leaning a shoulder against the wall to face Wade directly. "But don't lose sight of what she made very clear before she told you that. She said she'd never regretted bringing you into the world. She loves you, Wade. She told you what she'd done to let you know that she understands your pain. Don't go twisting it in order to make the problem worse."

"What do you mean by that? I do *not* want the problem to be worse."

"Not consciously, perhaps, but—"

"You're going to throw some of that truth at me, aren't you?"

"I was going to try."

Wade shook his head. "How is it that you know so much?"

"I don't know any more than what life has taught me. I pray a lot and try to listen."

"Okay, let me have it."

"Fine. I can't help wondering if, at some level, you really don't want this to get better. Maybe there's a voice in your head leading you to believe that finding more excuses to be angry will justify your anger." Wade looked so startled by the suggestion that Alex knew the idea had been inspired. He certainly wouldn't have come up with something like that on his own. "But maybe," Alex said more gently, "if you can get past being angry and really *try* to consider everything that's been said in there, you could start to grasp that there are other voices, Wade; voices that will lead you to forgiveness—of yourself and others. And that's the only way you'll find peace."

Alex put a hand on Wade's shoulder. "Now, why don't you go back in there and get the air cleared over this, once and for all. I know there are some things you want to know. Take advantage of having a mediator present who might be able to help it make sense."

Wade looked into his eyes, and then said, "Okay. Let's get it over with."

They went back into the room to find it completely silent; there wasn't even a feeling that everyone had stopped talking abruptly to avoid being overheard. They'd barely sat down when Wade said, "I have a question."

"Okay." Hadley motioned for him to go on.

Wade looked directly at his mother, and Alex could see her trembling, but she faced him with courage. "You were excommunicated for this," he stated as if she were on trial. But he didn't sound angry.

"That's right," she said.

"It's my understanding that when a disciplinary council for something like this is held, the religious leaders responsible for making the decision are required to know every aspect of the situation in order to make an appropriate decision." He turned to Hadley. "You're a stake president. Would that be an accurate statement?"

"I believe so," Hadley said.

Wade turned back to his mother. "Did you tell them the baby you were pregnant with did not belong to your husband?"

Marilyn looked hesitant, or perhaps confused over the purpose of the question. "Tell me the truth," Wade said. "I need to know if the decisions associated with your restitution were based on *all* of the truth, or just part of it."

"Wade," Brad said kindly, "please don't speak to your mother with—"

"It's all right," Marilyn said, putting a hand over Brad's. "It's a valid question, and he has a right to know the answer." She looked at Wade firmly. "I told them everything, Wade. They knew the baby was not my husband's. My concern at the time had nothing to do with appearances, or getting off easy. My concern was my eternal salvation. I had no intention or desire to withhold anything from these men. They told me they had made the pregnancy a specific part of the fasting and prayer related to their decisions on my behalf. The council agreed in unison that I was to be excommunicated. They also agreed, at least in this case, that it was better for you to be raised without having to wonder over things a child could never understand. We discussed the concern of your finding out eventually, but we all felt that the decision was right, and that the matter had to be put into God's hands. And that's where we left it. If the children we had at the time had been older, it probably would have been necessary for them to know the truth. But they were too young to understand. When you came home asking for blood tests, we knew what the answers would be. But we both had a sense of calm over the matter, as if God were letting us know that the time had arrived for the truth to come out." She sniffled and added, "I knew it would be hard for you. But I never dreamed it would be *this* hard. Deep inside I suppose I'd hoped that our love for you would outweigh your doubts."

"Okay," Wade said when she was apparently finished. "I have one more question. Was it not also a requirement of your repentance process to notify the father of the baby?" Marilyn was clearly unsettled over the question. Wade motioned to Neil and asked, "Why did he not know of my existence? Didn't he have a right to know? If I were him, I would want to know something like that. As I see it, he had no opportunity to make restitution with *me* because he didn't know I existed."

"I can explain," Marilyn said.

"Well, I hope you can," Wade said, "because . . ."

Alex put a hand on Wade's arm and said softly, "Let her explain, and then you can say what you need to say."

Wade took a deep breath to calm his anger and leaned back in his chair, waiting for an answer.

"They made it very clear to me that I needed to notify the father. I sent letters that were returned. I sent more that were certified in order to prove my efforts. I tried every possible avenue to find him. Unfortunately, I didn't know that many people who knew him. Our relationship had not been prone to social circles or family gatherings. His home number had been disconnected. His office told me he was gone and refused any explanation. I even called Ruth."

Alex bristled slightly at the mention of his mother's name. He couldn't help wondering how that conversation might have gone, and what pain it might have brought to his mother at the time. He wondered for a moment how she might feel about all of this if she were still alive.

"I didn't tell her my reasons for needing to find him," she went on. "Apparently she had no idea that he and I were not still together until she heard from me. She had no idea where he was. As I recall, she asked that I let her know if I *did* find him. She was angry at the time for not receiving any child support."

Neil winced at the comment, and then looked at Alex, regret showing deeply. Alex nodded toward him, hoping to silently convey that it was all in the past, all forgiven. They both knew that Ruth had fully come to terms with these things as well. Ruth and Neil had become good friends prior to her death, and Neil had given a great deal of financial help to her and the children.

Marilyn sighed and added, "I simply could not find him. Months after you were born, when I was baptized again, the council officially made the decision to put the matter to rest. The stake president suggested that I might be open to trying again in the future, but as far the Church was concerned, it was over and done. There were moments during the ensuing years when I wondered if I should try to find him, but I just couldn't feel good about it. Maybe I was just afraid; I don't know. And then . . . when years passed, it became easier and easier to forget that everything was not as it appeared. Truthfully, I'd believed that if I hadn't been able to find him, you probably wouldn't either. Obviously I was wrong." She turned to Neil and said firmly, "Again, I am truly sorry. I should have made more of an effort to tell you."

Wade seemed to take in his mother's words, then he turned to Neil and asked, "So, where were you? It didn't take much effort for me to find you last month."

"I took an extended leave of absence from work and went out of state to stay with a friend. My intention was to stay a few weeks and try to get a grip on my life. It ended up taking many months. I had enough clout with the company that I was able to stay connected and keep my place there. The truth, Wade, is that I had a complete breakdown. I'd had problems buried inside of me from long before I ever married Alex's mother, or became involved with yours. And my methods of trying to solve those problems had only made everything worse. It took me months of inpatient counseling to come to a point where I wasn't daily tempted to end my own life." He took a deep breath. "I didn't have the courage to use a blade. I took pills, a lot of them. Then I got scared and called my friend. Had my stomach pumped, ended up in the psych ward for so long that I lost track." He said, more to Marilyn, "I'm sorry I wasn't reachable. I had no idea, never would have dreamed."

Marilyn just shrugged. "I'm sorry you suffered so much. I didn't know."

"And vice versa," Neil said. Then to Wade, "I too understand the level of desperation you've experienced, if that's worth anything."

Wade sounded only slightly cynical as he said, "Well, attempting suicide certainly gives me a common bond with my parents, now, doesn't it."

Silence prevailed, making it clear that everyone had run out of words. "Does anyone else have anything they want to say?" Hadley asked. "Any questions before we end this session?"

"I have a question," Alex said when no one else seemed prone to speak. He turned to Marilyn and asked, "Why Moses?" She looked surprised, and he clarified, "When I gave Wade a blessing and he told me his full name, I had an impression that the middle name Moses had some significance. Wade said he didn't know. I was just . . . wondering . . . why you chose that as his middle name."

Marilyn reached for her husband's hand. New tears filled her eyes. "It was Brad's idea," she said, briefly meeting Wade's eyes across the room before she looked down. She became too emotional to speak for several seconds, and Alex realized that the significance of the name was close to her heart. "You see . . ." she finally said, "Moses was raised by people other than his own in order to protect him."

Alex took a sharp breath and noticed Wade straightening his back, his brow furrowing deeply. "Eventually Moses discovered his true identity, and in our hearts we knew that eventually Wade would likely do the same. For Moses, both aspects of his life, both families, were important to him in fulfilling his mission in this world. Brad hoped that the example of Moses would help Wade find his own strength."

Wade came to his feet as if to leave, then he hesitated.

"Was there something you wanted to say?" Hadley asked.

"Yeah. I just want to say that . . . I'm sorry for all the grief I've put you through, all of you." He moved toward the door. "I need to be alone."

In his absence, Brad asked the doctor, "Should we be concerned about him?"

"I believe he's come to terms with being suicidal, if that's what you mean. I also believe he's capable of moving forward with his education, his life. How much he chooses to hold on to the way he's feeling is really up to him. I think he should go home tomorrow, and I'll set up some outpatient time with him. He knows that you all love him and care about him. That's all anyone can do at the moment. From a spiritual perspective I'd just like to add that you should keep doing what you've done all along. Pray for him. Stay close to the Spirit and listen to it. That's the best way to know if he's okay."

Hadley thanked them all for coming and said that he was available if anyone should come up with questions or concerns. After he left the room, Marilyn stood and moved toward Alex. He stood to face her, and she hugged him tightly. "Thank you, Alex," she said. "Promise you'll never stop being a brother to him."

"Never," he said firmly.

"Whether he comes back to us or not, I can find peace in knowing he has you."

Brad offered a hand, and Alex shook it. "Yes, thank you," he said. "Please let us know how he's doing."

"I will, of course."

Marilyn turned toward Neil and took his hand, squeezing it tightly as she said, "Again, I'm sorry."

"It is I who am sorry, Marilyn," he said, "for all the grief I brought into your life."

"All of that is in the past," she said. "We need to leave it there."

Brad and Marilyn left the room. Alex turned to his father and got another hug. They walked together to the parking lot, saying very little.

Chapter 16

The minute Alex got in his car, something shifted in his brain and he felt a deep dread, perhaps even panic. He called the hospital only to be told that Jane wasn't in Barrett's room; no one seemed to know where she was. He called the house, and Susan assumed Jane was at the hospital. He arrived and hurried to Barrett's room, where nothing had changed. The child was sleeping deeply. He noticed the scriptures open in the chair near the window. He was wondering where to begin looking for Jane when he heard her say, "The doctor wants to talk to us." He turned to see her sitting on the floor in the shadows, her arms wrapped around her knees. "He should be checking back shortly to see if you're here."

"I'm here," Alex said, for lack of anything better to say.

"We both know what he's going to tell us," she said in a voice that was void of any emotion. "It's been more than forty days, Alex."

"I know," he said in the same toneless quality, gazing helplessly at Barrett.

"Until I hear him say it, I don't think I can believe it."

"I'm still holding out for a miracle," he said, but he didn't sound convincing enough to convince even himself.

"I don't believe in miracles anymore," Jane said. "I don't even believe that . . ." She stopped when they heard someone coming into the room. She came to her feet when they realized it was the oncologist.

"Good, you're here," he said, and Jane reached a trembling hand toward Alex. He wrapped an arm around her shoulders and held her close. The doctor looked at them directly and said it with compassion. "There's nothing more we can do. The important thing now is just to keep him comfortable. Do you have any questions for me?"

"No," Alex said, but he couldn't bring himself to say thank you—even though there was no measuring all this man had done for them, for their son. And his compassion and kindness had always been evident.

The doctor put one hand on Alex's shoulder, the other on Jane's. "I'm so sorry," he said. "You know where to reach me if I'm needed."

He left the room, and Alex felt Jane's entire body start to shake. Or was it his own? Both, perhaps. She turned her face to his chest, took his jacket into her fists, and let out a mournful cry that was muffled by the fabric of his shirt. She cried helplessly while he couldn't even come up with a single tear. He felt drained of strength and horrified with shock.

With no warning, Jane moved away from him, breathing as hard as if she'd just run a mile. She began ranting about how God had betrayed them, and no religion was worth so high a price. Even in her raging she kept her voice low, conscious of the fact that they were in a hospital, and Barrett was sleeping. But she cried and cursed and paced the room while Alex's sense of horror deepened. *Who was this woman disguised as his wife?* he wondered. He'd never seen her like this, never heard such language come out of her mouth. And then she picked up the scriptures and threw them with a vengeance to the floor where they slid and landed at Alex's feet.

"I don't believe anymore," she snarled as if it were his fault. "I don't believe in prayer, or faith, or even God. If there is a God, and he's taking my son, then I don't want anything to do with Him."

Alex watched as if through a fog, realizing that to hear her say such things hurt worse than the prospect of his son dying. He wanted to tell her that she was upset and hurt and angry and she didn't really mean it. But something in her eyes made it clear that she *did* mean it, and there was nothing he could say to change her mind. And if Barrett's mother had stopped praying for him, stopped believing in miracles, what chance could they possibly have of getting one?

Before he could come up with a single syllable, she grabbed her purse and rushed from the room, saying, "I can't stay here any longer and watch him die. Let me know when it's over, and I'll see if I can make it to the funeral."

For minutes after she left the room, Alex just stared in the direction she had gone, feeling more alone than he had since she'd been in a coma. He finally bent down to pick the scriptures up off the floor. He meticulously straightened the few pages that had been crumpled by the way the book had landed. He set the book in the chair and then sank to his knees beside Barrett's bed.

"Dear Father," he cried softly, pressing his head into his hands, "how can I pray for Thee to spare my son, if it is Thy will to take him? Please help me to understand Thy will, Father, and to accept it even if I don't understand it." The shock began to subside, and he heard himself sob. "Please, Father, show me . . . guide me. Whatever Thy will, help me put my family back together." He sobbed again and again without tears, and then he just listened— to the sound of Barrett's breathing, to the distant hospital noises that were so familiar to him. And there in the midst of those sounds came a still small whisper in his mind. *There is nothing you can do for Barrett right now. It is Jane who needs you.*

Alex shot to his feet, taking only a moment to touch his son's face. In the car he called the house. "Did Jane come home?" he asked Susan.

"Yes, but . . . she just ran up the stairs and locked herself in her room; wouldn't say a word. What's happened?"

"They told us . . ." He swallowed hard. "They told us there's nothing more they can do."

"Oh, I'm so sorry, Alex," she said with tears in her voice.

"So am I," he said, not willing to let the shock subside at the moment. "I'm on my way home. If Jane tries to leave, you call me immediately."

"I will," she promised.

At the house, Alex took the stairs three at a time and wasn't surprised to find the bedroom door locked. "Open this door, Jane," he called.

"I need to be alone," she called back.

"Well, I need to be with you," he said firmly but got no response. "Open the door, Jane, now!" Still he heard nothing, and he shouted, "I broke down a door last week; don't think I won't do it again! You've got ten seconds to . . ."

He heard the lock turning, and then the knob. The door slowly opened to show her standing sullenly, her face red and swollen, her eyes afraid and careworn. Alex stepped into the room and closed the door behind him. He took her shoulders firmly into his hands and pulled her face close to his. "Don't you *ever* shut me out again," he growled quietly. "I don't care how bad life gets, or how much we may have to lose before it's over, I will *not* be left to face it alone. Do you hear me?"

She only gazed at him with a hollow stare that reminded him of Barrett. He shook her gently and spoke in a hot voice. "Remember me? I'm the man in your life, Jane. I'm the one you exchanged sacred vows with. Remember? I'm the one who helped create this child, and I have stood beside you every step of the way through every joy and horror in his life. We are in this *together!* We brought him into this world together, and if it is his time to go, we will usher him out of it—together. Do you understand what I'm saying?"

Jane nodded and hung her head, pressing the backs of her hands to her face as if she could hold back the fresh onslaught of grief that rushed out of her in heaving sobs. She wilted like a rag doll, and Alex let go of her shoulders to catch her in his arms. He carried her to the bed and laid her there, stretching out beside her. She wept inconsolably while he pushed her hair back from her face and wiped at her tears. When she finally calmed down to an occasional whimper, he lifted her chin with his finger, fully tilting her face to his view. He kissed her hard and held her tight until she responded with a wordless beckoning, entrusting herself to him completely. With little effort he drew her with him into a brief but perfect sanctuary where nothing mattered but the love they shared. And the love they shared replenished the strength they needed to somehow keep putting one foot in front of the other for one more day, one more hour.

The magical silence between them gradually merged back into reality as she began crying again, and her grief filled the air around them. But even that felt sacred to Alex. Her tears clearly expressed his own anguish that refused to come beyond the wall of shock that was presently holding it back.

"I can't stop crying," she muttered.

"And I can't start," he said. She looked at him, puzzled. He pressed a hand over her face and into her hair. "I'm terrified of having it hit me. Right now I just feel . . . numb."

"I envy that," she said, setting her head to his shoulder. "I feel as if my every nerve is going to burst from the pain." Her weeping accelerated again. "It's too much, Alex. First my father, now Barrett. How can I go on? I just don't know . . . how to go on."

"We'll find a way," he said. "I don't know how, but . . . somehow . . . together . . . we will."

She wrapped her arms tightly around him as if she believed him. And a few minutes later she was asleep. He found it funny that the moment he knew she was resting peacefully, he had the impression that he needed to return to the hospital. He eased carefully away from her and covered her with a blanket, then he wrote a note and taped it to the bathroom mirror. *I'm spending the night with Barrett. I'll call in the morning. Get some rest. I love you, Alex.*

Alex found Susan playing with the children. He hugged each of them, thanked Susan for all that she did to keep them glued together, then he hurried back to Barrett's side. Nothing had changed, and he almost hated feeling compelled to be here when he felt so thoroughly helpless. He sat for a long while, leaning against the edge of Barrett's bed, not certain if he was praying or just sporadically bouncing silent pleas around in his head. Perhaps it amounted to the same thing. He touched Barrett's little face, relishing the evidence of his being alive, while he wondered how it would feel when that evidence no longer existed.

"Alex?" he heard a voice say and lifted his head.

Recognizing the transplant director, he came to his feet. "Yes?" He couldn't figure why she would be here this time of day.

"We've found another donor for Barrett," she said.

Alex felt himself teeter, and he had to grip the edge of the chair to steady himself. The tears he'd been unable to find suddenly surfaced. Hardly daring to believe it, he asked in a cracking voice, "Are you sure?"

"Yes, I'm sure. I wouldn't give you false hope now, Alex. It's for real."

"Who?" Alex squeaked. *He couldn't believe it!*

"Actually, it's someone who came in as a volunteer and asked to be tested a while back, but we didn't want to move forward until we knew for certain this graft wasn't taking. He just said he felt like he should be available and try. Logically this should not be a match, Alex. But it is. Between you and me, I'd call it a miracle." She motioned toward the hall. "He'd like to talk to you."

"Of course," Alex said and followed her down the hall and around the corner, trying to remain calm even though he was trembling from the inside out. At first, seeing Wade leaning against the wall made Alex think he'd just come to visit, then the connection struck him, and he couldn't take another step. Wade stood up straight and looked toward him, alert, maybe nervous, as their eyes met.

"I believe the two of you know each other," the director said. "I'll leave you to talk. We'll get the details worked out."

She left at a brisk pace. Alex found it difficult to breathe as his vision of his brother became blurry behind the tears gathering in his eyes. He was glad they were alone in the hall when the tears fell. He forced his voice enough to say, "I thought you weren't up for parole until tomorrow."

"The hospital left a message for me. I told Hadley there was something I needed to take care of." Wade glanced down. "I didn't want you to know . . . unless I was a match . . . and unless it was needed. They told me it wasn't likely I would be a match, but I wanted to try anyway. They tell me the matchup is a miracle."

"In more ways than one, in my opinion," Alex said. "What made you decide to be tested?"

Wade shrugged. "Maybe I was inspired," he said facetiously.

"I'm absolutely certain of it," Alex said firmly before he stepped toward his brother and hugged him tightly. "You could save his life," he muttered, still holding tightly to him.

Wade whispered in a quavering voice, "I'm sure going to try."

Alex drew back from their embrace and demanded quietly, "How did you pay for the testing? I know it's not cheap."

"You can thank Dad for that. I felt like I should ask, so I did. He just wrote out the check."

Alex smiled. "He's a good man."

"Yes, he is," Wade said and smiled in return.

* * * * *

Alex pushed open the bedroom door, certain he'd find Jane asleep. But the lamp near the bed was on, and she was standing near the window, looking out into the darkness.

"Hi," he said, and she turned toward him.

Jane felt her heart quicken to see Alex standing in the doorframe. How could she ever tell him what his love meant to her? His words of earlier, his affection, his commitment to her even when she had declared to have lost faith in all that was precious to him. She sensed expectancy in him, as if he needed to tell her something. But his expression was unreadable. Her stomach tightened as he closed the door and leaned against it, as if he were too weak to move.

"He's gone, isn't he," she blurted. "He's gone and I wasn't there, and I'll never see him alive again and—"

Alex quickly crossed the room and pressed his fingers over her mouth. "No. He's not gone. He's stable."

"Then what's wrong?"

"Sit down," he said, and she did. He knelt beside her and took her hands into his. "Driving home," he said, "it occurred to me that . . . hope is a very fragile thing. I realized that through my experiences of trying to save lives, the longer you can get them to hold on, the more intense your hope becomes. And if you lose them after all that hope has been invested, the loss is all the more devastating. It's ironic really. It almost makes you want to give up sooner, to avoid the letdown. But that wouldn't be right. To save a life, every effort must be filled with hope. And sometimes . . . sometimes, Jane . . . the hope pays off, and a life is saved. For me in the ER, we usually know in a brief period of time if our efforts have paid off or not. For Barrett, it's taken many months to come to this point. And I wonder . . . if he had another chance, would we be willing to invest more time, more energy . . . more hope . . . at the risk of making it harder up the road? Would we take the risk of putting hope into another chance, believing that it might pay off? That's faith, don't you think? To hope for something and do it even though it might bring yet a deeper heartache."

"What are you saying, Alex?"

"Oh, Jane," he touched her face, "please tell me you didn't mean it. Please tell me that you still believe in miracles, that somewhere deep inside you still believe that God is there for us, even if we can't understand His ways."

She looked away. "I don't know what I believe anymore, Alex."

"You're hurt, and scared, and angry. And that's understandable. But I know you, Jane. You're the one who carried me through all those years of anger and bitterness, leading me to the light. In your heart, Jane, you have to know it's true. You have to believe in miracles, Jane. At the very least, you must find some inkling of hope inside yourself, even if it's simply the hope that we can go on living without him and find happiness."

She looked searchingly into his eyes, but all she said was, "You mustn't give up on me, Alex."

"You never gave up on me," he said, and then he smiled.

Jane began to realize that something was incongruous about this conversation—or his attitude. "Why are you smiling?" she demanded, as if it were criminal. His smile widened and tears formed in his eyes. "Tell me!" she insisted.

"Oh, Jane," he said, and the tears trickled down his face, "we've been given a miracle, a second chance."

"What do you mean?" she asked breathlessly.

He made a noise that was a combination of sobbing and laughter. "We have another donor, Jane." He sobbed again. "They're doing the graft first thing in the morning."

Jane sucked in her breath and couldn't let it out. She gasped again and again until Alex feared she would hyperventilate. "Breathe," he whispered, taking her face into his hands. "Come on, breathe."

She finally let out a breath on the wave of a stifled sob. Tears of hope flowed as freely as her tears of grief had earlier. She clung to Alex and wept, and this time he cried with her, praying that their newfound hope would not be in vain.

* * * * *

Alex picked up a hospital courtesy phone and punched in a number, and then he waited for the phone to be answered. Hearing a teenaged boy say hello, Alex asked, "Is your mother there?"

"Yeah, just a minute."

"Hello," Marilyn Morrison said into the phone.

"Marilyn," Alex said.

"Yes?"

"This is Alex Keane."

"Hello," she said with hesitance.

"There's something I think you should know about Wade, about this situation. I know it's been very difficult for you . . . for your family. And I know you've wished that it had never come into the open. You said as much."

"Yes, I admit to that."

"Well, I think you need to know that . . . Wade is having a medical procedure done at the moment."

"What?" she demanded, obviously wondering what the problem was, and what it had to do with their previous conversation.

"He's fine. He's donating bone marrow." She became very silent, and he continued. "My son has leukemia, you see. He's six." He heard her gasp, then become silent again. "He's been getting heavy chemotherapy for about two years. When I met Wade, my son had just been given a transplant from my bone marrow, and he's been in isolation in the hospital for several weeks. But the graft didn't take, and we thought we were going to lose him. Wade had the tests done without our knowing. He's a match, a *miraculous* match. He's giving my son another chance to live, Marilyn. If your secret had remained a secret, Barrett would not have survived until a possible match could have been found elsewhere. Wade is a miracle to us. I just wanted you to know that. I'm truly sorry for the hardship you've gone through because of this, but you need to realize that your sacrifice has not been in vain. Whether this graft takes in my son or not, we will forever be grateful that Wade came into our lives and gave us another chance . . . and more time."

There was only silence on the other end, and then a sniffle. And another. "I'm glad you told me," she said. "We will pray for them—my son, and yours."

"Thank you."

"Please . . . let us know."

"I will," Alex said and ended the call.

He returned to his seat in the surgery waiting room, wishing he could care about anything in the magazines lying around. His thoughts were consumed with what was taking place, and how his son's life was hanging in the balance. Once he'd come to some degree of resignation in losing Barrett, it was almost frightening to feel himself investing new hope. He prayed again that his hope would not be in vain, for Jane's sake if not his own. He felt grateful, at least, that his other children were too young to comprehend the full depth of what was taking place. Katharine saw her brother as much as it was possible, but that was usually through a window these days. And she could hardly remember actually playing with him. In spite of how much they talked about him, she had quickly become accustomed to not having him around. And Preston. Would Preston grow up only knowing his brother through pictures and stories? Alex prayed that would not be the case. He wanted them to be brothers for life, in every sense of the word.

Alex turned to thoughts of his own brother. He felt somehow as if they had shared a lifetime together, as if they had known each other so much longer than they had. Thinking back to their first meeting, he was amazed to consider how quickly they had come to bantering with complete honesty, as if they had immediately found a brotherly relationship just in knowing the blood they shared. They had been through much together, and now Wade was giving him new hope where he'd given up *all* hope.

Alex heard his name and lifted his head. "Marilyn," he said, coming to his feet.

"It took a while to find you. I hope it's okay that I came."

"Of course," he said. "Sit down."

They sat side by side, and she said, "Is he still in surgery?"

"Yeah, but I don't think it will be much longer."

"Do you think he would be upset if I saw him?"

"I don't know," Alex said. "But I think it would be a risk worth taking. Maybe he'll be more humble in a hospital bed."

"Or more grumpy." She gave a wan smile, then looked down. "I didn't know about your son. I'm certain all of this drama with Wade hasn't been easy for you. When I think of your dealing with this on top of your son's illness, I just . . ."

"It's okay," Alex said. "I guess it gives us something in common."

"What's that?"

"We've both been struggling with losing a son and wondering if the loss would be permanent. If we had . . ." He stopped when the surgeon appeared. Alex came to his feet, and Marilyn followed his example.

"Everything went without a glitch. He's a little groggy, but he's coming around. You can see him if you like."

"Thank you," Alex said and took Marilyn by the arm, leading her to where he knew Wade would be. She hesitated at the door of his room while Alex moved close to the bedside and put a hand on Wade's arm. He opened his eyes and showed a lazy smile.

"How do you feel?" Alex asked.

"Like a pin cushion," Wade said. "But then, you've been here. You shouldn't have to ask."

"There's somebody here to see you. Are you up to company?"

"I'm talking to you, aren't I?" he said, still sounding groggy.

"I'm not company," Alex said. "I've seen you puking."

"So you have," Wade said, then asked, "Who's here?"

Alex turned and motioned Marilyn into the room while he kept a close eye on Wade's expression. When he saw his mother he looked surprised but not upset. Marilyn hesitated as if to gauge whether she should come any closer.

"Hi, Mom," he said.

"Hi." She took another step.

Wade reached a hand toward her, and Alex could see Marilyn struggling to keep her emotions under control. She took another step and slipped her hand into Wade's. Their eyes met, and Wade smiled at her. A little joyful noise involuntarily escaped her mouth before she said, "I'm so proud of you. When Alex called and told me what you were doing, I had to come."

"It's not a big deal, Mom," Wade said and glanced at Alex, adding facetiously, "Can't a guy keep a secret around here?"

"Nope," Alex said. "Maybe I should leave the two of you alone a few minutes to—"

"No, it's okay," Wade said. "Please stay."

Alex wondered if he was fine with his mother's visit, but not comfortable enough to be left alone with her. Did he fear some kind of argument starting, perhaps? Or at the very least, maybe he didn't want any uncomfortable topics to come up.

Alex just sat down and watched as Marilyn pushed Wade's hair back off his face and kissed his brow, showing visible relief when Wade didn't resist her affection. His heart quickened to see the silent signs of healing taking place. Wade was clearly very sleepy, and neither of them seemed to have anything to say, but the absence of words didn't feel important.

Marilyn touched his face again and said, "I'll let you rest. Would it be all right if I check back to see how you're doing?"

"Sure," he said, and she gave him a tender smile before she squeezed his hand and moved away.

"Thank you," she said to Alex on her way to the door. "You stay. I need some time."

He nodded, and she hurried out of the room. Alex eased closer to Wade and asked, "How do you feel?"

"You asked me that already."

"That was before you saw your mother."

"I'm fine," Wade said. "Thank you for calling her."

"I thought she should know. I called her because I wanted her to know that something good had come out of all of this. Your giving my son another chance is a tremendous blessing, Wade. I thought she should know."

Wade took hold of Alex's hand. "Knowing you're my brother is a blessing to me, Alex." He added more lightly, "So, I bet you're glad I didn't die last week, eh?"

Alex was firm in his response. "For a number of reasons, yes." His voice lightened as he added, "I guess I can tell you now that you never would have died from that cut on your wrist."

Wade's eyes widened. "Why not?" he asked as if the idea of not dying would have been a tragedy.

"I'm assuming you're past being suicidal enough that if I tell you the reasons you won't ever go trying it again."

"Never," he said firmly. "If I ever start feeling *remotely* tempted, I am going to call you and make you come and hold my hand."

"Good boy," he said. "And if I'm not available?"

"I'll call Dad," he said, and Alex smiled. "So tell me. I wouldn't have died, really? But . . . you were so upset. I thought . . ."

"You thought I was upset because if I hadn't gotten there when I had, I would have found you dead?"

"That's right."

"So let me clarify something. If you hadn't died from that attempt, but you still wanted to die, you likely would have tried something else. It was more your state of mind that scared me, as opposed to the amount of blood you were losing."

"I see," Wade said. "So, what did I do wrong?"

"Well, you got the direction of the cut right, but it wasn't nearly deep enough to do any real damage. Your arms were elevated, and . . . it really doesn't matter. Just know that your blood would have started to clot long before you would have bled enough to even lose consciousness."

Wade took a deep breath. "I must admit that I'm somewhat relieved to hear that."

"You are?"

"Yeah. At least I know my own ignorance would have saved me, even if you hadn't shown up. I don't think I would have had the nerve to try something else."

"I'm glad to hear that." Alex smiled and tousled Wade's hair. "I'm going to take your mom's advice and let you rest. But I won't let you go too long without seeing me."

"Okay," Wade said. "Just remember, when you take Barrett to the zoo, I get to come along."

Alex briefly choked on a rise of tears. "I'll be counting on it."

Chapter 17

Alex hurried from the room, fighting for control, suddenly wanting to see Barrett, just to make certain nothing had gotten worse. He passed Marilyn as he turned a corner, and she looked as surprised to see him as he was to see her. She gave an embarrassed laugh, then said, "Thank you, Alex."

"I'm glad it went well."

She appeared slightly tense, then said, "I . . . would like to talk to you about something, but . . . I can see you're in a hurry. Perhaps you could call me when it's convenient."

Alex sensed her need to talk and said, "That would be fine, or . . . you could walk with me."

"Are you sure?"

"Of course," he said and motioned for her to join him. He slowed his pace a little and asked, "So, what's on your mind?"

"Well, there are some things I've wondered about a great deal; things that I've always assumed I would have to be content not knowing, but . . . now that you and I have gotten to know each other a little, I feel like perhaps I could talk to you . . . frankly. I don't want to be . . . inappropriate or . . . presumptuous. I just have a couple of questions, and . . . if you're not comfortable telling me something, just say so. I'll not be offended."

"Fair enough," he said.

"I know we're talking about a sensitive issue here," she said, "but I've long ago gotten over being embarrassed or fragile over it. Emotional, perhaps," she added with a little laugh.

"Go on," Alex encouraged her, and she looked surprised as they stepped into the skywalk. "I need to go next door, if that's okay. I can help you find your way back."

"Oh, it's fine," she said and returned to her purpose. "The thing is, first of all, I would just like to know how your father is doing. I mean . . . I know this has been hard on him, but beyond that, before that. Has he been well? I know now that he was baptized again, but beyond that I haven't known anything. Keeping a safe distance was important, even though I should have tried harder to contact him about Wade. But those issues are really irrelevant now. Now we know we share a son, and I have a feeling we might keep popping up in each other's lives—perhaps the way divorced parents might. I'm rambling now, but . . . I just wonder how he's done. I've worried about him."

"Well," Alex said, "I don't think your concern or wondering is inappropriate. I think he's wondered and worried about you, as well. I had no contact with him for many years. When he first showed up in my life I was angry; I wanted nothing to do with him. Gradually some things happened to open my eyes. Maybe that's why I relate to Wade. I've been where he's been, and I really believe he'll come around."

"He seems to be."

"Yes, I think he's making progress. Anyway, when I finally reconciled with my father, I learned that he'd had a long, hard road following his separation from you. He hit rock bottom . . . like you did. I'm not sure I know much more than what he talked about in that session. He told me he was suicidal before he got the help he needed to come to terms with his reasons for leaving his family in the first place. He went through a lot of counseling, and eventually he found Roxanne. The man I know now is firm in the gospel, positive, and happy—in spite of the recent drama. He has regrets, but he's come to terms with them, I believe. This situation with Wade has opened old wounds for him, as it has for you, I'm sure. But overall I think he's doing very well."

"The two of you are close."

"Yes, we are. He's one of my best friends." He laughed softly. "Something I never would have dreamed possible at one time."

"And what of your mother, Alex? I hurt every time I think of her. She never got her husband back. When I think how all of this must have been for her!"

"She passed away several years ago," Alex said, and she was clearly surprised.

"I didn't know. How?"

"Heart attack. No warning." Even now, memories of losing his mother were difficult. "But prior to that," he went on more positively, "she was doing very well. She had some tough years, but she too came to terms with it completely. She and my father became good friends, actually. He tells me that she helped get him through some tough times, that perhaps they'd been better suited as friends. He said he was afraid to try and reconcile with her, in a way; perhaps he was afraid that he might end up hurting her again."

Marilyn nodded and looked thoughtful as they stepped through the door to Primary Children's. Alex felt compelled to take this opportunity to make an important point. "Marilyn," he said, and she looked up at him, "you need to know that you were not what came between my parents. My father had some serious issues from his own upbringing; he was deeply troubled and felt unworthy of my mother's love. He sabotaged the marriage. And if it hadn't been you, it would have been somebody else. He's certain that for him it was inevitable he would take that path. I think his biggest regret, beyond the hurt he caused his family, is that he took you down with him."

Marilyn sighed, looking both pained and relieved. Alex stopped walking and looked at her, sensing she had something to say. "I made my own choices, Alex. He needs to know that he's not accountable for that." She put a hand on his arm. "Will you tell him I said that?"

"I will," Alex said.

She drew a deep breath as if she felt relieved of a great burden. He added, "If you'll just give me a few minutes, I'll walk you to your car."

"Oh, that's not necessary if—"

"I'd be happy to," he said. "Sometimes even I get lost around here."

"Where are we?" she asked, looking around as if she'd just taken notice of her surroundings.

"I need to check on my son," he said and took her arm, leading her through the first set of doors. He asked her a couple of questions and explained the routine. She insisted that she didn't need to go in, but when Alex told her he'd love to have her meet his wife, she agreed and washed up.

Outside Barrett's room they could see through the window that a nurse was checking on him. Jane was there, holding Barrett's hand. "Wait right here," Alex said. "We can't have too many people in the room at once."

"Of course," she said. "Take your time."

Alex went in and greeted Jane with a long embrace, then he touched Barrett's little face while the nurse told him he was the same. That nurse left and another came into the room, saying, "Dr. Keane. You're here for the big moment."

She'd come with the bone marrow taken from Wade and was ready to feed it into Barrett's central line. She hung the bag and began the process of converging Wade's offering into Barrett's bloodstream. Alex kept his arm around Jane while they watched in silence as the process began.

"We'll keep a close eye on him," the nurse told Alex and Jane. He knew they would be watching him for any possible negative reactions. He prayed there would be none, that all would go well, and that this truly might be the miracle that they desperately needed.

Certain he'd go mad watching the IV, he was relieved to remember that he'd left Marilyn in the hall. "Come out here for a few minutes," he said to Jane. "There's someone I want you to meet."

"Okay," she said and followed him into the hall.

"Jane, this is Wade's mother, Marilyn. This is my wife, Jane."

"It's so good to meet you," Jane said eagerly.

"And you," Marilyn said. She glanced toward the window into Barrett's room. "I didn't know about your son . . . until today. I hope he comes through all right."

Jane said nothing, and Alex had to ease the tension by saying, "We hope so too."

Jane added, "We're very grateful for what Wade is doing."

Marilyn just smiled, seeming close to tears, then asked, "Is there a ladies room around here?"

Jane pointed it out, then said to Alex once she was gone, "How *is* Wade?"

"He's fine; I'm sure he'll be tender for a while."

"You would know."

"And he had a few tender moments with his mother, I believe."

He saw Jane's eyes smile. "Perhaps there are many good things happening in our lives today."

"Undoubtedly," Alex said and hugged her briefly before she went back into Barrett's room.

Alex waited in the hall until Marilyn returned. "How is he?" she asked, still watching through the glass.

"He's getting Wade's bone marrow right now," Alex said, unprepared for the way his own voice cracked.

Marilyn asked quietly, "How long before you know if it works?"

"The first step is getting it into his system without any reactions. That could take up to a few hours. And then we wait."

"How long?"

"A month or so. Although . . . if it doesn't start working, he may not last that long."

"I'd like to stay, if that's all right." He turned to her, surprised, and she added, "Just for a while, not a month." He smiled. "And you really don't have to walk me out when I go. I can find my way. You should be with your family." She paused, then asked, "Is there anything I can do, Alex?"

"Just prayers," he said.

"Do you have other children?"

"Yes, two; they're younger than Barrett."

"Are they okay? Can I help with—"

"They're fine," he said. "We've been staying with my mother's cousin, and she takes very good care of them while we scramble back and forth."

"If there's anything I can do, you only have to ask."

"Thank you," he said and impulsively kissed her cheek. "Maybe," he added, feeling an unexpected closeness to this woman, "you haven't lost a son after all. Perhaps you've gained one."

She smiled. "Yes, it seems that Wade may be coming back to me."

"I was talking about me," Alex said. Her smile widened, and her eyes sparkled.

"Maybe," she said.

"I won't be far. Let me know if you change your mind about needing an escort."

"I'll be fine," she said, and Alex walked away to call his father and Jane's mother with an update.

When the transfusion was complete, Barrett was showing no adverse affects to his new bone marrow. Marilyn slipped away once it was evident that the first stage of the process had gone well.

As much as Alex wanted to see immediate results from the new transplant, he knew it would take time to see a difference. And he knew they had to accept the possibility that this graft might fail as well. Two days after the transplant had taken place, Alex finished his shift in the ER and hurried to the other hospital to see Barrett. He had expected to find Jane there. Instead he found Wade, his forehead pressed into the palm of his hand, his eyes closed. The other hand was holding the scriptures open on his lap. This particular set of scriptures had come into the room new and unopened even before the first transplant, and the book had never left the room. Alex entered quietly, not wanting to interrupt whatever Wade might be pondering—or praying about. He leaned up against the wall and considered the scene before him. Whether or not Barrett lived, perhaps his struggle to survive had found its way into Wade's heart. Had Wade's giving a part of himself on Barrett's behalf made the fight more personal?

Wade sighed and leaned back, opening his eyes to gaze at the sleeping child. Alex said softly, "I thought you didn't believe in that stuff."

Wade turned to look at him. "How long have you been there?"

"Only a minute," Alex said, scooting a chair next to Wade's. He took the scriptures from Wade's lap and asked, "So what are you reading? Is it any good?"

Wade made a noise that indicated some kind of turmoil, but he said nothing. Alex noted the book was open to John, chapter eight. His eye was drawn to the chapter summary, curious about what topic Wade might be studying. And his heart quickened as the first words he read were, *The woman taken in adultery.*

Not wanting to pry or be pushy, Alex simply asked, "How long have you been here?"

"I don't know. I lost track. I told Jane to go home; she looked exhausted."

"Thank you," Alex said. "I'm sure she appreciated the break."

"I couldn't think of anywhere else I would rather be, and I didn't see any point in both of us sitting here and wondering."

"Sometimes it's just nice not to be alone," Alex said. Wade said nothing, and he felt the need to add, "On the other hand, sometimes you just need to be alone. If you want me to go then—"

"No, it's okay," Wade said. "I think my brain is going to explode if it's left alone any longer with the same thoughts."

"You want to talk about it?"

Wade said nothing for a full minute. Alex just waited. Wade finally made an anguished noise and pressed his hands through his rumpled hair. "Where did it all begin? Where does it end?"

"What do you mean?" Alex asked.

"I just . . . can't stop wondering . . . what was behind it all. My mother married a man who didn't treat her well, refused her pleas to solve the problems. And she what? Puts up with it to a point that she's driven to do something stupid instead of dealing with it effectively? Was her self-confidence so lacking that she couldn't handle it? Or did she just not have the skills to face it appropriately? How do you suppose she was raised . . . what kind of influence made her believe that jumping off a cliff was the only answer? And how was Brad raised if he believed that being an arrogant jerk was the only way to run a marriage? And Dad admits that his own upbringing had problems; he hasn't come right out and said it, but I get the impression there was some ugly abuse in his childhood."

"Yeah, I think there was."

"So, where did it begin?" Wade asked. "How many generations of dysfunctional garbage led up to this? And where does it end?"

"It ends with you," Alex said, and Wade looked surprised. "It ends with somebody having the courage and the strength to say it stops here. You have to decide that you will take what *you* have been given and respond appropriately. All three of your parents have been marvelous examples of reversing the cycles and undoing the damage. Unfortunately it took some hard choices to bring them to that. It's up to you to say that your life will be lived in a way that will keep the next generation free from the kind of heartache you've experienced. It's up to you to take the steps to be free of any pain or heartache that could potentially be perpetuated."

"How?" Wade asked intently. "And yes, I'm ready to hear the answer."

Alex thumbed through the book in his hands until he found Mosiah, chapter fourteen. He cleared his throat and read a few select phrases. "'Surely he has borne our griefs, and carried our sorrows . . . he was wounded for our transgressions, he was bruised for our iniquities; the chastisement of our peace was upon him; and with his stripes we are healed.'" He flipped backward through more pages and came to Second Nephi, chapter twenty-five, where he read, "'. . . As the Lord God liveth, there is none other name given under heaven save it be this Jesus Christ, of which I have spoken, whereby man can be saved.'"

He set the open book back in Wade's lap. "You'll find the same message over and over. It's the bottom line of all we are and all we believe in. You were raised with the gospel; you served a mission. In your heart you know the answers. Either you're a Christian, or you're not. Either you know in your heart that what He did was real, or you don't. And if you know it's real—and I believe you do—you have to be willing to reach out and take the gift He gave. Humanity is overflowing with grief and sorrow and pain. Some of it is the result of sin or poor choices; some of it is simply the result of life's circumstances." He motioned toward Barrett. "Nobody did anything to warrant Barrett having to go through this. It's just life. And no one can logically take away the results of your parents' poor choices. Your existence cannot be undone. Time cannot be rolled back to change the results. But a situation like yours is where the Atonement performs its greatest miracle, Wade." He lowered his voice to an imperative whisper. "It makes up the difference. It picks up where any degree of logic leaves off in matters that will never make sense." Alex put a hand on Wade's shoulder and leaned closer to him, looking him directly in the eye. "There is no need for you to suffer any more for this, little brother. The suffering has already been done. Give the burden to Him. Let Him determine the accountability and judgment of other people's choices. *He* knows where it began, and He knows the string of innocent lives that have been damaged by false beliefs, and abuse, and dysfunction. The only life you have to worry about right now is your own. Forgive them, Wade. Let it go."

Alex saw tears pool in Wade's eyes before he turned away and pressed the heels of his hands over them. He heard Wade sniffle a couple of times before he said, "And what *about* my life, Alex? I've been such an idiot. I said such awful things. I tried to kill myself, for heaven's sake."

"It's all forgivable, Wade. And you don't need me to tell you how that's possible, or the process to make it happen. You know the answers. You just need to accept that they apply to you as well as the rest of humanity." He sighed loudly and added, "Do you have any idea the things I once said to my father?" He chuckled without humor; Wade turned to look at him. "When he suggested that I let go of my bitterness and give it to God, I told him he had a lot of nerve bringing God into it when his hypocrisy in such things had ruined my life. And that was nothing compared to the things I'd said *about* him for years. I can only tell you that a miracle occurred when I looked him in the eye and asked his forgiveness."

"*His* forgiveness?" Wade asked, as if he thought Alex had transposed the words.

"Absolutely. I needed his forgiveness for being so stubborn, so self-righteous, so slow to forgive him. I'd wasted years blaming him for *my* problems. I finally realized that whatever life had dealt me, it was my responsibility to make the most of it."

Wade's emotion increased, and he buried his face in his hands. Alex put an arm around him and held him close while he wept without restraint. He finally calmed down and wiped his face dry on his shirtsleeve. He sniffled a couple of times and asked, "Why do you do it?"

"Do what?"

"I cry like a baby. I bleed. I puke. And you're always right there, never condemning or judging me."

"I don't know," Alex said. "I've been pretty harsh a few times."

"You were just telling me the truth when I needed to hear it." He looked at Alex as if he expected an answer. "Why?" he repeated.

"You're my little brother, Wade."

He let out a bitter chuckle. "Yes, well . . . I have two *other* big brothers, and I can assure you they would not do for me what you have done."

"Maybe they just don't understand."

"You got that right."

"Which doesn't make them bad people."

"I know that, but . . . even before all of this came out in the open, I just . . . never felt close to my siblings. I mean . . . we didn't fight or anything. We just didn't really have anything in common. My older brothers both served missions, but whenever I'd try to have a spiritual discussion with one of them, they just didn't seem interested." Somewhat facetiously he added, "How can anyone not be excited about the eloquent language Talmage uses in *Jesus the Christ?*"

Alex laughed softly and couldn't resist quoting one of his favorite passages. "'But of all His passions, however gently they rippled or strongly surged, He was ever master.'"

Wade looked at him in astonishment, then shook his head. "There you go again."

"What?"

"You just . . . say things, and . . . do things that . . . that . . ."

"What?" Alex asked again.

"You *feel* like my brother, Alex. The way you think and talk, the way you know how to say things in a way that I'll understand. Do you know what it's like to have a conversation with someone that doesn't always come down to sports or cars? I grew up with my nose in a book while my dad and brothers sat in front of whatever game might be on TV. I've tried to be connected to Brian, since our older brothers were married and not around much. We'd do things together occasionally, but he's still more like the others; his interests are just in a different vein than mine. I've just always felt different from *all* of them."

"But you said your parents treated you no differently."

"My parents *honored* the differences among their children. I would never connect my illegitimacy to that."

"That's good then," Alex said, motioning for him to go on.

"When I announced my intentions to be a doctor, everyone but my parents thought I was crazy, that I could never do it. I always thought my fascination with the human body was weird or something." He looked at Alex hard. "Do you know how I felt that first day we met when I realized you were a doctor? When you weren't afraid to talk about what was going on? And it's been that way ever since. I don't necessarily think that's because we share the same blood, because I'm as much related to my other siblings as I am to you. Full-blooded siblings can have entirely different personalities. And I know that people can find friends who share no blood at all and feel strong connections. I guess I'm just trying to say that . . . it's nice to have found a brother, who is also my friend, and to have found a friend in my brother."

Alex could never articulate what that meant to him. He could only say, "The feeling is mutual, kid. I only had two older sisters, and they thought I was crazy when I said I was going to be a doctor.

Now they appreciate free medical advice. I've never really had close friends, to be truthful. Since I met Jane, she's been my best friend. But this," he motioned between himself and Wade, "is different."

Wade gave a subtle smile. "You know, when Charlotte and Becca were talking about how we look like brothers, act like brothers . . . I somehow felt more connected than I ever had before. I can't explain it more than that. It just felt . . . right."

"I know what you mean," Alex said.

He watched Wade turn to look at Barrett, his expression becoming thoughtful. A minute later Alex said, "I've had a thought that I keep forgetting to share."

"Okay," Wade said.

"You told me once you'd always been fascinated with genetics—obsessed, I believe you said."

"That's right."

"Seeing how all of this has turned out, I can't help wondering if God didn't give you that obsession as the means to uncover the truth . . . when the time was right." Wade sat up straighter as if the idea struck him deeply. "Not every person in your genetics class took home capillary tubes to do the experiment. You did because you were passionate about it."

"Good heavens," Wade said breathlessly, "I think you're right." He chuckled. "I *know* you're right." Again he became thoughtful, and Alex remained silent. While he pondered the impact of their conversation on many counts, he wondered if Wade was doing the same. He saw Wade's brow furrow and his eyes become distant, then he turned to look at Alex as if he might have the answer to some unspoken question.

"What?" Alex asked.

"What you said about . . . my parents not treating me any differently . . . and I said that . . . they honored our differences and . . ."

"Yes?"

"I just remembered something." He straightened his back and smiled, as if the memory had given him some level of joy that Alex had never seen in him before.

"Are you going to share or—"

"I was a teenager; I don't remember how old exactly. I remember reading in my room and coming across something I wanted to share with my parents. I knew I could talk to them about anything, and Mom especially just . . . she always said I was more like her, that I understood her, that we were friends. I found them in the front room. Nobody else was around. I don't even remember what we talked about. I only remember sitting there for a long while, just talking to them, like we were equals, like they understood me. I remember leaving the room, and in the hall I recalled something else I wanted to tell them. I turned around, but before I went back in I heard them talking about me and stopped to listen; they couldn't see me."

Wade looked at Alex and laughed softly. "I can't believe how clearly I remember it. It's like I can . . ." He hesitated, struggling to explain.

Alex said what he instinctively believed had happened. "Like the Spirit just illuminated the memory in your mind, perhaps to show you something important?"

Wade's expression turned inquisitive, then thoughtful, then thoroughly enlightened, while at the same moment tears welled in his eyes. "Yeah," he said in a cracked voice, and the tears fell. He moaned as if he felt a joy that was almost painful and wiped a hand over his face.

"What did they say?" Alex asked in a subdued voice so as not to detract from the powerful spirit in the room.

Wade fought for composure and closed his eyes as he spoke, as if he could more fully embrace the memory. "Dad said, 'He really is amazing, Marilyn. There truly is something special about him. I can hardly look at him without feeling like he's some remarkable gift God has given me to remind me every day of how thoroughly blessed I am, a gift I often feel so unworthy of.' And then Mom said, 'You're such a good father to him, Brad. And you're so good to me. Your acceptance of both of us means so much to me.'" Wade laughed softly and went on as if the memory were playing like a movie in his mind. "And Dad said, 'It's no sacrifice to love him, Marilyn, or you. Most people could never understand, but in my opinion, your bringing him into our home is one of the best things that ever happened to this family.'"

Wade opened his eyes and looked at Alex. "I remember going back to my room, feeling loved and secure. Now I realize I had no idea what the undertones of that conversation meant."

Alex smiled. "They really love you; they always did."

"Yes, they did; they do," Wade said as if another epiphany had just overwhelmed him. His countenance darkened as he said with a tone of self-recrimination, "Oh, Alex. I've been such a fool, such an idiot. I said such horrible things to them, about them." He looked hard at his brother. "What do I do?"

Alex just smiled. "You don't need me to tell you that. You already know the answers."

Wade bolted out of his chair and took a step toward the door, then he turned back and Alex stood to meet him, accepting an embrace that left Alex breathless.

"Thanks, Alex," he said. "I've got to go."

Alex just watched him hurry out of the room, and then he laughed softly, sensing a miracle in the air. He turned to look at Barrett and prayed that they might be granted more than one.

* * * * *

Jane walked into the house, wishing she could shake the guilt that lingered with her. She couldn't bring herself to feel any guilt for the absence of prayer or scripture study in her life. On that count she felt more angry than anything, even though she tried not to think about it all. In truth, she felt so thoroughly out of sorts with herself that she hardly knew what to think or feel at all anymore. She felt as if she were simply putting one foot in front of the other, going through the motions of being a wife and mother. But even in that she felt distanced and weary. And that was perhaps her greatest source of guilt. More and more she found it difficult to spend time at Barrett's side. To her he already felt dead, and she couldn't bring herself to hope that it would ever change. The loss of Barrett seemed to have cut off a degree of the love she felt for her other children—and for her husband. She felt incapable of reaching past the aching hole inside herself that felt as if it might swallow her completely. Sometimes she just wished that it would. Disappearing into some dark, mental void was beginning to have its appeal. She wondered at times if she was truly on the path to a complete emotional break-down. At times the idea frightened her; at others she longed to be freed from the thoughts that plagued her night and day.

Jane spent time with the children, did some laundry, and helped Susan in the kitchen. They shared typical conversation, but she felt detached and knew she must seem like very poor company. The phone rang, and Susan answered it, then she handed it to Jane, saying, "It's for you."

"Hello," Jane said.

"Sister Keane?" a woman's voice asked.

"Yes," Jane said, feeling wary. At the moment she was grateful not to have a Church calling, and she couldn't remember the last time she'd gone to church. Most of the time, being with Barrett had been necessary, but she knew she'd taken to using it as an excuse to stay away. Just being called *Sister* Keane rubbed her the wrong way, and she wanted to hang up. But she didn't.

"This is Lisa Lamb, from your old ward. I know we didn't know each other well, but I hope you'll remember me."

"Of course," Jane said, feeling less wary knowing that it wasn't someone in the ward where she lived now. That eliminated the possibility of some kind of assignment.

"Anyway, this is going to sound very strange, but I really feel like I was supposed to call you. The thing is, I'm on the stake activities committee and we are putting together a big adult dance, romantic date night kind of thing."

"Okay," Jane drawled, wondering what on earth this could have to do with her.

"I know your son is still in the hospital, and the timing must seem horrible, but . . . I really felt like I should call you."

Jane said nothing. She was waiting for the punch line.

"The thing is," Sister Lamb began again, "we want to put together a really great floor show for entertainment halfway through the dance. But we don't want it to be like a second-rate talent show. We want it to be really great—professional, classy."

Jane still couldn't even fathom what this would have to do with her, until the bottom line came. "That's why we would love to have you and your husband perform a couple of ballroom numbers."

It took Jane a second for her brain to register that she had once done ballroom dancing. And Alex had done it with her. That part of her life felt like a dream, too distant and obscure to even grasp as a part of the woman she'd become. Once she had adjusted to the request, she had to ask, "How did you know? That was so long ago."

"I was one of those who helped pack up your house when you moved and Barrett was sick. I wrapped and boxed the dance photos of you and your husband . . . and the trophies. I've been racking my brain—and praying—for the best way to put this together. I remembered seeing them and just . . . really felt like I should ask. If you can't, I certainly understand, but . . ."

She left the sentence unfinished. But Jane didn't even have to think about it. Trying to be diplomatic she said, "Your offer is very sweet, but . . . Barrett's not doing well, and I'm afraid it would just be too much. We haven't danced together like that for years. We just wouldn't have the time to do the rehearsing."

Sister Lamb was kind, even though her disappointment was evident. "I understand," she said. "Thank you anyway. We keep praying for Barrett. Even though you've moved out of the ward, we hear regular reports over the pulpit, and he is kept in many prayers."

"Thank you," Jane said and ended the call. Before Susan could ask about the call she'd obviously overheard, Jane hurried up the stairs and shut herself in the bedroom, crying until she slipped once again into that dark oblivion that threatened to swallow her.

Chapter 18

Alex came home to find the children playing in Preston's room, making a typical mess of the toys. He spent a few minutes with them, and then went in search of his wife. He found her curled up on the bed, her back to the door. He entered the room quietly, certain she was asleep. His chest tightened with dread as he walked around the bed to see first a pile of wadded tissues on the floor, and then the hollow glazed look in her eyes as she stared at nothing. He'd seen that look on patients who had come into the ER on their way to the psych ward.

"Jane," he said, almost fearing she wouldn't respond, momentarily terrified that she had gone over the edge. She jumped slightly, startled by his voice.

"Hey," he said gently as their eyes met. "What's wrong?"

"Nothing," she said, sitting up abruptly.

"And this is just . . ." He motioned to the pile of used tissues.

"Nothing is wrong that hasn't been wrong for months, Alex. I don't want to talk about it."

"Maybe we should anyway."

"There's nothing to say, nothing to be done." The despair in her voice broke his heart.

"We can't give up hope, Jane," he said. "As long as he's still breathing, we have to believe he's going to make it."

Jane gathered the tissues from the floor and stuffed them into the wastebasket. "Barrett is lost to us, Alex. The sooner we both accept that the better." She moved toward the door. "I'm going to the hospital. Are you off tomorrow?"

"Yes."

"I'll see you in the morning sometime then, and we'll do the standard changing of the guard."

"Okay," he said, and she was gone. He debated going after her, forcing her to talk, reminding her of how he loved her. But in his heart he knew there was nothing he could say to make any difference. More and more she had these moments of receding somewhere inside herself to a place unreachable to him. He heard the kids fighting and rushed to act as referee, praying at the same time that some miracle would occur to help him find his wife again.

Later that evening Alex had just gotten Katharine and Preston to bed when the doorbell rang and Alex hurried down the stairs to answer it, knowing that Donald and Susan were out visiting friends. It took him a moment to recognize his brother.

"You shaved," Alex declared.

"Yeah," Wade said, rubbing his face. "I had the urge for a new look."

"A new look for a new man?" Alex asked, motioning him inside.

"Maybe," Wade said with a little laugh.

"It looks good," Alex said, not missing the light in Wade's eyes that he'd never seen there before. He'd seen a glimmer of it earlier at the hospital, but now his countenance truly sparkled.

Standing in the hall, Wade asked, "Do you think it's too late to go talk to Dad?"

"No."

"Would you go with me?"

"I'd love to, but I'm the only one here with the kids, and they're in bed."

Wade looked disappointed but said, "Okay, well . . . I guess it can wait."

Alex moved into the study and picked up the phone. Wade followed.

"What are you doing?"

"Seeing if Dad's busy. If he is, it will *have* to wait."

"You don't need to—"

"Hey, Dad," Alex said into the phone, "what are you doing? Good. Do you think you could come over for a little while? I'd come over there, but I'm in charge of sleeping children. Okay, thanks." Alex hung up the phone and said to Wade, "He's on his way."

"I don't know if that's really necessary," Wade said. "It's not an emergency or anything."

Alex shrugged and sat down. "I'm sure he knows that. Being spontaneous keeps life exciting."

"I think we could all stand to have life a little less exciting," Wade said, sitting as well. As if to clarify what he meant, he added, "Any change with Barrett?"

"Not so far," Alex said, hoping that represented some measure of trying to be positive. Again he took in Wade's countenance and had to ask, "What's up, kid? You look different."

"I shaved," he said as if it hadn't come up before.

"Besides that."

Wade laughed as if he were bursting with joy and just couldn't hold it all in. "Well . . . first of all, I called my bishop. Actually, it's the bishop in my parents' ward; he was my bishop until I moved out a year or so ago. He's been leaving messages for weeks, telling me I was in his prayers, and to feel free and come and talk anytime I wanted. I finally took him up on the offer. Funny how fast he was willing to see me. We had a good talk. He told me my parents had been in to talk with him about what had happened. He gave me a blessing and a new temple recommend."

Alex smiled and said lightly, "But I thought you'd stopped going to church."

"Well . . . I was sneaking in for sacrament meeting more often than not. I couldn't seem to stay away."

"Old habits die hard, I guess."

"Yeah," Wade chuckled. "Anyway, I left the bishop's office and went to see my parents."

Alex pretended to be more surprised than he was. "Really? And how did that go?"

"It was incredible, Alex. They are the most amazing people, you know."

"Yes, I know."

"I can't believe that I would be so blessed, to be raised by such great people."

Alex couldn't hold back a little laugh himself. He couldn't resist saying, "Just tell me one thing. What have you done with that other guy who has been impersonating Wade Morrison all this time?"

Wade apparently thought that was extremely funny by the way he laughed. "I can only tell you that what you see now is the real me." He added somewhat histrionically, "'I once was lost but now am found.'"

Alex repeated the next few lyrics from "Amazing Grace," "'Was blind but now I see'."

"There you go again," Wade said.

"What?"

"You're thinking the way I think. How do you know that song? It's not your typical Mormon hymn."

"Maybe not, but it's pretty familiar and famous. I've always loved that song." He paused and said, "So tell me about this miracle that's taken place in you, Wade."

"It *is* a miracle, Alex," he said, his eyes glowing. "I can only tell you that since those days of counseling, I have been praying and fasting and studying more than I ever have in my life. I begged God over and over to help me understand, to find my place, to feel peace—to forgive and to be forgiven. I started feeling some little glimmers of something here and there, but it still just felt so. . . overwhelming, so out of reach. Then after we talked at the hospital, it was just like something inside started to . . . understand. And it was like . . . one minute I was on one side of a line, and the next on another. Something literally changed inside of me, Alex." He said it fiercely, with a passion that made Alex's chest burn. "I could never explain what changed in me, or how. I only know that it doesn't matter any more; none of it matters. It doesn't matter who I was born to or who raised me or whose blood is in my veins. I mean . . . it *matters,* but . . . not in the sense of having to wonder who I am or what my purpose may be. I'm still me, the same person I always was. God loves me, Alex. I know it beyond any doubt. The fact that I have you in my life is evidence of that. He loves me. He always did. He always knew. And He's forgiven me for being such a fool. And everything else related to all of this is in His hands, and it was wiped clean a long time ago." He leaned forward, and his intense look matched the vehement quaver in his voice. Tears burned into Wade's eyes and fell down his cheeks as he said, "It's real, Alex. The Atonement is real. I don't know how it's possible, but I thank God from the depths of my soul that it is. All the suffering, and the heartache, and the grief . . . they're just *gone.*"

Alex came to his feet and Wade did the same. As if drawn by a force beyond their own, they met with a firm, brotherly embrace that silently expressed all they had gone through together, and the contrasting joy of this miraculous outcome. Then he took Wade's face into his hands, saying firmly, "I love you, little brother. You're amazing."

"No, not me," Wade said.

"Oh yes. Do you have any idea how many years it took me to get to where you are now? I know these weeks have been hellish for you, but it's a credit to who and what you are that you were able to come to this in so short a time. Your spirit is strong, Wade. Don't ever let go of that."

Wade smiled. "I love you too, Alex," he said and hugged him again. "I never could have made it without you."

Alex felt overcome with a hundred things he wanted to say. He wanted to tell Wade how much it had meant to discover he had a brother. He wanted to try and explain the depth of the bond he felt with him. He wanted to thank him, still again, for giving Barrett another chance. But no words would form, and he could only hope that Wade might understand. He smiled, and Alex felt sure that he did.

The doorbell rang, and they both wiped at their tears as Alex left the study to answer it.

"Hi, Dad," he said, pulling the door open. "That was fast."

"Hit every light green," Neil said, stepping inside. "So, what's up?"

Alex closed the door. "Actually it was—"

"It was me," Wade said, stepping into the hall. Neil looked toward him, surprised. "It's really not an emergency or anything. I told Alex you really didn't need to come all this way."

"Nothing wrong with being spontaneous," Neil said. Wade and Alex exchanged a sly glance. "You shaved," Neil added. "It looks nice."

"Thanks," Wade said, rubbing his face.

"Shall we sit down?" Alex said, motioning toward the study. He took the desk chair and the others moved to the couch.

They were all seated before Neil said to Wade, "So, what's up? Have you finally decided to swallow your pride and let me help pay for your education?" Wade let out a surprised laugh but said nothing. "It's just between us, if that's the way you prefer it. I know money can't compensate for what you've had to go through, but maybe it will help balance things out a little."

Wade turned to Alex as if for a cue. Alex just shrugged. Wade faced his father and chuckled. "It's okay, Dad. There's no need to compensate for anything. It is okay if I call you Dad, isn't it? I mean . . . all kinds of people these days have two sets of parents, right? I figure it should be okay to have two dads."

Neil gave an emotional smile. "That's more than okay with me. It's an honor to share that title with Brad; he's a good man."

"Yes, he is," Wade said. "And so are you."

Now Neil turned to Alex, as if he might be able to give some kind of explanation. Like countless times before through all of this, Alex wondered how he got the job of supposedly having all the answers. Or perhaps he'd just inadvertently ended up being the mediator between Wade and everyone else. Again he just shrugged.

Neil turned back to face Wade, who took a deep breath and said, "Thank you for coming tonight. I really was anxious to talk to you, and I wanted Alex to be here. The three of us have had quite an adventure together. It only seemed right that we all be together now, because there's something I need to say, but it's not necessarily easy."

Neil leaned more toward Wade. "Say whatever you have to say, son."

Alex saw Wade's visible joy fade into something mildly pained, troubled. He looked down and sounded nervous as he said, "The day we met . . . you asked me a question. Do you remember what it was?"

Neil looked taken aback, but said, "I remember it well." Wade gave him an expectant stare, as if asking him to repeat it. Neil's voice was strained as he said, "Can you ever forgive me?"

"That's the one," Wade said, looking down again. He leaned his forearms on his thighs and pressed his fingers together nervously. "I don't remember what I said; I know it wasn't very kind. And I'm here to say that I'm sorry about that, for the cruel things I said . . . for being so difficult. You've been very good to me in spite of all that, and I want you to know that I'm grateful."

Alex recognized that look on his father's face—completely stunned and dumbfounded. Alex had first seen it when he'd shown up after years of bitterly keeping his distance, to ask his father's forgiveness. Neil said gently, "Your difficulty with all of this has been understandable, Wade."

"Perhaps," Wade said, "but I still need to ask your forgiveness."

"Of course," Neil said. "It's done."

Wade smiled at him. "That's that, I guess. Now we can just . . . put the past where it belongs—in the past. And we can make a fresh start."

Neil looked puzzled as he asked, "Does this mean that you *have* forgiven me?"

"For what?" Wade asked. "For being my father?" Wade shook his head. "Your sin was not against me. It's not my place to hold any judgment on that count. God forgave you a long time ago. As I see it, that makes everything else irrelevant . . . except for the fact that I *am* your son. And I will never be ashamed to admit that."

Neil put a hand over his mouth, and tears pooled in his eyes. Alex recognized *that* look as well. For Alex, seeing his father's response to similar words several years ago had been the starting point of a whole new life for both of them. Alex watched through his own tears as Neil and Wade stood and embraced. Neil laughed through his tears and said, "And I will never be ashamed to call you my son."

Wade laughed softly and hugged his father again. They sat back down, and Neil said, "There's something I need to say. Maybe it's irrelevant, but I have to say it."

"Okay," Wade said with the same caution that seemed evident in Neil's attitude.

"What happened between your mother and me . . . we went about it all wrong. We were both bound by marriages elsewhere, and it never should have happened. So, what I want to say likely sounds hypocritical and contradictory. But sometimes we can't put human feelings into categories of black and white. I just want you to know that I loved your mother, and I know she loved me."

Alex couldn't help feeling some mixed emotions to hear his father's confession. While he'd certainly come to terms with all of this a long time ago, it was still difficult to think of his own mother losing her husband, and to think of the relationship he'd shared with Marilyn. Still, for Wade's sake, he understood how important this was.

Neil went on. "That doesn't begin to excuse our choices, and . . . really, I don't know that it makes any difference. For you, your existence is valuable and good no matter what might have been behind your conception. No matter how a child is conceived, that does not diminish the fact that *each and every one of us* is a child of God, and His love is real and complete. Still . . . I just wanted you to know."

Wade simply said, "Thank you," and hugged his father again before he shared with Neil the miracle that had taken place within himself. More tears were shed as they discussed at a deeper level the elements of difficulty and dysfunction that had been behind the circumstances surrounding Wade's birth. Alex mostly watched and listened in awe. He felt the conversation become distant as his mind was drawn to the hospital room where his sweet wife endured yet more hours of horrific waiting and wondering. The tragedy of Barrett's illness, and the possibility of his death had taken a secondary concern for Alex. In his heart he was most troubled over Jane's broken spirit. Her commitment to her family was evident, but her spirit seemed to be dying, as surely and slowly as

Barrett had suffered. But what could he possibly do about it? He felt deeply concerned over her disconnection from spiritual matters, especially knowing they had always been a deeply integral part of her. But if he even thought to be upset with her over this, he only had to recall her years of perfect patience and acceptance while he had stubbornly resisted going to church. He'd told her then that she couldn't possibly judge or understand his reasons for holding back. How could he not allow her the same respect? Barrett was his son too, and he too had lost a parent to unexpected death, albeit many years ago. But he could never fully grasp how these events, and their timing, had affected Jane personally. He could only stand by her and pray that with time she would find peace over this—whether they lost Barrett or not.

Alex was drawn out of his reverie when Neil declared that he needed to leave. Alex and Wade sat for another hour, talking about all that had happened in the weeks they'd known each other. He was surprised to hear the conversation turning to his thoughts of Jane. He poured out to his brother his deepest fears and concerns, and wept as he tried to reconcile the possibility that Barrett could still die, after all that could be done. Wade's simple wisdom and spiritual insight left Alex stunned as he heard his brother give the same advice that Alex had given him. "You just have to give it to God."

Wade ended up spending the night since he was there so late, and he had nowhere specific to be the following day. Alex woke up with a strong impression and asked Wade over the breakfast table if he would be willing to help. He readily agreed and, as always, Susan was only too happy to watch the children.

Alex and Wade entered Barrett's room to find Jane looking typically dazed and lost. She smiled when she saw her husband, but it was a weary, lifeless smile. Alex kissed her in greeting, then he took a deep breath, uttering one more prayer that she would not reject his offer, given her present state of mind.

"How are you?" he asked. Her only response was a weary shake of her head, and tears in her eyes. He hurried to add, "I've asked Wade to help me give you a blessing. Is that okay?"

She looked skeptical as she glanced at Wade, who was hovering in the doorway, out of earshot. She looked at Alex and said, "I don't know if I even believe in that stuff any more, Alex. Do you know how many blessings you've given Barrett and—"

"I know," he said. "I don't have the answers, Jane. I know it's hard to come up with faith when you can't find a good reason to have any. I'm just asking you to give us this opportunity. I think God has something He wants to say to you. You don't have to believe it, but I ask that you at least listen with an open mind."

She sighed, and something softened in her eyes. Perhaps putting it that way had made it possible for her to accept the blessing without feeling that she was required to have faith in it. In truth, Alex believed that her faith still existed in there somewhere. She just didn't know how to find it through all the grief and fear that had worn her down, month after month.

"Okay," she said softly.

"Okay," he replied and kissed her before he turned to smile at Wade.

As familiar as they'd become with the hospital, it wasn't difficult to find a private place to give the blessing. Jane was seated, and they began. Alex sensed her surprise when she realized that Wade would be giving the main part of the blessing. Did she know him well enough to know that he purposely wanted the blessing to come from someone other than himself? He didn't want Jane to wonder if the words that came out of his mouth were more from his own wishes or personal concerns. And while Alex had shared his concerns with Wade, he knew little of certain aspects of the situation. He reminded himself of miracles already evident as Wade put his hands on Jane's head, radiating a confidence in his own priesthood worthiness, when not so long ago he had felt so uncertain and unworthy of even being alive. Alex put his hands over Wade's, who began by speaking Jane's full name. Alex was momentarily struck with the huge circumference of this priesthood power and the continuity of being able to give blessings the same way that men in Old Testament times had done. He felt grateful to be part of a religion that offered those same keys and gave an understanding of something so eternally profound.

Following a long pause, Wade said firmly, "At this time, Jane, your Heavenly Father wants you to know of His love for you. He knows how difficult the burden of these trials has been for you, and He wants you to know that for this purpose He gave His Son, that in such hardship we might have peace and hope. He wants you to know that Barrett's life is in His hands, and only when Barrett's purpose on this earth has been fulfilled will he be taken home."

Again Wade paused, as if to attune himself to more information that the Spirit might impress upon his mind. Alex couldn't help wishing that some reference of time might be added to this promise. Through all of the blessings he'd given Barrett, he'd never been able to feel anything to indicate whether he would die as a child or grow into adulthood. He wondered what exactly Barrett's purpose on this earth might be.

"Jane," Wade said with a voice of tender compassion, and then a stretch of silence followed. "It is important at this time for you to find balance in your life. Your time with your son is important; however, moderation in all things is also important. Take time to find aspects of your life that have been lost through this lengthy trial. Take time to replenish and rejuvenate yourself by doing things that once gave you great joy. Don't be afraid to rely on those who surround you, who are there to offer the love and support you need to get beyond this difficult time. You can be assured that Barrett will always be well cared for, whether you are at his side or not. A time will come when Barrett will need a mother who is strong and renewed, not depleted and weary."

Alex was grateful for another lengthy pause, which allowed him to internalize that last sentence. While Barrett was mostly unconscious, he had little need for his mother. And if he were to die, he certainly wouldn't need her to be strong and renewed. Was this God's way of letting them know Barrett *would* recover, that he *would* need his mother again?

Wade continued. "Turn to your husband, Jane, for the sustenance you seek. Trust in him. His love for you is true and eternal, as is your love for him. It is within the bonds of the new and everlasting covenant of marriage you share with him that you will find the power to withstand the struggles of this world." The blessing came to an end. Together Jane and Alex echoed Wade's amen.

Alex squatted down beside Jane, taking her hand. He felt some relief to see tears in her soft eyes. He hugged her tightly, and she whispered, "Thank you." But she said nothing more. She stood and hugged Wade, thanking him as well. "I'm going home for a while," she said and kissed Alex quickly before she left the room.

"Thank you," Alex said to Wade.

"It was an honor," Wade said. "I hope it helps."

"I hope so too."

* * * * *

Nothing changed over the next couple of days. Alex encouraged Jane to do as the blessing had admonished and take some time to do something for herself. She spent less time at the hospital, but she mostly just sat in front of the TV, or spent more time in the kitchen when Susan had made it repeatedly clear that she enjoyed cooking and did not in the least consider it a burden.

Alex was almost glad to have to work, if only to distance himself from the problems he felt so helpless to solve. At least while he was at work he felt like he could make a difference, most of the time at least.

During his lunch break, Alex got a call on his cell phone from a number he didn't recognize. He answered in the usual way. "This is Dr. Keane."

"Hi," a woman's voice said, "this is Lisa Lamb. I was in your old ward."

"Of course," he said, and they exchanged some chitchat. She asked how Barrett was doing, and he told her.

"I'll get to the point," she said. "I really feel like I was prompted to call you, but if you say no, I'll understand." She explained how she knew that he and Jane had once been ballroom dance partners and had won awards, then reiterated her need for a few more numbers in the floor show she was putting together.

"I know your lives must be pretty strained right now," Lisa said, "but I just felt so strongly that I should ask. I keep thinking that maybe a diversion might be good for the two of you, something you can work on together. I'll bet you haven't been on a date with your wife in months."

"You got me there," he said, while memories of Jane's blessing and his ongoing concerns marched through his head.

"So, what do you say?" she asked.

Alex felt so good about it that he had to refrain from being overzealous. He hadn't admitted to anyone how his memories of dancing with Jane had been prominent in his mind; he missed that part of their lives and longed for an excuse to spend time with her in a way that might connect them to their falling in love. "I think it's a marvelous idea. I believe you might be right. It could be very good for us, for my wife especially."

"I'm glad you feel that way," she said, "because I talked to Jane about it, and she said no."

"I see. Well, that does complicate it."

"I really tried to settle for that answer, Brother Keane, but it just wouldn't leave me. I'm not trying to be pushy or cause problems in your marriage. I just felt I had to call."

"Let me talk to her and I'll get back to you."

"Okay, but . . . I hope she won't be upset or feel like I went behind her back."

"I'll clarify that," he said and took down her name and number.

Throughout the rest of the day, Alex pondered the situation. He felt increasingly good about how important this opportunity could be for him and Jane. And proportionately, he felt a tight dread about bringing it up. He prayed for guidance, and after work he found Jane in Barrett's room. Making sure all was well, he said, "Come on. Let's get out of here."

"Where are we going?" she asked.

"To get something to eat . . . somewhere besides the cafeteria."

He took her to one of her favorite restaurants, which wasn't crowded due to the early hour. They got in quickly, and the service was good, but Jane still acted nervous and impatient.

"Relax," he said. "The kids are all fine; they're in good hands. Nothing is going to change while you eat that steak."

"Okay," she said, taking a deep breath. "I guess you're right. I'm just . . . in the habit of . . ."

"Being busy, exhausted, and constantly worried about Barrett—if not the other two children."

"Yeah," she admitted.

"I think we've lost something of ourselves through all of this," he said. "It's been bothering me lately. I miss you."

"We see each other all the time."

"That's not what I mean, and you know it."

"Yes, I know," she said sadly. "I know you're right."

Alex took a deep breath. "I know you're struggling with spiritual things right now, Jane, and that's okay. You always accepted me through my spiritual lows, and you never judged me for having them. I'll stand by you no matter what."

She smiled faintly. "That's an ironic twist, isn't it?"

"Yes, I suppose it is. The point I'm trying to make is that . . . I still hope you can respect the words of that blessing you were given. They didn't come from Wade, Jane. But I felt their importance as he spoke them. You need balance in your life. You and I need to spend time together away from hospitals and children. It's like . . . we're parents to the same kids, and we devote everything to doing all we can for them, but . . . we've lost being husband and wife. Our children are the most precious things in this world to me—beyond you. But you and I need to keep the love between us alive and strong in order to be better parents. Would you agree with that?"

"Yes," she said, and he breathed a sigh of relief. They were making progress.

He finished eating and waited until she was almost done until he said, "I've been thinking about how you and I fell in love." She looked intrigued, but also suspicious. "You do remember, don't you?"

"Of course I remember."

"You told me when we shared that first waltz that you knew we would be partners for life. And so we are—in ways we never would have comprehended. What we have shared and faced together is incomprehensible to me, Jane. And I wouldn't trade the life we share now for anything—even with all its challenges. But sometimes I miss those days, when it was just you and me, the music, and a very large floor."

She took a deep breath, and he felt sure he was appealing to her nostalgia. He hurried on. "Given the train of my thoughts lately, you can imagine how thrilled I was when I got a call today that would give us an opportunity to dance together again."

Anger immediately flared in her eyes. "She called you."

"Who?"

"That . . . *woman.* I told her no, and she called you to manipulate me into—"

"Jane," he put a hand over hers on the table, "she is not trying to manipulate anyone into anything. Her call was an answer to my prayers, Jane. It's the—"

"Well, it's not an answer to mine," she snapped and came to her feet. "I'll be in the car."

Alex left enough cash on the table to cover the check and a tip, and then he hurried outside to find her pacing beside the car. He approached her and said, "You can't wait in the car. You don't have the keys." He dangled them out of her reach.

"Give them to me," she demanded.

"I'm not drunk, and you're not taking the keys." He stuffed them in his pocket and kept his hand around them. "We are not getting in that car until you hear me out. And maybe you could tell me how you could have an answer to your prayers, Jane, when you've stopped praying." She glared at him but said nothing. "You have moments of being more angry and belligerent these days than Wade was when I first met him. I'm trying to have a reasonable, adult conversation with you, Jane. Now, do you think you could just wipe the defensiveness out of your brain for a minute and listen to what I have to say?"

"Okay, fine," she said begrudgingly. "I'm listening."

"Sister Lamb called me because she felt strongly prompted. I think she felt that way because this is exactly what you and I need.

It wouldn't take that much practice for us to put something together that's workable. But it would get us away from this eternal waiting and wondering that's making us both crazy." He looked at her hard. "Please, Jane, do this for me."

"I do *not* want to dance, Alex. I have never been less in the mood to dance in my entire life."

"Maybe that's why it's so important," he said, and she made a frustrated noise. He pulled the ace he'd been saving and said, "Remember when you asked me to go to church with you? It was one of the hardest things I'd ever done. But I did it."

"You left in the middle."

"I did the best I could at the time, and that's all I'm asking of you." She said nothing, and he added, "Remember how you refused to marry me unless it was in the temple? I took you to the temple, didn't I?"

"I was under the impression that you wanted to be there. You didn't do it just for me."

"No, I didn't do it just for you. But the steps I took to get there were taken because I knew it was important to you."

She shook her head. "You planned this, didn't you? You had this all mapped out to manipulate me into doing this."

"Yes, I did," he said proudly.

"You are unbelievable!" she said, clearly angry.

"Yes, I am. But you know what? I'm doing this because I love you, because it's for your own good. So why don't you just swallow your pride and admit that I'm right, Mrs. Keane?"

She said nothing, but she looked like she wanted to deck him. He asked quietly, "Why are you so angry?"

"I feel . . . manipulated."

"Okay, I'll give you that. But all I really wanted to do is get you to think about what's important here. Please, Jane."

Again she was silent, but she looked more calm.

"Okay, I'll give you a choice," he said. "You can either do this dance thing with me, or we can go to the temple. We're long overdue."

Alex expected more argument or protest. Or maybe he'd hoped that she would have such an aversion to dancing in her present state of mind that she would choose a visit to the temple in order to get out of it. And he would have been great with that. But she said quickly and firmly, "Okay, fine. I'll do the dance thing. Can we go back now?"

The drive back to the hospital was completely silent. Jane still seemed mildly angry, almost pouting, and he wondered what was really going on inside of her. Oh, how he ached to know her, heart and soul, the way he once had. This spiritual protest she seemed to be on left him utterly disoriented. It was as if they no longer lived the same religion and she was just humoring his beliefs—beliefs that had always been her highest priorities.

Alex pulled the car into a parking place and turned off the ignition, but he made no effort to get out. After a minute Jane opened her door, but he put his hand on her arm to stop her.

"I need to ask you something," he said, and she closed the door. He turned to look at her. "Why are you so angry, Jane? And don't tell me it's about the dance thing. That's just an excuse, and we both know it."

She looked offended by the question, and then she looked away. He tightened his grip on her arm, hoping to imply that he wasn't letting her go until she told him the truth.

"My son is dying, Alex," she said.

"He's my son, too."

She turned toward him. "And why are you *not* angry, Alex?"

"I've had my moments, as you well know. But what good does anger do, Jane? I mean . . . sometimes we just have to . . . cry and scream and break something if we have to, but . . . holding onto anger isn't going to solve anything. Anger festers and turns to bitterness, Jane."

"Oh, and you're an expert?"

"You bet I am," he said in a tone of voice that seemed to prove it. "I wasted a lot of years being angry over my father's choices, Jane, and where did it get me? You're the one who told me how to get past all of that." He softened his tone. "You have to give it to God, Jane."

"What you really mean is that I have to give my son to God."

Alex couldn't help sounding cynical as he said, "Well, at least you're admitting you still believe He's there. I guess being angry with Him means you still have some kind of relationship." She scowled at him, and he took a deep breath, saying more sincerely, "Whether Barrett lives or dies, Jane, we have to trust that He knows what's best."

"Well, I don't trust that anymore. And I can't . . ." she started to cry. "I can't . . . make myself believe . . . he's going to make it. Sometimes I feel almost . . . guilty for . . . just wishing he'd . . . die and get it over with. And then . . ." she sobbed, "I feel like such a . . . horrible mother . . . for even thinking such a thing."

"You're not a horrible mother," he said, pulling her into his arms, grateful that she didn't resist. "I've had moments of wishing the same thing. You can't be hard on yourself for being human, Jane."

"But you're hard on me for being angry," she muttered, "and I can't help it, Alex. Right now, it's . . . all I've got inside of me."

"I'm not trying to be hard on you," he said. "I just . . . I'm worried about you, Jane—about us. Sometimes I . . . don't feel like I even know you anymore. What happened to *us* in the midst of all this?"

"I don't know," she said and eased away, wiping at her tears. "Thanks for dinner," she added as if it had been a date between casual acquaintances. Then she got out of the car and slammed the door.

"That went well," he said to the emptiness she'd left behind.

Through the next few days, Jane was quiet and apparently thoughtful, but she didn't seem angry. On the surface everything seemed normal, but Alex felt an underlying tension between them that he didn't know how to erase. He reminded himself that she'd agreed to this dance performance, and that meant the need for some rehearsals. He'd called Sister Lamb to let her know they would do it, but he felt the need to call her back and see if she could help him out a little. And with any luck, he might actually be able to find his wife again.

Chapter 19

Right after the evening shift change for the nurses, Alex said to the one now in charge, "You see that beautiful woman over there?" He pointed at Jane on the other side of the room.

The nurse looked at Jane, then at him as if he'd lost his mind, clearly knowing Jane was his wife. "Yes," she sniggered.

"Would you ask her if she'd consider going on a date with a guy like me?" He smiled at her and added, "You will tend Barrett for us, right?"

"Sure," she said, her smile widening as if she sensed his purpose. "I'll ask her."

Jane turned to the nurse as she approached. "See that guy over there?" she said, pointing at Alex, who was looking their direction almost timidly.

"Yes," Jane drawled, wondering what this was all about.

"He wants to know if you'd consider going on a date with him. He did say you were beautiful." Jane met Alex's eyes across the room and couldn't deny that she hated the distance between them. The nurse added, "I'll tend Barrett, of course. I can assure you that I'll take very good care of him."

Jane smiled at the nurse then looked at Alex again. She knew she'd been difficult, and her agreement to do this dance thing had been grudging at the very least. He was good to her, and she knew he deserved better than this. With a mock severity in her voice she said to the nurse, "Tell him I only go out with guys who know how to dance."

Jane watched closely as the mediator crossed the room and gave her message to Alex. He listened, and then his face broke into a smile before he said loudly enough for her to hear, "Do I have to prove it to you?"

"Maybe," she said. He lifted his brows dramatically, and his eyes took on a comical, seductive glow as he took a few steps toward her, then did an abrupt turn followed by a smooth succession of rumba footwork that made the nurse laugh. He shot an arm around Jane's waist and abruptly lifted her hand into his. He left her hand in the air and pressed his hand down her arm before he lowered her into a dramatic dip, provoking a gasp from the nurse, then more laughter.

"Okay, I accept," Jane said, and he eased her back up, leading her into a simple waltz step while he looked into her eyes. He brought her to a graceful halt, then pressed a quick kiss to her lips.

"I don't kiss on the first date," Jane said.

"I know better than that," Alex smiled.

"That wasn't a date," she corrected. "We were just . . . dancing."

His smile widened. "Let's get out of here."

"Bye," the nurse said, looking as if she'd just watched a romantic movie.

"So where are we going?" Jane asked once they were in the car.

"Dinner and dancing."

"Dressed like this?" She motioned to the fact that they were both wearing jeans.

"Our dancing shoes are in the backseat. What else do we need?"

She glanced back as if to assure herself, then she just looked out the window. Alex sensed that she felt distracted and nervous, that she was mostly doing this to humor him. But that was fine. At least she was doing it, and she wasn't being belligerent about it.

Alex pulled into the completely empty parking lot of a church building in their old neighborhood. She looked at him askance, and he said, "I made reservations." Before they got out of the car he made sure they both changed their shoes.

He unlocked the church door, while her gaze became increasingly skeptical. "I have connections," he said, making sure the door locked again so no one else could get in without a key. He took her hand and led her up the side stairs to the stage, where only a few of the colored spotlights had been left on, giving it the effect of a dim restaurant. On the floor was spread a blanket, and there in the middle was a beautiful picnic basket.

"Who did this?" she asked, but with a smile.

"I told you. I made reservations. Let's eat."

Jane took a good, long look at her husband and wondered why he should be so good to her. She'd been stubborn and difficult, and she knew it. Yet, his love for her was clearly evident. And she loved him.

They sat on the blanket together and shared the perfect picnic. Alex pointed out the fact that there were no bugs to bother them, the food was delicious, and the company perfect. Jane had little to say, but she did feel more relaxed about being away from the children. She couldn't remember when she hadn't been with either Barrett or the others, or driving back and forth in between—or feeling guilty because she wasn't.

After they had eaten and cleaned up the mess, Alex pulled the cord to open the curtains on the stage, revealing the empty cultural hall on the other side. It too had been left dimly lit.

"Voila," he said, jumping down from the stage. He turned to help her. "Perfect dance floor, all to ourselves."

He pushed the button on a CD player that had been left on the front of the stage, and Jane immediately recognized the music they had first waltzed to.

"Oh, Alex," she said as he put his hands into position, silently inviting her to join him. "It's been so long."

"No, it hasn't," he said, leading her into a simple step. "We've danced in the kitchen and the—"

"But we haven't played this song since . . ."

"Our wedding reception," he said. "I know. It's long overdue."

"I'm sure you're right," she said, and he smiled.

"Now," he said, carefully guiding her, "we just do a little turn, and . . . very good. And a pose," he added as she leaned gracefully away from him, his hand supporting her back. "That's lovely,

Jane," he said in a voice that mimicked their dance coach of many years ago. She laughed softly, and they resumed their waltzing. After a minute he pushed his left hand hard against her right and said, "Relax, Jane. You may be the boss at home, but on the dance floor, I lead."

"Sorry," she said and willed herself to become focused on his lead rather than trying to predict his moves. A minute later she pulled away from him and turned her back, insisting, "I can't do it, Alex."

Alex took a deep breath and said a quick prayer. "I'll be right back," he said and hurried out to the car where he dug out a few of the CDs he had there. He went back inside and put in Bruce Springsteen.

"What are you doing?" Jane asked.

"We're going to dance," he said, searching for the right track. "We're not going to think or talk. This is not about rehearsal or performance. We're just going to dance." He pushed PLAY and the room filled with a lively beat. He held a hand out toward Jane. She took it and quickly picked up on doing the swing. It was casual and spontaneous and took no effort or thought.

"Just feel the music," he said close to her ear before he moved away to broaden the footwork.

Alex couldn't help feeling drawn to the lyrics, especially when the title of the song seemed so metaphorical to all that lay between them. It certainly felt like they were in the dark; in fact at times it felt so dark he wondered if they could see each other at all.

I get up in the evening, and I ain't got nothing to say. I come home in the morning. I go to bed feeling the same way. I ain't nothing but tired . . . Hey there, baby, I could use just a little help. You can't start a fire without a spark. This gun's for hire, even if we're just dancing in the dark.

He felt Jane starting to relax and move more fluidly. He threw in an impulsive turn and a couple of variations on the repeated steps, and she stayed with him. She still looked depressed, but at least she was dancing. He watched her face closely, wondering what might be going on in her mind, while the lyrics filled his own.

Come on baby, give me just one look. You can't start a fire, sitting around, crying with a broken heart . . . You can't start a fire, worrying about your little world falling apart. This gun's for hire, even if we're just dancing in the dark.

When the song ended they were both a bit breathless, but not as bad as he might have expected, considering how little exercise they'd been getting. Of course, those brisk walks from parking lots and through long hospital halls probably gave them each at least a mile a day. Before she had a chance to lose the mood that he'd ignited, he hurried to change CDs, and another song started. She gave him a skeptical glance and asked loudly enough to be heard above the music, "Neil Diamond? Isn't this a bit retro for you?"

He stopped it when he realized he had the wrong song. "My dad left it in the car," he said, "but it's pretty good stuff." He pushed PLAY, and a gentle acoustic guitar began to play. Alex urged Jane into a simple slow dance that was in essence a slower version of what they'd done during the previous song. She seemed a little more relaxed, but he doubted she had any idea how many times he'd listened to this song, thinking of her—in an abstract kind of way.

Stones would play inside her head, and where she slept they made her bed, and she would ache . . . A good day's coming, and I'll be there to let the sun in. And being lost is worth the coming home . . . You and me, a time for planting. You and me, a harvest granting me every prayer ever prayed . . .

He looked into her eyes while they danced, but she only seemed lost somewhere inside herself, that place she'd spent most of her time for many weeks now. She put her head to his shoulder, as if to avoid his gaze. But he just held her and kept dancing. The song ended, and another began. She stepped back, obviously expecting him to change it. When he took her hand and it became evident he wasn't going to, she looked skeptical. The song had an unusual beat with unpredictable rhythms; not typical dance music, but he liked it.

"Just feel it," he said, guiding her into some semblance of a waltz step. "Don't think; just dance."

She made a frustrated noise, and he added, "Remember how Coach would sometimes put weird music on and tell us to just dance."

"Yeah, I remember," she said scornfully.

Alex repeated words their dance coach had said many times, "Dance is an art form, Jane. Be an artist. Become a visual enhancement of the music."

"But I . . . don't know the song," she said as if she wanted to get out of it.

"I do," he said, making it clear she wasn't going to. "Let me lead you through it; let go."

He felt her attempting to relax as they moved into the first chorus, which was a lively African-type beat that went beautifully with a basic rumba step they had once known well. They fumbled a little, but he just laughed and kept urging her on, even though she hadn't yet cracked a smile. The verse slowed down a little, and he urged her through a couple of simple turns, then back into the chorus where he felt a sudden exhilaration as something changed in her. It was as if only her body had been dancing, then her spirit had suddenly awakened and rushed in to become a part of it. She closed her eyes and lifted her face as if to more fully breathe in the music. They were synchronized, attuned, mutually fluid, moving together like one. Impulsively he threw her into a spin, but instead of bringing her back, he let go of her hand, giving the command, "Freestyle, Jane."

He was glad to see her respond to it with no hesitation. She took off on her own, dancing like he hadn't seen her dance for many years. She'd clearly picked up on the music enough to allow herself to become an instinctive extension of it. He knew that before he'd met her she'd had many years of experience in ballet and modern dance that had eventually led her to ballroom. He'd never questioned that she had a unique gift and a great deal of experience, but it had been lying dormant for years. And now she had tapped into that part of herself with more intensity and vibrancy than he'd ever seen. Alex actually felt breathless watching her. He leaned against the edge of the stage, feeling as if he'd just come face-to-face with the Mona Lisa.

"You are so beautiful," he muttered, but the words became swallowed up by the music. He watched her fade with the music, coming to a graceful halt before she turned to look at him. Without moving his gaze he reached over and turned off the stereo, not wanting any sound to alter the spell she had just woven around him.

Alex watched her attempting to catch her breath. She was breathing so hard that he felt sure adrenaline had been pushing her far beyond her own capacity as a mother of three who hadn't danced like that for years. She squeezed her eyes closed and bent over, pressing her hands to her thighs. Then he heard a sob break through her breathing, and another. He moved toward her, then quickened his pace when the sobbing suddenly overpowered her efforts to breathe. She wrapped her arms around her middle and teetered as if she might fall. He caught her in his arms just as she dropped to her knees, and he knelt with her, holding her close while she sobbed and gasped for breath. It seemed that whatever part of herself had been tapped into through dancing was interconnected with the place where her grief and sorrow had been stored away. The floodgates had opened, and she cried harder than he had ever witnessed. She wept violently, hysterically, emotionally regurgitating the fear and pain she'd been swallowing since the possible death of a child had violated her heart and soul.

Alex could only hold her, too shocked by her exhibit to know how to respond. Her crying became so volatile that he realized she was starting to hyperventilate. She bent over suddenly, gasping for breath. He took her face into his hands and shouted in her face,

"Breathe, Jane. Breathe!" She focused on his eyes, looking helpless and scared. "Come on, breathe," he said. "Do it with me." He blew out a long breath in her face. She tried but couldn't do it. "Just breathe!" he ordered. "Do it with me!" He inhaled and exhaled slowly and she began to follow his example. "That's it," he said. "Keep breathing. Just breathe." They began breathing together in unison, reminding Alex of coaching her through labor pains. The most traumatic birth for her had been the first, and Alex became drawn into memories of their bringing Barrett into the world. He wondered if it would become necessary for them to usher him out of the world, and if so, would it be so traumatic, so painful? Would they be able to keep breathing together if they were forced to see their son take his last breath?

Now that Jane was breathing she pressed her head to his shoulder and continued to cry, but more calmly. The tears gradually receded into silence while he sat on the floor, holding her in his arms, wondering if the venting of her pain might have opened any of the doors that had been closed between them. He was startled when she jumped to her feet, saying, "I'll be back."

Alex lay back on the hardwood floor, wondering how long she might hide in the ladies room. She came back a few minutes later and stood above him for several seconds before she said, "Should we try that waltz again?"

"Okay," he said, wondering if this was the same woman who had just emotionally crumbled in his arms. She held out a hand and helped him to his feet. He looked into her eyes, searching for some kind of connection, but she only motioned impatiently toward the CD player. So he turned on the music and stood to face her, holding up his hands. She put her right hand into his and placed her left on his shoulder. The first few steps went smoothly, but as soon as he tried to introduce something different, they fumbled.

She said with chagrin, "We were more in tune to each other when we were strangers."

He nearly reminded her that they hadn't been doing so badly a little while ago. Instead he said, "We didn't have issues between us then. But I wouldn't want to be sharing my issues with anyone but you." He guided her carefully through another turn, then said, "All we had then was what I saw in your eyes."

"And what was that?" she asked as if she didn't know. Or maybe she was testing him.

"I saw exactly what I had been feeling since I'd first laid eyes on you. I was head over heels in love, and with no effort at all I found you waltzing with me."

Jane struggled to focus on the dance while allowing her mind to wander back to that first waltz. She closed her eyes and attempted to feel the music as opposed to thinking too hard. The memory of where their relationship had begun suddenly became clear, almost palpable. She opened her eyes and met his gaze, surprised to feel her heart quicken. *It was still there.* She would never forget the way he'd looked at her the first time they'd danced, nor the way it had made her feel. And it was still there. That consummate look of love. *And the way it made her feel.* Her heart quickened further, and her stomach fluttered while he held her gaze until they came to a graceful halt, even though the music was still playing. And then he kissed her, so much like he had that first time. Then the magic of remembering their first kiss melted into something even more wonderful. A warm familiarity and sweet passion crept in, making it the kind of kiss shared by two people who had been husband and wife for many years, people who had shared every joy and crisis of life. And in the midst of his kiss a marvelous idea occurred to her. If they lost Barrett it would be devastating; she simply couldn't comprehend such a loss. But no matter what happened, she knew that Alex would be by her side. At the moment, she was finding it difficult to believe that God was there for her, but Alex was. And if he could carry her through something so horrible as watching their son slowly die, perhaps he could carry her back to a place where she might find God again. As hard as she'd tried, she couldn't find even a grain of faith within herself. But she knew that Alex had faith, and he had committed himself to her, heart and soul. If he could have enough faith in her to still love her so completely, even when she'd lost faith, then maybe there was some measure of hope that they could navigate through the future after all.

The music was still playing when Alex drew back from a kiss that he considered absolutely perfect, and then he saw something in Jane's eyes that reached deep into his heart. "What are you thinking?" he whispered.

She just smiled and said, "I remember you. You're the guy who rescued me at a restaurant on a Saturday night. And you sent me home with the most wonderful chocolate dessert in the sack with my leftovers."

"So I did." He didn't even try to hold back the joy he felt to hear her speak to him about such things. "I was tempted to put my phone number on the box."

"You didn't need to. I met you again two days later."

"It was destiny."

"Yes, it was."

Jane smiled again. "Do you know what I thought when I found that dessert?"

"What?"

"I remember thinking, 'Wow. Maybe he's in love with me too.' Then I laughed because it sounded so absurd." She touched his face and added with intensity, "Oh, how I love you, Alexander."

He kissed her again until the next song began to play, a lively Cuban beat that provoked them both into soft laughter. Alex kept his arms around her as he moved his feet to the rhythm, and she started to do the same. They both blew it and laughed again. But oh, to hear her laugh!

"It's been too long," she said. "This one's harder."

"It's okay." He urged her to try it again. "You step on my toes, and I'll step on yours. And eventually we'll get it figured out. We won an award for this number. And you were stunning."

"No, *you* were stunning." She kissed him while they continued to dance. "Your form is excellent, Alex." Now she mimicked the coach.

"I think my feet can't remember what my brain is trying to tell them."

She kissed him again. "I wasn't talking about your feet."

"I think we'd better stick to dancing at the moment," he said.

"I suppose," she said and focused on what her feet were doing. They kept messing it up, so she turned off the music and said, "Okay, let's walk through it. Count it out for me."

"I start behind you," he said, moving there. "We're facing the same direction, so we do it together. Left, right, one two three. Right, left, one two three." He repeated it over and over until they were doing it quickly in perfect synchronization. "Okay," he said, "now I turn you to face me, so the steps have to be mirrored."

"Am I changing or are you?" she asked.

"I am," he said, and having no sooner said that, stepped on her toes, which made her laugh. And he laughed just to hear her laugh. "I should step on your toes more often," he said.

For more than an hour they worked through the basic steps of the rumba number over and over, until their footwork came naturally to the rhythm of the music. They took a break while Jane lamented about how old she was getting, reminding him that she'd had three babies since they'd last danced this intensely. Alex just said, "I had three babies too, you know. And I'm older than you. That's why we both need more exercise."

Following their break they worked another hour on remembering the dramatic poses and turns they had done in this number. Their first try on a few of them was so awkward that they both fell into peals of laughter. But with some effort it began to flow the way it once had, and Alex said, "As easy as riding a bicycle." His words were followed by a series of elaborate turns while he held one hand above her head.

While he was pressing his hands down her arms, Jane recalled something else the coach had said and mimicked her perfectly. "Dance like you love each other with a love that is forbidden."

Alex chuckled and turned her abruptly to face him, while the meticulous footwork continued. "There's a problem with that."

"What?"

"We're married," he said and dropped her into an unexpected dip. "There's nothing forbidden about it."

"How delightful," Jane said as he lifted her back up and whirled her immediately into another spin. "However," she spoke breathlessly as they continued to dance, "marriage has a way of complicating life."

"Yes, it does," he said. "So, what should we do about it?"

The dance ended with her leaning into his chest, her leg poised behind her. In the absence of music Jane said, "We should take the time to dance."

Alex actually felt choked up as he contemplated the change in his wife. He'd found the connection he'd been hoping and praying for. Given the broad perspective of challenges in their lives, he felt sure they had a long way to go. But they'd made glorious progress. At least at some level, they were in tune with each other again. And he was grateful.

They continued to practice both the rumba and waltz until it was very late. The reality of how long it had been since they'd done this was evidenced by the need for frequent breaks. But by the time they turned out all of the lights and left the church building, they both felt that they had relearned the numbers they'd once known so well, and with a few more rehearsals they could do a performance that wouldn't embarrass either one of them.

"What about the picnic stuff?" Jane asked as they were getting into the car.

"She'll pick it up in the morning," Alex said.

"Who?"

Alex said facetiously, "That *woman* who went behind your back to manipulate us into doing this. I called to ask if she could arrange a church; the picnic was her idea. I was going to buy a pizza or something."

Jane smiled sheepishly. "Tell her thank you . . . for me."

"I will," he said and took her hand. "And I'll tell her thank you for me too."

A few minutes later Jane took notice of the road they were on and asked, "Where are we going?"

"Home," he said. "Linda's staying with Barrett until morning. Tonight we get to sleep in the same bed."

Jane smiled. "Oh the things that most married couples take for granted."

"Indeed."

"Just don't snore," she said. But she laughed when she said it.

* * * * *

Alex called Wade the following morning, simply to say, "I only have a minute. I just wanted you to know that Jane and I went out last night and had a wonderful time. It was just the two of us for hours. I think she's doing better."

"That's great," Wade said. "I have some news too, and something I need to talk to you about. When would be a good time?"

"Can you meet me in Barrett's room this evening?"

"Sure."

"I'll be there after six. What's the news? I can't wait that long."

"I got a job. I'll tell you about it later."

"That's great," Alex said and felt that maybe things were looking up.

When Alex arrived at Barrett's room, Wade was already there. He told Alex about the job he'd gotten, and they both agreed that it was better than either of the jobs he'd recently lost. Wade was back in school, and by all accounts doing well, but Alex could tell something wasn't right.

"What's up, kid?" Alex asked.

Wade sighed loudly. "You know I've worked hard to come to terms with all that's happened."

"I thought it was all taken care of."

"Not quite. I'm having a problem with that restitution thing." He sighed again. "The day I confronted my parents about the blood tests. It was . . . a Sunday. You see, every fast Sunday, all of the family would get together for dinner and a big home evening thing. Brian's the only one left at home, but the rest of us would come over, and . . . well, I went over early to talk to my parents. No one else was there yet. Brian was up in his room. After they told me the truth, we were all just trying to pretend that everything was normal. We sat there at dinner, and all I could think was how I didn't belong anymore, that it had all been a lie. I got up to leave. Mom begged me not to go. She was upset enough that everyone could see something was wrong. One of my older brothers got angry with me, wanted to know what I'd done to get her so upset." Wade hung his head. "Well, you can imagine how it went from there. I've already told you they all know because I told them. I said horrible things."

"But your parents are okay with that now," Alex pointed out.

"Yeah, well . . . my siblings aren't. I started wondering about it and asked Mom yesterday how it was going with the rest of them. The ones that will have anything to do with her at all treat her like some kind of tramp. And it's my fault."

"Your telling them doesn't make you accountable for their behavior."

"Maybe not, but I sure didn't set a very good example of how to treat her. And Brian's not doing well at all. He's getting into trouble; nothing serious as far as I know. But he's not on a good path. I feel responsible. I feel like I need to make restitution somehow. I'm just not sure how to do it. How do you go back and gather up words you've said that have caused so much hurt?"

"You got me there," Alex said. "I do know that you've been given a lot of miracles. Surely you'll be led to a way to find peace over it."

"I hope so," Wade said and visited a few more minutes before he insisted that he had things that needed attention.

Twenty minutes after he left, Jane arrived. She smiled and kissed him, but he sensed that she was in one of her dark moods. In spite of the progress they'd made, she still often felt distant. While they sat together in silence, Alex prayed for a way to help her reconnect with the spiritual strength that he knew could carry her through when nothing else could. When the silence grew unbearable, he picked up the remote and turned on the TV.

"What are you doing?" she asked. For all the time they'd spent in this room, they'd rarely had the TV on except when Barrett had been watching something he liked. And he hadn't cared about anything at all for weeks now.

"I don't know. Can't stand the quiet."

"Well, good luck finding something better than quiet," she said cynically.

Alex flipped through all the channels twice, finding nothing but sports, obviously stupid programs, and commercials. When he started going through them a third time, Jane said, "Oh, just turn it off. You're not going to find anything worth watching." He then came to something that looked biblical and decided to give it a try. A few minutes made it evident this was a portrayal of Mary, who was now trying to explain to Joseph why she was pregnant. A dream sequence followed where Joseph was having a nightmare about people wanting to stone her and goading him to throw a stone at her. The dream merged into a voice telling Joseph that the child Mary carried was the Son of God.

Jane made the comment, "Sometimes these TV movies are so cheesy."

"I've seen much worse," Alex said, reluctant to admit he was really taken with it. "I'll take the Bible over whatever else might be on."

As the movie progressed, Jane appeared disinterested, haphazardly thumbing through magazines she'd already read. Alex became thoroughly engrossed. The film's focus was on the mother of Jesus, and therefore His life was only shown in the snatches where Mary would have been present, but for the most part it was well dramatized and fairly accurate, although Jane made the comment, "They got the baptism all wrong." But at least she was watching it now.

"Yeah, well," Alex said with a chuckle, "you can't expect these filmmakers to know who to consult on such things. Most of it's actually pretty good."

The ministry of Jesus was skipped over rather quickly, since there was no account in the Bible of His mother being present through most of it. The conversation Jesus shared with His mother prior to the last supper was touching and reverent. Alex couldn't help being intrigued with thoughts regarding the relationship between Jesus and His mother that he'd never considered before.

Through the dramatization of the trial and the crucifixion, Alex had moments where his heart pounded in his chest and he felt near tears. He was surprised to hear sniffling and turned to see Jane crying her eyes out.

"What's wrong?" he asked, taking her hand.

"I don't know," she said. "Watch the movie."

The film ended with Mary's determination to carry on with all that Jesus had exemplified through His life. Alex turned off the TV and was surprised by the thought that surfaced in his mind as he watched Jane wiping her eyes. Feeling compelled to ask Jane some thought-provoking questions, he first set the tone by saying, "That movie would be pretty hokey to watch if you weren't a Christian."

"It really was pretty good."

"Oh, come on. Changing water into wine. Causing the blind to see. Coming back from the dead. You have to admit it all seems a little hokey."

She looked at him as if he'd sprouted horns. Feeling a bit like the devil's advocate for just a moment, he smiled at his own analogy.

"What are you saying?" she asked.

"Do you believe that stuff is true?" he asked.

"Of course it's true," she insisted.

"Then you must be a Christian," he said.

"As you are," she pointed out.

"Of course I am," he said. "I just wasn't certain if you were anymore or not." She looked astonished, maybe angry. He added firmly, "Tell me, Jane, is it true or not? Is Jesus the Christ? Or is it a myth?" She said nothing, but her expression had softened. "If you believe He changed water into wine and came back from the dead, why can you not believe that He will carry you through this?"

Alex got up and left the room, feeling it was better to leave her alone with the thought, rather than giving her an opportunity for an argument. Alone in the hall, he whispered, "Thank you, Lord." It was nice to know that He was keeping track of when something good would be on TV.

Chapter 20

Later that evening when Alex saw Jane, nothing was said about their conversation, but she did seem a little more relaxed. They went to the church building to rehearse and had a good time together, even though they didn't stay nearly as long as they had before.

In the car on the way back to the hospital she said out of the silence, "Can I talk to you, Alex?"

Alex tried not to appear surprised, "Anything in particular? How about flavors of ice cream?"

She let out a little laugh, which he considered a good sign. "Perhaps we could work our way up to ice cream."

"Okay," he said, and still she hesitated. He made no attempt to fill in the silence, allowing her the opportunity to continue when she was ready.

"I've been thinking," she finally said. "You know . . . we did everything right. We got married in the temple, and we both saved ourselves for marriage—even though we had a long wait. And then we created life, Alex. We did it the right way at the right time, but did we have any comprehension of the ramifications of what we were doing?" She chuckled without humor. "I'm absolutely certain when Barrett was conceived that we were *not* thinking about chemotherapy and bone marrow transplants."

"No, we certainly weren't," he said, not particularly enjoying the conversation, but grateful to have her talking. "But you know what? I'm grateful that we did it right. Think of all the children out there who are born into difficult circumstances, often with only one parent to raise them as a result. I'm grateful that we're in it together, Jane. Beyond you, there's no other person in this world who loves Barrett the way I do, and who understands the pain at the same level that I feel it."

"I can agree with that," she said and took his hand. He was wondering if that was all she'd wanted to say until she added, "I don't think I want to have any more children, Alex."

Alex was so stunned he could hardly think straight. He pulled the car over to the curb and put it in park. "What are you saying?" he demanded, turning toward her.

"I'm saying that I don't want to have any more children. Obviously, if you're going to stay married to me, that's something you're going to have to live with. If you can't live with it, you need to let me know."

Alex felt like he'd been kicked in the stomach. How dare she throw a choice like that in his face? He told himself to stay calm and stated what he figured was most important. "I am committed to this marriage, Jane. I will be by your side no matter what, whether I agree with you or not. But I have a hard time believing what I'm hearing. Are you saying that Barrett's life was not worth living? Would you deny another child that right just because one child's life has been a struggle?"

"A struggle?" she echoed. "Oh, Alex, the word *struggle* could never begin to describe it. I could never live through it again, Alex. Never!"

"So . . . what? If something happens to Katharine or Preston you're just going to write them off?"

"Obviously I'm committed to seeing life through with the children we have, but I don't have to make the choice to raise the odds."

"So, the joy we've found in our children is now . . . what? Irrelevant? Does it not balance out? There has been nothing so wondrous in my life, Jane, as marrying you and bringing these children into the world. Nothing has ever felt so right and good as making the choice to give these children life. I'm not suggesting we should have a dozen, but I don't believe we're done yet."

Her voice became fierce without being angry. "How can something feel so right and turn out so horrible, Alex?"

"I don't have all the answers, Jane. But I suspect when parents set out to cross the plains they knew in their hearts it was the right choice. It was hard, but they did it."

"Well, you can't very well turn back when it's a thousand miles either way to civilization," she countered. "How right do you think they felt it was when they started burying their babies in the snow?"

Alex exhaled slowly, reminding himself that an argument was not going to solve any problems. "I don't think we can imagine how difficult that would be, Jane, but—"

"Oh, I don't know. I think we could probably imagine. But do you think those kids who froze to death were puking up blood for weeks?"

"Probably not." He forced composure into his voice. "But what about the kids who got frostbite and had their feet cut off? Or the kids who didn't get enough to eat and were hungry and cold for hundreds of miles? However, if we're making comparisons, don't forget that not a single person in those handcart companies that suffered the most ever lost his or her testimony."

Jane turned away abruptly. "Well, I'm certain they were better people than I am."

"Not necessarily," Alex said gently. "I'm sure there were moments of anger and struggling to understand. No human being could endure such horrors without struggling to understand."

"Well, I'm certainly struggling to understand, Alex. What purpose can there be to such suffering in children? I grieve for what I've lost through all of this, Alex, and I don't even want to think about losing him, even though I can't comprehend that we won't. But the worst pain is seeing him suffer. He's already lost to us, Alex. What do you think is going on in that little head of his when he looks right through us? He probably hates us, Alex. He trusted us and we took him there and signed him over to a depth of suffering that you and I have no comprehension of."

Alex squeezed his eyes closed and looked down, grateful that they were having this conversation but at the same time hating the way she was saying things he'd never wanted to think about, let alone speak aloud. Through a grueling stretch of silence his mind wandered back to the days preceding the discovery of Barrett's cancer. He thought of the moment when the Spirit had let him know that trusting in God would see his family through any possible trial. At the time, Alex would have never dreamed what they were about to embark on. But he had to believe the promise held true. He'd done his best to trust in God, but he wasn't feeling very confident at the moment about his family coming through this trial unscathed. Then he recalled words that Jane had said to him that same day. He felt compelled to bring them up, even though he suspected she wouldn't swallow them easily.

"Do you remember before you had Preston, and I was having those uneasy feelings?"

"Yes," she said warily.

"You told me then that we both needed to trust in the Lord, do our best to stay close to the Spirit, and have some faith. You said that whatever the future might bring, God would make us equal to it, that He would get us through."

She looked even angrier than he'd suspected. "Clearly I didn't know what I was talking about."

"Or maybe you did," he countered. "What is this condition you've suddenly put on your faith, Jane? You can stand back and have firm convictions about living the gospel as long as your trials don't descend below a certain point? And then to heck with it? How can you believe in something for more than three decades of your life, and then suddenly you don't believe it anymore because life doesn't turn out the way you think it should?"

She came back hotly. "How can you keep believing in something when it all falls out from under you like a mudslide? At this point the *best* I can hope for is that my son will die without suffering any further, Alex. *If* he lives," she went on, "will he ever fully recover from the trauma? Physical complications are one thing, but what have we done to his mind, his spirit? And if he dies, then all we have put him through will have been entirely in vain."

"We knew it would be tough, but we knew it was the right thing to do, Jane."

"I'm not so firm on that anymore. I'm not so sure I even know how to feel the answer to a prayer—if He's even listening at all. Maybe it's all just a delusion we've created to justify the choices we don't want to take accountability for."

"Are you saying you truly don't believe in God any more?"

"No, I believe in Him. But He's not the God I thought I knew. My whole life I've stood back and watched life go by, people having trials and struggles, and I'd think, 'As long as they have faith, they'll be okay. They'll find peace.' Do you know how many people have said such things to me since Barrett got sick? And I want to knock their lights out. They stand on the outside and believe that going through the motions will solve every problem. But how can I judge them when I used to be one of them? I realize now that I've never had any comprehension of trial and struggle. What *is* a trial to a normal woman, Alex? Having a washing machine break down when the laundry piles are deep? A car repair that you can't afford? A kid with the flu? Still, trials are relative, aren't they? How can I not have compassion for a tough day in the life of any parent for any reason? How can I not hold a profound love and respect for the countless people who have stepped out of their comfort zones to help carry us through this?" Her voice betrayed the threat of tears for the first time in this conversation. "I don't know if God is there for me, Alex, and I don't know if He will take my son from me. But for as long as I live, I will never look the other way when others are suffering—for whatever reason, for whatever definition they put to their struggles. I will never take for granted living under one roof as a family, the health of a child, the life that we breathe in every hour of every day. I will never look at a sunset or a Christmas tree or a puppy without marveling at the simple beauty of life that is shut out when one is forced to exist within hospital walls. I'm forever changed, Alex. I look back at the woman I used to be, who believed she had it all figured out with a simple formula, and I would not want to be her again."

Alex pondered the change of tone in her words that she was hardly conscious of. Did she have any idea the contradictions she had just stated? He realized then that, while she was too clouded by grief and anger to see it, her faith had not died. She was a good woman with a good heart, and in spite of the way this nightmare had put issues of disagreement between them, he had never loved her more than he did in that moment. He took her hand and kissed it, pressing his other hand to her face as he whispered, "Then Barrett's suffering has not been in vain."

She turned toward him, clearly startled by the comment. Impulsively he pressed his mouth over hers, preferring to remind her of the love they shared, as opposed to giving her an opportunity to counter his words.

"Jane," he murmured, holding her face in his hands, "I know this is hard, harder than either of us could have ever predicted. But I love you, Jane. As much as I love our children, they are the product of the love we share. It was you and I before anything else. We need to remember that. We need to hold tightly to each other. It's the only way a marriage can survive something like this. Whatever you may or may not believe doesn't make me love you any less, Jane. I may not agree with you, but I will always be there for you, and I will respect whatever your beliefs may be. I only ask that you do the same for me. I'm not going to try to change you, and I know you would never try to change me. I can accept you for who you are now, and the place you're at, because you taught me the power of unconditional love a long time ago. Promise me, Jane, that no matter what happens, we will not lose each other— figuratively or literally. Promise me."

She nodded firmly and put her arms around him, holding him as tightly as he held her. Alex rejoiced in her nearness, grateful that the love they shared still existed in the midst of all their disagreement and flailing aspirations. If he thought about it, he could find all kinds of reasons to be afraid or concerned. But he loved her, and she loved him, and for the moment, nothing else mattered.

* * * * *

A few days later Alex had a shift that began at two P.M. He left for work, dreading the twelve-hour shift but feeling grateful for the lack of tension he felt between him and his wife. They'd shared no further serious conversation on any topic, but he felt a closeness between them that he didn't take for granted.

On his way to work, Alex had a phone call from Wade, asking if he would go on an errand with him on his dinner break. A little after eight, Wade picked him up at the door to the ER. Alex got in the car to hear "Collective Soul" playing loudly on the stereo. Wade turned it down and handed him a sack with a burger and fries in it, and a drink to wash them down.

"You eat. I'll drive," Wade said.

"You think of everything. Thank you."

"You were . . . what? Going to go without eating to be with me?"

"Maybe. Where are we going?"

"Shopping," he said. "I need a gift for my mother. I think I found the right thing, but I need a second opinion. It's not cheap, but I've been saving some money and I have enough, but . . ."

"You sound nervous."

"Well . . . it feels right, but . . . logically I fear it might be . . . awkward. That's why I need your opinion."

"Oh, so it will be *my* fault if it ends up awkward."

"That's right," Wade said with a smirk.

"So, what is it?"

"I don't want to say anything first. I just want you to see it and try to imagine how my mother might see it. You've gotten to know her. I want to know how you think she might feel about hanging it on her wall."

Alex made a noise of interest then said, "Turn it up. I like this song."

Wade grinned at him. "You like 'Collective Soul'?"

"Absolutely," Alex said. "Nothing wrong with some good, clean rock and roll. Start the song over."

Wade began the track again and turned up the volume, and Alex wondered if Wade had considered the lyrics in relation to himself.

Change will come, change is here. Love fades out, then love appears. Now my water's turned to wine, and these thoughts I have I now can claim as mine. I'm coming home.

Change has been, change will be. Time will tell, then time will ease. Now my curtain has been drawn, and my heart can go where my heart does belong. I'm going home.

When Wade started that song over again, Alex just smiled at him. They didn't need to say anything to know their thoughts were the same.

He drove to an LDS bookstore, and Alex just needed a minute to finish eating in the car before they went in. Once inside, Wade walked directly to the framed art section and pointed upward. It only took one glance for Alex to feel the impact of the beautifully framed print both in his heart and in his spirit. He sucked in his breath as if a gust of wind had rushed into his face. He knew Wade was waiting for a reaction, but he couldn't force his eyes away, and he couldn't find his voice. The painting of Jesus with the woman taken in adultery had magnificently captured the profound moment of the Savior's perfect compassion and acceptance. Looking at the artist's depiction, it was easy to imagine the richly clothed bystanders skulking away when confronted with Jesus' challenge, "He that is without sin among you, let him first cast a stone."

"It's too much, isn't it?" Wade said.

"Too much for what?" Alex asked, unable to take his eyes away. "I thought you said you could afford it."

Wade made a disgusted noise. "Tell me if it's too . . . *bold*, I guess. I don't want her to feel like I'm trying to advertise her past by implying that she should hang this on her wall. But its message just has a way of . . ."

"Speaking to the spirit in a way words never could," Alex said.

"Yes!" Wade said, clearly thrilled to hear that Alex understood what he couldn't say.

Alex finally turned to look at Wade. "I think it's perfect. For those who see it who don't know the truth, they'll just think it's beautiful art with a powerful message. For those who do know, it will be a constant reminder of charity and acceptance."

Wade let out a little laugh of relief. "That's exactly what I was thinking. It's like we're brothers or something." Alex smiled, and Wade added, "I'm going to get it now."

Alex waited while Wade asked for the print to be taken down and then paid for it. They drove away with the gift carefully tucked into the trunk.

"When are you going to give it to her?" Alex asked.

"I've been thinking about that, and I think I've figured out the best way to go about it. As usual, whenever I'm facing anything uncomfortable in my life, I would like you to be there."

"Okay," Alex said with no hesitance.

"The thing is . . . all my family lives within an hour or so of here. I told you how we would all get together on fast Sundays; we'd all have dinner together and then have a big family home evening thing. Since all of this flared up, it hasn't happened. So, fast Sunday is coming up, and . . . I want to ask if we can all get together, and . . . well," he said it as if it were so obvious, "I'll give the lesson."

"It's brilliant," Alex said.

"Inspired, I think."

"Absolutely."

Wade looked panicked. "Do you have to work Sunday evening?"

"Nope. I go in Sunday late for a night shift. I'll get some sleep in the afternoon and be there."

"Great," Wade said. "I guess I need to make sure everybody can be there. If everybody isn't there, it won't be quite right."

Alex pulled out his cell phone. "You can start with your mother," he said and found her number in the phone's memory. He pushed the button to call it and handed it to Wade without waiting for permission.

Alex listened as Wade said brightly, "Hey there. How you doing?" He paused to listen, then said, "That's not so bad. How's school?" Alex realized he was talking to Brian. "Yeah, I hear you. But high school doesn't last forever. Then you can go to *college.*" He was silent while listening, and Alex sensed his concern for Brian. "Well, maybe we need to talk about that. Don't do anything until we talk, okay? Yeah, thanks." Wade whispered to Alex, "He's getting Mom. He says he's going to drop out of school so he can work at some fantastic job."

"Great," Alex said with sarcasm.

"Hi," Wade said into the phone. "I'm good. How are you? Listen . . . Mom. I have a favor to ask. Do you think we could have one of those big home evening things this Sunday? I'd like to get everybody together. I'll give the lesson." Wade whispered to Alex, "She's crying." Alex smiled, and Wade said into the phone, "It's okay, Mom. I realize we can't force them to come, but . . . I'll just call and ask them, and we'll do the best we can. It's a place to start, I guess. We'll just see what happens. Okay. I'll let you know." He paused, and then said, "I love you too, Mom."

Wade turned off the phone and handed it to Alex. "She said to tell you hi. She was expecting it to be you since it was your number."

"You've come a long way, kid."

"Yes, I suppose I have . . . thanks to you."

"I didn't do anything," Alex said firmly. Wade looked at him askance, and he added, "I'm just the messenger."

"Well, thanks for giving me the right message."

"What are brothers for?"

Wade sighed. "With any luck I can get the right message to Brian before he completely screws up his life."

"I'm sure he'll be fine."

"You know, coming from you," Wade said, "I think I believe that."

"Why?"

"If nothing else, you've taught me the power of a big brother with a good example."

Alex said humbly, "All I did was care, Wade."

"Exactly."

Wade called Alex the next day to tell him he'd spoken to all of his siblings. He only told them he wanted to get all of the siblings together, along with their spouses, for those who had them, to share some feelings he had about all that had occurred in the family. He requested that other arrangements for grandchildren be made in this case, and the entire family could get together another time. His oldest brother, David, said he'd try but didn't sound very positive. The brother and sister between him and David in age said they would be there. He had a younger sister in college who promised to come, and Brian, who still lived at home, said he would be there as well.

"How's Barrett?" Wade asked, as he did in every conversation they had.

"The same," Alex said. "It's the weirdest thing, you know. It was like . . . before he went into PICU, he was so sick all the time. He couldn't keep down the tube feedings. He was puking all the time whether he'd been fed anything or not. He was in horrible pain. But he was there, you know. We could talk to him, and even though he couldn't say anything, he looked at us, he knew us, and he spoke with his eyes. Then he was put into that induced coma, and he came out of it a different child. The tube feedings are working fine. He doesn't act sick or in pain at all. Before it was like somebody had to be right there every second, and the anxiety was horrible. Now it's like he doesn't need anybody there at all, and sitting there watching him is a completely different kind of anxiety. He just sleeps. And sleeps and sleeps. And when he's awake, he's just . . ." Alex heard his own voice crack, "he's just . . . not there anymore."

Wade was genuinely compassionate and encouraged Alex to keep talking. He cried as he speculated over the reasons for the change and the hopes and fears of what the future might bring. When they finally got off the phone, Alex couldn't deny that it had been good to have a chance to voice his feelings. Sometimes talking about it with Jane just felt like he was adding to her burdens by simply not being strong enough to hold them both together. How grateful he was to have found a brother—and a friend!

* * * * *

Alex got off work in the middle of the night and checked on Barrett to find him sleeping soundly, and Jane sleeping in his room. He went home and straight to bed, waking up a little past ten to the sound of his cell phone ringing from the bedside table. "Are you awake?" Jane asked after he'd answered.

"I am now. What's up?" He didn't have any indication from her voice that anything was wrong, but he couldn't help fearing every day that the worst possible news would come.

"Are you sitting down?" she asked.

"I'm in bed. Just cut to the chase."

"The most recent blood work results are in."

"And?"

Her voice became strained with emotion. "The cells are grafting, Alex. The bone marrow is working."

Alex couldn't hold back tears as he muttered quietly, "Oh, thank you, God."

"Amen," Jane said through the phone, and Alex felt like his heart would burst. He knew this didn't mean Barrett was guaranteed a full recovery. Things could still go wrong, and a certain period of time had to pass before they could be sure that cancer wasn't still hiding in his body somewhere. But they'd just made a huge stride. And even if they ended up losing him, the fact that the new bone marrow was working would buy them some time. Either way, Alex felt a glimmer of hope that his wife might be coming back to herself. How could he not be grateful?

Focusing on the joyous news she'd just given him, he said with fervor, "I think you just made my day—maybe my whole year."

She laughed. "Yeah, I know what you mean."

They talked for a few minutes about the ongoing waiting and wondering, and their concern for Barrett's lack of enthusiasm for life, during the very little time he was awake at all. But they wholly agreed that they'd come far, and they had hope, and maybe, just maybe, they could see a light at the end of the tunnel.

After Alex ran downstairs to share the good news with Donald and Susan, he called Wade before calling anyone else. He was lucky to catch him between classes.

"Guess what, little brother?"

"I don't have time to guess. Just tell me."

"The graft is working, Wade."

"Really?" He laughed. "Wow! That's wonderful."

Alex went on to quickly explain that this wasn't a guarantee, and it would still take time. But they agreed it was cause for celebration.

The following day Alex once again started work at two P.M. When he'd finished his shift twelve hours later, he went to Barrett's room, surprised to see Jane at his bedside—and open on her lap were the scriptures she had once thrown at him. His heart quickened, and he recalled once finding Wade sitting in the same spot, the same way, the same ponderous expression on his face. It seemed that Barrett's bedside had become a place of spiritual reconciliation. As late as it was, he wondered why she wasn't sleeping.

"Hi," Alex said, and she looked up—with tears on her face.

"Hi," she said, wiping them away.

"Is it any good?" he asked, motioning to the book as he sat down.

She smiled slightly and said, "If you weren't a Christian it would probably sound kind of hokey." She sighed. "But I'm enjoying it."

"Good," he said and took her hand to kiss it, attempting to be nonchalant about the evidence of a possible miracle taking place.

"That movie we saw the other day," she said.

"Yes?"

"You know what struck me the hardest?"

"What?"

"The scriptures tell us that Mary was there when Jesus was on the cross. He spoke to her. But I never stopped to consider what it must have been like for her to see him suffer that way." Jane became emotional, and Alex put an arm around her. "I just couldn't stop thinking about it. And if . . . if . . ."

"What?" he urged gently.

"If Mary could give up her Son, I should be ashamed of myself for being so stubborn and angry over giving up mine." She cried long and hard against his chest, and Alex cried with her, feeling the Jane he knew and loved coming back to life in his arms. Whatever happened, he knew they would get through it together.

When she had calmed down, they talked for nearly an hour about the way they were feeling, their fears and hopes. And Alex felt his gratitude deepen. She had found herself again.

* * * * *

The following Sunday Alex got off work just past dawn. He went to the hospital to see Barrett as well as Jane, who had spent the night there. He attempted to ignore the familiar bleak mood surrounding them. The hope they had in knowing the bone marrow had started to work was counterbalanced with the stark lack of life in Barrett's eyes. He was awake when Alex arrived, but the child made no eye contact, no indication whatsoever that he was even aware of what was going on around him. The concern in Jane's eyes clearly expressed Alex's own fears. Even if he recovered physically, would they ever be able to undo the emotional abuse of what they had put him through? Seeing the hollow look in Barrett's eyes, Alex could almost wonder if the radiation had caused brain damage, except that exhaustive tests had shown no physical evidence that gave any credence to that theory. Personally, Alex just believed he was depressed. And why wouldn't he be?

Holding to the hope that his son still existed in there somewhere, Alex sat close to him, stroking his little bald head, speaking to him in gentle, animated tones. He talked about going to the zoo and eating ice cream, and he told him what Katharine and Preston had been doing at home, and how they couldn't wait to have Barrett come home from the hospital. Alex heard sniffling and turned to see Jane crying. He gave her a tender smile and kept talking to Barrett until he drifted off to sleep, then Alex held Jane close, whispering, "It's going to be okay. No matter what happens, we will always love him, and I will always love you."

She tightened her arms around him. "Keep telling me that, Alex . . . no matter how this ends."

They sat together in silence, watching Barrett sleep, soaking up the love they shared that could sustain them through wherever the path ahead might lead.

Alex knew Jane was making spiritual progress when she insisted that he leave and take the children to sacrament meeting. Their church attendance had been sparse through the course of Barrett's illness, but it was a joy to hear Jane tell him that one or the other of them needed to be there whenever possible—and to set an example for their children.

After sacrament meeting Alex slept until late afternoon. Wade came by to pick him up, and Alex noticed as soon as he got in the car that Wade was nervous.

"Hey, it's going to be okay, kid," Alex said. Wade just made a dubious noise. "You know what you want to say, right?"

"Yes, but . . . actually saying it might not be so easy. I want to make an impact, but I don't want it to be too . . . sappy. Or too harsh. I called Mom and told her that some of what I had to say might sound harsh, and she needed to trust me."

"So, she's been warned," Alex said. "Was she okay with that?"

"Oh, yeah. I think she's gotten good at people saying harsh things to her—or about her."

With no warning Wade pulled over to the side of the road. "Can we say a prayer?" he asked.

"Sure."

"Would you say it?"

"I'd be happy to," Alex said and proceeded with a heartfelt prayer that Wade would be calm, that the Spirit would guide his words, that they would come from the heart with the purpose of doing good and helping others follow his example of healing and finding peace. He prayed that hearts would be softened and spirits receptive to what Wade had to say. When the prayer was done, Wade thanked him, and they drove on. He seemed more relaxed.

"I've been praying very hard on how to handle this, Alex. I feel like a drama has been shown me in my head, but acting it out feels frightening."

"You need to trust the Spirit to guide you. It will."

"I know, and I believe it's the right course. It just feels so . . . dramatic."

"Maybe God knows that it needs to be dramatic to shake some sense into these people. Their attitude is hurting your mother deeply. It's a dramatic situation. Just go with your feelings."

Wade nodded thoughtfully. When he pulled up in front of the house, Alex noticed him taking a long, deep breath. "I haven't seen anyone but Mom and Dad since the night I found out . . . and I blew up." He chuckled with no humor. "The prodigal son returns, eh?"

"Been there, done that," Alex said, and Wade looked intrigued. Of course he knew that Alex had reached a point of reconciliation with his father, but he'd never heard the details. According to the car clock they were early, so Alex gave him the brief version. "Knocking at our father's door to make peace with him was one of the most difficult things I've ever done. I'd only spoken to him once through the course of many years, and it had been a very ugly conversation—at least the things *I* had said were ugly. I left his home that night a different man." He put a hand on Wade's arm. "It's going to be okay."

"I'm really glad you came with me," Wade said.

"I'm glad to be here if it helps."

Alex figured they would get out of the car. He knew they were expected for dinner, and the clock now read six exactly. "I should warn you," Wade said. "No one but Mom and Dad knows that you're coming . . . and our connection."

"You think that will bother them?"

"I don't know. I don't really care. I just don't want it to cause grief for you."

"I'm pretty tough. It doesn't bother me, but . . . you can tell them I'm a friend if you think it will be easier."

"No." Wade shook his head, his gaze thoughtful. "I don't want any secrets. I don't want there to be any aspect of this situation that I have to be afraid of people finding out. If they can't accept you as my brother, that's their problem." He smiled and added, "My mom loves you. She thinks you're amazing."

"She doesn't really know me," Alex said lightly. "Personally, I think *she* is amazing."

"Yeah, she is, isn't she," Wade said, and Alex felt deeply warmed by the changes that had taken place in him.

"Come on, kid. We're going to be late."

Chapter 21

Wade sighed and opened the car door. He got the wrapped painting out of the trunk and handed it to Alex so he could pick up a small sack.

"What's that?" Alex asked.

"A visual aid," he said, "for my home evening lesson." He made a dubious noise. "Let's hope it doesn't turn into family home screaming."

"I'll referee," Alex said, and they headed to the door.

They went in without knocking and found the front room void of people. Wade hurried to slide the painting behind the couch, and he put his sack discreetly under its corner. Alex wasn't surprised by the coziness of the Morrison home. It was well kept and comfortable, with plenty of evidence that a large family had been raised here. Pictures of family members completely filled one wall of the front room. He also noticed Brad and Marilyn's wedding portrait, and a large print of the Salt Lake Temple.

Noise from the distance made it clear that dinner was being put on. They were heading in that direction when Marilyn appeared in the doorway. "Oh, it's you," she said, her eyes sparkling with a happiness that Alex had never seen in her before. She hugged Wade tightly, and Alex noticed his chin quivering as he held to his mother.

"It's so good to have you here," she said, touching his face.

"It's good to be home," he said and smiled.

Marilyn turned to Alex and hugged him as well. "It's good to have you here as well. How is your family?"

"Doing well, actually," Alex said.

"I heard that Barrett's improving." Her eyes glowed. "It's truly a miracle."

Alex glanced at Wade. "Yes, it truly is."

"Come in," Marilyn said, taking hold of Wade's arm, but he held back. "What is it?" she asked quietly.

"I don't know. I just . . . I can't explain it. I feel . . ." He looked at his mother. "It's that feeling of . . . wondering if I belong anymore. I thought I'd dealt with it, but . . ."

Marilyn put a hand to his face. "Whatever any one of them may say or do, you're my son, and your place in my home and my heart will never change. It's all right."

Wade nodded and drew courage. He tossed a wan smile at Alex, and they walked into the dining room. Alex took in the scene of several people seated around a lovely dining table, set beautifully, with a fine meal spread out. Only Brad and Brian were familiar to him, but he was able to assess where the others fell into place in the family simply by their ages, and the ones who were with spouses.

"Wade is here," Marilyn said brightly, and all eyes turned toward them. Alex hung back slightly as the room became silent. Brad came to his feet and greeted Wade with a big hug, saying firmly, "It's good to see you, son."

"It's good to see you too, Dad," Wade said, and Brad smiled. Alex wondered if Brad had once feared never hearing Wade call him that again.

The ice was broken somewhat when the others all gave various greetings as they were seated, but there was no denying the tension still in the air. Brad shook Alex's hand and greeted him warmly. Marilyn motioned Alex to a chair between Wade and Brian as she said, "And this is Alex."

"Hello," Alex said and received some nods and casual greetings in return. They all looked curious but afraid to ask about his presence there.

"Hey, I know you," Brian said to him.

"I know you too," Alex said.

The others looked especially curious, and Marilyn said, "We met him at the hospital when Brian was in that little accident."

Brad offered a blessing on the food, in it expressing gratitude to have their family together again. While food was being passed around the table, Brad made introductions. "Alex, this is our daughter Sadie and her husband, Ted. They have two children at home. This is David and his wife, Marie. They have three children." Alex nodded toward them, knowing David was the one who said he might not come. "And this is our son Lance and his wife, Brianna. They're expecting their first baby; we just found out about that."

"Congratulations," Alex said.

"Thanks," they both said, and Brad continued.

"This is our daughter Robin. She's going to BYU at the moment. Of course, you know our son Wade, and our son Brian."

Alex noticed the way he casually, but firmly, called Wade 'our son,' just as he did the others. "It's a pleasure to meet all of you," Alex said. Then to Marilyn, as he ladled dark gravy over his mashed potatoes and roast beef, "And this looks absolutely wonderful. Wade's told me what a marvelous cook you are."

Marilyn just smiled humbly. Robin asked, "So, Alex, I'd like to hear more about how you met Brian at the hospital. What were *you* doing there?"

"I work there," Alex said. "I'm the one who gave him the stitches."

"Alex is a physician in the ER," Marilyn explained.

"You're a doctor," Lance said, as if it were a great surprise. Expressions around the table made it evident he wasn't the only one surprised. Sitting there amidst the heavy silence, Alex understood Wade's concern. There was an undeniable current of negativity and judgment. Glances were filled with silent insinuation and mistrust. He uttered a silent prayer that Wade's "lesson" would go well, and wished that someone would say something to break the horrible tension. He decided he'd prefer some level of arguing over such silence. Then Sadie spoke up. "I hope I'm not being obnoxious, but . . . I can't help wondering why the doctor who stitched up Brian's head is here for Sunday dinner when we were under the impression this was strictly a family gathering."

"It *is* a family gathering," Wade said without hesitation or apology. "Alex is my brother."

The shock wave didn't go unnoticed. It was Lance who said to Wade, "I can't believe you'd bring him here when—"

"Before you get all hot and bothered," Wade said, "I think you just need to give me a chance to say what I need to say. But it can wait until after dinner. I bet we can all tolerate each other that long. Then everyone can have a chance to speak."

"That sounds fair," Brad stated, as if to put an end to it.

Again silence fell, this time amidst even more heavy unspoken judgment. Alex thought of Marilyn tearfully saying that she wanted to gain back the love and respect of her children. He couldn't even imagine how heartbreaking it was for her to feel their disdain for herself and for Wade. Again he prayed that the outcome would be favorable.

Marilyn ended the silence by saying, "Alex, I think this would be a good time for you to tell everyone a little bit about what's been happening with your son."

Alex felt somewhat put on the spot, but he wasn't opposed to talking about it—or anything—to deflect attention from the under-lying issues. "Um . . . well . . . my son, Barrett . . ." He hesitated and scanned the faces looking at him. They all showed varying degrees of boredom or skepticism. Did they think he was going to share a story about his son's soccer team winning a championship or something equally unimportant to these people? He wasn't one for dramatics, but he felt a desire to help these people gain some perspective. "Barrett is six," he began, "and he has leukemia." Already he sensed a subtle softening in some more than others; or at the very least they were slightly more receptive to what he might say.

"We discovered the illness the day after my wife gave birth to our third child, about two years ago. At this point, Barrett has been in the hospital for months now. He's gone through extensive chemotherapy and radiation. He was given a bone marrow transplant, but it didn't take, and we were certain we were going to lose him because the likelihood of finding another suitable donor was next to impossible. But we had a miracle. We *did* find another donor, and the second transplant appears to be working. He's still in the hospital and struggling, but he's showing signs of improvement, and we are very grateful."

"He's only six?" Brian asked, incredulous.

"That's right," Alex said.

"Can people like . . . go visit him?" he asked, and Alex noticed Marilyn showing pleasant surprise. He knew that Brian had been extremely difficult for many weeks. Was his apparent compassion for a sick child a complete surprise to his mother?

"Right now he's in a special room that's kept completely germ-free because his immune system isn't able to fight any possible infection. But when he gets past that, I would love to have you meet him."

"Okay," Brian said, and Wade gave Alex a subtle smile.

"Tell us more about the bone marrow transplant," Brad said, as if he were genuinely curious. And maybe he was. But Alex knew Wade's parents were manipulating the conversation toward a particular point. And that was fine. Alex agreed that Wade's siblings needed to know the whole story. And he was prepared to tell it, preferably with some dramatic impact. It had certainly been dramatic for him; why not for these people?

"Well," Alex said, "in essence, the only chance we had to get rid of the cancer in Barrett's body was to completely kill all of his bone marrow through intense radiation and chemotherapy. Then, before too many hours passed he needed a transplant. The donor bone marrow feeds new, healthy cells in to replace the old ones, so to speak. A donor has to be a careful match, and a lot of testing and preparation has to be done to pair up the right elements."

"Does it have to be a relative?" Robin asked, sounding genuinely interested.

"It doesn't have to be, but the chances of finding a match otherwise are difficult. Even among relatives it's hit and miss. In our case, I was the only one out of the entire family who was a close enough match. But my bone marrow didn't graft with his, and we thought he was lost."

"But you did say you got another donor?" Sadie asked.

"That's right," Alex said. He put a hand on Wade's shoulder. "I have your brother to thank for saving my son's life."

Another silent shock wave went through the room, but no one had anything to say, so Alex added, "At this point, tests show that the new bone marrow is grafting and starting to work; however, Barrett has been so sick for so long that he's physically and emotionally exhausted. We still have a long way to go, but we're glad to have some hope."

Marilyn said, "We're so grateful he's doing better. It's nice when something good can come out of a difficult situation."

"Yes, it is," Brad said. Then he asked Wade about the classes he was currently taking. The conversation was somewhat stilted beyond that, but it remained in untroubled territory.

When dinner was over Alex did his best to join in the well-practiced custom of each person taking their own dishes to the kitchen, and helping to clear the table and load the dishwasher. He volunteered to scrub the mashed potato pan, since he didn't know where other things needed to be put away. Marilyn smiled at him as he set to work, and he wondered if either of them might have ever predicted such an event as him washing dishes in the kitchen of the woman his father had been sinfully involved with. He chalked it up to the miracle of forgiveness and just kept working, glad to have a task that kept his hands busy and gave his brain some space to digest the scene at the dinner table and the possible reasons for so much tension within a family that Wade had repeatedly told him used to be fairly close.

When the work was done, Marilyn announced that, as usual, they would be having dessert after the lesson. They all moved into the front room and were seated. Alex noticed Wade sitting where he'd tucked his visual-aid sack beneath the couch. He motioned for Alex to sit beside him. Brad asked Alex if he would give an opening prayer. He gladly agreed but kept it brief and general, not wanting to put anyone on the defensive by outlining Wade's purpose for being here. Brad then turned the time over to Wade once he'd expressed gratitude for having the family together under one roof.

Wade turned to Alex, who gave him an encouraging gaze. Moving to the edge of his seat so that everyone in the room could clearly see his face, Wade began by saying, "I already told you that my purpose in bringing us together tonight was my need to say some things related to the drama that's come up in our family. There is no point pretending that we don't all know the truth about what happened many years ago, or the results we're dealing with now. And there's no point pretending that we haven't all been—or still are—angry and upset over this. Except for our mother, I have probably been more upset and angry than any of you. I can only excuse myself in that by saying that it was quite a shock to learn that I was misbegotten, to put it politely. I've had trouble trying to figure out who I really am and where I belong. I've had trouble with feeling such extremes of anger, and hatred, and loneliness, and despair that I . . . well, I thought I'd found the answer to all my problems with a box cutter."

He held up his wrist, displaying the scar that was still visibly pink. Alex saw some of their expressions growing dark, while others just looked so thoroughly uncomfortable that it was difficult to tell how Wade's confession might be affecting them.

"What are you saying?" Robin blurted, horrified.

Wade looked directly at her. "I'm saying that I cut my wrist with the intent to die."

"Did you know about this?" Robin asked her mother.

"Yes." She spoke firmly but without anger. "And don't lecture me about not informing any of you." Her eyes scanned the room. "Each of you, in your own way, has made it clear that, whether it was right or not, you had a hard time seeing Wade as anything more than a reminder of what a terrible disappointment I'd become. You've been politely disdainful toward me, at best. I had no reason to call and tell you anything, to be quite frank."

"I can't believe it," Robin said, looking back to Wade. She apparently had no rejoinder to her mother's accusations.

Wade said, "Mom felt prompted to call Alex. He found me and stopped the bleeding and stitched it up. I spent a few days in a suicide management clinic. I'm not telling you this to get you to feel sorry for me. I made the decision to do this, and I'm grateful I didn't succeed. I'm simply trying to make the point that this has been difficult for me. Not one of you can tell me that I don't understand how it feels to find betrayal and heartache at the core of a family that you had always believed was close to ideal. The facts are that I am only a half brother to each of you, because our mother committed adultery and—"

"I don't know why we even have to talk about this," Sadie interrupted hotly. "It happened. We all know about it. Let's just . . ."

"What?" Wade asked. "Brush it under the rug and try to pretend it's not real so we can go on believing we're the ideal Mormon family?" Her eyes said that he'd hit the nail on the head. "You're obviously upset over it, Sadie. Do you think not talking about it will make you feel any better? You may be able to go back to your own home and pretend that it didn't happen, but I don't have that luxury. I have to look at the results every day in the mirror." Sadie looked even more uncomfortable, and Wade added more gently, "What are we afraid of? Our Church leaders are not afraid to frankly discuss sin and human mistakes. If repentance and forgiveness are preached over and over from the pulpits, what purpose would there be for them to do that if sin were not a part of the human experience? Jesus was not afraid to talk about sin. What makes it so difficult to discuss?" He motioned toward Marilyn. "She's not uncomfortable talking about it. Not now, anyway. Do you know why? She's been so thoroughly humiliated and degraded over it that she has nothing left to lose."

Wade met his mother's tear-filled eyes and said softly, "Sorry, Mom."

"It's okay," she said and smiled, holding tightly to Brad's hand.

"Our mother is an amazing woman," Wade said. "Not so long ago I couldn't fathom ever feeling that way toward her again. I could only see the bad choices she'd made and how they had affected me. But I've come to see things differently now. Whether or not each of you ever decides to come to terms with this is up to you. However, I need to take the opportunity to just share a few thoughts with you, and then you are welcome to leave if you choose."

Wade took a deep breath as if to sort through his thoughts. "When I finally realized that I needed to put some effort into finding peace with this, I forced my way past the anger enough to pick up the scriptures for the first time in weeks. I found a story that I believe is worth sharing. In the New Testament it tells of a woman taken in adultery, in the very act, it says. I find it odd that the man she'd been with wasn't mentioned. The scribes and Pharisees brought her before Jesus, apparently testing Him to see what He would do. Obviously any intention this woman might have had to keep her sin a secret had been blown. Her sin had been declared publicly, no doubt with a great deal of humiliation and degradation. Now, by Jewish law, she should have been stoned . . . to death. I think she was probably hoping for a fatal blow early on to end her misery quickly."

Wade gave his mother a cautious gaze, and she returned it confidently as he crossed the room and squatted down in front of her. He took hold of her left wrist and looked into her eyes, asking softly, "Is it okay if I tell them?"

She nodded firmly, without hesitance. Wade turned her wrist to look at the scar, then he kissed it before he glanced around the room and said, "I believe our mother would have hoped for a fatal blow early on." He shifted his position to put his wrist next to hers. "I think she's the only person in this room who knows how thoroughly desperate I felt when I put that blade to my wrist."

The horror felt by Wade's siblings became readily evident in their faces. "But given a second chance," he went on, "she chose to live." He touched his mother's face and returned to his seat.

"Going back to my story . . ." he said. "You've all heard it before, many times. But maybe it wasn't so personal the last time it came up in Sunday School." Wade reached beneath the corner of the couch and pulled out the little sack. He drew from it a large stone, irregularly shaped but relatively the size of a softball. Alex heard a few soft gasps in the room. He had no doubt that Wade had been inspired. Just seeing it in regard to the present situation was chilling.

Wade held the stone contemplatively, his fingers wrapped around it like he might be preparing to pitch it like a ball. He looked at it while he said, "The story is very brief in the way it's recorded, but Jesus' response speaks volumes. He simply said, 'He that is without sin among you, let him first cast a stone.' And they all slithered away."

He looked around at his siblings, and Alex noticed that their expressions were now troubled and unsettled, rather than angry and uncomfortable as they had previously been. "These days," Wade said, "our culture and traditions are much different. Less barbaric perhaps, but in a sense more cruel. We use words instead of stones."

Wade stood in the center of the room and turned slowly while he held the stone. "Okay, so now's your chance to say all that stuff you were itching to say at the dinner table." He held the stone toward Lance, who had been so boldly defiant earlier. "Go ahead. Tell her what you want to say. Tell her she betrayed you and she's responsible for ruining what's left of your life. Or maybe there's something you want to say to me. Tell me," he challenged. "Tell me you'd prefer that I not come around any more because my face is an ugly reminder of things we don't want to look at, and we certainly don't want to talk about them. Am I suddenly a different person? Am I not the same brother you grew up with because you found out that my blood has different DNA from yours?" He motioned toward Alex. "Is there something you want to say to him? Or to me about him, perhaps? Now's your chance."

Lance said nothing, didn't move. The gaze he gave Wade was mostly unreadable, but more humble than angry. Wade walked around the room, holding the stone out to each of his siblings and their spouses. "Anyone?" he asked. "No takers?"

In a softer voice he clarified, "I'm not here to cast stones at any of you. I said horrible things to our mother, and about her, things I wish with all my heart I could take back. I had the mistaken idea that I had the *right* to condemn her because my hurt was so deep, and in my opinion, clearly her fault. And I felt angry with our father. He'd admitted that he hadn't been a very good husband, that he'd driven her away. I felt justified in believing that their self-ishness and poor choices had ruined my life, and if anyone had the right to cast a stone, it was I. I called my mother . . ." He squeezed his eyes closed, his expression filled with torment. He drew courage and said what he had to in order to make his point. ". . . I called her an adulterous tramp . . . to her face." He turned to look at her directly. "Now I can only beg her forgiveness."

"Of course," she whispered tearfully when his silence made it evident he expected an answer.

Wade smiled at her. "And I would like to say that I forgive you, but it just doesn't seem right, because . . . there's no need. Your sin was not against me. I have no place or right or need to offer forgiveness, because I know God forgave you a long time ago. And I may not have known the truth, but He did. So I would simply like to follow the example of my Savior and borrow His words for a moment." He penetrated his mother's eyes with his own. With the hand holding the stone he motioned around the room, then met her eyes again, saying gently, "Woman, where are those thine accusers? Hath no man condemned thee?" He dropped the stone to the floor where it landed with a hard thud. "Neither do I condemn thee."

Marilyn put a hand over her mouth and began to sob. Brad wrapped his arms around her and smiled up at Wade with tears in his own eyes.

Wade glanced around again at the others in the room as he motioned to their father. "Look at him," he said. "See how much he loves her, how he stands by her without question. Do you have any idea what an incredible example he is? He, who had more right than anyone in this world to condemn her and turn her out, chose to look at the beam in his own eye, and he never passed judgment on the mote he found in his wife's. Our father is a man among men, and I consider it an honor to call him father, just as Jesus surely would have called Joseph His father, even though they both would have known that Jesus had none of Joseph's blood in His veins."

Alex saw Brad's tears flowing freely as he rose to his feet and hugged Wade tightly. He only let go when Marilyn stood beside him, and he moved back so that she could have a turn at hugging her son. Brian left the room, and Alex felt a little nervous about his absence until he returned with a box of tissues that he handed to his mother as she sat back down, then he returned to his own seat. Brad and Wade also returned to their seats, and nothing was said for a couple of minutes.

Wade finally spoke. "I'm not suggesting that it isn't good to express our feelings and talk about them. I think you *should* talk about it. But if we have anything to say to each other, we should say it with love, the way we were raised to speak to each other. I wouldn't expect that any of you can snap your fingers and make all the difficult feelings go away. But the answers are only going to be found inside yourselves, not by placing blame." He took a deep breath and added, "There are just a few more things I want to say. I know this is a difficult and sensitive situation. We don't need to advertise the fact that we've discovered we're a unique family, but I don't think we should be ashamed of it either. Obviously I have to accept that in truth I belong to two families, and as much as I have grown to care for Alex and . . . our father, this will always be my primary family. I will not keep secrets about who I am and why, which is part of the reason that I brought Alex here with me today." He smiled at Alex. "Beyond needing his moral support."

Wade sighed and went on. "I am not ashamed to call Alex my brother, any more than I am ashamed of my mother for how I was conceived. If any of you are uncomfortable with that, I can accept your feelings for what they are; you're certainly entitled to them. But I ask the same in return. Don't ever question my decision to embrace both of my families and openly accept who I am. This is a decision I've come to through much anguished prayer and fasting. I will not back down on it. If you're uncomfortable with that, then we will just have to be tolerant of each other. I think we all need to be grown-up enough to accept that it's okay to have different opinions, different ways of dealing with pain or hardship, and different ways of interpreting what happens to us. But we were taught to honor and celebrate our differences. That's all I'm asking of you as I try to move forward and make the most of the changes in my life." He looked at his mother. "My only concern is that it might be difficult for you if people find out."

Marilyn shrugged comfortably. "It really doesn't matter anymore, Wade. I've gotten beyond feeling ashamed and embarrassed or caring what people think. If anyone asks me, I'll just tell them the truth. I had an affair a long time ago. It was a stupid thing to do, and the price was high, but I did get one great thing out of it. I have a wonderful son."

Wade smiled at her and went on. "Last of all," he said, "I would like to just toss out some food for thought regarding a different perspective on all of this. Let's just ponder a few 'what ifs' here. What if . . . our mother had not become involved with another man? Dad told me that her leaving him was such a shock that it changed him very deeply. He admitted that his upbringing had been difficult, and prior to that time he hadn't been a very good husband and father. What kind of man might we have been raised by if these events had not occurred? Sometimes hardship brings out the best in people. Our father is a shining example of that."

Wade was silent a few moments, then went on. "What if . . . our mother had never come back? Dad would have raised David and Lance and Sadie on his own. Or he might have remarried. That certainly could have changed the family dynamics. That would eliminate the existence of some of the people in this room. Or . . . what if . . . either or both of our parents had left the Church over this? What do you suppose our lives would be like if we had not been raised with the gospel? What if they had held on to bitterness because of the betrayal? What if our mother had no penitence over her mistakes? The list could go on and on. The point I'm trying to make is this. If you really start looking at what might have been, scenarios that many other people in this world have had to deal with, we have no conclusion beyond being extremely blessed." He turned to his parents. "I just want to say, for the record, how deeply grateful I am that the two of you chose to patch it up and stay together. I know it took a great deal of courage and hard work, and in some ways it probably would have been easier to get a divorce. But you didn't. You chose to stay together and to raise your family the right way. Mom, you could have chosen to remain outside the Church once you were excommunicated. I know the road back couldn't have been easy. But I'm deeply grateful that I was raised in a home where the gospel was not only present, but strong. I believe that added strength was in our home because you knew what it was like not to have the blessings of living righteously. I want to thank you for that, and to say that in spite of certain bad choices you made, you followed them up with a lot of really good ones. Thank you for staying alive, for staying married, for bringing me into the world, and for loving me in spite of myself. You are a woman among women, and I love you." He turned more toward Brad. "And thank you . . . Dad . . . for taking her back, for being humble and forgiving and tolerant. And for raising me with the same love and acceptance that you gave to all of your children. You are a man among men, and I love you too." He looked around. "That's all I have to say."

Then, a minute later, Wade added, "Now that the stone is on the floor, anyone is welcome to speak up."

More silence followed until Alex said, "I'd like to say something, if I may."

"Of course," Marilyn said, wiping at her eyes with a tissue.

"I'd like to clarify something from my perspective. As I understand all of this, from what Wade has told me, David is the oldest and the only one old enough to even remember his mother's absence, and even that is vague. Is that right?" he asked David.

"Yes, that's right," David said.

Alex nodded. "While my being here this evening has appeared to be as an innocent bystander, I want to point out that I'm much older than the rest of you. I was thirteen when my father left us. Not only do I remember it well, I was at a very impressionable age. I stopped going to church. I smoked. I drank. I was angry and snotty and belligerent over it for about twenty years. In my heart I hated and cursed the woman who had taken my father away from us. But I know now that it's much more complicated than that, and I'm grateful to be able to say that I long ago came to terms with ill feelings regarding this situation." He looked directly at Marilyn and said, "I want you to know that it's a privilege to be in your home, and to see the beautiful family you have raised. Wade is a fine young man and I am grateful to have him as my brother, and my friend. I honor you for your courage, your commitment to your husband and children, and for your faithfulness in living the gospel." He smiled. "And thank you for dinner. It was incredible."

Marilyn laughed tearfully. "You're welcome, Alex. You and your family are welcome in our home any time."

When no one else spoke, Brad said, "Maybe it's time for that dessert." Alex sensed his wisdom in allowing the family to have some time to let all that had been said settle in and take root. They couldn't be expected to come to terms with all of this immediately just because they'd been given a different perspective.

"That sounds great," Marilyn said and stood up.

Alex nudged Wade. "The gift," he whispered.

"Oh, yeah. Mom, first . . . I almost forgot. I have a gift for you."

She sat back down. "That's really not necessary," she said.

"I know, but . . . I wanted to." Wade drew the wrapped package out from behind the couch, and Marilyn gasped. Its size and shape obviously indicated this was something to hang on the wall. Wade set it on his mother's lap, although it was big enough to spread over his father's as well.

"Before you open it," Wade said, "I want you to know that I debated over whether or not this was right. I felt good about it, but if you don't like it, I won't be offended if you exchange it. I have the receipt."

Wade remained standing in front of his parents. As they pulled away the paper, Alex thought it was perfect that no one else could see the front of the painting from this angle. Their eyes both immediately said that they had grasped the message of the gift, and they were both clearly pleased. Wade repeated what Alex had told him. "For most people who come into your home, they will look at this and see a beautiful depiction of a touching story. For those of us who know the meaning of this in our family, it will be a constant reminder of the Savior's example of compassion, acceptance, and tender admonition. You might prefer to hang it in a more private part of the house."

"It's beautiful, Wade," Marilyn said. "It's perfect. I love it. And I'm going to hang it right there." She pointed to the wall above the couch.

"It *is* beautiful," Brad added.

"Let me see," Robin said and came to her feet, as if she couldn't stand the suspense. She moved to her mother's side and caught her breath as it came into view, then she turned and hugged her mother tightly, saying through a rush of tears, "I love you, Mom. I'm so sorry."

"So am I," Marilyn said, returning her embrace with fervor.

Robin then approached Wade and hugged him just as tightly, whispering an apology in his ear. Brian was right behind her, hugging his brother in a way that most teenaged boys would be mortified to do. A minute later it looked like a receiving line as the rest of the family gathered around the painting and commented on it, each in turn hugging Marilyn, and Brad, and Wade, while quiet apologies and regrets were spoken, and tears flowed. The box of tissues was passed around. Alex just sat and observed the culmination of a miracle. Marilyn had gotten her wish. She had her children back, and more importantly, she had their love and respect.

They all returned to the table for berry cobbler and ice cream, and Alex couldn't help noticing that the mood was entirely different than it had been at dinner. Tension and disdain had been replaced by warmth and acceptance. The love in the room was almost tangible. It was the miracle of forgiveness. Alex noticed Wade leaving with Brian. They came back twenty minutes later, both laughing comfortably.

Brian left again, and Wade sat down by Alex, who was just basking in his observation of a beautiful family made whole again. "How is he?" Alex asked.

"Good, I think. He promised to stay in school, get rid of his stupid friends, and stop skipping seminary."

"Ah, the influence of a big brother."

Wade grinned at Alex. "Indeed."

"You did great, kid," Alex said, focusing on Marilyn and Brad, surrounded by their children, talking and laughing.

"I was inspired," Wade said with a serenity that nearly made him glow.

"It can take a lot of hard work and courage to act on inspiration. You did a great job."

"Thanks for being here."

"I wouldn't have missed it. Let me be there when you tell Dad about it."

"Okay," Wade said. And he smiled.

Chapter 22

When they finally left the Morrison home, even Alex got some hugs from people besides Brad and Marilyn. They were going to drive together to Neil's home and tell him about their experience, but when Alex called Jane at the hospital, she said that Neil and Roxanne were there.

"Tell them not to leave," Alex said, and they arrived to find Barrett sleeping, with no reported change. Wade quietly shared the experience he'd had with his family. Neil told him how proud he was of him. Wade just smiled and said, "Thanks, Dad. I'm proud of you too."

* * * * *

A new level of the nightmare occurred when Barrett's condition worsened dramatically due to what they officially called Graft Versus Host Disease. Again he spent time in PICU while the cells in his new bone marrow attacked his body, and the battle became ugly. Days merged into nights with a familiar loss in the sense of time while Alex wondered how long they might have to go on like this, waiting and wondering, not even knowing what day it might be or if Barrett would live to see the next one. The difference he felt now was that Jane had gained a new level of strength, making him feel that they'd drawn closer together instead of further apart. Alex took as much time off work as he dared, and they spent every possible minute together in Barrett's room, talking quietly of what they would do should he die—or live. Jane suggested that if the scriptures said, "If ye are prepared ye shall not fear," then perhaps they'd do well to prepare for the worst and then let it go. With that much stated, she spent a couple of hours talking about every detail of Barrett's funeral and what she would do with his things should he no longer need them. Alex listened and gave an occasional suggestion; they cried together, and prayed together, and hovered close to their son, wondering if their time with him was truly drawing to a close.

And then another turnaround came—quickly and dramatically. Again the word *miracle* flew around in the sentences spoken about Barrett's condition, and he was soon returned to his usual room. All the tests showed improvement, but still Barrett looked at the world through lifeless eyes, apparently lost in another world, and far preferring to be there. And who could blame him?

Wade kept close track of Barrett each and every day and quickly became as familiar with the nursing staff as Jane and Alex. He asked questions of doctors and nurses at every opportunity, and Alex felt something innately wonderful about Wade's profound interest. He wasn't at all surprised when Wade quietly announced one evening, while they sat together in Barrett's room, "I've decided on a specialty."

"Pediatrics?" Alex asked, almost lightly.

"Yes, but more specific."

"Okay, don't keep me in suspense."

Wade looked at him firmly. "Pediatric oncology."

Alex didn't know whether to laugh or cry. He felt a mixture of emotions over such an announcement. Trying to keep the mood light, if only to avoid any tears, he said, "You have a sick fascination with bald-headed, puking kids?"

Wade looked at Barrett. "Maybe I do. Or maybe I just hope to make the tiniest difference in saving some lives, or making their lives a little less miserable."

"Wow," Alex said. "It sounds trite to say that I'm impressed. I couldn't do it. I hate to point out the obvious, but you realize you're going to see a lot of suffering in order to meet such a goal."

"Yeah, I know," Wade said, looking down. "I only know that it feels right, Alex. The first time you brought me in here, I felt like I'd come home, like this is where I belong. And I'm sure you realize this is one of the leading hospitals in the nation for treating kids with cancer."

"Yeah, I knew that. I've thanked God for that a thousand times."

"Well . . . I want to work right here . . ." He looked again at Barrett. ". . . Where angels walk the halls."

Again Alex felt like he might cry, and he had no desire to get started again. He countered it by saying, "Well good. We can meet for lunch. But if it's all the same to you, I think we should meet here. The food's better."

Wade looked enlightened and said, "The food *is* better here, isn't it."

"Well . . . duh," Alex said with a little chuckle. "You can't get a sick kid to eat if the food tastes nasty. This is probably the best hospital cafeteria in the world."

They sat in silence for a few minutes before Alex asked if Wade had heard any more from his brothers and sisters. The strain of Barrett's illness had pushed other things to the back of his mind, but now he couldn't help wondering. Wade told him that he'd had long conversations with each of his siblings. Some were still struggling more than others with coming to terms with all that had happened, but their attitudes had changed dramatically, and Wade was pleased and grateful to see that his family was healing.

Wade was extremely busy the next couple of days, but he called Alex often to remain informed of Barrett's condition. Late one evening Alex was grateful for an opportunity to discuss with his brother a summary of the present situation. From all outward appearances, nothing had changed. Barrett slept almost constantly, and when he was awake his spirit felt absent. But blood tests were showing a steady improvement on the inside. His immune system was getting stronger, and there was no evidence of cancer. Of course, it would take time to be certain that they'd really conquered the plague, but hope was increasing. They were being told that they could work toward taking Barrett home. And while Alex knew Jane shared his longing to have Barrett back beneath their roof, he knew that it would likely be just another difficult adjustment with its own challenges. During his residency he'd been involved more than once with the preparations to send a patient home following something like this, and they had to take a good portion of the hospital with them. Still, it could have its payoffs.

Alex found Jane in Barrett's room, reading in the book of Job. The pages were heavily marked and well worn. While this set of scriptures had stayed in Barrett's room all these weeks, they'd both pored over certain passages. Jane's hiatus from the book had ended, and she had once again immersed herself in Job's struggle to understand and come to terms with the horrendous suffering and hardship that had been placed upon him.

Alex kissed her in greeting, and then they went together to the cafeteria to get some lunch. Returning to Barrett's room, they sat close together and continued to talk quietly while Barrett slept. Alex stopped talking when he heard an unusual sound. They both turned at the same time to look at Barrett and found his eyes wide open, watching them closely.

"Hey, Barrett," Alex said, moving closer, looking into his eyes as he'd done hundreds of times, longing to see some kind of response. He drew a ragged breath when he realized that Barrett *was* there, gazing directly at his father, seeming to take in the connection. Alex glanced at Jane just long enough to be assured that she had caught on. She was watching with wide eyes.

"Barrett," Alex said, "did you have a good rest? Do you know that pretty soon we're going to get to take you home, and you can play with Katharine and Preston? What would you think of that?" His eyes sparkled in response, and Alex couldn't keep from laughing through the tears that rolled down his face. Barrett reached up a hand to touch them. "Those are happy tears," Alex said. "I'm so glad we get to take you home from the hospital."

Jane made a joyful noise, and Barrett looked at her a moment, then back at his father. He looked expectant and intrigued, as if he'd simply been absent all this time, and he'd truly just come back. He touched Alex's beard as if he'd never seen it before. Of course he had, but he'd been horribly ill since Alex had taken to wearing it.

"Daddy's face feels funny, huh," Jane said. Barrett turned toward her, and his eyes smiled. With their gaze connected, she added gently, "Maybe we should have a party when you come home from the hospital. What would you think about that?"

Barrett turned back to his father and asked in a quiet, raspy voice, "Can we go to the zoo?"

Alex and Jane both laughed deeply and cried harder. Alex took Barrett into his arms and held him close. "You bet we can, buddy," he said, then Jane took a turn at holding Barrett close. Alex encircled them both in his embrace, thanking God for yet another miracle. Apparently they wouldn't have to give up their son after all—at least not yet. They knew that it would take time to know for certain if the cancer had been completely annihilated, but that was a bridge yet to be crossed. In the meantime, they had their son back, and Alex was determined to enjoy every minute of it.

* * * * *

Through the afternoon an excited buzz surrounded Barrett. His sudden turnaround had left the doctors and staff all in awe. Even those who weren't religious were calling it a miracle. Alex called his father, then Jane called her mother, to give them the good news, and they promised to call family members and spread the word. They let Barrett talk to each of them on the phone for a minute, even though he only managed a couple of words.

Barrett slept a little here and there, but he seemed anxious to be awake, taking in his surroundings with distinct awe. It was as if his little body had just been in some kind of long-term, sedentary state, preparing for a reawakening. And now that his enormous period of sleep had given his body the downtime it needed, Barrett seemed eager to be a part of the world again.

After Jane and Alex had taken turns going to the cafeteria to get some dinner, things quieted down a little, and Alex called Wade. He'd made it clear to their father that he wanted to tell Wade himself, but he knew his brother had been in classes and working.

"Are you busy right now?" Alex asked.

"Nothing that can't wait, why?"

"I know it's kind of late, but do you think you could come to the hospital?"

"Which one?"

"Barrett's room."

Wade sounded wary as he said, "Sure, I'll be right over."

"Thanks," Alex said and hung up. He sidled up next to Barrett on his bed, then urged the child onto his lap when it became evident that's what Barrett wanted.

"I have something special to tell you," Alex said.

"Is it the miracle everyone's talking about?" he asked, his voice weak but alive and real.

"It is," Alex said, smiling at Jane, who was sitting at the side of the bed. "Do you remember how we talked about bone marrow? And how you needed new bone marrow in order to get better?"

"You gave me some of your bone marrow."

"That's right. But mine didn't work, and that's why you got so sick that you've hardly even known we were around for a long time. We thought you were going to die, Barrett. But we found someone else who had bone marrow that matched yours, and that person gave you new bone marrow. And because it worked, you're going to get better. That's the miracle."

Barrett looked up at his father and asked, "Was it Preston?"

"No, buddy. It wasn't Preston."

"Preston is my little brother."

"Yes, he is," Alex said. "And the thing is, while you were sick I found out that I have a little brother too. I didn't know because he had a different mother and we grew up in different homes. But now I know I have a brother, just like you have Preston. Except

Wade is all grown up. You met Wade for just a minute, but you were very tired, and you might not remember."

"Is Wade my brother too?"

"No, Wade is your uncle. And he's coming to visit you so that you can meet him. The thing is, Barrett, it was Wade who gave you the bone marrow. If I hadn't found out he was my brother, we would have never known that he had the kind of bone marrow that you needed to stay alive."

Barrett laid his head against Alex's chest, clearly weak but not sleepy. "I'm glad I get to stay alive, Daddy."

"So am I," Alex said, exchanging a poignant glance with Jane, who once again had tears in her eyes, but they were tears of perfect joy.

"I have to stay here so I can be baptized," Barrett said, his eyes closed. "When I'm eight years old, can I be baptized?"

"You sure can," Alex said.

"Grandma and Grandpa said that I needed to get baptized and grow up and go on a mission."

"When you talked to them on the phone?" Alex asked.

"No," Barrett said and yawned.

"Was it before you were in the hospital?" Jane asked.

"No," he said again. "The other grandma and grandpa."

Alex and Jane exchanged a wide-eyed glance. "What do you mean?" Jane asked.

"Grandma Angel," he said matter-of-factly. That was how they'd always referred to Alex's mother, since she had died long before Barrett was born. "And Grandpa that lived in California."

Barrett rested his head against his father, apparently too sleepy to talk any further. But Jane squeezed Alex's hand while they silently contemplated yet another facet of the miracle they'd been granted. Could it be possible? Had Barrett truly been told by his loved ones on the other side of the veil that he would grow to adulthood?

A moment later Wade rushed into the room. His expression looked terrified as he took in the scene. Alex didn't realize how it must have appeared until Wade asked, "Is he . . ."

Alex just smiled and nudged Barrett, who opened his eyes and turned to look at their visitor. "This is your Uncle Wade," Alex said.

Wade let out a burst of breathless laughter and moved closer.

"Are you my dad's brother?" Barrett asked him.

"Yes, I am," Wade said with pride. He looked at Alex with moisture in his eyes, silently expressing his awe over the evidence that Barrett had come back to life. He turned again to Barrett. "I've been waiting a long time for you to get better so I could see you again."

Barrett gave a weak smile and said, "Thank you for the bone marrow, Uncle Wade." He closed his eyes and relaxed again.

Alex saw Wade's chin quiver as he reached out and touched the child's face, then he took Alex's hand and squeezed it with trembling fingers. "You're welcome, kid," Wade said. Then to Alex, "I think this is the greatest moment of my life."

"Nonsense," Alex said, "your life is just beginning."

* * * * *

Alex arrived in Barrett's room following a long, hard shift, to find only a nurse changing the sheets. "He's in the playroom," she said with a smile.

"Thanks," Alex said and quickly found Barrett there with Jane—and Katharine and Preston. It was the first time all of his children had been together—and playing—in months. For a long moment he just leaned in the doorway, soaking in the scene that almost made him feel like they actually had a normal family. Barrett's weakness and frailty were evident, but his progress was unmistakable. He actually looked smaller in size than Katharine, but they had every hope that he would make up for the growth he'd lost and eventually be completely healthy.

"Wow," Alex finally said, and they all turned toward him. He winked at Jane and sat down on the floor where the children overwhelmed him with hugs. He tickled them and made them laugh.

And how could he not laugh with them? Never had the laughter of children struck him so deeply. He finally lay back on the floor, and Barrett lay beside him, putting a head on his shoulder, quickly tired.

Katharine and Preston climbed on Alex's belly in an attempt to retaliate for all the tickling. Barrett matter-of-factly quoted a line from his favorite storybook. "Stop! You must not hop on Pop!"

Alex and Jane just laughed.

* * * * *

Neil and Roxanne came to sit with Barrett, presenting him with a new Batman action figure that made the child's eyes light up. Once they were settled, Alex and Jane took the other kids home to be with Donald and Susan. Together they went to their own church building, just down the street, where Alex had arranged to get in and use the floor for a rehearsal.

They had gone through each of the numbers just once when Alex's cell phone rang.

"Where are you?" Wade asked from the other end of the phone. "You're all out of breath."

"I've been dancing, if you must know."

"Dancing?" Wade asked dubiously.

"With my wife. You know, dancing. You move your feet around while you listen to music."

"Ha ha."

Alex chuckled. "We're practicing for a floor show for some stake thing that's coming up. It's part of trying to achieve balance in our lives."

"And . . . since when are you and Jane into dancing?"

"You and I need to have a little chat, kid. Jane and I fell in love through the course of a waltz. We were paired up on a ballroom dance team."

Wade let out a laugh. "You're kidding."

"No, I'm quite serious."

"You're like . . . a dancer. Seriously. For real."

"For real," Alex said. "Did you call to make fun of my hobbies or is there a point to this?"

"I don't remember. I want to see you dance."

"Fine. We could use an audience. Hurry up."

"Serious?"

"Sure," Alex said and told Wade where they were. "Call when you're here, and I'll let you in."

They decided to take a break when Alex told Jane that Wade was coming over. "We can see if we're still up to the pressure of an audience," Alex said.

After Wade arrived, Alex got a chair for him and told him to sit down and shut up.

"Yes, sir."

"We have two numbers, and we need to run through them and see if you make us nervous."

"Great," Wade said as if he were about to see his favorite band in concert.

Alex took Jane to the center of the floor, then said, "The real reason we need you is to push the button so I don't have to do it then run to get in position. Just push PLAY if you think you can handle it."

"Okay," Wade said, turning to see the player at his side.

"The Waltz," Alex said with drama, and the music began.

While they danced he was only vaguely aware of Wade watching, apparently consumed with absolute fascination. As they came to a graceful halt when the music ended, Wade rose to his feet, applauding and whistling.

"Okay, that's good," Alex said and stopped the player. "Now we need to do the rumba." He set the player and went back to the center of the floor. "Hit it, maestro," he said, and Wade pushed the button.

Again Wade became enthralled with watching the dance. When it was finished and Jane and Alex were both out of breath, he turned off the player and said, "Why didn't you tell me? That's amazing."

"There's probably a lot you don't know about me, little brother."

"And vice versa," Wade said.

"Give it time," Jane interjected, smiling at them both.

* * * * *

A couple of days later Sister Lamb called to tell them the stake dance had been postponed for a few weeks due to a scheduling mix-up. She was thrilled to hear that they would still be able to do the floor show, and Alex was pleased with the excuse to have a weekly dancing date with his wife. He told Jane it was a habit they would be wise to stick to, and she agreed.

Barrett's recovery suddenly took off, and it was a great day when he came home from the hospital. Alex carried Barrett into the house and set him down. Within a minute he had found Katharine and Preston, who were coloring in coloring books; Preston was mostly scribbling, but having a marvelous time at it. Barrett immediately picked up a crayon and opened a different coloring book to carefully color a dinosaur bright green. Alex put his arm around Jane as they took in a moment that felt almost surreal by its very normalcy.

As Alex had predicted, bringing Barrett home was complicated and challenging. Every part of the house where Barrett would be spending time had endured a cleaning like it hadn't seen since its renovation, according to Susan. A hospital bed was rented and set up in Alex and Jane's bedroom, and the room quickly took on a unique aura. Jane called the decor "early anachronism," with modern medical mixed into early Victorian.

With Barrett at home, his parents had to make up for much of what the nursing staff had done to see that he got all of his medications in the right way at the right time. And he still had a feeding tube that had to be maintained, among other issues. When Alex needed to work, that responsibility fell fully to Jane, even though Donald and Susan were there to help with the other children. He could tell she was nervous and concerned about the responsibility in his absence, when his medical training made all they had to do much easier. But Jane took on the assignment with courage and determination. She was eager to learn how to care for her son, and Alex found a new bond with her as she got a taste of certain aspects of his career.

In spite of the challenges, Barrett coming home was a huge milestone, and the support of others was as strong as it had ever been. They needed to continue to be very careful about exposing Barrett to any germs, which meant that Katharine and Preston were pretty much confined to the house along with their brother, but it was a joy to see them playing and interacting. They did things together as a family in a way they'd completely lost through these horrendous months. And the children were full of delighted laughter when Alex turned on some music and started dancing with Jane in the middle of the family room. From the way the kids were acting, he felt like they were performing some kind of circus act, but he just relished their laughter, threaded into the joy of dancing with his wife.

Barrett's improvement was fast and furious. In record time the feeding tube was removed, and he was gradually reintroduced into the world of eating. This brought on a few challenges, but they worked through them and pressed forward. Regular outpatient visits kept up a less intense but ongoing chemo regime as a standard precautionary measure. Periodic blood work kept them posted on Barrett's improving immunity, and they put a date on the calendar to go to the zoo.

Alex and Jane both knew it wasn't over yet. The chemotherapy would go on for months yet, and there were still the omniscient tests on the horizon that would determine the absence—or presence—of any cancer cells. One result would mean an eventual clean bill of health and a ticket to life, and the other would mean a certain death sentence. Alex and Jane had talked about both possibilities, speculating how it might feel in either case. While losing Barrett after all they'd been through would be difficult in no uncertain terms, they both agreed that somehow they would survive it. They would move on. And they would always be grateful for the years Barrett had spent in their lives—and for the extra time they'd been given through Wade's life-giving gift. The joy they found in having their son back, even if it was temporary, was beyond description. For Alex, just having all of his family under the same roof was a miracle in itself. And it was nice to be sleeping in the same bed with his wife again.

Donald and Susan thoroughly enjoyed having Barrett back in their home. Now that the worst of the leukemia drama was over, they began making preparations for a mission, and Alex and Jane were thrilled to officially purchase the house.

Wade came around regularly, seeming happy and at peace with his life. He enjoyed his job and was doing well in school—especially since he made Alex help him with his homework when it got tough. And Alex was pleased to hear that Wade and Neil had come to an agreement over the money. Neil had paid off Wade's existing student loans, and he had committed to helping with the remainder of his tuition as long as he stuck with his goals to keep a job and get successfully through medical school.

Alex loved to see the warm relationship Wade had developed with the children—especially Barrett. The bond they shared could never be described, but never denied. Wade had saved Barrett's life, and they loved each other dearly.

When the night for the stake dance arrived, Alex told Jane just to get herself ready. He promised to make certain the children were all arranged for and left it at that. They both knew that Donald and Susan would be attending the dance, insisting that they didn't want to miss this. Alex also promised to pick up the costumes they would be renting, and have them in the car. They'd made the decision to rent clothes for the event, rather than going to the expense of buying clothes they wouldn't be likely to wear again.

"You nervous?" he asked as they were driving to the church.

"Not really," she said. "Are you?"

"As long as you're holding my hand, I'll be fine."

Through the first hour of the dance they hung out on the dance floor, dressed in their usual Sunday attire. They laughed and danced without getting too showy, but having a marvelous time. When it was time to get ready, they went to separate rooms to change, and Susan helped Jane with her hair. When they met in the hallway outside the cultural hall, they just stood and stared at each other before they both broke into smiles at the same moment.

"Wow," Alex said, glad that she'd chosen to rent the white ensemble. Wrapped in satin and sequins, she not only looked stunning, but he couldn't help being reminded of how she'd worn white for the waltz they'd shared at their first competition—and the day he'd married her.

"Will you marry me?" he asked.

She laughed and said, "Already did."

"What a relief," he said.

She smiled and said, "You look absolutely adorable in tails, Dr. Keane."

He lifted his brows comically. "It's a Fred Astaire thing."

Susan pulled them aside so she could take a couple of pictures of them, then Donald and Susan went to find a seat.

From the hallway they could hear Sister Lamb introducing them. Following an accurate list of their dance experience and awards, she announced that they had met when they were put together as partners on a ballroom dance team. "Alex and Jane dated for four years before they were married in the Salt Lake Temple. They've now been happily married nearly eight years, and have three beautiful children. Alex is an emergency room physician, and before she had children, Jane was teaching kindergarten. And as you're about to see, they haven't lost their touch on the dance floor. I'm told this is the same waltz they first fell in love to, and they also shared it at their wedding reception. Ladies and gentlemen, Alex and Jane."

A roar of applause went up that in itself brought back vivid memories. Jane took a deep breath and met the sparkle in Alex's eyes before they walked onto the floor. The number went beautifully.

Jane felt oblivious to the crowds surrounding them while they danced in the center of the cultural hall. She could only see Alex and the love they shared. She was the happiest woman alive.

Following the waltz, they were met with huge applause that accompanied them through an elaborate bow and a graceful exit off the floor. They hurried to change while a clogging group performed, then they met again in the hall to wait for their cue.

"You look incredible," Alex said when he saw her in the burgundy dress and satiny shoes.

She smiled and touched the fabric of his shirt that matched her dress. "So do you," she said and kissed him quickly.

After they were announced again, Jane was surprised to have Sister Lamb hand the microphone to Alex. He kept hold of Jane's hand as he spoke. "Before we perform our other number, there is something that I felt needed to be said. About two years ago, when Jane was expecting our third baby, we had a fire in our home, and we moved in with my cousin. That same day Jane went into labor, and the very next day we discovered that our son Barrett had leukemia. I can't begin to tell you how difficult these years have been. Barrett has not only endured extreme levels of chemotherapy and radiation, but he's been given two bone marrow transplants, which left us pretty much living at the hospital for months. On top of that, Jane's father passed away unexpectedly, and members of my family were faced with some challenges. Even though we had moved out of this stake, however, the love and support never stopped. Many of you helped put our home back in order, and then helped us move our belongings out when it became evident we needed to sell it. We had people who were willing, even eager, to sit with our son when we couldn't always be there and to help with the other children, and to bring us meals, even though we now lived elsewhere and it was a twenty-minute drive. We also know that many of you helped raise funds and contributed generously to help pay for the enormous medical costs of saving Barrett's life. And most importantly, I know there were many prayers, and ward and stake fasts on behalf of our son, even though most of you probably had no idea who you were fasting for. But we felt the power of those efforts. Even when we thought we would lose Barrett, we were often buoyed up by strength that we didn't even comprehend completely until we were beyond it. We want to formally thank you for that, and we are thrilled beyond words to tell you that Barrett is recovering well. He will need to continue with chemotherapy for about another year, and while his complete recovery isn't certain yet, we have every reason to believe that he will be fine. We have been blessed with many miracles, including the prayers and support we received here. You have truly shown us the power of mourning with those who mourn."

Jane heard some sniffles in the room as he paused and kissed her hand before he added, "I want to dedicate this number to my beautiful wife. A while back, when we believed that we would have to let our son go, she pointed out very poignantly that there is a time to weep and a time to mourn. The opportunity to prepare for this event has replenished much of what we had lost in our marriage through the course of trying to keep our son alive, and it has given us great joy in the midst of our challenges. We are very grateful to be here tonight and want you to know that there is a time to laugh . . . and a time to dance."

Alex handed the microphone back to Sister Lamb, and the crowd applauded as he led Jane to their beginning position for the rumba. They pulled it off without a glitch, and when it was finished the applause was almost deafening. They took an elaborate bow, and then Alex motioned to his left toward the crowd. Jane caught her breath to see Barrett move out of the audience, carrying a dozen red roses. He looked thin and pale and his hair was barely a quarter of an inch long all over his head, but he was here—alive and well. She laughed and said to Alex, "You *manipulated* this."

"Yes, I did," he said as Barrett gave the roses to his mother, who hugged him tightly. Alex lifted the boy into his arms, and the audience all rose to their feet with a standing ovation.

Alex laughed and said to Barrett, "Wave." And he did.

Alex took the microphone from the stand and said, "Barrett wants to tell you something."

He held the microphone up for Barrett, who said, "We're going to the zoo in two days."

Everyone laughed and applauded again.

"Who brought you?" Jane asked Barrett as they were walking back toward the hallway.

"Everybody's here," Barrett said, and he held up a finger for each person. "Grandpa, and Grandma," which meant Neil and Roxanne, "and Susan, and Donald, and Katharine, and Preston, and Uncle Wade, and Wade's mom, and Mom, and Dad," he finished triumphantly, holding up all ten fingers. "That's you," he added, and they laughed, then he looked distressed. "I don't have another finger."

Alex chuckled. "Ten is all you get, buddy."

"But how do I count me?"

"Start over," Jane said and held up one of his index fingers. "Barrett. There. That's you."

He smiled and held up the other index finger, saying proudly, "And this one is for Wade's girlfriend."

"Who?" Alex and Jane both said together, then were met by the crowd that Barrett had just been counting.

After Alex had greeted everyone close by with a hug, graciously accepting compliments about the dancing, he noticed Wade hanging back, holding the hand of a lovely young lady. She had short, dark hair, and a definite sparkle in her eyes when she looked at Wade. Alex approached them and got a quick hug from Wade, along with a burst of laughter.

"You shaved!" Wade said.

"Yes, I did," Alex said, rubbing his hairless face that still felt a little strange.

"You look like a new man."

Alex smiled. "It seemed like a good thing to do on the brink of a new beginning."

"I know what you mean," Wade said. "Hey, that was amazing out there, big brother. If I had known you were so talented, I wouldn't have been embarrassed to be your brother all these years."

Alex smirked at the hidden meaning, then said, "You harass me for keeping secrets? Where have you been keeping this sweet thing?"

"This is Elena," Wade said. "Elena, my brother Alex."

"It's a pleasure to meet you, Elena," he said.

"And you," she said. "I've heard so much about you. And the dancing really was fantastic."

"Thank you," Alex said. "So, how long have you known this brute?"

She laughed softly. "About ten days, I believe."

Music began to play from the cultural hall. Now that the floor show was over, the dance had begun again. Wade took Elena's hand and said to Alex, "Excuse us. This is a great song."

Alex watched them move onto the dance floor, settling quickly into the slow, gentle rhythm of a sweet love song. He quickly made certain the children were in good hands and took Jane's hand, leading her onto the floor for a simple, slow dance. Half a minute into it he said, "Remember the way we looked at each other during that first dance we shared?"

"How could I ever forget?"

"If you turn to your left you will recognize that look, I believe."

Jane turned quickly and scanned the crowd until her eyes focused on Wade and Elena, and then she laughed. She said conclusively, "They're going to be together forever."

"I would have to agree wholeheartedly on that."

"Wow," Jane said and laughed again. "That's wonderful."

"Yes, it is," he said and guided her through a quick, unexpected twirl, pulling her attention away from Wade and Elena. He brought her back into his arms, where they exchanged the same kind of heart-stopping gaze. "I love you, Jane."

"I love you too, Alexander."

"You know what's *really* wonderful?"

"What?"

"We're going to be together forever."

She smiled. "I would have to agree wholeheartedly on that."

Chapter 23

The excursion to the zoo for a lengthy family home evening was a glorious event. Unlike the last time they'd taken Barrett to the zoo, he was alert and animated, taking in every animal they saw with excitement. He still rode in a wagon to keep from getting worn out, but he regularly climbed in and out to get a closer look at all there was to see. Neil and Roxanne and Wade and Elena went along as well. Alex felt a joy beyond words to observe the interaction of these people he loved. Wade had grown so close to Barrett that no one could ever see them together and not believe they hadn't been close for a lifetime. At the zoo, Wade was often picking Barrett up to point something out to him. He would occasionally tickle and tease him, making the child laugh.

Alex realized Jane had read his mind when she quietly said to him, "Look at them. You would think they shared a special bond or something."

"And the same blood—literally."

"Sometimes," Jane said, "I just want to get down on my knees and kiss Wade's feet."

"Yeah, I know the feeling. But it might be kind of awkward."

Jane laughed softly, then eased away from Alex and moved close to Wade as he was putting Barrett back into the wagon following a lengthy viewing of the elephants. She wrapped her arms around Wade and gave him a long, tight hug.

Wade laughed and hugged her back. "What was that for?" he asked. "Not that I'm complaining . . ."

"For giving my son life," she said.

Wade looked startled by the tears in Jane's eyes. He said quietly, "It was nothing, Jane. It was a privilege."

"It was everything to us," she said. "I just want you to know that I'm grateful."

She hugged him again, and they moved on to catch up with Neil and Roxanne, who had wandered up the trail, pulling rented wagons that held Katharine and Preston. Alex walked next to Wade, who was pulling Barrett in the wagon, and said, "Ditto . . . to everything she said. And thanks for being such a great uncle too."

"You make it sound like it's some kind of sacrifice." Wade glanced over his shoulder. "Barrett is one of the greatest people I've ever met."

Alex tossed a smile toward his son. "Yeah, I know what you mean."

* * * * *

Alex was thrilled when Wade called to tell him that he'd asked Elena to marry him, and she had accepted. Elena knew all about the scandal related to Wade's life, and she'd spent time with both of his families. Wade was pleased to report that she'd never even batted an eye over it. They had set a date to be married in the Salt Lake Temple, and Wade wanted to be certain that Alex and Jane could be there.

"We wouldn't miss it," Alex said. "You keep in touch, and if there's anything we can do to help with the wedding plans, let us know."

"Thanks, big brother," he said and let out a little laugh.

"You sound happy."

"Yeah, I am," Wade said.

"That's great. You deserve to be happy."

He also let Alex know that he had been accepted to a medical school back east. While Alex dreaded having Wade and his wife live out of state, it was obviously the right course, and he was pleased to know that Wade's goal was to eventually come back here and settle down.

A couple of weeks before the wedding, Alex struggled through an afternoon where he had rarely seen the ER so busy. Nothing serious or life-threatening; just a continuing throng of stitches, infections, broken bones, and a nasty migraine. He was told the waiting room had finally cleared out at the same moment that he was handed a chart and was motioned to one of the exam rooms.

"Stitches," was all the nurse said. "The stuff's already in there. Baker insisted you take this one. She's been waiting a long time."

Alex knew what that meant. The patient would likely be grumpy as well as needing medical attention. And if Baker wanted him to take this patient, what exactly might Baker be trying to get out of? As standard procedure, he glanced at the paperwork in his hands just long enough to get an idea of what he was dealing with. His focus was more on the papers as he opened the door, saying absently, "Hi, there. I'm Dr. Keane." He pushed the door closed and set the paperwork on the counter. "Sorry about the wait. It's been crazy out there and—" Alex stopped mid-sentence and froze where he stood. "What are you doing here?"

"Waiting," Jane said.

For a moment Alex wondered if this was some kind of practical joke to be sent into an exam room and find his wife waiting. She was wearing a hospital gown, leaning against the bed that was elevated to a sitting position. Her long legs were bare and stretched out in front of her, and over one thigh she was holding a piece of gauze with blood soaking through it. The blood didn't look like a joke, and Alex asked, "What did you do?"

"It's not so serious," she said. "But seeing you walk through the door like that, I have to say it was almost worth it."

"And why is that?" he asked, putting his hands on his hips long enough to hear what she had to say.

"I was thinking about the night we met. Do you remember?"

"How could I ever forget?"

"We had that brief encounter at the restaurant, and then we both spent the next couple of days obsessed with each other but not even knowing each other's names. Destiny brought us back together at that dance rehearsal. But you were an intern then, and I was just thinking how funny it would have been if the next time we'd seen each other had been like this."

Alex chuckled and went along with her. "Hello again. My name is Alex."

"Hi," she said while he pulled sterile gloves onto his hands. He sat on a stool and rolled it next to the bed, reaching out a hand to pull the wheeled tray closer that had everything on it he would need.

Jane moved her hand, and he peeled away the bloody gauze to see a gash that was more deep than long. "Ouch," he said, soaking up blood with a fresh piece of gauze so he could get a better look at it. "What did you do?" he repeated.

"It was stupid," she said with self-recrimination.

Alex chuckled and glanced at her face, feeling his heart quicken as he tried to imagine falling in love with her all over again. It wasn't difficult to comprehend. "I've never heard a story about an injury that was necessarily smart. Accidents happen. If they didn't, I'd be out of a job." She smiled until she saw him pick up the needle and pull off the cap. As always, he gave fair warning. "This is the only part that's going to hurt worse than actually cutting your leg open." She looked away as most people did. "Just count to ten," he said, then counted for her as he quickly and carefully inserted the needle to inject anesthetic around the wound. He heard her gasp and saw her fists clench. By the time he said "ten" he'd already put the needle in the sharps container. "You okay?" he asked.

"Relatively speaking," she said.

Waiting for the anesthetic to take effect, he repeated his question, "So, what did you do?"

She laughed sheepishly. "I was experimenting on a craft project and the knife slipped."

"I see," he said, liking the idea that she had come back to a place in her life where she had the time and motivation to do a craft project. "Did you drive yourself here?"

"I did."

Alex glanced at the clock and knew the anesthetic still needed another couple of minutes before he could begin. "This is weird," she said. "Other than when you've helped deliver our babies, I've never actually *seen* you working."

"Well, it's a little weird to be sticking a needle in *you,* if you must know. I don't find it pleasant to inflict pain on my wife."

"Since that shot is over with, I'm actually thinking maybe I'm glad the knife slipped."

"Why?" he asked with a little laugh.

"It's nice to see you in the middle of a shift."

"It's nice to see you too, but I really think I'd prefer different circumstances." He lightly pressed a needle around the wound on her leg and asked, "Can you feel that?"

"No," she said.

"We're ready then," he said.

"Ooh, I can't watch," she said and looked in the other direction. He chuckled, and she added, "Are you any good at this?"

"The best," he said. "And just for you I'll make a house call to remove the stitches."

She laughed and said, "While you're there, you can take out the garbage and bathe my children."

Alex laughed, then focused on his work while his mind wandered. He wondered what it might have been like if he'd encountered her this way all those years ago. He couldn't resist saying, "Would you go on a date with me?"

She shot him a look of mock astonishment and said, "I'm a married woman, Doctor."

Alex chuckled and looked down to take another stitch. "Well, if he doesn't treat you like a queen, you let me know, and I'll give him a bloody nose."

"I'll let you know," she said. "And since you put it that way, I would love to go on a date with you."

"Great," he said. "I'll look forward to it." He finished what he was doing and almost felt disappointed. He would have liked to drag it out much longer.

"There," he said triumphantly, swabbing around the wound to clean all the excess blood away. "All done."

Jane leaned over to look at the results and said, "Very impressive."

He impulsively pressed a quick kiss to the wound.

She laughed softly. "Is that standard, Dr. Keane?"

"Oh, no. That costs extra." He took the gloves off and tossed them in the trash before he rolled the stool over to the counter and wrote on the paperwork that went with the patient. He then scribbled on a prescription pad. "I'm giving you a few pain pills, just enough for a couple of days. After that, Tylenol or ibuprofen should be sufficient. They shouldn't make you terribly sleepy, but if you take them during the day, don't drive. You can shower but don't bathe; we don't want it soaking in water."

"Okay," she said and chuckled.

"What's funny?"

"You sound like a doctor."

"How many years have you known that I'm a doctor?"

"I don't know. I've lost track."

Alex continued. "I'm also giving you an antibiotic. Take it until it's gone. We don't want any infection."

"Okay," she said again. He handed her the prescription and asked, "No place else that needs stitching?"

"Not that I can think of at the moment."

"No medical problems you might like to discuss extensively?"

"Sorry." She shrugged. "If anything comes up we could talk about it when you make that house call. But for the moment, my mind is blank"

"That's too bad. I would much rather sit here and talk to you about toe fungus or something than go face whatever is in the next room."

"Come to my place when you get off, and we can talk about anything you like."

"What a great idea," he said and couldn't bring himself to leave. He was thoroughly enjoying this little oasis in the middle of a crazy day.

"So, Dr. Keane," she said, "why don't you tell me what you're thinking while you're staring at me like that."

He smiled and said, "I want to kiss you so badly it hurts . . . almost as much as it hurt to give you that shot."

Her eyes smiled as she said, "I can assure you, *Doctor*, that in both cases, it hurts me a lot more than it hurts you."

Alex put one hand on the elevated bed, next to her shoulder, and carefully leaned toward her, pressing his lips to hers. In the time it would take to draw a deep breath, their kiss mutually drifted from meek and timid to soft and warm. He drew back but kept his face close to hers while he could hear her breathing sharply near his ear. With his lips almost touching hers, he whispered, "You should see a doctor about that strained breathing, Jane." He kissed her again.

"Do you know one who makes house calls?" she asked and kissed him.

"Absolutely," he said. "And if I go into cardiac arrest, call 911."

She looked at him with a puzzled smile. Impulsively he took the stethoscope from around his neck and put it in her ears, pressing it to his own chest as he leaned forward and kissed her longer and harder.

"Wow," she said and reversed the stethoscope so that he could hear *her* heart.

Alex limited himself to just one more kiss, then eased back. He pulled the stethoscope from his ears and asked firmly, looking into her eyes, "Will you marry me?"

"Yes," she said just as firmly, and he kissed her yet again.

The door came open, and he turned to see an astonished nurse who hadn't been on the staff very long. "It's okay," he said. "This is my wife."

"Oh, good," she said. "If you're . . . finished here, we've got a heart attack coming in."

"I'll be right there," he said. "Thank you."

The nurse left, and Alex kissed Jane once more. "I'll see you later, Mrs. Keane."

"I'll look forward to it, Dr. Keane," she said, and he reluctantly went back to work. But in his heart he felt a warm depth of gratitude for this wonderful woman he shared his life with. And everything they had been through together only made him love her more.

* * * * *

On the day that Wade and Elena were married, Alex was thrilled with the opportunity to take Jane to the temple. But he felt something quite profound when he saw Wade there. He could never put into words what it meant to him to know they were brothers, and to know that in spite of all the challenges of life, they could come to this place that was closest to heaven on earth.

Alex put his focus elsewhere as he escorted Jane into a sealing room in the Salt Lake Temple, and memories of the day they had been sealed here overcame him like a warm wind. They sat close together, holding hands, and a minute later his father came in with Roxanne. They exchanged whispered greetings, and then Neil sat next to Alex and briefly squeezed his hand, as if to communicate some inexpressible joy.

Alex watched as Wade's siblings all came into the room, faces he recognized from his visit with their family. They were all there except for Brian, who was still too young. But Alex knew he was waiting outside the temple, helping keep an eye on his nieces and nephews until the ceremony was over. Charlotte and Becca came in together, and they exchanged smiles across the room. Alex's sisters had flown in the day before, and they had all shared dinner the previous evening.

Brad and Marilyn came in, holding hands. Alex watched them exchange a few quiet words and a quick kiss before Brad took his place in one of the witness chairs, and Marilyn sat in her place as the groom's mother.

"I never would have imagined a moment such as this," Neil whispered to Alex, the peace in his voice quietly evident.

"Funny where life takes us, isn't it."

"It certainly is."

"How's Barrett?"

"He's great," Alex whispered then laughed softly just to be able to say such words.

A hush fell over the room as the bride and groom were escorted in and took their seats. Alex saw Wade scan the faces in the room, and he paused for a moment when their eyes met. They exchanged a smile before Wade turned to look at Elena as if they could take on the world together and conquer whatever it might give them. Alex felt sure that they could.

Alex turned to look at Jane and thought about the vows they had exchanged in this very room. He had believed at the time that he could never love her more, that he could never be any happier. He'd been so wrong. The enormity of all they had shared since that day was as incomprehensible as the depth of the bonds that continued to grow between them.

While Wade and Elena exchanged vows over the altar, Alex and Jane looked into each other's eyes, silently internalizing those vows all over again, understanding now more than ever how profound and powerful they truly were. While everyone else in the room watched the bride and groom exchange a kiss over the altar, Alex kissed Jane, then whispered against her lips, "Forever is a wonderful thing, Mrs. Keane."

Epilogue

"Okay, Barrett, smile," Wade said and snapped the picture.

"Let me see," Barrett said, running toward Wade to look at the back of the digital camera. Alex followed more slowly and looked over Barrett's head to see the picture of himself and Barrett, dressed in white.

"I'll print a copy for you," Wade said to Barrett. "And then you can always remember the day your dad baptized you."

"Okay," Barrett said and took Alex's hand. "Come on, Dad. Mom's already in there."

Alex chuckled and went with Barrett, saying, "Come on, Uncle Wade."

The baptismal service was beautiful. As Alex lowered Barrett down into the water, then lifted him back up again, he was instantly struck with the impression that he had seen this moment at some previous time. The sensation felt like déjà vu, but it was more clear, more real. In the space of a heartbeat the memory came back to him with clarity. They'd just been told that a donor match had been found for Barrett, but Alex hadn't yet known it was him—or that the graft would fail. But he had seen in his mind Barrett's being baptized, receiving the priesthood, getting his Eagle Scout award, going on a mission, getting married in the temple, having children of his own. Only now, when the images repeated in his mind, did he realize that it hadn't just been a hope or a wish—it had been a vision. The Spirit had shown him in the length of a long breath that Barrett would survive and grow, but

Alex hadn't recognized the event for what it was. But now he knew. In the time that it took Barrett to wipe the water from his face and throw his arms around Alex, he knew. He looked up to see the faces of so many people he loved surrounding them, setting his eyes firmly on Jane. And she smiled.

After Alex and Barrett had changed into dry clothes, they entered the room where everyone was waiting for the confirmation to take place. Alex scanned the room and did a double-take when he saw faces that were familiar but unexpected. He took hold of Jane's arm and ushered her across the room where Bruce and Karen were hovering at the edge of the small crowd.

"We have company," he whispered to her. She looked up and gasped before she hurried to embrace Karen, and Alex accepted a firm handshake from Bruce, and then a tight hug. There was an unspoken connection with these people that no one else in the room could ever understand.

They had kept in touch with Andie's parents, mostly through email. Alex had informed them of Barrett's baptism and had invited them, but he hadn't expected them to actually show up. He and Jane had discussed how it might be difficult for them seeing how Barrett had survived the torture chamber of bone marrow transplant, and their Andie had not. But here they were, all smiles and clearly thrilled to be there.

"You came," Jane said, embracing Bruce while Alex hugged Karen.

"We wouldn't have missed it," Bruce said.

"We're so glad you let us know," Karen added. She looked at Barrett, who was talking with his grandfather. "He looks so good."

"Yeah," Alex said, "he's doing great." He turned to them and asked, "And how are you?"

"We're very well," Bruce said. "We miss Andie, but we've been very blessed."

They talked quietly for a few more minutes before the service continued. When it was over, everyone met back at the house for a barbecue. Since Barrett's eighth birthday had been the previous day, they'd decided to just celebrate everything all together. Jane's mother had flown in from California, along with a couple of her sisters. Charlotte and Becca had come from out of state, along with their husbands and children. And of course, Neil and Roxanne were there. Donald and Susan had recently returned from a six-month mission on the east coast and they were preparing to embark on another one. And Wade and Elena were actually living with them at the moment. Wade was taking the summer off from medical school. Their first baby was due in the next couple of weeks, and they'd decided they wanted to be around family and friends for its arrival. Staying with Alex and Jane was an obvious choice, considering the size of the house. The irony was that Alex and Jane were due to have their fourth baby any time now. They'd been hoping she would wait until the baptism was over, but now that it was, Alex felt certain she'd be anxious to get the baby here. It had been Jane's idea to have another baby, and even though the pregnancy had been somewhat miserable, she'd never once complained.

While Alex hovered near the barbecue grill, attempting to keep a variety of selections from burning, he turned to take in the affirmation of how thoroughly blessed he was. The normalcy of life was evident in so many little things. Jane and Elena were sitting close together, laughing and talking, their feet up while they compared swollen ankles. The chatter and laughter of other loved ones floated across the yard, mingled with the sound of children playing. But Alex smiled widest when he saw Barrett steal a football from Wade and run, dodging chairs and children and people, dashing around the yard with Wade hot on his heels. Wade finally grabbed him and wrestled him to the ground, tickling him while they both laughed wildly. That was about all the strength Barrett could muster, but it was evident that he was on the path to becoming a relatively normal child. The chemotherapy was finished now, and ongoing tests had made it clear that no sign of cancer existed anywhere inside of Barrett. He was a walking miracle!

Alex checked the meat and took most of it off the grill before he paused again to just bask in the beauty of the moment. And it was made more beautiful just being in the shadow of this incredible home, built by his great-great-grandfather after crossing the plains to make a better life for generations to come. He couldn't help hoping that Alexander Barrett might have the opportunity to look down upon moments such as this. And his mother as well. She surely would have found great joy in such a day.

When the meal was over and cleaned up, everyone lingered in the yard as if being together was all that mattered and there was no need to want to go anywhere else. Alex sat close to Jane while Barrett opened his birthday gifts and blew out the candles on his cake. Alex was glad to see Wade taking pictures, since he wanted the memories well preserved, but he preferred to just sit and soak it all in.

While Roxanne, Charlotte, and Becca were passing out cake and ice cream, Barrett surprised Alex by showing up on his lap. He was small for his age but destined to catch up. He hugged Alex tightly, and the strength in him was evident.

"What's up, buddy?" Alex asked.

"Thank you for baptizing me, Dad."

"It's one of the best things I've ever been able to do," Alex said.

Barrett seemed content to just sit there, and Alex held him close while their attention was drawn to Wade getting Jane and Elena to stand up and pose for a picture. Alex couldn't help but laugh to see the two women holding their dresses beneath their bellies. They stood to face each other, showing a perfect profile of how hugely pregnant they each were. Wade took the picture and declared, "Perfect! In a couple of weeks we'll take *another* picture of the babies together."

Wade sat down next to Alex and showed the picture to him and Barrett.

"How perfect is that?" Wade asked.

"It's pretty perfect," Alex said, and hugged Barrett tightly.

About the Author

Anita Stansfield, the LDS market's number-one best-selling romance novelist, is a prolific and imaginative writer. Her novels have captivated and moved hundreds of thousands of readers, and she is a popular speaker for women's groups and in literary circles. She and her husband Vince are the parents of five children and reside in Alpine, Utah.

If this story has touched you, and you would like to donate to the treatment of childhood leukemia, donations may be sent to Primary Children's Medical Center Foundation, P.O. Box 58249, Salt Lake City, Utah 84158-0249.